THE
SHADOW'S
GRASP

Book One of The Dark Angel series

COURTNEY LILLARD

ISBN: 979-8-9859212-6-0

Cover design by Etheric Tales & Edits | MC Damon

ACKNOWLEDGEMENTS

This book is dedicated to everyone who contributed some fraction of their time to help shape the person I am today, including my parents, siblings, friends, teachers, and colleagues from across the country. I also must thank my husband, Darren, who not only gave me the push I needed to begin writing seriously and reads all of the drafts but who also listens to my ideas with honest, eager ears.

A NOTE FROM THE AUTHOR

The Dark Angel series has gone through several editions; however, this final version combines what used to be the first two books. Part One is what was previously just known as The Shadow's Grasp while The Guardian's Deception (originally a separate book) is now Part Two of this book. This decision was not made lightly considering the amount of effort it takes to rebrand a series, as well as my readers who were familiar with the original first and second books, but each story has been kept the same. Chapter titles have also been added, and the rest of the series will follow a new order, so to speak.

This note serves as a notice for those of you who may see The Guardian's Deception, whether online or a physical copy. That book will now be considered the second half of The Shadow's Grasp, and the rest of the series will be numbered appropriately. Other changes will be mentioned in future notes.

Contents

ACKNOWLEDGEMENTS iii

A NOTE FROM THE AUTHOR iv

Part One

A Fateful Encounter 1

The Journey Begins 12

An Unexpected Companion 36

Introductions in Verona...53

Surprise Encounters 67

Bid the Palace Farewell...82

Growing Unease...94

The Seer's Prediction 105

The Danger Angels Bring 118

Wings of Destiny 128

Who to Trust 139

Finding Answers 151

The Cost of Revenge..162

No Turning Back...175

Part Two

How to Heal a Scar 187

The Mage Service Law 205

A New Normal 227

Yeluthia's Ambassador 244

A True Test of Courage...261

Sharing Secrets...275

Widening the Circle 289

An Asteom Welcome 307

Harvest Festival Adventures 318

A Cruel Assignment..341

On the Road Again..355

Memories of the Past..368

The Southern Base 382

Danger in Dala 399

Friends or Foes..414

Deadly Ambitions 427

The Golden Dagger..439

About the Author..453

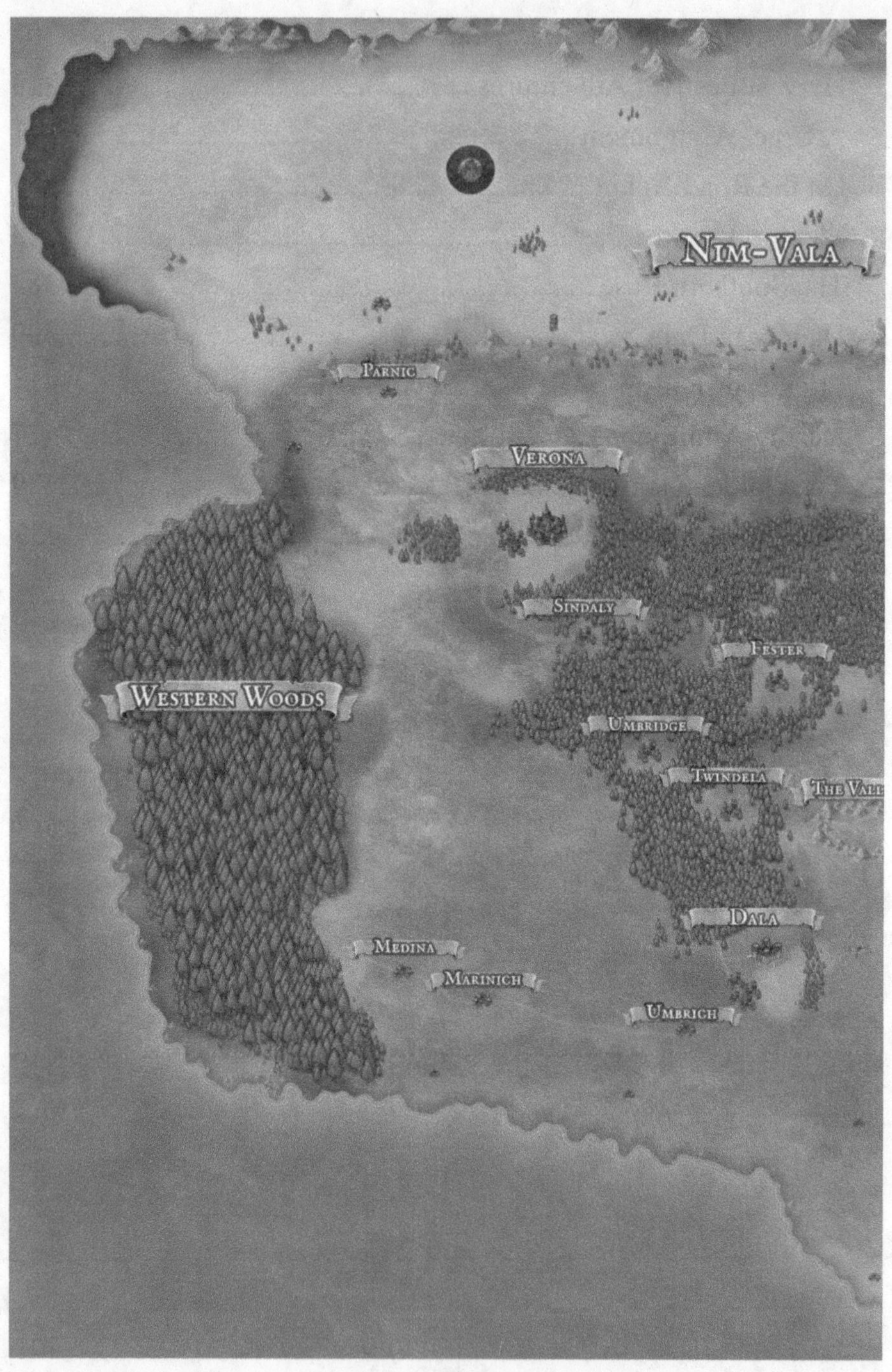

Nim-Vala
Parnic
Verona
Sindaly
Fester
Western Woods
Umbridge
Twindela
The Vall
Dala
Medina
Marinich
Umbrich

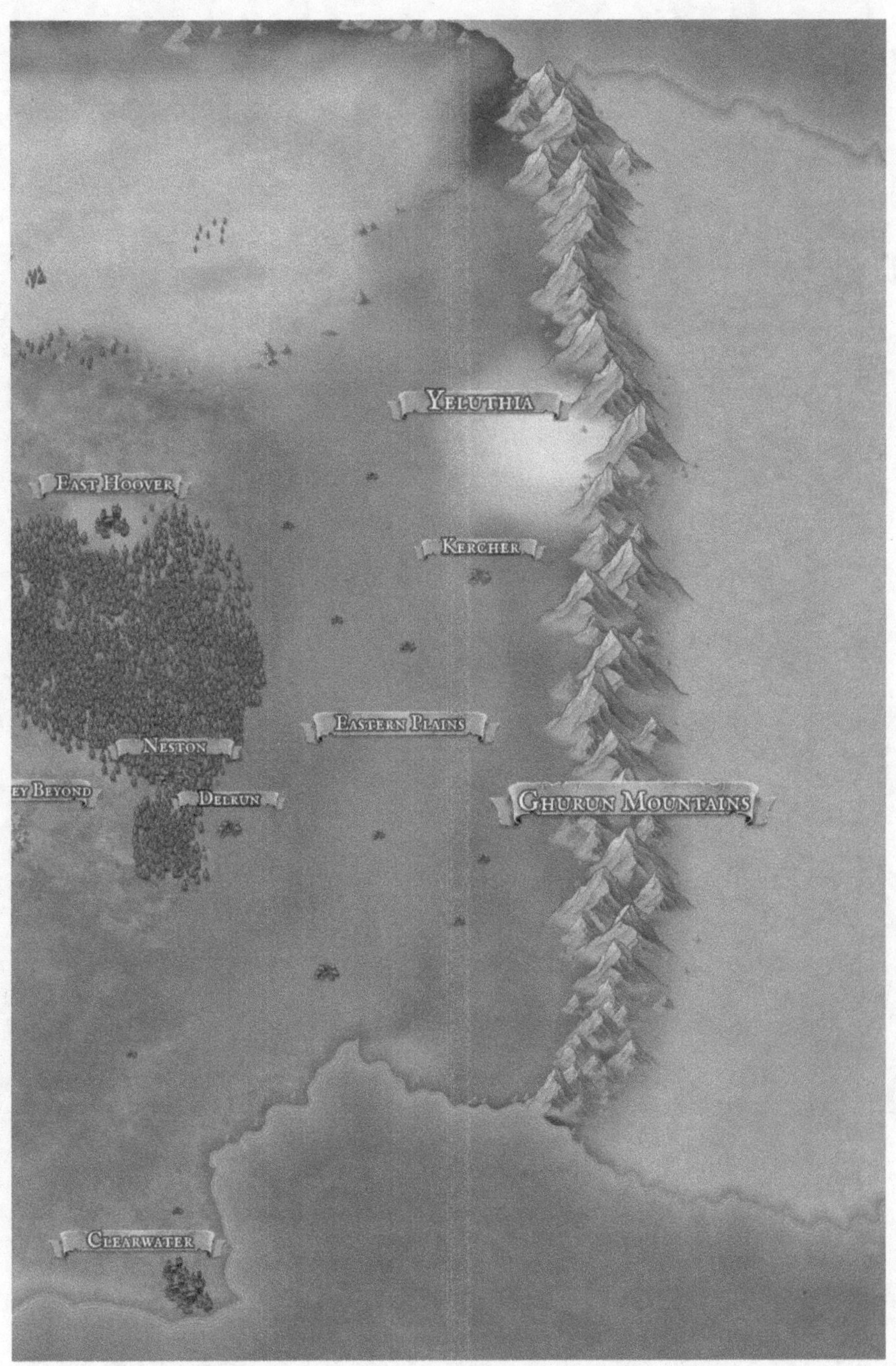

Yeluthia
East Hoover
Kercher
Eastern Plains
Neston
Ghurun Mountains
ey Beyond
Delrun
Clearwater

Part One

A Fateful Encounter

Against the setting sun spreading golden light across Neston, Paulina Galdwin stood in the doorway of her simple home while Coura ventured into the woods surrounding the quieting town.

"Don't travel too far now," the woman called. "Supper is almost ready, and it's getting dark!"

Although Coura heard her mother's voice, she continued to wander farther into the forest while waving to show she heard the order. *It's not like I haven't been lost before,* she thought absently.

Once away from the area, she burst into a full sprint, allowing her lungs to exercise with her legs. Soon enough, she recognized her goal: a fallen tree split at the roots. In fact, it was the largest tree she had ever seen, spanning at least three times her arms' length, making it the perfect landmark in the woods outside her home.

Her pace naturally slowed to a walk after she climbed over the giant log, as it always did when she passed that area. In another few minutes, she would be at her destination, which was a place her village labeled Sunrise Hill. Despite the name, Coura and both her parents found it to be the perfect location to watch the sunset as well since the sky above opened to both ends of the world, allowing for sunlight to constantly pass over on a clear day.

"I'll be just in time," she muttered to herself between breaths with a familiar eagerness and a glance at the indigo pieces of sky beyond the evergreen canopy.

Minutes later, she pushed through a wall of needled branches while wincing as they poked her bare arms and blinked in the light pouring over the hill overlooking miles of dense forest below. As she took a seat at the edge, the sun's bottom half began to touch the end of the earth. She released a content sigh before relaxing and listening to the sounds of various birds, insects, and other woodland creatures.

The sky soon transformed into shades of orange, scarlet, and gold, which melded together against the blue that darkened over the distance. It always proved to be a beautiful sight at the end of the long, summer months. All felt at peace, a difficult experience to find outside Neston according to those who traveled.

It's a shame only a few of us aren't afraid of what hides in the forest, she reflected in a glum manner.

In the town where Coura and her mother lived, everyone knew they would be safer during the day and within Neston's limits. No one ventured off the trails or into the trees unless they had to, and that was with their weapons. Even she kept a dagger buckled to her waist, though she never used it or would carry it with her otherwise. Absolutely no one was allowed out after dark because of the monstrous creatures prowling the woods. She only saw them a handful of times, and all but one were from a distance. The closer encounter had been the most recent, injuring the man who trained her how to fight with a knife and terrifying her for weeks after.

Before then, I didn't know how dangerous they could be. Mother, Father, and I watched them creep around below this hill every other instance.

The creatures became difficult to spot in the shadows as their elongated bodies appeared to be covered with slick, ink-like fur. Her father once explained how no two were similar and told stories of ones that took the shape of a giant dog or cat. He also made sure she understood the creatures possessed violet eyes with sense in them.

Before Coura could ask what he meant, her father scooped her up in his arms, and they hurried back to Neston.

The memory reminded her of the brief amount of time she had left to return home. With one, last glance at the nearly sunken sun, she made her way through the brush as the light started to fade. The fallen tree came within sight just when she abandoned running due to the approaching darkness, which hindered her steps. The woods would grow pitch black shortly, especially since the treetops blocked the moon and stars.

Despite the risks the woods brought, Coura never felt afraid. It helped that she knew how to defend herself and stay calm, two of the most invaluable characteristics, according to her parents.

"As long as you remain alert and steady-minded, you can prepare for whatever comes," her hunting teacher Gordon always reminded her.

Coura smirked at the man's voice while the order replayed in her mind. *I might not be as sharp as him, but sometimes I wonder if everybody might be worrying over nothing. No one goes looking for trouble, so why should we not do something to keep them away? Father never seemed too concerned when he was here...*

The expected tightness at the reminder of his disappearance gripped her heart after she placed a hand on the trunk and prepared to climb over. The lingering sensation distracted her enough that a new sound caused her to jump.

"It's a little dark to be wandering around, young one," said a smooth voice to Coura's right.

Every muscle grew tense in response, and she sprang back to face the stranger with her knife drawn.

How come I didn't hear or see anyone? she thought frantically and scrambled to assume the defensive stance Gordon taught her. Both feet spread apart while she leaned forward a bit so her arms would have enough space to swing if the stranger attacked.

Instead, the woman in front of her laughed sweetly and stepped closer.

"Calm down," the stranger chided and pointed a finger at the knife. "Put that toy away. I only want to talk for a moment."

Although the limited light hindered her vision, Coura could tell the woman wasn't human, at least not entirely. Silky, black hair flowed down in a wave to her waist, and her skin-tight outfit covered her entire body except for her face, hands, and feet. Three aspects soon revealed the stranger's identity. First, the eyes showcased a deep, violet hue as they studied Coura. Second, the tips of her pointed ears stuck out from underneath the voluptuous hair. Finally, and most frightening, the charming smile she flashed as she approached included sharpened canines. The realization caused Coura's knees to shake.

I've never seen a shadow creature take a human form, but this woman doesn't exactly feel human either. Is it something entirely new? she wondered while remaining frozen in place despite her fear.

The stranger waved a hand at the knife without hiding her amusement. "I told you already; I just want to talk, child."

"If you don't mind, I would rather be on my way," Coura countered in a weak voice while backing up and preparing to circle around the trunk still blocking her path home.

The unnatural creature startled her by swiftly climbing over the fallen tree, like a leaf dancing in the wind, to stand in front of her. Sweat began trickling down Coura's neck once she witnessed how fast the woman moved, and how it would be impossible to escape.

"You're from that town near here, aren't you?" the enchantingly smooth voice asked next.

Somehow, Coura managed to speak coherently, though the words poured out while her mind raced for an excuse to get away. "Who are you? We shouldn't stay in the woods after dark or else the monsters will come after us. If you're looking for the road, I can help direct you there."

The woman's eyes narrowed, then she peered in the direction of Coura's hometown. "Do not fret, Dear One. I already found what I desire." Her mischievous tone suggested an unpleasant fate awaited the people in Neston.

As they stood staring at each other in the resulting silence, Coura's hopelessness grew, and her head began to throb from the strain of remaining still. Never before did she picture herself in that kind of situation, one where fighting to escape was not an option.

The stranger crossed her arms, tilted her head, and addressed Coura once more. "You're all alone. Even though I can sense the beings around here, I visited this area quite enough to know you humans fear the creatures at night. Yet for some reason, you chose to leave." A wide, wicked grin graced her lips. "Lucky me."

Fear continued to paralyze Coura, and she became hypnotized by the woman's voice. The gentle tone lulled her into a trance, keeping her hanging on every word.

"Here's an idea," the stranger continued while tapping a finger on her chin, seemingly oblivious to Coura's internal struggle. "I'm rather bored, but I believe I can have some fun with you. What's your name, child?"

"Coura," she answered automatically since she still couldn't process the situation.

What's going on? This isn't like any creature I've seen or heard about. She can't be human, can she? What does she want with me?

The woman repeated it slowly, as if tasting the sound like the adults did with wines and ciders. "What a lovely name."

Coura couldn't even flinch when the stranger put one hand under her chin and tilted it up so their eyes met. Only then did she notice how the material she thought had been the woman's clothing was really the figure's skin, which reminded her of an animal's fur. The sleek coat could not distract from the muscles underneath, though.

Her breath caught at the stranger's next words.

"I am a demon, Dear One. You may call me Soirée."

The creature giggled after Coura's eyes went wide to reflect her sheer terror.

This can't be real, can it? Demons were in the stories, so... How is one here?

Only whispers of demons ever reached the children in Neston, mainly because nobody knew anyone who ever spoke of them outside the founding of their country. They were remote beings who spent their days alone seeking power and causing trouble. Additionally, they fought with angels who protected the humans in Asteom, though the demons were chased away. The angelic race became just as scarce soon after.

Coura recalled one, last piece of information. *Demons possess people by taking over their bodies and destroying their minds. That's why we never hear about them. If she said she wants me to keep her entertained, does that mean... But, I'm just a child! What could she possibly use a me for?*

While the thoughts continued racing through Coura's mind, the creature named Soirée merely smiled at her, and a surge of anger and annoyance at her situation began mixing with the fear.

"What do you want?" she choked out yet succeeded in showing that hint of frustration. Unfortunately, it only succeeded in making the demon chuckle.

"Why such hostility? I intend to have fun, and because I am so generous, you get to share in it too. What do you think? Will you let me borrow your body for a while?"

"It's not like I get a choice," Coura couldn't stop herself from mumbling, which the creature noticed and laughed at.

Her chest hurt from the pounding of her heartbeat while her knees threatened to give out. All she wanted to do was cry. *I'm just a child. Why would she do this? It has to be a nightmare... I wish Mother were here, or Gordon.*

At the thought of what chaos awaited her family and hometown, Coura suddenly felt curious about the demon's reasoning. She couldn't help herself from staring at the creature's face and noted a patient expression.

Does she expect me to respond? I might as well give up now. If she plans to capture me, I wouldn't even know what happened. Why does she hesitate? Could torturing me really just be for her own, sick entertainment?

Something about the encounter didn't sit right with Coura, about how the creature caught her alone on a regular trek away from Neston. Still, she knew in her aching heart the demon would not let her go.

If that is the case, I can't willingly let her hurt Mother and the others in town.

"Y-You're…asking me, right?" Coura began with feigned confidence.

"I suppose I am," Soirée responded lazily, as if the waiting grew tiresome.

"Do demons keep promises?"

The creature tilted her head in a curious, animal-like manner and raised an eyebrow. "A demon never lies. At least, I don't."

Coura attempted to swallow the lump in her throat and sheathed the knife against her protesting instincts. For her idea to work, she needed to believe Soirée. "If all you want is to entertain yourself, I will help under one condition."

The demon didn't even try to hide her amusement. "Oh? I'm quite interested to hear this."

All at once, the inevitability of her fate caught up with Coura. A single tear escaped her watering eyes while her bottom lip quivered. *After all, I'm only a child. I shouldn't die so soon, and all alone.*

"I would like to make a deal."

***

Byron Rinod paused his leisurely stroll to turn and peer into a nearby forest in the opposite direction. Something felt wrong, something only an experienced mage like himself could sense, and that worried him considerably. He glanced around, backtracked his steps until he found a path leading east toward the magical energy, and made haste.

That's a dark spell if I ever recognized one, but I don't remember encountering such a surge of power from this great a distance before. Another presence is there too. Could it be a demonic creature?

With that consideration in mind, Byron hurried his pace to jog down the worn road while manifesting a ball of fire in his hand to aid his hindered sight. Thankfully, the area remained clear so he could move without the possibility of stumbling into somebody else.

Yes, it must be from one, he concluded with more certainty as the source of the energy neared. *Only a demonic creature has that type of unnatural power. At least I didn't come all this way for nothing, even though I truly wish to avoid a confrontation.*

He spotted a cloud of gray smoke hovering against the star-filled, moonless sky before racking his brain for the possibilities.

I'm not terribly familiar with the southeastern section of these woods, but if I recall correctly, the towns are smaller, meaning none of our mages should be posted there. That leaves me to deal with either someone new to using their magic, a demonic creature, or a ritual to summon a demon. I doubt our scouts would overlook a person possessing such power instead of taking them to the academy for an evaluation. Besides, I can sense the wrongness of a demon's energy at work and must assume the worst.

As a master mage, one of his responsibilities included addressing harmful situations involving power stemming from humans, demonic creatures, or worse. His eleven years of training and teaching at the Magical Arts Academy provided him with plenty of experience in adapting to various levels of dark and light energy, though he could wield the former. Even so, Byron was not entirely comfortable in that area and noted the heavy silence lingering amid the increasing smoke and burning smell.

In a short amount of time, he approached the entrance to the town marked by a pair of stone buildings placed on either side of the road, which stretched wide enough for two carts to pass through side by side. A haunting glow loomed from beyond them, indicating a fire. Still, Byron made sure not to rush as he risked the chance of an ambush.

I don't sense demonic energy anymore, and it appears all the townsfolk are gone. What that implied could not be determined by standing at a distance, so he relaxed a bit and continued walking.

Additional stone structures, seemingly shops, lined the road while brick and clay houses were scattered in between. Most of the glass windows broke inward, roofs made from straw dwindled beneath dying flames, and many of the buildings' sides possessed scorch marks. Inside the homes, only a few pieces of furniture caught on fire, which intrigued Byron.

From what he observed as he made his way past the remaining buildings, no bodies, nor the stench of burning flesh, tainted the scene. *If the person or creature responsible didn't destroy everything, raid the empty homes, or kill at first sight, why would they be here in the first place? Unless they can somehow hide from me, I should be safe to explore.*

He glanced up and down the final alleys and appreciated how the entire town consisted of about thirty businesses and homes. After a couple minutes, he reached the edge and turned around with a sigh.

There's nothing left under my jurisdiction to investigate. If I can't sense magic, the mage or creature must be long gone by now, Byron concluded. *I should send a scout to this place when I return to the MAA. It's a shame the army doesn't post soldiers in these independent towns. In some cases, they could use the protection more than the cities.*

A sudden yet weak brush against his mind signaled the presence of magic. The sensation proved to be fairly indescribable, but when he needed to explain it to the younger students, he told them to imagine someone tickling their brain. It sounded near enough to the truth and lighthearted, and they often laughed at his outrageousness. With how faintly most mages could sense energy, it got the point across.

Only an experienced mage like himself could do so at a distance while distinguishing certain features, such as its light or dark essence.

He instinctively traced the trail back toward the middle of the town and behind the first two homes where he overlooked a figure crumpled in the shadows until the energy led him there. Carefully, he knelt beside the body of a girl he thought no older than twelve and put a hand on her trembling arm. When she didn't respond to his touch, Byron decided to brush away the hair covering her face and check for breathing. He found the child alive but suffering from shock and knew exactly what that meant.

She isn't hurt, and the energy stems from her, which means something triggered the release of power. It makes sense; after all, a lot of mages discover their magical potential around this age and without warning.

"Hello? Is anybody here?" he called in the direction of the main path while rising. "I am a master mage from the Magical Arts Academy in East Hoover. The danger has passed, but I need to speak with someone."

Only the crackling of the dying flames answered.

He swore under his breath and tried to figure out what to do. *A whole town disappears and leaves this child behind. They probably became afraid of her spells, which I must admit were strong if they caused such damage. I can feel the dark energy stirring, but it seems normal compared to what I picked up before. Could a demonic creature be responsible for startling her into using magic?*

As he looked down at the girl once more, Byron wiped the sweat from his forehead and wondered what he should do next.

According to the MAA's policy, any individual with the ability to wield dark or light magic must be taken in by the academy to foster their maturing power. The rule protected both the individual as well as vulnerable onlookers.

This isn't the first time an inexperienced mage caused damage to their home or frightened their family away. Usually, I would need permission from the child's guardian to intervene; however, I cannot in good conscience let her stay here or go on without training. Her destructive potential must be reined in as soon as possible, even if it means leaving the situation as it is for the moment.

By the time he decided his next course of action, night covered the land, and Byron had grown exhausted from the full day of travel, meaning there was no use in trying to get to East Hoover before morning. He stripped off the packs he still carried on his shoulders and set up a makeshift camp in the middle of town.

At least I won't freeze to death, he reflected a bit cynically once he noticed the fires going out on their own and the smoke continue to rise instead of crowd the space. *On a positive note, if anyone returns or comes to help, we will be here to explain the situation. Then, I can let them know I'll be taking her. It shouldn't cause trouble that way.*

After preparing his bedroll on the ground and placing an extra blanket next to it, Byron carried the girl over and laid her on the former while accepting the latter for himself. His last thought before sleep took him related to the safety of the area in the morning, and how the townsfolk should return.

To his dismay, when Byron rose at the first sign of sunlight, he and the girl remained alone. After waiting until midmorning, he needed to move on with the still-unconscious girl.

When I get the opportunity, I can return here or send a messenger to relay the news and her status. By then, I expect there will be survivors who can confirm my suspicions about what happened last night.

The Journey Begins

Coura stood with her back to the metal door of the spacious, circular workspace serving as a classroom. The stone area held a limited amount of furniture consisting of a wooden chair and an empty table at one end for the instructor, who left to tend to a call from another teacher. Because of the lack of objects, the space could hold her entire dark spellcasting class of twelve mage trainees with a ring at the center for combat demonstrations and shielding practice. At the moment, she seized the chance to demonstrate her abilities to the rest of the class, mainly for two students in particular.

Joshua and Selma always brag about their control over a fire spell, but their opinions will change once they see mine. Master Leni picked the perfect time to disappear for a while, she thought with a smile at what she planned to do.

After inhaling a deep breath, Coura extended her right arm in front of her body, faced the palm outward toward the opposite end of the room, and focused on the energy humming in her center. Four years of training with the top dark mage at the academy made spells easy to learn. In fact, she'd been told how she developed into the most skilled trainee among her peers on multiple occasions, just not by them.

I would be jealous too if another classmate towered so far above me, she reflected without feeling ashamed of her vanity. *After all, I'm the only student Byron has worked with individually for so long.*

"Well, what are you waiting for?" the rosy-cheeked girl named Selma asked in an impatient tone while standing off to the side by their other classmates.

Joshua, the tall, lean boy at her side, bobbed his head twice. "Master Leni will be back soon if you don't hurry."

"If you would shut up, I could concentrate," Coura mumbled loudly enough for them to hear. Then, she tapped into the energy within herself.

Casting a spell worked like releasing a dam holding the power in her center. Once the user triggered it, they would need to lead the energy to their hands and manifest a spell; otherwise the power found another way to exit, which was often painful and uncontrolled. Given her years of practice, this took less than a few seconds for Coura to achieve, and with only a bit of recoil afterward.

'Manifesting a spell simply requires you to pull forth your own energy and command it to take a physical form, say fire, lightning, ice, or a wall. A mage's responsibility is to control the power within themselves, along with what's around them. Without control, they destroy their body and soul while tampering with the natural energies around us.' Byron sure hammered that lecture into my head during my first year.

A bright fireball the size of a melon grew and shot from her hand. After soaring across the space, it connected with the stone wall on the opposite side and broke apart into tiny flames. This earned her slight gasps from some of the students, but most waited eagerly for more. Just as the sparks from her previous spell touched the ground, Coura launched two more blasts in the exact same spot.

The room fell into a stunned silence.

She turned with a smirk, knowing such accuracy proved difficult for even advanced mages to accomplish; however, Joshua, Selma, and a few others gave her unimpressed looks.

This time, she became determined to silence their doubts, even if it meant extending the display, and the wooden chair that had been pulled away from the table when Master Leni exited appeared tempting enough. With another reach into her center's pool of energy, Coura swiped her hand horizontally through the air, releasing a straight shot of flames directed at her target. The chair rocked back from the blow but didn't fall over. Instead, the flames engulfed it, charring the wood beneath.

When she remembered they stood in a sealed room, leaving no opening for the smoke to escape, she expended more energy, this time into the form of an ice spell. The crystals blew in such a unique way that they joined together to create a snow-like blast of air. Not only was the chair saved from burning up, but a thin layer of frost crept along its surface.

Coura prepared to face her fellow trainees once more until the door to the training space opened. Every student jumped at the sound before turning with wide eyes to see Master Leni frozen in the entryway. An expression of surprise graced her wrinkly face before a rage Coura recognized only too well replaced it.

"What is going on here?" their instructor demanded in her shrill voice as she stormed inside without closing the door.

Of course, no one spoke up. If they assumed Coura would, they should have thought better. She had been caught in this type of situation often enough to know Master Leni wouldn't listen to reason since the woman reprimanded disobedience.

The instructor's eyes went straight to the damaged furniture, then to Coura, who remained alone in the center of the room.

"I should have known," Master Leni grumbled, biting off the end of each word in disgust. "Everyone, we will pick up with this tomorrow. I expect better behavior from all of you by then."

The older mage watched the class leave with a hawk-like gaze. Her skinny build and long face were made more menacing with her graying hair pulled into a tight bun on top of her head. Each trainee kept their head down and silently hurried away before they could draw her wrath. Meanwhile, Coura stayed behind. Experience taught her a lecture was imminent, and possibly a worse one compared to those in the past. Once everybody else exited, Master Leni slowly closed the door and released a frustrated sigh.

"This is the fourth time this year, Coura," she began and held out her hands to emphasize her plea. "I don't understand why we keep having this issue."

She waited for some sort of reply and scowled when Coura didn't give one.

Of course she's upset, but any excuse I give won't be acceptable. I can't tell her I'm bored in this group again or she'll tell me to find something else to keep my mind occupied outside our class. If I mention how far above the other students I am, she'd just yell at me for 'overstating my abilities.'

Master Leni had no tolerance for what she couldn't control or supervise, which meant she and Coura didn't get along. After a few more seconds of silence, the instructor gestured for Coura to follow her out into the hallway. They both knew the way to the headmaster's office, so the older mage made no effort to keep track of her. Master Leni had certainly not been the only instructor who felt it necessary to send her there.

She ignored the curious glances of the students scattered around the academy halls at this break in the afternoon classes. Too many seemed to shoot her knowing glances, as if to say, "Coura's in trouble? What a surprise," while they snickered behind her back. Their reactions never bothered her, though, especially since they understood nothing of the issue bringing about her misbehavior. The two soon approached the office and slipped inside without a word.

Headmaster Symon's main room was past a waiting area where his secretary named Jann busied herself with stacks of paperwork. A window behind her desk let in plenty of light, and Coura wished the woman would open it to let some fresh air into the stuffy space. Jann sat up straighter at their arrival and finished what she had been writing but relaxed a trifle when she saw who entered.

"Master Leni, good afternoon to you," she greeted the instructor with a genuine smile.

Coura's teacher acknowledged the gesture by dipping her head in a sharp nod. "Same to you. Is the headmaster in?"

"Yes, ma'am." Jann waved a hand at the door to her right. "You can head on in."

Master Leni looked over at Coura, who already took a seat in one of two, wobbly chairs against the wall farthest from the headmaster's room. "Remain here, and do not cause trouble for Jann."

Coura gave a mock salute as the woman marched through the doorway to see Headmaster Symon. "Master Leni, I wasn't expecting you," she heard the man say before the door closed and faint murmuring began.

She huffed to show her displeasure and caught Jann offer a sympathetic smile. Then, the secretary returned to what business waited on her desk. Although the two crossed paths often enough, Jann always worked without feeling the need to make conversation.

Then again, how do you talk to somebody in trouble? Coura wondered absently. *I wish this didn't warrant a visit to the headmaster. Do the instructors think they can't address me directly aside from scolding my behavior? What do they worry I'll do when I leave this place?*

The notion pulled her mind in another direction.

The entire academy essentially taught three types of students until the age of sixteen: scholars, soldiers, and mages. Most scholars consisted of the children whose parents were noblemen, craftsmen, merchants, or others demonstrating high enough skills in reading, writing, geography, and history. Not many of these students enrolled at the academy, for the well-off could afford tutors or schools closer to the capital city of Verona, and merchants or craftsmen took on apprentices instead.

Other children not destined to inherit a position within a family business or who preferred physical work, an honorable title, and serving the country went into the army. Coura heard about families who considered it a tradition to have at least one child from their generation bring glory to their name by making that their livelihood. The academy taught the basics of fighting with a variety of weapons before those trainees were sent off in graduating classes to the capital for specific training. About a dozen students left every spring, so the option became fairly common around East Hoover.

The remaining classes consisted of magic users with the potential to be light or dark mages. Since the academy was the place for beginners to go for training, they made up most of the MAA.

Then, graduating mages selected one of four options based on their varying skills before they prepared to leave.

Those with the intellect and patience, or who grew too old or weak to do much else, could stay at the academy or return at a later time to teach future mages. Others with the drive for combat were encouraged to serve in the army, especially since all students learned how to wield a weapon, whether to defend or attack. Another option, and the most popular, involved acting as a guard for the cities and towns across Asteom where they worked alongside posted soldiers to protect and keep the peace. Students who favored staying close to their homes or who, more often than not, were not physically or emotionally fit to handle frequent violence chose this path. A final option had been reserved for individuals showing special talents useful to the king, generals, and master mage in the palace. Not too many students were recommended for these positions, which included spies, assassins, ambassadors, and other, unique jobs, but the trainees all knew it remained a potential route.

By the time a student turned sixteen, they usually possessed some inclination as to what they hoped to do. The country needed both dark and light mages, so a trainee could do whatever they set their heart on.

Unfortunately, Coura had no vision for her future.

Because I grew up here surrounded by combat and magic, I don't have a home or a family to influence my decision. It would be boring to stay in one place, and I doubt anybody would vouch for me if I wanted to teach. That leaves the army, which I could tolerate if I had to, but the idea of taking orders from a stranger bothers me. It would probably be the best fit, though.

The longer she thought about the decision, the more uncertain she felt. What was worse, she recently started her final year, meaning she would soon graduate and be forced to choose.

I'm almost certain you're placed before your seventeenth birthday, whether you agree with the assignment or not. By then, you should already know what you need in order to survive and are just wasting another trainee's spot.

Muffled yelling from the headmaster's main office caught Coura and Jann's attention, causing them to involuntarily glance at the door.

"Symon, I don't care about policies!" they heard Master Leni shout.

Softer, inaudible words followed, undoubtedly from the headmaster.

"…can't comply! I've never… She should be removed and … send somewhere. It would be easier on us all!"

More mumbling and hysterics took place before the two quieted. Coura's face flushed from a mixture of frustration and embarrassment when they continued a minute later with Master Leni emphasizing Coura's abilities and lack of responsibility.

At the desk, Jann cleared her throat in an uncomfortable manner to draw Coura's eyes. The woman's cheeks also appeared scarlet, as if she didn't believe she should be eavesdropping. "I'm going to deliver these documents to the messengers' department. Please, behave while I'm away. It shouldn't be much longer…"

They nearly fell over when Master Leni cried, "And another thing!" before diving into a rant regarding Coura's placement in that particular class as opposed to another with less students. Coura got the impression her teacher used this opportunity to complain about the other instructors and the drama going on with the faculty. Jann collected various papers and exited while pretending to ignore the headmaster's door, leaving Coura alone to unwillingly listen.

The conversation became more civil within the next minute, so Coura had to strain her ears in order to hear the headmaster's verdict. If he felt sympathetic toward her because of Master Leni's attitude, she'd receive extended, outside work or additional chores, which were punishments she became familiar with over the years.

She had no idea what his decision would be if he didn't pity her.

Upon further reflection, Coura realized every time she had been sent or escorted to his office, Headmaster Symon never spoke *with* her. He gave a brief lecture on what he considered to be the duties of a mage her age, then he shared his conclusion.

He should be used to assigning my punishments, yet I've never heard any of my instructors yell. Did I go too far by scorching the furniture? It wasn't the worst thing I've done, but why do I sense this time is different?

She caught Byron's name and immediately focused on listening to the conversation. When their words were still too muffled, Coura tiptoed to the door and pressed an ear against the crack in the thick wood. If Jann intended to avoid being involved, she probably would not return until Master Leni decided to leave.

"He's shirking his responsibilities, and we have no idea why," came Master Leni's high-pitched voice followed by the headmaster's soothing yet firm tone.

"I understand your frustration, but this is a private matter with the king and his council. We can't place trainees with Byron since he will be departing this afternoon. Every other spellcasting instructor has full classes."

"He is the only one who can tolerate her misbehavior. Now that he's running back to Verona, I will not stand for any more outbursts. This time, it was a chair; last time, she almost struck another student with a bolt of lightning while we were practicing shielding!"

Coura winced at the memory and remembered her desire to practice an advanced spell Byron started her on. After, Master Leni proceeded to recall another incident that left bruises and a shallow cut on a student when Coura chose to work with real swords instead of their wooden practice blades while the instructor assisted a new trainee.

What bothered her the most wasn't the talk of her past troubles nor the lack of places for them to move her; learning her favorite, preferred teacher planned to leave, as well as the lack of compassion from her instructors, hurt.

She stepped away from the door to stand in the middle of the room, unsure of what to think. *Byron is the only person who actually cares about me, not just about obedience and potential. I never misbehave when I'm with him because of that. Well, and because I make progress when I study under him instead of toying around with the basics. I can't believe he's going to the capital so soon after returning. Last time, he was gone for two weeks, and before that, he stayed here for just a week and a half.*

Another consideration came to mind. *He also avoids confronting anybody when he departs. He didn't train many students, at least no one who needs it like I do, which means he isn't leaving much behind. Since the headmaster made it sound as if the other instructors don't know about his visits, I doubt Byron makes an effort to tell anyone else.*

Coura glanced around the empty office and debated what she should do.

Jann might be taking her time, and too many eyes will notice me in the hallway outside. Byron could still be in his room, though. If I speak with him about this issue, maybe he can give me some advice for handling Master Leni. In any case, I really don't feel like listening to another lecture on responsibility.

***

Headmaster Symon held his tongue while his subordinate continued venting about her student, Byron, and the faculty's inability to cooperate and communicate effectively. Beneath the annoyance with her dramatics, a genuine interest blossomed from what Leni revealed.

I can't believe he didn't explain what he's been doing at the palace. That fool! Now I'm the one who must deal with the master mages' backlash.

In a way, it was better for Byron to avoid mentioning why he traveled to Verona so frequently, yet Symon had not considered how this could lead to suspicion and hostility among the other instructors. After all, what his friend's work dealt with would determine the future of their graduating mage trainees.

Once the woman stopped to breathe, Symon pounced on his opportunity to rectify the situation. "Leni, would you like to know why Byron is leaving so often?"

She tried to hide her curiosity but failed. "I suppose it's better late than never."

The woman is just concerned, as I hear all the master mages are. These changes hide an issue going on right under their noses. I figure I would be anxious as well, he told himself to remain neutral. Symon's ability to rationalize with a level head had been one of the reasons his peers recommended he accept the position of headmaster for the academy.

"Byron is our most powerful dark mage and has always trained the fewest number of students. He lived in the capital during his service in the army and can make the demanding trek between Verona and East Hoover. Also, I personally acknowledged him as our representative for King Hernan's council because of his critical thinking skills and patience." Symon paused to wait for any additional comments.

"Get on with it," Master Leni muttered with an edge to her voice.

"To put it in plain terms, Byron is constructing a contract of sorts with King Hernan and the generals." He went into detail about the proposed law and what both sides, the academy and the army, had to say.

By the end of his response, the old mage hunched forward with her fingers laced across her lap. She wore a thoughtful expression then spoke with a calmness that startled him a little.

"I see. There is much more happening outside these walls."

"I'm glad we had this discussion," Symon admitted while rising from his seat to conclude their meeting. His legs grew stiff from sitting nearly all morning, so he paused to stretch his back. "I'm going to ask you to spread this news to your fellow instructors and apologize on my behalf. Please advise them not to speak of this to the trainees yet. I'm sorry it took this long for you to find out, but I believe it's better for all of you to hear it now while it is just a possibility."

Leni stood as well, appearing drained from the discussion, and nodded.

The poor woman. Ranting really wore her out. She must have been suppressing her suspicion up to a boiling point. Speaking of which, we ignored Coura.

"I suppose I should deal with your student sometime today too," he joked. To his relief, she laughed.

"Oh, I forgot about her! My mind is leaving me fast lately, Symon."

"I'm sure it's making room for more important matters," he reassured her with a chuckle.

Leni pinched the bridge of her nose. "I don't know what to do with her. What I told you from the beginning is true. I have never dealt with a student who seems determined to disobey instructions from every teacher."

The bags under her eyes were evidence she hadn't lied about the burden of the extra students in her classes due to Byron's absence, and their consistent troublemaker.

Every child shifting into a young adult goes through a period of time where they act independent. With that being said, I can't recall any student who caused this level of stress in their instructors. Could it be because she has a unique past without a connection to her family or hometown?

As Symon ushered the weary woman from his office, he thought about the first time he encountered Coura four years ago. Byron, of all people, had been the one to bring the confused, senseless girl to the MAA for recovery. Even a lesser mage like Symon noticed the amount of dark energy surrounding her at the time.

I don't believe the scouts we sent to Neston a few weeks after her arrival reported anyone claiming her as their relative. There may have been a mother who disappeared, but nobody came looking for her within the last four years. Besides, from what Byron told me, Coura possesses no memories of the place or interest in visiting, which was why he never pursued an investigation. Such an odd turn of events that brought her to us indeed.

Of course, Byron volunteered to take the girl under his wing, giving her private tutoring to nurture her abilities that far outdistanced the other trainees her age. With no knowledge of her schooling background, Coura went through the basic exams for academics, combat skills, and magic. She became passionate about everything except the textbook courses, such as history, geography, and mathematics, but picked up on spellcasting as naturally as breathing. This came from her teachers' observations when they would update him, especially Byron during their private conversations.

"It's just that attitude of hers," his friend would complain. "She has all the potential in the world and no interest in controlling it. She accomplishes one task, hones one ability, before leaping into five others without completely understanding why it's necessary to do things a certain way or take the process step by step. When I tell her to relax and focus, she becomes upset with me and argues why our pace is slow. In her eyes, if it isn't keeping her entertained, it's not worth the time. The worst part is she learns the 'how' so quickly, faster than any of my previous students, yet couldn't care less about the 'why.' If she put in the extra effort and time to do that, she wouldn't be messing around in her classes."

I believe I referred to him as a borderline parent for Coura after he made that last comment. Even so, Byron tolerates her mischief because he understands her personality, abilities, and progress since he's been her primary teacher. With him traveling, though, she is unable to train properly at the same level, leading to a lack of interest in simpler classes and her unintentionally causing trouble.

Symon still had no idea what he could say to help Coura's situation, but at the moment, he needed to provide some sort of response to satisfy Master Leni. He opened his office door to exit with the woman close behind and stood alone in front of his secretary's desk.

"Where is she?" he asked as he moved to the door leading out into the hallway.

"I cannot believe this," Leni exclaimed from where she stood at his side. "I give her one, simple order, and she disappears!"

Against his own disappointment in Coura, Symon wondered how long they conversed and peeked into the hall. He saw Jann leafing through the stack of papers in her hands farther down yet not out of earshot.

I bet she felt uncomfortable with the yelling. I recall her mentioning her home life involved constantly bickering relatives, so I understand why she needed a break at the first sign of a verbal argument.

Symon cleared his throat, a sound that filled the empty space. "Jann?"

The lady looked up without hiding her relief and hurried over. "Headmaster, forgive me. I wanted to run these to the messengers' office, but they had their own meeting. I wasn't sure how long it would take for both rooms to clear."

He placed a reassuring hand on her shoulder accompanied by a smile she returned, then he led them inside his office. As Jann returned to the desk to rearrange the sheets of paper, Leni tapped a foot after crossing her arms. Symon noticed the movement and grew curious if Jann saw Coura sneak out. When he decided to ask, she shook her head with a worried expression.

"I lingered in front of the door for a while," she started. "I would have seen if she left."

Leni threw up her hands, as if her patience for the situation finally ran out. "Coura couldn't have just vanished!"

After a moment of confused silence, a warm, summer breeze blew through the room. Symon closed his eyes to savor it while figuring out his next approach when Jann begged his pardon.

"Headmaster, I'm not sure what Coura made of your words, but I do know that when I left, the window was closed."

***

A sturdy pack filled with clothes, rations, and various tools lay in front of Byron, and he nodded in approval at the contents. In the back of his mind, the master mage told himself not to worry since he completed the five-day trip to the capital numerous times. The palace servants also knew him well enough to keep extras of what he would need stored away until his arrival.

"You're leaving again?" an irritated voice from behind addressed him, one Byron had become accustomed to hearing.

A glance up from his bag showed his primary student Coura sitting on the sill of his open window with an unamused look. He matched the expression in an attempt to hide his disappointment at being caught heading out once again without mentioning it to anyone.

"You should be in class," he countered.

Coura crossed her arms and frowned. "You were planning on sneaking out at the busiest time of the day to avoid seeing anyone. How selfish of you."

When Byron closed his bag instead of answering, she hopped off the windowsill and strolled over to where he remained kneeling next to his items. Only then did he respond.

"You realize you're almost finished with your training, right? Skipping the extra practice hinders your progress."

"I already know every lesson in those classes," his student proclaimed arrogantly. "They can't teach me what you can."

Byron didn't need to ask who she was referring to. Both Coura and Symon informed him when her instructors grew impatient with her attitude, usually resulting in her being sent to the headmaster's office. *I'm only thirty-six years old, yet all this work and these constant trips to argue with royalty are taking their toll on my body. Not to mention my own lack of training, both physically and magically. If Coura could just wait until my business is done, or she graduates in the spring, life will become more interesting.*

He rose and reluctantly decided to face the conversation he'd put aside for weeks. With as stern a look as he could muster, Byron took in the most powerful yet troublesome student he had the pleasure of mentoring. In the four years since he brought Coura to the academy, she developed into a tough fighter and gifted mage. Unbound, black hair trailed down her back and blew slightly in the gentle breeze from the window as her sapphire eyes shone with unfavorable emotions directed at his leaving. He noted the rarity of her combination of physical characteristics on more than one occasion.

Typically, a mage who can wield dark energy carries similar features to their ancestors, Byron reflected while running a hand through his ink-colored hair. *Black or coppery hair, pale skin sensitive to sunlight, and green eyes are key indicators. I'm a pretty accurate example.*

In addition to those with dark blood, meaning somewhere in time their lineage traced to the demons living beneath the planet's surface, were ordinary humans and light-blooded mages. The first humans in the country were said to possess chestnut eyes and hair complementing their tan skin, which scholars believe resulted from working in the eastern plains. Since they couldn't manipulate magical energies, typically someone bearing those features was not destined to be a mage.

The other type, those with light blood, descended from the angelic race who live in the hidden city of Yeluthia, otherwise known as the 'city in the clouds.' Hundreds of years ago, the angels protected humanity by sealing the demons beneath the surface. Anybody sharing their power could wield light magic and often possessed blond or white hair, fair skin, and their signature, blue eyes.

The bloodlines became so mixed over the decades that features hardly mattered when judging whether a person has the ability to use magic; however, he'd never met anyone with Coura's set of eyes and hair color before.

Byron appeared as one would expect, showcasing cropped, black hair and emerald eyes. He stood a head taller than his student, who continued studying him, and shaped his body for combat during his younger years, resulting in muscular arms and a broad chest.

After the long pause while all of that came to mind, he finally caved in. "Why aren't you in class?"

Instead of answering, she held her ground, as usual. "Why are you leaving again?"

"I asked first," he retorted with a knowing, crooked smile.

"We were let out early." She said no more, giving Byron the impression she hid part of the truth.

"You got yourself in trouble again, didn't you?"

A brief flash of surprise passed over her face before the stubbornness returned, causing her to hesitate. "I didn't do anything wrong. I just didn't do exactly what Master Leni expected."

Byron rubbed his tired eyes. *If I'm counting right, this marks the eighth time this school year I heard a similar reason from either her, Symon, or another instructor.*

"Coura," he began before she cut him off.

"It's not my fault! I'm bored in these classes, Byron. You and I know my magic's stronger than the rest of the trainees'. I do what I'm supposed to, but I'm wasting my time."

"Have you really learned about the spells, or just how to cast them?" he asked without hiding his skepticism.

She nodded, showing more confidence than he expected. "I can cast the types of spells. I've been practicing how much energy to put into them and played around with the form each takes."

His student went on to explain the situation that landed her in the headmaster's office. Despite her disobedience and the risks involved, he felt a sense of pride in her progress and how she manipulated her power.

As she neared the end, he deduced another issue had prompted Leni's decision to visit Symon. *While Coura's actions were unnecessary, I wouldn't deem them horrible enough for her to see the headmaster. Also, for Leni to blow up on him loud enough for Coura to overhear is unprofessional and uncharacteristic of the woman. I'm assuming since she brought up my name, the faculty is curious about my temporary assignment in Verona. How will Symon react to this?*

Coura finished her account and appeared to be waiting for some sort of reassurance, which he didn't feel inclined to give at the moment.

"Do you not trust your instructors?"

She gave him a confused stare before answering. "Well, of course. I suppose, but-"

"Did you ever stop to think there's more to magic than learning the spells?" he interrupted without restraining a portion of his own, personal frustration. "Their age and experience allow them to prepare you and the other trainees for the future. If you bothered to practice in those classes, you would improve your aim and exert less energy. I told you that on multiple occasions. Your problem is, you can't see the bigger picture, the *why* of what you are taught in class and what opportunities are available to develop your abilities. Without the right mindset, we're no better than careless workers thoughtlessly going through life."

Coura did not take criticism well. He knew that much as he saw her whole body grow tense and face flush with repressed anger and shame; however, he dealt with her enough by that point to know when he seriously pushed her limits.

Although Byron refused to step down and returned her glare, he continued in a patient tone. "I am telling you this because, by disobeying their instructions, you're not only flirting with potential danger to others who are less skilled, but also showing your classmates it's possible for them to test their power unsupervised and disobey authority. We've had plenty of accidents, both here and out in the field. People died because they lost control while experimenting with the simplest of spells."

Coura paled a bit and averted her eyes.

Byron stopped himself from adding to the subject once he remembered her past. A sudden headache brought about by the conversation forced him to try calming down by inhaling deep breaths. Meanwhile, his student mumbled to her feet and turned her gaze toward the wall on her left.

"What was that?" he inquired and hoped for some cooperation.

"I guess I didn't consider the risks," she replied at a volume he could hear.

"You usually don't."

When he reflected on his relationship with Coura, Byron found he cared about her for two reasons. Primarily, he had been the person to find her alone and helpless against the frightening power inside her body. He didn't have children since his job filled the need for any, but never before did he feel obligated to assist and teach an orphan with nothing else except the MAA. The second consideration, as he realized shortly into their training, had to do with the fact that Coura's personality didn't fit what one expects or encourages in a mage.

She's headstrong and defiant, always willing to jump out of line if it means proving a point. When she doesn't understand a lesson or problem, she gets frustrated and often uses force instead of her brain. If this behavior doesn't stop, she'll avoid reaching her potential and need to be restrained because of how strong and skilled she's become. In today's case, she refused to listen in favor of showing off. I understand she tires at a slower rate than most people and the classes seem beneath her abilities, but that's no excuse for acting up.

His mind cleared when he believed his point reached her, but another thought came to him immediately after. A glance at the bag by his feet reminded Byron he was supposed to be on the road to Verona. He suppressed a groan at the idea of another trip, which he seemed to be doing more frequently.

Every other week for the past four months, he visited the capital to meet with King Hernan and the man's council and discuss the possibility of a new law involving the graduating students at the Magical Arts Academy. It had been an uneventful series of ventures, but having time to settle in to one spot tempted him often. Still, Symon recommended him as the spokesperson on the academy's behalf, so he couldn't say no.

"Byron?"

He shifted his eyes away from the pack and back to his student's gaze where he caught her concern and interest. "Hmm?"

"You look like you want to fall on the bed and sleep for the rest of the day."

"Is it that obvious?"

"Only to someone who sees you enough. Tell me why you're always gone."

Byron chuckled and rubbed the back of his neck while Coura visibly relaxed. She leaned against his desk with her arms crossed, and the hint of a smile settled on her lips. The stark difference in her tone and mannerisms from a minute ago was like day and night. That, as he learned over the years, meant she took his words to heart and moved on.

"I don't believe that's any of your business," he teased.

"Fine, but how much longer are you going to be doing this?" she pressed then hurried to add an additional comment. "Not because I miss you. We're both aware you're the only dark mage who can train me properly, and the only one who's willing to put up with me."

I can't argue with that.

"I don't know," he admitted. "It shouldn't be too long. Also, you can't expect to learn everything from me. It might do you some good to cooperate with your peers and instructors. As I mentioned earlier, it'll be worth your time to practice basic spellcasting anyway."

"Are you sure you're not saying this because your abilities are going stale? Because if-"

A knock at the door cut off the rest of her sarcasm before Byron could. He prepared to shout for the guest to enter until he remembered he locked his office door while packing to avoid unwanted company.

I'll need to remember to lock the window next time as well.

While he approached the door, Byron intentionally ended their conversation. "We can continue this discussion when I return, but I'd appreciate if your behavior and attitude improve. You're about to graduate. I won't always be around to keep an eye on you or bail you out of trouble. A master mage should be able to think critically about a situation before making decisions while following the law. Remember that, Coura."

Without waiting for her response, he unbolted the lock and opened the door. His longtime friend Symon slid inside a second later, as poised as ever.

"Headmaster, to what do I owe the pleasure?" Byron asked while closing the door.

"We've been through this enough to dismiss the formalities," Symon replied with a wave of his hand. After, he noticed Coura, now standing straight, placing her arms at her sides, and wearing the guilty expression of a criminal expecting the hammer to fall. "I came to see you off before you left, though I imagined you would be alone."

Byron apologized and turned to Coura. "Do you mind?"

As she stepped toward the door in a motion to leave, Symon shook his head. "There's no need. I just need to give you these and wish my friend a safe voyage."

He handed over a satchel after. A brief glance showed the bag held signed documents on various matters. Byron usually offered to transfer papers for the capital because nobody made the trek as often. Symon shot him a grateful smile, lifting his spirits a bit, yet he intended to poke fun at the job anyway.

"I see. You must confirm your requests are taken care of, and the messenger boy follows through with his duty. I remember the days when people would ask before shoving papers in my face."

Byron held his chin higher while wearing a grave expression he knew Symon couldn't stand. The headmaster tried not to laugh and failed. Seconds later, Byron joined in before noticing Coura's slight alarm at their behavior.

She must have forgotten our history. Thinking about when we graduated from here has me feeling old. My preference always leaned toward offensive magic and combat, which led to my decision to join Verona's army for further training. Meanwhile, Symon enjoyed life behind his desk where he strives to better the future of younger generations. He's organized, honest, and as personable as necessary with a fair sense of judgement comparable to most of Asteom's leaders.

When the MAA sought instructors, Symon had been one of the first to volunteer. A few years later, the previous headmaster opted to retire, opening the position to the rest of the faculty. Their unanimous vote went to him, and despite his uncertainty about upholding the academy's standards, it didn't take long for him to adjust.

"You're worth far more than a messenger boy," Symon responded while assuming a thoughtful expression. "I believe you're comparable to an ox. It suits both your build and personality."

Byron rolled his eyes. "So, I'm an animal now? If I am to be an ox, you must be some sort of colorful bird that spends all morning chattering."

Symon pretended to appear offended before composing himself and casting a gaze at Coura with a frown. "Indeed, I did a lot of that today. I seem to be hearing a rather extensive list of problems from Coura's instructors. As you know, I'm obliged to inform you."

Coura blushed and looked away from them. While Byron knew how to craft a conversation to get the message across in the easiest way possible, Symon always followed a straightforward approach with his words. In this case, Byron chose to address Symon directly, as if Coura wasn't present, in order to ease the tension.

"I spoke with her about the issues she's been having and those she created for others. It seems I will need to spend some time with her when I return, though additional practice outside class is just what any student could use before leaving the academy."

Symon sent Byron a questionable look. "Yes, I understand. In fact, I remember you mentioning how much you appreciated your lessons after you graduated. You relied on them when you began in the army, right?"

The headmaster gazed upward in thought, leaving Byron to wonder what the man was planning. After a moment, Symon nodded to himself, eyed Coura, then smiled at Byron.

"Coura is at the age to become an apprentice."

Byron shot his friend a wary gaze in response. "Yes, and?"

He better not suggest assigning her anywhere. I've had this talk with him and several instructors more than once. I won't allow her raw potential to be put into practice without the proper training, especially since she doesn't remember her life outside East Hoover. Unfortunately, the likelihood of this happening to our students is growing thanks to the law King Hernan wants to put in place...

A few months ago, Symon received a notice from His Highness stating the generals hoped to form a contract with the academy. They proposed the mages would train until the age of seventeen before being integrated into the army for three years. After their service is fulfilled, they could choose to stay in the palace or leave for one of the other career options available to them. The reason for such an idea, according to the generals, stemmed from fewer mages joining the army. In case of a war with the neighboring, northern country, they desired fully prepared troops.

Our dilemma has to do with most trainees naturally not showing interest in that life because they either aren't built to handle the stress and sights or they lack the skills for combat. Pressure, fear, and raw emotions are dangerous for mages since they impact our control over our energy. My explanation sounds too ridiculous to the king and his generals, though.

Symon's next words pulled Byron out of his thoughts before putting him in a sour mood. This time, the headmaster intentionally addressed Coura, who remained wide-eyed and apprehensive.

"Have you considered where you would like to go once you graduate?"

"I went over my options, but I haven't decided what to do," she answered honestly and without any trace of the nerves she displayed earlier.

"What would you say to tagging along with Byron on his visit to the capital city?" Symon asked, to both Byron and Coura's surprise.

Before Byron could wrap his head around the idea, and possibly dissuade his student, she agreed to the request. The pair glanced at him while wearing matching grins, as if the suggestion had been planned. He met their looks with a disapproving stare and tried to figure out his own stance on the invitation; however, Symon sent Coura off to pack for the journey.

The headmaster closed the door by the time Byron processed the whole affair. Then, his friend faced him with an air of defiance in preparation for a challenge.

"What prompted you to do that?" Byron asked instead of arguing. Although he trusted Symon, the man acted impulsive at the best of times and intolerable at the worst when it came to dealing with these types of situations.

"As I mentioned, her instructors have been complaining to me for weeks when she's not under your supervision. Normally, I shrug off a misbehaving student once they learn their lesson or consider dismissing them from the academy if the problem continues. However…"

"Coura's not exactly normal."

Symon tapped a finger on his lips. "We would have nowhere to send her, but I must say, the idea of her wandering around Asteom with such potential is concerning. Nonetheless, both her attitude and abilities need your hand, and yours alone. On top of that, she *is* of age for apprenticing. Don't assume I forgot our talks either. I wouldn't let her graduate unless I was sure she could control herself and not tarnish our reputation."

"All right," Byron agreed in defeat. "Besides the obvious, why else do you want her accompanying me?"

Symon sighed and appeared sympathetic toward Byron. "I worry about my friend, you know. Every time you return, I can tell this assignment has placed more burdens on your shoulders. Also, with the risk of a war upon us, at least according to what you mentioned, I need to believe you'll stay safe. Even though Coura seems ready to graduate, this should be a worthwhile experience for her. I'm hoping it will give her a glimpse into why we're so serious about our training."

Byron lightened up at the response. "I like the idea; it just caught me off guard."

The headmaster placed a reassuring hand on his shoulder. "There's another reason too."

"And what would that be?"

Symon stepped back to begin opening the door. "I can imagine how lonely you must be. A little company could do you good. Your morning breath wards off any living creature nearby, and I won't even go into your cooking. I only hope the young woman can tolerate smoke and burnt meals, or else she'll starve to death."

"Why you…"

Byron didn't have enough time to grab a light object to throw since the headmaster slipped into the hallway and closed the door after his final remark.

So, that's his way of saying goodbye? Then again, it was all Byron needed from his friend.

An Unexpected Companion

"I thought our adventure would be a little more exciting," Coura commented from behind Byron.

He turned his head to address her from where he led a few steps ahead. "What did you expect? Remember, it takes a few days to get to the capital."

"You don't even get a horse?" To her amazement, he laughed at the question and faced forward to continue at a leisurely pace.

I guess that's a no then, she concluded as she adjusted the bag on her shoulders before trotting to walk beside her teacher. Although he would never mention it, Byron seemed to enjoy her presence more than he initially let on.

The two set out from East Hoover on their journey to the palace a few hours ago. Byron took extra steps to make sure she behaved, a decision Coura couldn't blame him for. He even lectured her during the first part of the day on traveling safely, proper manners in a public setting, and whatever else he deemed important. She continued nodding and promised to not cause trouble, but eventually he caught on to her excitement spurred by finally leaving the academy. The positive emotions eased his tension, and they fell into conversations about casual topics, such as the local wildlife and climate conditions for the area.

In the evening, they settled in a clearing off the road. Byron assigned Coura the task of starting a fire, feeding it, and collecting enough wood to last through the night while he set up their bedrolls and cooking supplies. With no more than a wave of her hand and a touch of the energy in her center, she created sparks to catch on the tinder. Once a basic fire rose, she stood and walked away to fetch some branches.

"Just a moment," Byron called.

When she turned around, it startled her to see him stomping out the fire with one foot. "What are you doing?" she demanded.

He rummaged through his bag, removed two stones, and tossed them over. "Make it again."

"Why?"

"Because I said so," he answered while dropping to sit and pull out bread, fruit, and dried meats that would serve as their supper.

Coura cocked her head, waiting for more, and chose to raise a hand and repeat the fire spell. To spite him, she enlarged the flame so it could catch on to the smashed kindling.

Instead of rising, Byron picked up a blanket at his side and beat the flames until they disappeared into the dirt. She watched without comprehending and immediately grew irritated with his actions. Only after nothing except charred tinder remained did he set the blanket aside before gazing at her with a challenge in his eyes.

"Make it again," he repeated and gestured to the stones in her hands.

Her lips curved into a sardonic smile. "I did."

"Let me be clear. Make it again but with the fire-starting stones you're holding, unless not using magic for this task seems too daunting."

She knew this game far too well. When Byron wanted certain results, he would find a way to appeal to her competitive nature; however, this time she became more curious about the purpose of his order than determined to prove herself. "I will when you tell me why."

"Because I said so."

Coura narrowed her eyes at her mentor, who remained unphased by her attitude. "That's a stupid reason."

"Perhaps, but it's still mine. Now hurry up before we're fumbling in the dark."

Coura knelt next to the remains of the previous fires with a displeased grumble, arranged what she could collect into acceptable tinder, and began scraping one flint stone against the other until a spark on the dry material produced smoke. She coddled the weak flame for a few minutes until it rose enough to not go out.

"There, are you happy?" She dropped the stones on the ground in front of Byron and hurried to the edge of the campsite to grab as many twigs and branches as she could carry.

"You'll find the heartier pieces if you head farther out," her instructor called from his spot.

Coura ignored him and continued her task. When she collected a sufficient amount of wood, she returned to set the armload into a pile before feeding their fire. Only after they ate a simple supper of the tough meat, toasted bread with butter, and an apple for dessert did she feel like making conversation.

"Why did you have me use flint stones instead of magic?"

"For two reasons," Byron began as he wiped his hands on the grass. "First, we typically never use those to start a fire. I needed to see you do it in case you had to learn."

"Why should I? You taught me mages manipulate the energy inside our center. That power stays in us as long as we're alive, right? Why wouldn't I be able to use it?"

"What do you know about light and dark energy types?"

Coura bit her lip. "Light energy allows some people to wield light magic, and dark energy lets us wield dark magic."

"That's putting it in an extremely simple way, but fine. What if it isn't possible to use magic?"

She pondered the notion for a moment. "When do we experience that? I've never seen or heard of a mage lacking the ability to manifest a spell."

"Try not to think of the question in terms of a mage not possessing enough energy. We can cover what happens when you drain your reserves another time. What I'm referring to is rare, but some situations involve certain circumstances when we shouldn't use our magic, or it would be better not to. What if you had to avoid detection or were assigned to a group of people unfamiliar with mages? I can share multiple stories of when using spells became more dangerous than avoiding them."

"You never told me that," Coura replied as she found her interest in the subject growing.

Byron nodded and went on. "In my earlier years stationed in Fester, a fire started outside the city in an old farmhouse, and the family had been terrified. At first, I tried to put it out by using ice blasts while holding a shield to keep the flames contained, but the owners of the farmhouse went mad when I did. You see, magic caused the mess, so wielding it connected me to their suffering. Not to mention, it made me a suspect."

"So, what did you do?" she pressed, unable to imagine anyone panicking after witnessing a basic spell at work.

"I brought down my shield and grabbed a bucket like the rest. It may have taken longer and caused more damage in the end, but it stirred less chaos around the family." Byron gave her a sidelong glance, as if expecting her next question.

"I understand the first reason. What's the second?"

His lips bent into a frown. "Obedience."

"What?"

"It's no secret you struggle to follow directions, Coura. I promised the headmaster and my fellow instructors I'd work on that with you."

Something about the way Byron phrased his words bothered her. "Do *you* have a problem with my behavior?"

He paused to look past her. "I do, and before you complain, just listen. There are appropriate times to follow your own judgment or speak out but also instances when you should respect authority, trust others, and obey instructions."

"What if they're wrong? What if they don't understand the full situation?" Coura countered while remembering her issues at the academy. "How can you sacrifice your own needs to follow someone else, especially if you don't know them personally?"

"As I said, you should be able to understand when to follow your own instincts, let somebody lead, or adapt. In your classes, instead of using the extra time to practice or seek advice, you disrupted the other trainees' progress. Tonight, you disobeyed my request because you didn't trust my intentions. In the army, that's treachery."

"If you would have told me this before, I'd have done it right away," she argued and tried to wrap her head around his logic.

"You're missing the point. There won't always be an opportunity to talk, and sometimes you don't get an explanation because there isn't one. Believe in your comrades and their decisions. It might not turn out how you predict, but no one knows for sure. Most importantly, how can you expect to earn others' loyalty if you're not willing to give yours?"

"I'll earn it through my own actions and decisions."

"Look where that lands you with your instructors," he added, showing a hint of his frustration. "What if your choices and actions cause harm or worsen the problem? The generals you'll work under in the future have experience guiding troops toward a goal. Soldiers risk their lives for beliefs embodied in their superiors."

"When did I ever mention I planned to be a soldier?"

The question stopped Byron in his tracks. He stared at her for a moment before realizing what his lecture implied and apologized. While she wrapped her blanket around her shoulders, Coura wondered what drove him to assume she would join the army.

"No matter what, I trust my own judgement over a stranger's," she concluded matter-of-factly. "If they give me the information I need to make a decision, I can work with them, but I would never lend anyone my abilities unless I know their intentions."

She lied down after and faced away from Byron when he continued to study her. After a few moments passed, she heard him moving around, then silence.

His lack of a response stirred a bit of guilt. *I don't regret what I said at all. No one should ever be forced to obey someone else's orders without understand why they should. Then again, I guess I see what he means about having faith in those who are experienced.*

Byron's voice in the quiet evening air startled her out of the self-reflection.

"Do you trust me enough to follow my advice?"

She wanted to laugh. *Of course I do. I wouldn't come along if I wasn't willing to work with you. Is he asking if I believe in his intentions enough not to question them?*

After a moment of thought, Coura noticed his even tone suggested more beneath what she heard. In response, she replied honestly with what she figured he hoped to hear. "Yes, I trust you."

*

The second day of traveling proved uneventful. They wandered through a town where none of the people paid them any attention, then the pair made camp outside the area in another clearing populated by merchants with carts and others on their own business.

As they settled away from everybody else, Byron explained his usual route to Coura and how they should reach Verona over the next three days. Each field he planned camp in was one he occupied several times over the recent months. Since the roads would only grow busier as they neared the capital, he expected the clearings to contain additional travelers, who provided a sense of protection and left firepits to make their preparations easier.

The following morning, the duo set out; however, instead of taking the populated road leading through another town, Byron directed them along a rough path in the thicker part of the woods.

"Why aren't we moving with everyone else on the better route again?" Coura asked as she pushed aside a branch covered with pine needles. Plenty hung over the dirt trail to prevent a leisurely stroll.

"This is more scenic," Byron answered in a carefree manner.

They saw much of the wildlife in and through the trees, which varied in color from bright and darker greens to the browns and whites of tree bark and spots of floral colors. Since Coura didn't remember her years outside the academy, the sights, evergreen scent, and sounds of water, rustling leaves, and creatures scurrying around seemed practically new. The weather complemented the scenery as sunlight poured through the canopy above, shining on the plants and covering the branches all around them. The downside, besides the path's solitude, proved to be the biting bugs constantly buzzing near her face. When her temper got the better of her, she started slapping at them with no remorse.

"You sure know how to make a lot of noise in a forest full of it," Byron commented from where he hiked in front of her.

"I can't help it! I'm being bitten all over," Coura snapped and swatted her cheek as a fly landed on it.

"Hang on just a little longer. I remember a break in the trees coming up soon," he reassured her.

As promised, the trees thinned so more light poured on the land before they emerged into a grassy field. She stretched her arms upward and released a content sigh when the bugs remained behind.

"Finally, I thought we'd never-"

Byron stopped Coura with an arm, freezing her in place. She understood something was wrong by that action alone and scanned the seemingly ordinary space. Foliage surrounded the space as a wider trail cut through to the opposite end. Near the middle, an assortment of wildflowers grew just off the path. She squinted at a purple bunch and noticed a figure lying on one side and facing away from the two. The arm in front of her lowered as Byron hurried toward the person.

She followed without rushing and watched the edge of the trees, reaching out her mind as she did so in order to sense any possible, unknown presences. Her imagination conjured scenarios of bandits and beasts hiding beyond while using innocent bodies as bait. Byron knelt next to the figure, so she remained standing to continue keeping an eye out around them. Still, the forest chimed on. After a moment, she settled down enough to focus on the waking stranger.

***

Byron's initial thought after spotting a boy in the clearing and confirming no unnatural power lingered nearby was to check if

42

the stranger had been harmed. He already swept the area for suspicious activity by instinct and allowed Coura to do so on her own. That way, she could independently learn what should be done in that kind of situation; however, in such a secluded area as he knew the place to be, he didn't expect they would need to fret over much.

"Are you all right?" he asked and gently pressed the back of one hand against the boy's forehead. After a brief inspection, Byron realized the stranger was not as young as he guessed.

Shaggy, brown hair covered the stranger's face enough to barely hide a set of round glasses pressed to his cheek in an awkward position. Despite a scrawny build comprised of short, skinny limbs, he didn't appear older than the students at the MAA. No physical injuries were present, and his breathing remained deep and steady.

"Is he asleep?" Coura inquired in a surprised tone from behind his shoulder.

"It seems that way," Byron muttered with some amusement before shaking the young man's shoulders to wake him.

The stranger started, blinked up at them, and wore a dazed expression. After realizing he wasn't alone, he let out a startled yelp and pushed himself away from Byron.

"I-I-I just… Who are you?" he stammered in a frightened manner. "How did you f-find me? I don't have anything!"

In response, Byron held up his hands to erase any concern regarding his intentions. "We're not here to harm you. We came along the trail and found you lying in the middle of the grass. Are you hurt?"

The young man stared at him before leaning back to stare up at the sky, seemingly reflecting on his situation. "I don't remember."

Byron waited while the stranger began looking around and muttering to himself before exclaiming, "That's right!" Then, he searched the ground and lifted one of the violet flowers bearing wilted petals.

"I came here to study this."

"What is it?" Coura asked.

"It's a purple fly-lily. These only bloom in areas where direct sunlight, lots of rain, and warm temperatures are available. I heard a rumor in Fester claiming they grew in these woods, so I set out to find them."

Byron pushed himself to his feet and offered the young man his hand. When the stranger accepted his gesture, Byron noticed a satchel, papers, bottles, and various utensils scattered around their location. "What happened to you? Were you attacked?"

The young man flushed and gave Byron a sheepish look. "Oh no, not at all. I needed to make sure this actually is the right flower, so I ground it into an edible paste. The purple fly-lily's pollen is said to act as a sleeping agent, which can be useful in many potions."

Coura stepped forward and pointed at the flower. "So you figured the best way to test its pollen was to taste it for yourself? That's idiotic!"

Byron nudged his student with an elbow to stop her from scolding the stranger further. Although she glared at him while rubbing her side, she didn't offer an additional comment. "My name is Byron, and this is Coura. We're mages from East Hoover on our way to Verona."

"I'm William Shairp, but you can call me Will," the young man replied before offering a genuine smile.

Byron returned the friendly gesture. "It's nice to meet you, Will. As long as you're okay, I suppose we should leave you to your work."

"Actually, I'm heading to Verona as well. Would you mind some additional company for the remainder of your journey?"

Will bobbed like a rabbit as he gathered his belongings without waiting for an answer. Meanwhile, Byron contemplated taking him along and couldn't come up with any reason not to.

"I suppose it wouldn't be a problem," he responded before returning to their route.

"Just try not to slow us down," Coura commented with her arms crossed.

If she meant any offense, Will didn't seem to notice. He only bowed his head to hide an embarrassed blush.

"Come along, you two," Byron called. "We'll set up camp before the sun sets as soon as we reach the edge of these woods and see the main road." He took the lead after, leaving Coura and Will to follow.

***

Coura knew Will's type from her interactions with the scholarly trainees at the MAA, and they hadn't been her favorite people to talk to. As the trio trekked through the forest, she became annoyed with his constant analyzing of each tree, plant, root, and berry in the woods. Byron seemed more inclined to listen after sharing a little about their journey and even asked a question or two.

"Coura, you're awfully quiet," her mentor addressed her from the front of their line. Once they began moving together, the two mages made sure to keep Will between them.

"What do you want me to say?" she responded in a harsher tone than she intended. A flying bug landed on her arm, so she slapped it flat, taking satisfaction in seeing its crushed body on her skin instead of another bite.

"You should try this for those insects," Will interjected and reached into the satchel he carried to dig out a bottle of an orange liquid.

Byron halted to observe their interaction but appeared more interested than concerned.

Hesitantly, she accepted the strange-looking potion. "What is it?"

"A bug repellent," he answered while showing a touch of pride.

Coura removed the cork and cautiously sniffed the mixture. To her surprise, it smelled like peppermint. "What's in it?" she asked before deciding to pour a healthy amount onto one hand and applying it to her arms and face.

"It's a favorite of mine," Will began and readjusted his glasses with some enthusiasm. That seemed to be a segue into the next topic of conversation as he described the various leaves used in the mixture. After, he continued with his findings for several other plants in the area, which didn't possess medicinal properties on the skin and caused rashes or pain.

Throughout the afternoon, Will told stories of experiments that left him vomiting, dazed, numb on parts of his body, itchy, or hallucinating. By the time the trio reached Byron's chosen campsite, the sun reached the point of setting, and Coura's stomach growled, even after hearing about the repulsive concoctions and their side effects.

How can someone willingly risk their safety and comfort like that? Coura wondered as their new companion went on. *I mean, it might be useful in the end, but I would never rub an unknown plant on my body, let alone eat it!*

"How's the itching?" Will asked when they set their bags down and stretched before preparing camp.

She raised her eyebrows and inspected her skin. The bites no longer irritated her, and the bugs had stayed away during the rest of their hike. Even without a verbal response, Will believed his solution worked, and he beamed at her while pushing his glasses up the bridge of his nose.

"Works great, huh? It really is the scent that gets the bugs to stay off your skin. Like I mentioned earlier, the plants help with the itching. I put a few harmless berries in for color, but I'm planning on sharing the recipe once it's tested more. I'm still not sure how long it lasts or if it has other properties, useful or not, so there's plenty of room for experimenting. Actually, there's a fern I-"

"I'll go get the firewood," Coura interrupted. Her patience ran thin when people rambled, so she turned her back on Will to jog toward the edge of their area and clear her head.

***

As his student moved away from the camp, Byron criticized her lack of manners in his mind, even against his better half as her mentor. *How can Coura be rude when speaking with someone so intelligent and good-natured?*

Although he talked a lot, Will sounded honest and proud of his profession as a herbalist, two qualities most people didn't share regarding their work. He understood some of what the newcomer brought up, but Byron found himself learning as Will prattled on about the plants' different medicinal properties.

Yes, he can lecture for a while, yet it's valuable information. What's more surprising is how young he is. I would venture he's Coura's age, or close to it. I should have a discussion with her about picking up relevant bits and pieces through these sorts of conversations, and also how to avoid offending everyone she meets.

Will watched her move to the edge of their camp with his mouth hanging open from stopping mid-sentence, so Byron put a reassuring hand on the young man's shoulder.

"I apologize for my apprentice. She's not the best at holding a conversation."

"Don't worry. She's definitely not the first girl I scared off after talking about my experiments, but she sure is one of the prettiest, even if she is blunt."

Byron raised an eyebrow at Will's easygoing nature and the compliment directed at his student. His eyes followed Will's to where she knelt to gather twigs and branches.

I never even considered anybody finding her attractive, Byron thought while smiling to himself as he recalled Coura's attitude toward her fellow trainees. Her physical features looked normal for that age, which became accentuated by a fit lifestyle. Even so, her personality had potential friends and admirers turning on their heels. Memories of fights, dominating magical and physical obstacles, and verbal bouts flooded his mind.

He patted Will's shoulder to express his sympathy before starting to unpack, letting the idea fade.

The young man brought his own supplies, which consisted mostly of foraged items, a bedroll, and utensils in addition to the satchel full of research materials. When Coura returned to drop the armful of firewood, Byron tossed her the flint stones.

She shot him an annoyed glare in response. "Seriously?"

Although she didn't refuse this time or opt to use her magic, a stream of mumbled insults filled the silence until she created a spark that caught on to the kindling. All the while, Will described some of his tools to Byron until she cut him off.

"Do you ever shut up?" she snapped before discarding the stones near their belongings.

"Coura," Byron warned while hoping she could avoid losing her temper.

Fortunately, Will just chuckled at her question. "Sorry. I guess I'm used to being alone in the woods and keeping myself company."

Byron expected his student to make some sort of retort, but she merely rolled her eyes and reached for the pack containing their food. The trio ate their bland dinner, which seemed a bit better when Will contributed a pouch of sweet elderberries, and slept only after the newcomer thoroughly explained what edible types grew around the region.

***

The next morning, Coura felt much more energetic as the thought of reaching the capital city made her eager to be out of the woods and around new buildings. While her companions slept, she packed their belongings and practiced her shielding and elemental spells at the farthest end of the campsite. As the morning wore on, though, she decided to wake Byron in order to get them on the road. He groggily rubbed his eyes, yawned, and rose, but it took even longer for Will to prepare for the final leg of their journey. By the time they actually started moving, it was around noon.

"You said we were planning on arriving in Verona today," she reminded Byron and attempted to suppress her irritation brought about by his sluggish pace.

He shrugged from the front. "Why hurry?"

"Because I'm tired of sleeping on the ground in a forest. I'm ready for an actual bed, warm food, servants, and a little more civilization."

"I'm not sure we'll stay in the palace tonight."

Coura released a sigh in resignation. "I guess an inn is fine. I've never actually spent the night in one, but I'm sure it's a similar experience."

"You've never stayed at an inn?" Will asked and cocked his head in her direction. He acted less enthusiastic that afternoon yet would talk when spoken to or when the group fell silent.

"I never needed to since I've lived at the academy for as long as I can remember."

"I travel all over the country, so I stay at inns often, though I prefer to camp out. There's something about being away from people that's calming."

His words triggered a dozen questions she contemplated asking; however, her impatience won out, and she stretched her arms in the air to emphasize her stance. "Well, *I* would rather stay in a building with a wide, comfy bed."

"You'll stay wherever I tell you to," Byron cut in while removing their breakfast from his pack. "Let's get going. We can eat on the way."

Coura accepted the nearly stale bread and a piece of fruit from him and mumbled, "*Now* you want to hurry."

*

After an hour on the road with no conversation, Coura decided to learn more about their new companion. She tapped Will on the back without a word, causing him to stumble forward and almost fall on his face.

"What exactly do you do again?" she asked once he recovered.

He gave her a puzzled glance. "What do you mean?"

"You travel to research plants, so is this your job? You don't seem that old."

Will nodded and perked up at the sudden attention. "I studied with an herbalist in Clearwater, the southernmost city in Asteom; it's where I'm originally from. When I was a child, my parents assigned me to train under him in order to test if I could use magic. After a few months, it became obvious I couldn't. They prepared to transfer me to another position, but I enjoy conducting research and crafting."

"You can do that without magic?"

He snickered. "Well, of course! My mentor could heal with his light power, but most of our work involves putting together various species of herbs, flowers, and other plant-based ingredients and producing medicines."

"I guess I didn't consider what people without magic do."

From the front, Byron groaned and turned to shoot her a displeased look. "What do you mean you didn't consider it? Should I have you explain your weapons training, or perhaps order you to start a fire without your energy?"

Coura shrugged and monitored the woods around them. "I can use magic, so I don't worry about that."

Whatever Byron muttered after became lost as he turned to continue leading them on the trail. When Will didn't pick up the discussion, she left it alone.

For most of the day, she stared into the trees around them and let herself grow lost in her own thoughts. The two ahead of her soon halted because the path stretched perpendicular to a busier road. Then, her mentor addressed them.

"At this rate, we should reach Verona and be able to set up camp before it gets dark," he informed the group in a satisfied manner.

Coura couldn't repress the urge to add her own input. "So, if we slow our pace and *don't* have time to make camp…"

"I guess the ground will be less comfortable to sleep on," he responded without skipping a step.

Reluctantly, she followed behind when they continued moving.

The woods thinned as the sun began setting later in the day. Before they knew it, the trio found themselves at the edge of an enormous field, the largest Coura had ever seen. A structure in the distance possessing twinkling lights all around caught her attention next, and she realized it had to be the palace.

Byron noticed her gaping at the sight and laughed. "Pretty neat."

"Neat doesn't even begin to describe it. That castle is huge! We can see so much from this far away too."

"Yes, and now that we're here, we can prepare camp." He dropped the bags on his shoulders after to punctuate his order. Will followed suit, plopping his belongings down with a huff.

As dusk darkened into night and their trio ate, Coura continued eyeing the magnificent structure between bites. It appeared to stand at least four or five stories tall with lamps glowing in numerous windows on each level, giving it a lively appearance. Shadows of tiny figures passed by frequently enough to cause the lights to blink often. The longer she observed the area, the more interested she became until she pried her eyes away to converse with her companions.

"Why were you so adamant about camping here?" she asked Byron out of curiosity rather than the restlessness she experienced earlier.

"What do you mean?"

"We could have reached the palace today, if not during the evening. I can tell you want to rest away from the city. If you're invited there on business, why is it so important we stay here instead of in Verona?"

Her mentor fell silent for a moment as he stored the items in his bag before answering with a straight face. "I prefer private company."

"That's it?"

"I think you'll understand once we go into the palace."

"I think you're crazy for choosing to stay outdoors," Coura retorted, shook her head, then turned to stare at the trees looming behind him.

What does he mean he prefers private company? We're just visitors, right? Every messenger sent to the academy has been kept away from the students and stays in their own chamber. I haven't heard of any threats or assassination attempts, so why would our capital be unwelcoming?

She noticed Will staring at her from across the fire and tried to ignore him. When he seemed to be debating whether to speak or not, she decided to address his behavior.

"What?" she snapped while shifting her eyes to meet his.

"Why don't you like the woods?" he asked, not at all bothered by her off-putting tone.

Confusion replaced her annoyance, and she fumbled for a response to the unexpected accusation. "I don't... Why would you say that?"

"Ever since I joined you two, you've been scowling into the trees and talking about how you can't wait to leave. That was my first impression."

Coura dared a glance at Byron, who kept his mouth shut and stretched onto his bedroll. Will relaxed on his own and gazed at the stars when she didn't respond right away.

"I don't know," she began before lying with her back to the other two. "I notice too many shadows, and there's not enough room or visibility. I can't stand the bugs either."

Will grunted in confirmation but abandoned the subject in favor of resting. Meanwhile, Coura reflected on the question after internally agreeing with his observation. Blurred silhouettes of monstrous creatures came to mind, and the faint imagery sent a shiver down her spine.

To be honest, I never noticed, she wanted to answer. *Now that I think about it, I can't stand the feeling of being in the woods, not what's in them. Maybe it's because there's no space. I bet that could be the reason since I'm used to fighting with weapons and magic.*

The excuse didn't sound entirely convincing.

No one else spoke, so she assumed they fell asleep. She stayed awake well into the night, recalling the shadows and picturing them closing in on her from the empty road leading away from the well-lit palace.

Introductions in Verona

The familiar sight of the palace's stone structure brought some comfort to Byron despite the stress awaiting him that day. He had been the first to stir with Will up and ready almost immediately after. When asked about his intentions once they reached the city, the young man sounded uncertain. Evidently, Byron could tell the capital intrigued Will, though the newcomer felt uncomfortable inviting himself along. He saw no harm and extended the invite, which Will accepted with obvious relief.

For all her urgency the previous days, Coura had been the last to rise, and with a start. He convinced her to eat breakfast, then they packed their bags and walked straight across the wide clearing until they encountered a space he remembered where the servants hung laundry just outside the palace. A tired-looking woman pointed him around the nearest corner toward the front gate and urged them on in order to continue with her chores.

There, he had the most difficulty keeping his companions steady.

"Can you two please hurry?" he pressed while stopping in front of the stone bridge leading to a set of oversized doors.

While Coura slowed her pace to gawk at the structure from various angles, Will couldn't seem to compose himself to his liking. Byron watched as the herbalist removed a tattered rag from one pocket and wiped his glasses before brushing his hair down. Since it was mid-morning, they missed the rush of workers heading in or out; however, those hanging around gave the trio odd glances and hurried in either direction. Finally, Byron grabbed both by the arm and pulled them in close enough to hold a private conversation.

"Listen to me," he began in the specific tone he developed when lecturing. "Once we pass through those doors, you are my students, observing me as apprentices should. I expect you to stay close by, do as I ask, and keep quiet. It'll be important for you to listen to everybody around us as well."

"Why?" Coura asked and fidgeted under his hold.

"While I'm focused on gathering information, I won't be able to pay attention to too much else. Servants talk; nobilities gossip. It's always imperative to keep your mind sharp and ears sharper. Think of this as a test of your concentration."

With that, he released his grip, straightened to break their huddle, and proceeded to enter.

Despite his various visits to the palace, Byron remained in awe of the pristine grand hall. The gates opened into a spacious room with marble flooring and an enormous staircase at the far end, which connected to the second floor. White pillars matching the floor, walls, and ceiling stood in parallel rows spanning the area, and statues of past kings and queens hid in alcoves along the outer sections. What made the space unique, aside from its beautiful simplicity, were the handfuls of giant, stained glass windows on the building's south side. Each window consisted of several colors, so when sunlight shone through, it painted the white surfaces.

Byron heard Will gasp and mutter from behind.

On an ordinary day, nobody lingered longer than necessary. Besides the soldiers in crimson jackets posted just inside, their trio proved to be the only motionless people. The area felt empty with three dozen or so others nearby, but Byron knew it filled to the brim with hundreds during ceremonies or public events.

It seems as if everything is normal. I was worried about King Hernan's council trying to meddle with my arrival, especially after how we ended the discussion last time, but this trip might not turn out as badly as I expected. Then again, once the council hears where

Symon stands on their final proposition, I doubt we'll leave on better terms.

That headache could wait until later. At the moment, he needed to make the king aware of their group's arrival. Without checking on Coura or Will, he started heading across the hall and toward the staircase. His footsteps, those of the wandering citizens, and their casual murmuring became the only noise in the room. Because he valued his appearance, Byron held his head higher to appear professional in case anyone recognized him or knew where he came from. The lazy atmosphere helped settle his nerves until they reached the bottom of the stairs.

A page boy lingered close by, and like most servants in the palace, he wore a plain, tan uniform, which looked a bit too large as it hung off his limbs. Byron recognized him because the boy's master sent him to fetch Byron during each visit. The recognition became mutual, as the servant's eyes showed a warm familiarity when the three approached.

"Master Byron, a pleasure as always," the page greeted him with a deep bow.

"I'm glad to see you too, Lyle. Would you be so kind as to escort us to our rooms? It's been a tiring few days of travel." Byron stretched his back in a dramatic fashion after, to the boy's amusement.

"Yes, sir! One moment…" With that, the servant scampered around the staircase to a door behind and disappeared through it.

When Byron remembered Coura and Will, he turned to face the two. He didn't expect them to converse, yet the former blurted out a question loudly enough to make him cringe.

"Why did you address him like that?"

"Like what?" he responded at a quieter volume and with a displeased look.

She caught his message and lowered her voice. "You seem so comfortable and said his name."

Byron shrugged. "He's just a person. Lyle always helps me when I arrive, so we speak casually."

"I guess I assumed it's their job. Why should you need to remember his name?"

He frowned and shook his head to show his disappointment, yet he understood how her sheltered life influenced her mentality in such a negative way. "Servants are people too. It may be their duty to assist us, but would you speak down to a shopkeeper or merchant? You never want to give anyone a poor impression of yourself by acting impersonal because of their life's work. Besides, it doesn't hurt to befriend somebody, particularly a person who hears the news and reports it to their master."

"I get it now," Coura responded without a hint of humility.

The sound of pattering footsteps caught Byron's attention before he could say more. Lyle descending the stairs in front of them, stood panting when he reached the bottom, then smiled with crooked teeth.

"Master Byron, thank you for being patient. I passed your message along. High Priest Hendal requests you remain here while the king's group makes their way to the hall."

As cheerful as the servant became, Byron's heart sank. It took years of control for him to keep his face unreadable and avoid growling in frustration. *What rotten luck. Meeting King Hernan now must mean speaking with me is a top priority. If that's the case, I can predict what kind of unreasonable mood he'll be in.*

"Thank you," he managed to respond as sincerely as he could.

That seemed to be Lyle's signal to leave, prompting the boy to bow a second time before exiting through another door farther away from the stairs. Will slid to Byron's side soon after.

"What's wrong?" the young man asked with some concern.

Byron couldn't keep from wincing and scratched the top of his head. *Will is rather observant. Either that, or I need to practice upholding my appearance better in these types of situations.*

"Nothing for you to worry about," he answered while Coura moved to stand on his other side.

"Did he say the king is coming to see us?" she inquired and gazed at the top of the staircase.

"That appears to be the case." For Byron, this became yet another hoop the king's council was having him jump through, but he realized then how Will and Coura might feel about coming face to face with royalty. Their stunned expressions confirmed it.

"The actual king?" Will whispered fiercely. "H-He's coming here?"

"If it helps, I doubt he'll pay you two any mind," Byron admitted to ease some of their distress.

Coura's head snapped to him. "Why is that?"

"This is a tactic intended to throw me off balance mentally," he began before Will interjected.

"We're in their home, not to mention a public space, and at a time of their choosing. Not only are they denying Master Byron a chance to relax, but they're giving us the impression they control the circumstances. What those are, I can't imagine."

Byron stared at the young man after the explanation without admitting his surprise at its accuracy. "That sounds about right."

"It's almost as if you know what's going on between them," Coura commented, narrowed her eyes to show mock suspicion, and poked Will in the arm.

In response, he pulled out the cloth to wipe his glasses again, then he blotted his sweating forehead.

While they continued to wait, Byron contemplated Symon's message and wondered if King Hernan somehow expected the plan regarding his proposed law to not go as smoothly as he hoped.

***

"Where is this group?" Coura muttered and rubbed the toe of her boot into the polished, marble floor to show how unimpressed she felt with their host's tardiness. Luckily, Byron and Will knew better than to try calming her rising irritation when they couldn't guess how much time it would take either.

Her stomach tightened from her nerves, in addition to hunger. Their measly breakfast wouldn't hold her over for long, and her patience ran thin. She could care less about Will's explanation or the king's motives for meeting them like that; at the moment, her concerns focused on finding a place to rest, then food.

57

I hate standing around. Why does every decision need to be politically calculated? Why can't we just go to our rooms and unwind first?

A muffled laugh from behind the set of doors at the top of the staircase interrupted the near silence hanging in the hall. Loud chattering followed. As she glanced across the room, Coura's body went tense at the sudden noise, and she noticed servants purposefully leaving through the nearest exits. A groan from Byron caught her attention before the doors opened at once to reveal a flock of men and women, who conversed as though nobody else could overhear.

A feminine chuckle rose above the voices from a woman near the front, and she craned her head to speak to someone behind her. "Your Highness is too funny!"

"We all enjoy your humor," a man dressed in a white and gold ensemble complete with oiled-down hair added.

"Such a pleasant palace," a hefty, makeup-covered woman threw in as she scanned the hall with a fan in her hand. "I always enjoy our visits."

Without even attempting to conceal her annoyance, Coura scowled at the dozen or so people fluttering down the stairs. Not only were their echoing voices insufferable, but their outfits appeared to match their personalities. The several women clinging to one another at the front wore dresses in flamboyant colors with skirts at least twice their width, and most sported hats and hairstyles as dramatic as their clothes. Coura's eyes widened once she spotted one with a stuffed bird dyed red nesting on a straw hat.

Honestly, this would be hysterical if it weren't so irritating, she could only think.

The men in the group didn't seem as outgoing with their own outfits or behave as obnoxiously; however, each cleaned up well and carried at least a single piece of gold or silver on their person. They trimmed and groomed their beards to show off their features or health as well.

Based on the characters and how they each spoke, Coura presumed the group consisted of the nobility in Verona.

As the cluster of colorful characters descended the staircase, two men near the back drew her attention next. Against the crimson, yellows, and various other combinations, the black-and-gold outfit of the first and the cream-colored robe of the second stood out. Still, their clothes had not been what caught her eye; the sheer presence of the pair demanded anybody nearby to notice them.

The crown on the first man indicated his identity. The king of Asteom, King Hernan, surveyed the trio below with an unamused gaze and a thin smile while following the crowd down to the first floor. Some of the nobility stood taller than their king, but none looked as broad, for the man's shoulders stretched twice as wide as Coura's. His blond hair had been combed to hang neatly at his neck, and a similarly colored crown bejeweled with gemstones rested on his head. Despite the title, his clothes didn't seem that elaborate. A black vest, pants, and boots were trimmed with gold and kept impeccably clean. Although the king clasped his hands behind his back, she had no doubt they remained calloused from years of combat training. The muscles and lean figure beneath showcased that experience, along with his poise while descending.

Then, Coura raised her eyes to his face, no doubt sculpted by years of practice in court. The square shape complemented his strong jaw and chin, and no scars or wrinkles marred his tanned skin, which provided some contrast to the dark outfit. His lips remained stretched into a casual smile, but even she could tell he was tolerating being the center of attention around the nobility. Overall, King Hernan proved to be one of the most handsome, commanding men Coura had ever laid eyes on, and she immediately disliked him.

The king's company reached the trio at last, quieted, and studied them before turning to whisper to one another. Hernan remained on the final step to address everybody from above. As his rich, sapphire eyes scanned over Byron and Will, she realized nothing about the man seemed genuine.

This is just a game to these people. Until he gets whatever it is he wants from Byron, we're merely guests to be managed.

Even as the thought crossed her mind, Hernan's gaze slid over to her. Coura's heartbeat pick up, and she couldn't breathe during those few seconds while she held a demanding stare. Somehow, she managed to narrow her eyes a bit at the arrogance behind his and swore the smile on his lips spread ever so slightly before he returned his attention to Byron.

"Welcome once again, Master Byron of the Magical Arts Academy, to you and your students." King Hernan's voice proved deep and powerful enough to prompt every individual in the grand hall to stop what they were doing. Despite his subtle disinterest, he sounded pleased to meet with them.

Coura noticed movement out of the corner of her eye from Byron as he bowed. She copied the motion and listened to their exchange with mixed feelings.

"The pleasure is certainly ours, Your Highness," Byron greeted the king. To the flock, he probably sounded composed; however, Coura had learned what it meant when his voice became strained into a controlled, steady cadence.

I wonder why he's so anxious? It's not like Byron to get nervous in front of people, and he's been here plenty of times before. Once she recalled Will's explanation, she understood her mentor's behavior better. *It must be because members of the nobility are here. They like to gossip; Byron mentioned that earlier. I doubt Hernan would talk about whatever it is they're working on in public, but perhaps he could use this group to influence us. I'm guessing there's more going on than I can tell.*

"As usual, you underestimate the significance of your visit," the king went on. "We are excited to hear what news you bring from the esteemed academy. Rumors have been flying wildly of what contributions can benefit the capital city."

Byron's face remained like a statue's, stiff and unmoving aside from his mouth. "There will always be plenty of ideas for improvements or benefits for certain people. As you might expect, I do bring news from the headmaster and my fellow master mages, though I politely request we speak in private after my students and I are able to freshen up in our room. I would hate to contribute to invalid assumptions."

"I find it hard to believe a morning's walk would wear out seasoned travelers," Hernan countered with that same, impassive stare.

Beneath his response, the noblemen and ladies spoke in hushed voices to one another. Coura strained her ears to discern their words but struggled. She couldn't hear anything clearer than their tones, which sounded confused, offended, or concerned.

Byron's expression lightened, though, and he even smiled in a natural manner. "You would be surprised at how much young men and women complain."

Coura expected Will to blush at the comment with his head bent forward and dismissed the urge to roll her eyes. *At least I know Byron has some humor left.*

The king's face softened as well before he replied. "Believe me, I understand."

At His Majesty's side, the bald man in the simple robe leaned over to whisper to his superior. Hernan nodded with a grunt and shifted his attention to the flock around them.

"My honorable guests, I apologize, but the representative and I have much to discuss this afternoon. I offer you my most sincere thanks for joining my wife and I for this morning's brunch."

The nobility picked up on the hint, stammered their gratitude and best wishes, then hurried to the front gate as one collective. Coura felt relieved to watch them go despite how they giggled until the entrance's double doors shut with a boom.

*

For two days, Byron met the king and his council in their meeting chamber from dawn until dusk. During that time, Coura and Will were confined to one room on the second floor in the western wing of the palace under the supervision of the servants who brought them their meals. As soon as Coura attempted to explore during the first afternoon, one of the older maids ushered her back inside.

"It'd be awfully frightening if you got lost in such a large castle," the servant explained while shooing her away with a broom and a forced smile.

The following hour, Coura moved in the opposite direction until somebody grabbed her by the arm. A middle-aged, plump woman possessing rosy cheeks and a no-nonsense attitude told her only the servants' quarters, laundry rooms, and one of two kitchens were located in that direction. When Coura lied and claimed she intended to go into the kitchen for a snack, the woman called over a boy, who looked scared to death at being summoned, and ordered him to bring the honored guest a plate of food. Obviously, somebody controlling the servants had warned them about her sneaking around since dozens of eyes tracked her as she returned to their room.

She found Will nibbling on a platter full of fruits, cheeses, and pastries delivered from the kitchen with books and bottles spread around one of two desks. She gave up for the day and went to sleep early while Will studied in the candlelight.

The next morning, Byron was still gone, and Will slept until the afternoon. Coura tried to traverse the floor but got caught four times by servants who soon grew tired of her escaping. The final instance, she reached a staircase and somehow made it into the entrance hall. She approached the guarded gate where she planned to select another direction before one of the kitchenhands from the previous afternoon popped up.

"Wait!" the young man shouted through his panting, as if he sprinted to catch her.

"What?" she snapped in reply.

Instead of scolding her like the others, he smiled and bowed while showing some hesitation. "Please, miss. You're not allowed to leave the palace."

Coura crossed her arms and glared at him. "Why is that?"

She wondered what expectations the kitchenhand had for this conversation before interrupting her, for his smile dropped, his cheeks shaded scarlet, and his eyes found the floor.

"I-I don't..."

"Tell me what you know," she went on to save him from needing to invent an excuse. "Why am I not allowed to venture outside the palace, let alone take ten steps from my room?"

"Because it's simple, palace protocol," said a cool, female voice from nearby. "That, and those of us who work here would like to be certain no one is sticking their nose in places they shouldn't."

Coura glanced behind to see a woman dressed in the all-white robe of a light mage coming to meet them.

"I'm sorry," the young man mumbled from his position to Coura's left. She became too preoccupied with the stranger to care about him anymore.

"Who are you?"

With a smile, merely a slight adjustment of her ruby lips, the woman gave Coura a bored gaze. "I am one of the palace's personal healers and the master light mage. Normally, guests fulfill their duties and only need a room for meals and rest."

Coura fumed under the condescending stare but didn't dare let her tongue slip.

The woman passed by before hesitating in the doorway, then she addressed Coura once more. "Servants should assist visitors while they are here, not play sitter. You would do well to remember that."

She left after leaving Coura with those words, ending their brief conversation. The two guards posted in front of the entrance inched closer together, as though they expected her to follow the mage. Instead, she turned on her heel and stormed away with the kitchenhand remaining at a safe distance.

"Who does she think she is?" Coura growled under her breath. "What an arrogant lady with her nose so high in the air. A true master mage wouldn't act so cold."

Insults continued to flow from her mouth, and eventually more than just the servant behind her heard them. When she felt sufficiently relieved of her frustration from the encounter, she went straight back to the room. Will was wise not to bother her for the remainder of the night as she practiced combat motions with an invisible sword in order to ease her restlessness.

*

"This isn't fair," Coura complained as she dramatically dropped onto her bed. The morning after spending a few minutes in the grand hall, she didn't even bother attempting to leave save for using the washroom.

Their quarters had a simple set up containing four beds, two desks, two dressers, and two windows along one wall. It held enough space for Coura to do simple exercises, even with another person present, but days without really training her body or practicing magic left her muscles twitching and dark energy humming. The whole while, Will studied a variety of books brought by the servants and toyed with his plant samples.

He half-glanced her way with a "Hmm?" in response.

She stared at the blank, stone ceiling in dismay. "We haven't seen Byron since we were escorted here. I wonder how he's doing."

"He's just fine."

Coura sat up at his monotone comment and watched as he carefully measured a white powder using a tiny spoon. "How do you know?"

After pouring the substance into a bottle, he swirled the mixture together, set it down, and faced her with a grin. "I've been staying up to read. He comes in and goes straight to bed, though he must eat there since he's never here when we get our meals. Unlike you, I don't mind sitting around all day."

She huffed a laugh. "That's because you're a bookworm."

Will shrugged off her reply and went back to his work. "Although I would rather conduct research in the field, I don't need to be outside. It's kind of nice to not worry about preparing my own food or keeping watch at night."

"Whatever," Coura muttered as she sprang off the bed and walked around the room. Then, she sat on its edge for another minute before moving to observe the potion-making process by standing over Will's shoulder.

He removed his glasses, rubbed his eyes, and released a weary sigh. "I wish you wouldn't do that."

"Do what?"

"Pace like a cornered animal," he answered before returning to his measuring.

"What else am I supposed to do?" she countered.

"I don't know, maybe ask a servant for a book or two. No one can predict what you might find in a library like theirs."

"You've been there?"

"Well, yes. They seem to trust me a little more than you since I understand what I want and where I should be." Will ended his statement with a smirk.

"Oh, shut up," she muttered and decided to open the door to the hallway. Before Coura took three steps, a servant turned the corner.

"Miss, is there something I can assist you with?"

"Actually, I do need your help. Would you bring me a few books from the library?"

The woman's hazel eyes widened upon hearing the request, then she nodded. "Of course! I will head there straight away. What sort of books are we looking for?"

Coura paused to consider the question for a moment because she didn't intend to be reading. "Bring me some you enjoy. If you don't have any, just pick whatever looks or sounds the best to you. Otherwise, ask the desk worker."

While the servant bowed and hurried in the opposite direction, Coura returned to the room and strolled past Will to the first window. Within a few minutes, there came a knock on the door, and the same woman handed over an armful of books. Coura kicked the door shut, dropped the stack onto the second, empty desk with a thud, then returned to the window.

"So, you're finally taking my advice?" Will chimed from her right.

"Not quite." After flashing a grin, she unlatched the lock on the window and pushed it open to meet a warm breeze that soon filled the space with fresh air. Then, she climbed onto the sill before swinging her legs over.

In response, Will jumped to his feet quickly enough to almost fall over. "Wait, what are you-"

"I'll be back before anybody notices," she assured him with a wink from the ledge.

"Are you crazy? If you get caught sneaking around, we could be in serious trouble! Not to mention what it could do to Byron's business…"

"Relax, Will. I just need some space. If they ask, I'll tell them exactly that."

Before he could continue protesting, she flipped onto her stomach and crawled out along the wall.

Surprise Encounters

Through the aching in her hands and fingers as they clung to the stone, Coura remained determined to reach a shadowy hiding spot as soon as possible in order to avoid being detected. Unfortunately, their window faced south, meaning sunlight covered most of that side early in the afternoon and would remain until dusk. No other buildings or trees could give her cover, though she considered using what sheets the laundresses hung out nearby.

A trickle of sweat tickled Coura's neck as it slid down her face and into the collar of her shirt. Her best option would be to climb the rest of the way to the ground, then she could sneak around to the eastern side. To her relief, their room was located closer to the opposite end from the main gate. None of the busy servants would notice, or at least she hoped they wouldn't.

After descending from the second story until her feet touched the solid earth, she leaned against the cool wall to catch her breath.

It's rather dumb luck the outer wall's stones jut out enough to climb. I'm sure only those with the skill can pull their bodies around, but I would be cautious about leaving any windows unlocked.

The intoxicating scent of fresh grass blew up on the wind. For a while, Coura stayed with her back pressed against the stone, cleared her mind, and enjoyed the freedom of being outdoors once again. When the sun moved higher in the sky and its heat beat down mercilessly, she pushed her body off to think about her next move.

"Now what?" she muttered aloud and scratched her head. "I should still avoid being seen, but I'm not staying here all day."

Without knowing where exactly she intended to go or what she planned to do, Coura began walking east. She reached what she figured had to be the back of the palace and turned the corner only to find another wall extending beyond what she just passed. This one indented inward, and the brick appeared grayer than that of the rest of the palace. It stretched for a distance, preventing her from continuing on unless she chose to traverse the entire perimeter. The strangest part happened to be how it acted like a fence, reaching about ten feet tall and possessing no roof from what she could tell.

This must be a new addition, she concluded after an inspection. *I wonder what's on the other side.*

The bricks had been more evenly placed but didn't make climbing impossible for her. In an uncomfortably lengthy amount of time, she managed to get herself over the top and onto the manicured section below before ducking behind a circular bush.

Unlike the outer side, which expanded into the open field, this area looked maintained and filled with all sorts of decorative plants, trees, and sculptures. In the emerald grass grew evergreen bushes trimmed into various shapes and trees that towered well above her head, bearing ripe apples, pears, and other fruits. Amid the greenery, paths laid out in brick matching the exterior branched in multiple directions.

As she approached a waist-high, stone wall lining them, Coura leapt over once she deemed the space empty. Every thought focused on the beauty of such a garden, for that proved to be the only way she could describe it. What she dismissed as random trails actually intertwined with one another and spread into different areas with unknown purposes.

The first path she chose led her farther from the castle. In fact, Coura became worried she would find herself leaving Verona without realizing it; however, the brick curved to the right and ended before a shallow pool decorated with pink and purple flowers. A cherry tree swayed in the gentle wind, and she savored its lingering, perfumey scent. No towels, brushes, or soap lied around, so she assumed the pond was meant for decoration, though she suppressed the urge to splash water on her face and wash away the accumulating sweat.

She turned from the pool and cut across an open area spotted with rose bushes to reach another path stretching even farther from the palace. All of a sudden, she heard a faint conversation and slowed her steps while continuing forward. A woman laughed, then a second, deeper voice spoke. Their conversation proved impossible to understand at a distance, so Coura decided she would rather get caught wandering than eavesdropping on potentially important people.

After backtracking, she wandered closer to the castle. The area widened into a decorated floral bed with carved, wooden benches. She found the spot absolutely relaxing, almost enough to forget she was trespassing. As she shrugged off the reminder, a glimmer in the distance caught her eye, drawing her toward the source. She soon discovered a fountain holding a statue of an angel in another space surrounded by bushes for privacy. Additional benches had been placed there, so she chose a seat in front of the piece, taking in the magnificent image before her.

The angel, seemingly constructed from pure, white marble, stood at least two heads taller than Coura. In his right arm, he poised a sword, which appeared sharp enough to be a real weapon, in a victory pose with the blade horizontally above his head. In his left arm, he held a vase covered with intricate patterns in gold. Water flowed from its tipped opening, as if the angel controlled how it poured. He wore armor, nothing Coura was familiar with, but the pair of wings behind him enraptured her. Instead of looking blocky or hard like a normal statue, each feather had been crafted with such carefully smooth lines and meticulous detail. Everywhere her eyes fell on them showed something different; no two feathers were identical.

The level of artistry is indescribable, she acknowledged in awe.

Behind the wings sat a structure built like a tree, and more water trickled from the tips of its branches to create a thin waterfall effect. She couldn't spot any imperfections. In fact, the harder she looked, the more intricacies she discovered.

As marvelous as the fountain as a whole appeared, Coura couldn't help but stare at the lifelike wings. For a long while, she fantasized about what it would be like to meet an angel.

Would their wings be heavy, like an extra set of arms, or as light as a bird's? How much effort does it take to carry a person my size? Are they as soft as ordinary feathers, perhaps a chick's? What if I had a pair of my own?

The last question struck a nerve.

Where would I go? I can't even figure out where I am going to go and what I should be doing. I can't stay with Byron at the academy forever, but I'm just not sure…

Her eyes dropped to the grass at her feet, and she sat like that for a while, content to be alone.

"Beautiful, isn't it?" a tenor voice suddenly said from behind.

Despite feeling startled, Coura managed to shift in her seat and glance at the stranger interrupting her peaceful moment. She considered expressing her annoyance upon being disturbed but paused instead.

The young man, who looked to be around her age, dressed similarly to the noblemen from her first day at the palace, though in a less abstract fashion. His loose, crimson shirt had been lined with silver thread, which gleamed in the sunlight and reminded Coura of the fountain's vase. Cropped, golden hair covered his head and ears, and on his head rested a metal band of the same color.

A crown, Coura realized with no small amount of shock. *I'm trespassing in a walled-off area after sneaking outside, and of all people, I run into a member of the royal family!*

Instinctively, she assessed the rest of his features to confirm his lineage: the lightly tanned skin, sky blue eyes, and square face. After racking her brain for what little knowledge she possessed regarding the king, she remembered a lone child, his only heir.

Still, something separated the person in front of her from the arrogant, haughty man, even though their appearances were similar. Across the prince's face stretched a smile so unlike his father's, Coura thought he might have been adopted, though the rest of his features suggested otherwise, especially his eyes. They appeared identical in shape and color, yet the king's were cold and calculating; his son's seemed full of life, absorbing as much of the world as they could.

That was when she could sense an awkward tension, which the prince picked up on too.

"You've been staring," he commented in an informal manner.

She couldn't help from blushing before making a silly retort. "I believe you were the one who interrupted me."

What a fool I am, a complete idiot! Looks can deceive, and if he shares this encounter with his father, there's no telling the consequences.

Her brash words visibly took the prince back, so Coura returned to studying the fountain to hide her face and wait for the hammer to fall. To her utter surprise, he chuckled.

"Forgive me, my lady. It's not often I'm able to speak first. Most people lead the conversation before I can greet them properly."

"I'm not a lady," she added over her shoulder and caught his eye. He seemed to already know.

"Every woman deserves to be treated like one."

She turned away again to conceal another blush before deciding to change the subject. "You're right. About the statue, I mean."

"This is one of my father's favorites, a gift from the Yeluthians at his wedding. Not that they actually attended the ceremony, but he and my mother never complained."

"I haven't seen such detail in a piece of art before," she admitted. "It's so lifelike. The sculptor is truly blessed with talent."

"They say the angels craft special tools to manipulate the material, making it more realistic. This is the only statue of theirs I know of belonging to a human."

Coura couldn't think of a way to continue, so they observed the fountain's flowing water in silence. Its trickling became the only sound in the garden for a few minutes until he cleared his throat.

"I didn't introduce myself. I'm Prince Aaron."

"I know who you are," she partially lied without making eye contact.

"Why do you address me so informally then?" he countered, revealing a hint of annoyance in his tone.

There it is. I overstepped my boundaries.

Even with his title hanging over her, Coura dared more conversation. After shrugging to suppress her nerves, she chanced another look at the prince and offered a hesitant smile. "I enjoy conversing with people when they don't have a hidden motive for talking to me. At least, I hope that's not the case now."

He returned her smile with an amused one of his own and clasped his hands behind his back. "I see. Well, I must be going."

Coura watched as he began walking toward the palace before halting to turn and meet her eyes again.

"I suggest you inform the guards next time you would like to visit the queen's personal garden. We'd hate to have any accidents in such a lovely place."

*

Coura's body trembled from her encounter with the heir for minutes after he disappeared because of his generous warning. *The queen's garden? I've never heard of such a place. I saw no guards on patrol to prevent me from sneaking in. Then again, how many people could climb over from the outside? I better go before anybody else finds me.*

She rose and immediately made her way to the outer wall closest to the fountain. Then, she followed it away from the palace until she selected a spot mostly hidden by fruit trees. After struggling over, she strolled away while pretending to have nothing to do with the area as her mind raced.

How long has it been? I doubt Will would hide the fact that I left, especially to Byron.

She paused to glance up at the sun in an effort to gauge the time. During her exit from the garden, she didn't climb the same wall she used to enter. Instead, she fled in the other direction, leaving her standing on the opposite side of the structure as their room.

It looks like I'll need to go around again unless I can manage to sneak inside, but I would probably get caught. Not to mention how the servants and their masters will react. I'd be locked inside with guards stationed at the door. I suppose if I'm going to be caught anyway I can continue exploring before my imprisonment.

She made it to the next corner of the building, which wasn't far considering the vast size of the queen's garden, and continued. The next side looked similar to its opposite in that it revealed a field with woods looming farther beyond; however, near the front of the palace were several stables with dozens of figures moving around. Some meandered in the open space, but most seemed to be gathered near the largest building. It took Coura a moment to realize a stone wall that looked to reach her shoulders surrounded the perimeter of the area before the edge of the forest beyond began.

As she strolled west while keeping close to the palace, she recognized echoes of thwacking between wooden weapons and chatter from the group nearby. Soon, she could see their movements better and noted the items in their hands.

This must be their soldiers' training ground, she realized with growing interest and glanced around. *If I get close, they're sure to notice, and I don't believe they'd allow a stranger to roam in from out of nowhere.*

Several doors lined the structure, yet people constantly entered or exited through the two farthest from her position. After weighing her chances of sneaking by or retreating to the other side before dark, Coura straightened and grinned.

Byron's going to kill me. If I'm in trouble regardless of which option I choose, I should satisfy my curiosity before his punishment.

Instead of moving toward any of the doors leading into the palace, she went straight to the group by the stable where about thirty men and several women practiced motions with practice blades and a partner. Coura recognized the moves from a distance as basic defensive maneuvers and wondered how educated they were.

She flowed around each pair to observe their work without commenting. Most people didn't care and focused on their own partners, but some glared at her with either arrogance or irritation. She ignored their looks in favor of concentrating on the exercises in order to compare them to what she learned.

Like I would let any of these soldiers intimidate me, she thought as she noticed many flaws and uncertainty beneath their skills.

"What are you staring at?" a man who appeared a few years older snapped at her. She had been studying him at the moment his partner successfully parried a blow on accident.

"Your swords," she replied without taking her eyes off his practice blade. At the academy, her original weapons master started them out with wooden swords too until they became competent enough to use actual, deadly ones.

"This isn't the place for strangers, especially young girls," the brute sneered and turned back toward his partner.

Coura thought about letting the comment go yet couldn't stop a retort from tumbling out of her mouth after his response. "That's probably for the best. I wouldn't want anyone to see me either if I were bold enough to pretend I could wield a sword."

Those around them who heard halted and grew invested in the argument; however, she noticed their eyes went to the man she insulted, as if to witness his reaction, and he did not disappoint. With an audible, animal-like puff of air through his nostrils, he spun around to face her.

In response, she kept her face neutral and met his glare.

"Who are you?" he demanded through clenched teeth.

She wondered what would happen if she told the truth and revealed her identity as a student from the Magical Arts Academy. In the end, she shrugged before deciding against it. "I just know a thing or two about sword work."

He raised an eyebrow and glanced at those around him who also showed a mixture of doubt and surprise. To her own amazement, he backed down with a grumble and faced his partner again. That seemed to be the others' cue to return to their own training and ignore the stranger.

Despite her luck, Coura felt more offended than relieved, prompting her to cross her arms. "You're less aggressive than I gave you credit for. It's no wonder you're not talented at fighting with a sword."

What self-restraint he had vanished as he spun around while fuming. "I was trying to be nice because you're new, but you must not be worth wasting manners on!"

Without hesitation, she approached his partner while the man yelled and extended a hand toward his wooden sword. "May I?" she asked in the resulting silence.

The boy, for he appeared no older than Coura, leaned closer. "Are you sure?"

She ignored him, and he eventually gave in.

All eyes fell on the stranger who challenged their comrade.

She reveled in the attention as she weighed the wood in each hand. "I've seen children pick up weapons and learn to wield them without possessing the heart to match their progress. Skills take time and effort to develop, but if you aren't able to put your emotions into them… Let's just say it's not going to end well for you."

Coura raised her blade to point its tip at the man as he studied her intensely. Then, she charged without warning with the intent to swipe right. The movement caught him off guard, though he responded instinctively enough to raise his sword, and the resulting crack of the connecting wood rang throughout the training ground. A second later, he stepped back to gape at his sword, which nearly split in two along the length of the weapon.

"How did you… It's broken!"

She handed the practice sword back to its wide-eyed owner as casually as she accepted it. The resulting stares didn't reflect fear, though. In fact, while she leveled a gaze at each person, Coura saw only curiosity and awe. That surprised her more than she was willing to admit.

For their lack of experience, these soldiers sure are made of tougher stuff.

"Do you remember what I said before?" she asked her opponent to bring the encounter full circle. "When you fight with a sword, you need to commit to a mindset. When I charged at you, I fully intended to break your arm."

The man's mouth hung open in disbelief, yet he remained silent. His lack of a reply allowed them to hear murmurs from behind Coura that drew her attention next. When she turned around, the soldiers had parted for a new person. He dressed in all brown, which matched his hair and eyes, and unlike her opponent, he appeared to be closer to her age.

"What's going on here?" the newcomer demanded, projecting some authority over the group.

While she kept quiet, the boy she borrowed the sword from answered before anybody else could. "Marcus, it was incredible! She showed up, took my sword, then struck a blow at Remy to split his sword. We all saw it!"

The group, including her opponent, nodded in an eager manner. Despite their enthusiasm, the younger man stared at Coura with narrowed eyes, obviously sizing her up.

Against her urge to do or say something in her defense, she remained silent and assumed a bored expression.

His stare shifted to the soldier, and his tense posture eased a bit. "Thank you, Jorge. Would you grab me two blades from the armor station?"

The soldier agreed before scuttling off to another stable, leaving Coura standing across from the newcomer as those surrounding them chatted with one another.

After a moment, she decided to break the tension. "I take it you're in charge of their training?"

The young man the soldier addressed as Marcus didn't reply, which irked her.

"Usually you introduce yourself when you burst into the center of a lesson."

"All right, go ahead," he countered with a sly smile.

The boy returned then carrying two, polished swords whose blades shone in the sunlight.

Marcus took one before stretching his wrists. "Please, give the other to..."

"Coura," she supplied and grabbed her own without removing her eyes from her next opponent.

I'll be glad to knock that smirk off his face, she thought as she prepared her stance.

Marcus mirrored the position.

So, he knows how to fight. I can already tell he'll be more of a challenge.

She expected to go on the offensive first; however, he charged before she could move, releasing a grunt as he brought his sword down diagonally to aim the slice at her neck. Coura blocked the blow with ease and pushed his weapon away after. He followed with three additional swings at each of her sides, which she sidestepped before knocking the third away with her blade. Then, she countered by lunging to strike his thigh. As she expected, he deflected the attempt.

That last attack had strength behind it, which means he either thinks I'm causing trouble and wants to teach me a lesson or he believes I actually know what I'm doing. Either way, he's too strong to take head on. I'll need to adapt a lighter strategy.

*

"There are three main categories of weapons work I've seen over the years," Coura's beginning instructor once explained. "First and most common is strength based. When you're on the offensive, you put a majority of your muscle behind attacks. For combatants who have muscle or are physically larger, this is the best way to knock your opponent off their balance. It's also intimidating for fighters without much experience. The blows are direct, so you cannot hold anything back. This category is for blunt weapons and swords.

The next focused on swiftness for those of you who can make up for a lack of strength with speed and agility. Usually fighters skilled with daggers, knives, or other smaller weapons find this to be the best for their style.

Lastly, there's the distance-based method. If you don't like being close to your opponents, this one's for you. Most of the time, you naturally have a preference for strength or agility, but this category focuses on avoiding all that with precision. Of course, you'll need to be trained to wield additional weapons, but this adds an extra means of fighting through throwing knives, a bow and arrows, or even javelins.

Now that you understand the basics, you need to follow two rules. The first is that you're all fit to use a certain weapon or two based not only on your physicality but also your own preference. I've seen sprouts who thought they were tough enough to stab an enemy with a sword but didn't possess the heart to put their weight behind blows. Likewise, brutish students often explode when their throwing knives don't hit a target because they expect them to, like they have the control. You *must* find the balance you're comfortable with and go from there. That's why your later years at the academy focus on what you can, and want, to work with.

The second rule is why we train you in them all right away. Each weapon can be wielded in multiple ways, but you'll never be well rounded unless you're flexible. If you lack strength, there's no reason for you to fight with a mace, and if you're too bulky, don't you dare assume you can dance around with only a dagger. You will have your specialty, but what if you lose your weapon or don't have access to one? Then what do you do? A competent fighter can select any option and figure out how to use it to his or her advantage. This requires accepting your strengths and weaknesses, then adapting."

After the lecture, he ordered the class to select what weapon they felt best suited for. Coura never hesitated when she chose a sword first.

*

The pair traded blows to meet each other with precision honed through years of training. They huffed in the afternoon sun, and both bodies began gleaming with sweat. Never once did Coura take her eyes off Marcus or consider how much time had passed. He swung for her right side while she rolled into his sword, sweeping under the blade and parrying with a similar blow. His reaction came too slow, allowing the tip of her sword to scratch his left hip. The cut didn't seem deep, yet it proved to be enough of a distraction when hand went to that spot and his weapon lowered.

Coura licked her lips in anticipation. *This is my chance. He let his guard down.*

She charged in an attempt to strike his right arm with enough force to cause him to drop his sword, and for her to claim victory; however, as her blade rose, she caught his lips curving upward.

Something's not right, she realized during the motion, but it became too late to abandon the effort.

Her sword began to fall as his rose to meet it. At the same time, her opponent threw his left shoulder forward, slamming into her chest and knocking the breath out of her. The flat side of his blade smacked against her right elbow in the process, seemingly on accident, and the sudden impact caused Coura to release her weapon while she fell onto her back.

***

The blade's metallic clang on the ground remained the only sound for what felt like minutes. No one around Marcus seemed to be breathing.

I'm sure they're loving this, he reflected and relaxed a bit to wipe the sweat off his brow. *They've never actually seen me seriously spar before now.*

He kicked the young woman's sword behind him and out of reach while he waited for her to rise. After a few seconds, she still didn't stir. His comrades murmured around him, and Marcus's stomach twisted.

I thought I restrained myself with that blow. I had no intention of harming her or laying her out. What did I do?

A growing sense of panic rose at the idea of hurting an innocent person, so he stepped over to where she dropped onto her back and hesitated to kneel beside her in case he startled her awake. Her eyes had closed to tell him she somehow lost consciousness, and a hand rested on her chest where he shoved her. Marcus also noticed the welt on her elbow beginning to swell.

"Should I get a healer?" somebody in the crowd asked.

The group's presence led him to decide to take the professional route and not leave her injured in the dirt.

"Yes," he began as he dropped to one knee. "Tell them it's not urgent, but-"

Without warning, the stranger's eyes opened before her right fist shot toward his hip and struck him on the scratch she delivered earlier. The wound didn't appear serious, yet it proved deep enough that the blow had him clutching his side. Then, one of her legs swung upward to kick him in the back of the head, sending him face first into the dirt and seeing stars. When Marcus pushed himself into a sitting position after, his opponent stood above him with his sword in her hand and touched the blade's tip to his chest.

Her behavior stunned him, along with those around them, until their audience began shouting insults.

"Disgraceful!"

"Where's your honor in a fair fight?"

"That's not how you duel!"

"How could you fake an injury?"

To her credit, the young woman ignored the jeers and kept her focus, and the sword, on him. Marcus released a defeated sigh and raised his hands while attempted to avoid letting his annoyance show too much.

"I yield," he announced a moment later.

When the sword lowered, he pushed himself to his feet and brushed off the dirt covering his clothes. She eyed the people around them as he did so. Most still appeared displeased, but the voices faded once he rose, except for a single word.

"Cheater," someone muttered under their breath loudly enough for everybody to hear.

The rest of the onlookers nodded in agreement.

His opponent shrugged indifferently. "It's not cheating. A fight is a fight. You go until one person forfeits, is actually knocked out, or dies."

Despite the blunt response, Marcus hoped his comrades would take the information to heart after observing his experience. He cleared his throat to draw their attention with the intent to break their group apart before questioning the stranger until a booming voice cut him off and startled most everyone.

"There you are!"

A visibly upset man shoved his way to the middle of the circle after and leveled a glare at the young woman, who hurried to hand Marcus the sword.

"Byron, I-"

"Let's go," the newcomer ordered. "Now!"

Reluctantly, she went to his side where he gripped her arm so tight everybody could see his fingers indenting her skin. Then, the man dragged her along as he returned to the palace.

Marcus didn't interfere with their business, though he instructed the group to pair up and practice their exercises again. Throughout the rest of the afternoon, he fielded various questions about his fight and began to wonder if being chivalrous had been the right choice in his situation.

Bid the Palace Farewell

"Ouch, stop! You're going to bruise my arm," Coura whined under Byron's grasp.

Only when they were well into the building did he release her, but he continued walking without commenting on her behavior. If he stopped for long enough, he predicted his temper would snap.

I'm already on a short stretch, and Coura likes to toy with my patience.

"Slow down," she called from behind to start a conversation.

He pointedly ignored her until they entered their guest room. Will stayed where Byron had left him: at his desk with his nose in a book and medicinal materials spread all over. When he returned earlier and found Coura gone, they reached a mutual understanding that when he brought her back, things would get heated.

Once in the private space, Byron went straight to the tray of finger foods brought in by a servant and selected a handful of options. His student closed the door behind her and stood with her arms crossed. Fortunately, she had been lectured enough to know he would be more reasonable after he cooled off and quelled his hunger. He scarfed down the snacks, opened the wine left with the food, and took a couple swigs. When he felt mentally prepared to deal with her accustomed lack of cooperation, Byron began.

"Why did you go outside the room?"

"Are you really that angry?" she replied while falling onto her bed and spreading her arms out.

"*Why* did you go outside the room?"

She refused to meet his leveled stare. "I'm not like Will. I can't stay cooped up in here all day."

"You were supposed to stay here," he snapped and let his frustration show; however, with Coura, revealing your own temper only served to draw out hers.

She sat upright on the bed and threw her hands in the air. "I can't believe you're making such a big deal about it! What is so wrong about wanting fresh air?"

"I requested the servants keep you both in our quarters for your own safety and for the sake of my assignment."

Her eyes widened in alarm before narrowing. "You ordered them to do that? Don't you think we're capable of handling ourselves?"

Byron let her vent for a moment before releasing a sigh. "I know you're smarter than this, Coura."

The disappointment in his voice came through clearly and stopped his student from complaining. That pause allowed her to look him over.

"You seem like you haven't slept since we got to Verona."

"I haven't. The hours I'm able to return here to rest are limited. This law could have a major impact on the academy, and negatively if it's not taken care of properly. King Hernan and his council don't understand our side, so I spent the morning arguing. I'd rather not spend my *whole* day arguing, if you mind."

She returned the sigh and glanced out the window in a calmer manner. "You know I've never been good at following directions."

"Do you not know why I needed you to stay in the room?"

Coura contemplated his question. "You're keeping us safe in case anybody attacks, maybe to use us as a tool to get you to agree to their terms."

"Not just that, but because your interactions could impact their emotions or impressions of the academy."

When she glanced away to hide a blush, Byron's heart dropped. *She's gone and done something foolish, that much I can tell. In any case, I don't need to hear about it right now. I'm barely able to stay awake*

The room fell silent as he gazed out the window, and Will continued working as if they weren't there.

"We've been requested to join the royal family's private dinner in a few hours," he shared while kicking off his boots. "Until then, I plan on resting. You should ask a servant for ice to help the swelling in your elbow."

She didn't give a vocal response, so he decided to end the discussion there. After climbing into bed, it took less than a minute for him to fall asleep when his head touched the pillow.

***

A formal dinner with the royals was cause for the three to clean up and dress their best. When Byron agreed to take Coura along over a week ago, he insisted she bring one, 'presentable' outfit for such an occasion. Most trainees didn't feel the need to keep their own formal clothing at the academy, or some, like her, didn't own any, so the MAA offered a wardrobe full of dress clothes for students to borrow. She had only ever utilized a gown twice, though she selected the same, emerald one both times, and didn't feel the need to change her decision.

As she adjusted the skirt before starting to braid her hair, Byron's voice interrupted the peaceful moment.

"Are you two almost ready?" The master mage stood in the doorway and tapped his foot to display his impatience. He wore a dark blue shirt, brownish pants, and matching, polished boots, courtesy of the servants. His inky hair had also been combed, yet his nap helped remove part of the strain on his facial features the most.

"Coming," Will called from the other side of the room.

Their new companion hopped on one leg as he slipped on a black boot while Coura finished tying her braid. Since he had been traveling, he didn't possess formalwear. Fortunately, a request from Byron resulted in a servant arriving with what she deemed acceptable clothes for the dinner, which consisted of dark pants and boots, a white, long-sleeved shirt, and an evergreen vest. The whole ensemble looked a size too large, but they hoped nobody would notice or feel the need to point it out.

"Let's get going," Byron urged while turning to head down the hallway.

Coura followed, and Will trailed behind.

"This is exciting," the latter chimed from the rear. His nerves made his voice's pitch unnaturally high in response.

Coura rolled her eyes. "Why? Byron's been eating with these people for days."

"Actually, the meals we shared between and during those meetings weren't extravagant," her mentor interjected. "Delicious, yes, but hardly what we'll be experiencing."

His comment added to Will's anticipation. "This is like in the songs and stories then, right? I heard many about the finest musicians playing for the royal family, and how sometimes they invite different types of performers to entertain their guests. Do you think the king might bring them here tonight, Master Byron?"

"I don't know, but I doubt anybody will be considering us."

"Why is that?" Coura asked without hiding her curiosity.

"Let's just say our council session grew heated, and not everyone agrees with the final decision."

"And what would that be?"

Byron shot her an unamused look over his shoulder, which she expected. As the trio approached a guarded door near what felt like the center of the second floor, he halted to face and address her and Will.

"I don't want you to speak unless spoken to. Keep your heads down and ears open. You'll most likely be ignored again, so you can enjoy the meal at your own pace. Will, let me know if you have any questions, and Coura..." Byron paused to rub his eyes. "*Please* behave."

Before she could reply, he spun around to approach the entrance. The soldiers posted at the doors opened them wide, revealing the aforementioned dining hall.

Compared to every other part of the building, the room showcased what Coura imagined when she considered the idea of a palace. The amount of light inside contrasted with the corridors drastically enough to blind her for a second. Its marble floor shined like glass under the many lamps and candles around the room, including those hanging on a chandelier in the middle of the ceiling.

A pair of sturdy, wooden tables had been positioned parallel to each other, and dozens of benches lined both sides, as well as the length of the outer walls. A slightly shorter one connected to the other two to form three sides of a rectangle, though it stood a head taller than the rest.

Despite the atmosphere, its setup nor its lively inhabitants caught Coura's breath like the artistry did. The walls and ceiling had been painted a warm, cream color and displayed realistic portrayals of natural scenes involving dancing, laughter, and more. Each design seamlessly weaved into the next while surrounding the space. She composed herself and let Byron lead them to their seats at the right side of the head table while vowing to spend the evening enjoying the artwork.

Just like their welcome in the grand hall, the lords and ladies took pleasure in strutting around to flaunt their finest dresses and robes, like showy birds. Everybody ignored the trio for most of the evening, just as her mentor predicted. King Hernan didn't so much as look in their direction, which was fine with Coura, yet she noticed his bald advisor glancing over several times.

The entire dinner tasted phenomenal and raised her spirits. Servants brought around trays bearing fresh fruit, pastries, and cheeses first, then vegetables glazed in a sweet sauce, roasted potatoes with herbs, and the juiciest venison roast she'd ever had. Finally, they poured more wine before the dessert course. By that point, she felt stuffed and used the resulting lull to marvel at the scenes decorating the hall.

"It really is something, isn't it?"

She looked to her left where Byron sat and found him watching her with a faint smile. His words were the first any of the three had spoken since entering the room.

"It's one of the few parts I truly enjoy about this place," he went on in a casual manner. "Queen Freya may be shy, but she supports the arts, presumably from her time at events as a noblewoman. From what I know, she practically forced King Hernan to redesign this space and even had the area at the back of the palace built to be her own garden."

"That's interesting," Coura mumbled before glancing at her empty plate to hide a blush.

The final trays arrived then, consisting of berry-flavored tarts, jams on crackers, and various, dainty pastries. She ate what she could then decided to sip on the last of her drink while surveying the hall.

Several musicians traded off to perform throughout the meal. All played some sort of instrument, and nearly half sang when they could. At that moment, a middle-aged man strummed a soft ballad while adding words she couldn't discern at a distance. A portion of the guests left before the end of the meal, and those who remained conversed with one another.

Coura prepared to ask Byron when they would retire for the evening; however, a glance at the head table had her making eye contact with the familiar face of Prince Aaron. In response, the royal rose from his spot beside his father while utilizing an envious amount of grace and wandered toward the trio. Every step raised her nerves until he stopped in front of Byron.

I hope he doesn't mention our meeting...

"Master Byron, we're honored you could stay tonight and dine with us," the prince began in a genuinely friendly tone.

"As you know, it's been a long week," her mentor began in the same manner. "I couldn't imagine leaving without a proper night's rest, though the food is reason enough to linger."

Perhaps it was her imagination, but the royal seemed to relax a bit as he chuckled. "You and your apprentices are always welcome. Speaking of which..." He paused to address Coura. "I'm pleased you admire the artwork, Lady..."

"Coura," she supplied while restraining a wince.

Aaron winked at her in response, offered a similar greeting to Will, then continued chatting with Byron about the city. To her right, Will decided to observe the musicians across the room when he could offer no input. She did the same for a minute before leaning over to whisper her thoughts.

"Doesn't it bother you how they ignore us?"

"Not really," he answered without removing his eyes from the entertainment. "They belong here. We *are* just Byron's company after all. They have no obligation to talk to us."

"I know, but I hate being left out. These people act like they're so much better than us too. If I wanted to, I could…"

Will faced her with a wary expression. "You could what?"

"Nothing. I'm just tired." To emphasize her words, she focused her attention elsewhere.

I could easily threaten them, and with both physical weapons and magic. It's true, though. Nobody would stick their nose up at us if we show them what we're capable of.

Coura dismissed the concept entirely but only after considering it, and that concerned her.

***

The morning after the extravagant dinner, Byron made sure Coura and Will were awake at dawn in order to begin their return to East Hoover. Against protests from the former and groans from the latter, he arranged for them to eat cold sandwiches for breakfast while they departed through the front gate instead of a hot meal that would have been brought to their room. They ate in silence as he stalled for their final companion: a guard issued by the king's council. He made sure to mentally prepare himself before letting the two know about the addition.

As he finished his food, Coura opened the second of her wrapped sandwiches and dug in with vigor.

"This place may be unbearable, but at least their food is decent," she commented around a mouthful.

"There's one thing I need to mention before we leave," Byron said to draw their attention.

"What is it?" Will asked while wiping his glasses.

"We're going to have another person joining us."

"What?" they both demanded, Will to project his worry and Coura to reflect her irritation.

He explained the reason at a lower volume, which settled their emotions.

88

In case anything happened to him or, more importantly, the documents he carried in his bag regarding the proposal, the soldier would either alert the king of the issue or deliver the papers to the academy on his behalf. He knew the council didn't trust him to follow through with his end of the agreement, though he would never go against his word even if the situation didn't favor him.

That part remained his secret. His student would overreact, and the young man wouldn't understand. Instead, he assured them a guard provided extra protection, which made sense given how vital the documents were to the academy. Despite the half-truth, the two accepted his response.

"Where are they?" Coura asked after finishing her meal.

Before Byron could reply, he noticed movement from the opposite side of the bridge. A soldier sporting Asteom's full uniform consisting of an all-black ensemble and crimson coat decorated with golden buttons and badges crossed to approach the trio. A pack hung over one shoulder while a sheathed sword and dagger were buckled to the belt on his waist. Once he halted, the young man extended a hand in greeting.

"Assistant General Marcus Tont, reporting as your escort for our venture to the Magical Arts Academy."

While Byron accepted the handshake, he heard a displeased huff from behind. When he glanced over his shoulder, Coura already left to start heading across the clearing.

"I guess we'd better be on our way," he added despite his confusion at her behavior. He motioned for the boys to follow his student yet noticed the newcomer attempting to hide a smirk.

*

The group stayed quiet as they moved along the road, so Byron decided to ease some of the unspoken tension by becoming familiar with their guard. "You seem to have accomplished an honorable title in a short amount of time, general. To earn such a place in the army is no easy feat."

Marcus, who visibly kept his eyes and ears alert, turned his head to address the compliment. "Please, call me Marcus. I'm actually considered an assistant general. I wouldn't lie about such an important role."

"Assistant general?" Byron raised an eyebrow when the young man nodded.

"Yes, sir. Do you know the military ranking system?"

"I learned the basics as a mage…"

"Nothing at all," Will interjected from the front. He slowed his pace to walk on Marcus' other side. "I'm interested, though. Can you start with the basics?"

At first, Marcus looked surprised by the request, then he shrugged. "The simplest way to view it is as a pyramid. The bottom consists of new recruits, then what we consider third-class troops, such as foot soldiers and advanced rookies. They make up the majority of Asteom's army. The second class has assistant generals, like me, cavalry soldiers, and appointed section leaders."

"The top class must be the generals," Will added.

"Right. You'll also hear them called captains or commanders. It's the same title for the highest rank."

"How many generals are there?"

"Five at the moment."

"Only five? I thought the capital holds hundreds of soldiers."

"It does, but most of the disciplining and delegating go to the section leaders. Each soldier is categorized into a single division with a supervisor who reports to the generals."

"So, you're in charge of your own division?"

Marcus shook his head. "I'm an assistant general. My duties are to work directly under the generals and pass along information. We're sort of considered the middlemen between the first and second classes. At the same time, we learn from our superiors in order to move up in our ranking."

Byron could sense Marcus avoided telling them the details and pressed the subject when the soldier didn't elaborate. "When are you promoted?"

"I wish I knew."

"What do you mean?"

"It's up to the judgement of my supervising general. When they deem you worthy as their partner or successor, you'll be appointed to a new position."

"That sounds unbearable," Will responded without attempting to hide his disbelief.

"They don't mention when you're close or if you're heading in the right or wrong direction," Marcus went on, though more to himself than to them.

"Think of it this way," Byron told them in a thoughtful manner. "A student's graduation and future assignment are up to the discretion of the instructors. That's because we work with them for years and understand when they're ready to move on from being a trainee. If the army is like the MAA, their leaders will use honest judgement based on actions and attitudes. As long as my students work hard, be honest, and are good-hearted, I believe they'll succeed."

The answer satisfied both Will and Marcus; however, Byron kept a close eye on Coura farther ahead. When he began to talk, he sensed her listening.

I only pray she remembers my words.

***

That evening, no one argued when Marcus offered to keep watch during the first half of the night and Byron the second. They prepared camp in a resting area often used by travelers, as the recently banked firepit showed. It didn't take long after dinner for Coura to hear Byron's light snoring and Will's heavy breathing.

As she tossed and turned, she caught a glimpse of Marcus perched against a log with a thin book in one hand. The crimson embers lit his hazel eyes while they focused squarely on reading. The forest nightlife remained active with insects and nocturnal creatures chirping, scratching, and whistling to each other. To most people, it would be a peaceful setting, but the noise against a dark backdrop made Coura restless.

When the moon rose high above and the coals faintly glowed, she decided a fulfilling rest wasn't going to happen. She got up while avoiding creating too much additional sound and stood beside Marcus.

He didn't remove his eyes from the book yet still addressed her. "Can't sleep?"

"I figure there's no sense in both of us staying awake when I'm meant to be up tonight."

After a moment, he closed his book and stretched with a yawn. "I'll keep you company until my mind settles."

Marcus patted the ground next to him and offered a tired smile, so Coura took a seat. From their initial meeting on the training ground to that evening, she began to like the soldier. He patiently answered Will's incessant questions and sparked casual conversations about the academy and mage training with Byron. Meanwhile, Coura had kept to the front of the group but still listened.

Every time he talks, it feels genuine. Even his expressions aren't feigned like everyone else's at the palace.

"Why do you want to be a general?" she decided to ask.

"That's a little out of the blue," Marcus replied and tilted his head at her.

"You spent part of the day explaining your position and the army's system, yet you never told us about yourself."

He chuckled awkwardly, which proved to be the first sign of discomfort he showed since they met. "I suppose I consider this assignment as more of a duty than a leisurely trip."

"What do you mean?"

He paused and grinned to himself. "This is the first time I traveled outside the capital city. When I received the request to accompany your group, I bet they could tell I was eager to see the country."

"I shouldn't be surprised. I can't imagine they let many leaders within the army leave unless it's for an important reason."

"That, and I'm leaving my father behind."

"Oh?"

"Actually, he convinced the council to send me instead of anybody else."

Coura narrowed her eyes at him. "Really?"

"I mean, he *is* one of the most experienced generals." His eyes danced to reflect his amusement at her baffled expression.

"Your *father* is a general? Why didn't you say so before?"

"I'm trying to be mindful of my responsibilities. This journey has been interesting so far. I'm learning plenty, but the council warned me about sharing my position and relationships in case they put me at risk."

"I can understand that," Coura added before dropping the subject. The two sat in silence for a minute until she thought of another topic. "You didn't mention our spar."

"Should I have?"

"No, I guess. I don't care what you do," she admitted with more aggression than she intended.

He covered another yawn and stood without commenting on her reply. "I should get some sleep."

As he settled in the grass near the firepit, Coura turned her face upward to the stars glimmering above.

"Hey," she heard Marcus whisper and glanced over to where he stared at her with a half-awake gaze. "About yesterday, I didn't want to embarrass you by lingering on how you cheated. You can promise me a rematch sometime, though."

His snores filled the air before she could growl a retort, so she returned her attention to the stars. After a while, she considered their fight and laughed quietly to herself.

I'll hold him to that.

Growing Unease

The majority of their return went as expected. Byron made sure to follow the same route he used to get them to the palace because it kept their group away from populated areas. Although he didn't mention this to Coura or the young men, he expected they shared his caution.

Not only are we carrying important documents straight from the king and his council, but they assigned a second-class soldier to act as our guard. If that doesn't raise suspicion, then I guess I would be losing my touch. I've also had a strange feeling ever since we left Verona, almost as if there's a magical presence in the air. I can't pinpoint a location, though. We're about a day and a half away from East Hoover, so if we can reach a familiar border by nightfall, I believe we'll be fine.

The idea of being followed concerned him, but he didn't want to panic.

"What's wrong?" Will startled him by asking from his left. As usual, the herbalist noticed when any of them became bothered.

Byron pushed his concerns to the back of his mind before answering. "I'm just thinking about when we arrive at the academy."

Will didn't look convinced yet didn't question him further.

The peaceful setting of the shades of green, colorful flowers scattered like gems around the forest, and chirping creatures lightened Byron's mood throughout the morning. Will begged the group to stop several times in order to collect samples of plants and other substances the young man spotted with a keen eye. Other than those breaks, the group made decent time.

At the next pause in their venture, Marcus and Coura nibbled on their lunches nearby while Byron knelt beside Will in a patch of tall grass.

"What is it this time?"

Without removing his eyes from the dirt in his hand, the herbalist spoke as he used a metal spoon to scrape the patch of earth. "It's a fungus called the silkshroom. For some reason, it only grows in the shade of lemongrass, which means it's pretty rare. I've never been able to experiment with it much since I usually can't stock up enough."

"Lucky for you then." With the other two out of earshot, Byron decided to confront Will about a thought that rolled in his head from the moment they entered the woods. "Once you finish, I need to ask you a question."

The young man caught on to his serious tone and looked over with the same worry he displayed earlier. "What is it, Master Byron?"

He attempted to reassure Will with a smile. "Please, just call me Byron. I'm wondering what you plan on doing when we reach East Hoover. That will be the end of our journey together, after all."

"Of course." Will paused to finish up with the sample. "I suppose I'll continue exploring these forests in the north. There's no reason for me to stay near the academy, what with the light mages." He let out a dry chuckle that caused Byron to wince.

"This must be one of the first times you traveled with other people."

"Actually, it *is* the first. Nobody needs an herbalist accompanying them. Besides, my duty is to my research. I only slow us down."

Byron sensed how disheartened Will felt about the subject and placed a hand on the young man's shoulder in a gesture of reassurance. "There's no reason to be discouraged. It's the innovation and dedication of people like you that lead to so many beneficial medicines and other creations."

"I appreciate the sentiment."

An idea came to Byron then, and he got to his feet. "That being said, I hate leaving you on your own without the skills to protect yourself. Perhaps we can resolve this at the academy, maybe by inquiring about combat lessons."

The suggestion must have been what Will hoped to hear, for he showed surprise, which shifted into elation. "Master... I mean, Byron, that would be fantastic!"

As he offered a hand and helped the young man to stand, he caught Marcus and Coura staring at them and ordered the group to continue moving. Will returned to his normal, talkative self, presumably because of the offer, and Marcus happened to be the next person to ask about the samples, leading him into a lecture on each one's properties. Byron cast the soldier a sympathetic look, which their escort acknowledged with a rueful smile, then he hurried his pace to where his student wandered several steps ahead.

"You're unusually quiet," he began to spark a conversation.

She merely shrugged and continued to scan the woods ahead.

"Is there something on your mind?" He knew her too well to know there was but didn't care to force it out.

Perhaps it's Marcus. I thought I recognized him, though it took me a while to remember I pulled her out of a fight with him a few days ago. She probably doesn't trust him because he's a soldier. Given time, he figured she would warm up to the young man like she did with Will.

"Coura, can you hand me a sandwich?" Will called from behind. "I'm starving!"

The group slowed to a stop before she removed a wrapped bundle from her pack. During the break, Byron noticed Marcus rubbing his eyes.

"Tired?" he asked the assistant general.

"I'm not used to keeping watch is all, but I'll be fine. I'm surprised Coura's still standing; she's the one who's been awake every night."

During their first evening on the road, Byron rose at dawn and found his student had taken his shift. At first, the gesture flattered him, yet she did the same ever since due to restlessness. He never knew her to skimp on sleep, though her reserved behavior made more sense.

"It's because she hates the woods," Will muttered between bites.

Marcus tilted his head. "What?"

"I do not," she snapped.

Will shook his head. "It sure seems that way."

"Why do you keep bringing it up?" she asked after a pause to calm down.

"I mentioned my reason before. You haven't slept well except at the palace and still glare into the trees, like you're scared a monster will jump out."

Byron decided not to add his opinion since he expected Coura to yell again, as was her nature.

However, she looked up at the sky instead with a mixture of exasperation and uneasiness. "I don't hate the woods. Every time we've been out here something doesn't feel right. I can't explain it."

While she shook her head, presumably to dismiss the topic, Byron's heart sank. *Just as I am unable to pinpoint what I'm sensing, she can tell there's a presence too. If it's bothering her this much, it's strong and most likely nearby.*

He met her eyes while hoping to project the severity of such a threat. "Is it magic you're picking up? I noticed the same ever since we left the capital, but I haven't been able to tell exactly what it is either."

She didn't answer. The three looked to him with anxious expressions, so he closed his eyes and attempted to locate the source again.

"Coura, I'm trying to see if I can identify where it's coming from and if it's hostile. Do the same."

After a moment, the familiar 'tickling' sensation met his mind.

There it is! Now, let's get a read on it...

Probing magical energy was like walking along a road and looking a stranger up and down, though only mages possessing a solid center with power to spare could observe other presences in detail. In several instances, Byron needed to check if a mage had died, where his comrades were, and if a spy hid within a group. There would always be a chance somebody could observe him too, but it proved to be a slight risk. As far as he knew, less than a dozen mages in Asteom possessed the energy and training to use this ability with Coura as the youngest. More importantly, one could discern demonic energy in an instant since it felt heavy and active, like breathing humid air around sparks of lightning.

He attempted to follow the source but couldn't figure out the location since the power seemed entirely new, which worried him the most. Unlike every other type of energy, this felt lighter and cool, almost the exact opposite of a dark mage's. Of course, it remained faint enough to not reveal any additional information. Finally, he abandoned the attempt and opened his eyes.

Marcus scanned the trees around them with a hand on his sword, and Will fidgeted in place.

"What did you discover?" the latter asked.

"I'm not sure. Coura?"

"I don't like it," she answered while still staring at the sky.

Byron chewed on the inside of his cheek for a moment. "It remained too dim for me to trace, but I didn't sense malice. It's definitely not a demonic creature, so that's positive news for us."

"I don't like it," his student repeated before meeting his eyes and shaking her head. "It felt wrong. I can't explain why, but it clashes against my own energy."

"I've never heard of anything like that."

"You're right too. I can't figure out a precise location. If I had to guess, I'd say it's following us by using the same method."

Byron bit off a frustrated curse and scowled in thought. *Coura's probing skills must be better than mine. If the presence bothers her this much, it must be dangerous. We had better hurry, though I wonder if this mage plans on stepping in before we get to the academy. There's no doubt it's watching us, but why? I'd rather not take a chance on being ambushed out here where we're alone.*

"What should we do?" Marcus asked in a tense voice when no one offered a suggestion.

Perhaps we can divert their attention elsewhere. We're approaching an intersecting road connecting Fester to East Hoover soon, and it's only a day's trip away. It might be wise to use a detour. Best case scenario, I'm just being overly cautious. Better to arrive later than expected than not at all.

"I have a plan," he announced and faced the group while keeping his tone and attitude neutral. "It'll take us longer to return to the academy, but we're changing our route to pass through Fester. I propose we travel straight there without a break. Then, we can rent a room at an inn and head out the next day."

Marcus nodded in agreement. "We'll keep eyes on us. No one would dare try to attack in a highly populated city with the guards posted."

"Exactly. Now, let's get moving."

***

The four reached Fester just before dawn the following morning. Imagining an unknown threat isolating them in the forest acted as motivation to pick up their normal pace. Coura felt exhausted yet couldn't sit still until Byron selected a decently sized inn near the western edge of the city. The friendly, plump innkeeper had been so charmed by Byron's incessive complimenting that she gave them the largest room with two beds and promised lunch on her.

Despite their luck, Coura grew more anxious.

Part of me dislikes lingering while we're being watched by somebody, or something, we can't identify. I would rather hurry to the academy or go after the culprit than run and hide. Then, the other part...

She shuddered.

This energy... I hate it! My blood begins to boil when I sense it.

As she stared out the window again to eye what trees loomed in the distance, she began to relax. Shopkeepers started to open their doors, wagons clattered across town, and the citizens stretched and grumbled to one another on their routes to work. Just knowing other people were present around their group eased the tension, and soon Coura stopped sensing the horrifically strange presence.

She yawned in response and sat on the edge of her bed a few minutes later. Marcus and Will set up their bedrolls on the floor once the group entered the room, leaving the cots available for her and her mentor. Evidently, the two figured out if it came to fighting a mage, Byron and Coura would need every bit of strength, just in case. It didn't bother her in the slightest.

Byron entered carrying a bundle of what smelled like sausage and pastry and placed it on the table to the left side of the room. After kicking the door closed and fastening the lock, he addressed her and their other companions.

"I mentioned we would be resting all day, and the kind lady offered us a gift. Sleep as long as you like. We'll plan on heading out tomorrow morning, unless plans change."

"What do you mean?" Marcus inquired, allowing his suspicion to seep into the question. Perhaps it was due to a lack of sleep, but that seemed to be the first time Coura noticed Marcus fulfilling his role as their guard.

The master mage shook his head and dropped onto the second bed. "There's a chance our stalker will attempt an attack before we leave. There is also a chance we may need to stay here another night to recover. Plans change. That's a practical concept I'd expect a general to understand."

She knew Byron's frankness resulted from his weariness. Thankfully, Marcus didn't argue with the response. Once everybody relaxed, they started to catch up on their lost sleep.

*

Coura woke at some point in the afternoon and felt immediately relieved by the lack of that mysterious presence, prompting her to rise and scarf down a few of the treats in the innkeeper's bundle. Marcus soon followed, then Will. They ate in silence before returning to their beds to rest with full stomachs.

The next morning, she woke in a half-aware state of mind when sunlight peered through the lone window in their room and smiled before pulling the blankets tighter around herself. She didn't know how long she had been in bed, but no one else made a move to rise.

Perhaps I better enjoy this comfort before the others get up.

After a few minutes passed, she sat up, stretched, and threw the blankets aside. Since their group expected to be on the road, she considered washing up and eating a proper meal as she rubbed her eyes; however, when she looked around the room, she found herself alone. None of their belongings had been packed, and a scrap of paper lay on the table beside a wrapped meal and a pouch.

Coura,

> *It's around noon now. Will left to explore some of the shops in town earlier, and Marcus wanted to meet a few soldiers stationed here. It looks like we'll be leaving tomorrow morning instead. I'm going to pay a friend a visit at Wilken's Tavern at the other end of town and see what information I can gather about this area. You're free to do as you please for the rest of the day, but return here around sundown or come find me if I'm not back by then.*

-Byron

She left the note on the table, picked up the wrapped meal, which proved to be a portable meat pie, and dug into it while glancing out the window. *I can't believe it's already after noon. I guess I needed more sleep than I realized.*

After preparing for the day, Coura tied her hair back before grabbing the small bag filled with a dozen coins. It wasn't much, but it would be enough to purchase a trinket or jewelry. She exited once she felt ready to explore the city.

Fester reminded her of Verona in size and possessed a main road holding shops, then plenty of trails leading to homes and farms near the outskirts of the city. During her leisure time, she entered what buildings piqued her interest and inspected their variety of wares. Along the way, she purchased roasted nuts from a bakery then gave the rest of her money to a street performer who juggled knives before throwing them at marked targets, including one just above his assistant's head. Although she couldn't understand why somebody preferred to play with weapons instead of wielding them, it entertained her nonetheless.

As the sun began to set and the sky filled with shades of warm colors, Coura made her way back to the inn. Byron must have requested the innkeeper replace their original package, for fresh food awaited her. Will was the only one in the room, and he already munched on a piece of dried jerky from the basket. They greeted each other and nibbled on the steamy, savory meats items together. Will informed her of his adventure in Fester while she summed up her day in a few sentences.

"Did you reach the potion and herbal shop? That's my favorite place, and I'm sure you would like their flowers. They're all for decoration, which is why the employees arrange them in such an extravagant fashion."

Coura shook her head and rose to light the candles. At first, she prepared to do so by casting a spell but ultimately decided it would be better not to risk using any of her power and attracting the unsettling presence. She instead exited to light the wick at a lamp in the hallway before dropping to sit on her cot.

"It's well after sundown," she mumbled thoughtlessly. "I wonder where they could be."

Will waved a hand in a dismissive manner. "I wouldn't worry. Marcus said he'd be with some soldiers he trained with, and I trust Byron is safe too."

Coura voiced her agreement yet wasn't entirely convinced.

Outside, the noise from the main street died down, and the sky grew dark.

"Would you like to see the books I bought?" he asked a moment later. "They're probably not what you're interested in…"

"Sure."

He glanced over without hiding his surprise. "You would?" Even as he spoke, Will pulled out the pair of light texts from his pack.

While he explained each and shared what information they held, Coura's mind wandered elsewhere. *Where could they be? Surely Byron didn't spend all day at a tavern just to talk, though he did mention meeting a friend. On the other hand, I still don't fully trust Marcus. I would like to, but I don't know how he would behave in a dangerous situation...*

"Coura?"

"Hmm?"

Will stared at her with his finger on a section of one chapter. "Is everything okay?"

"We should go look for them," she replied at last and jumped to her feet.

The herbalist returned his book to the bag with obvious reluctance before following her out of the room. "Are you sure you're not overreacting? Don't you trust Byron?"

Coura stopped just before the inn's exit to spin around and aim a glare at her companion. "You think I don't trust him? I'm his student, the one who worked with him for years, so excuse *me* for being the most concerned! If you would rather stay here and shut yourself away, then go ahead. It's not like you and your useless books are helping anyway."

She stormed outside without waiting for a response, leaving Will gaping in the hallway.

*

The tavern Byron mentioned proved to be the farthest building across Fester, nearly pressed against the woods beyond. Coura tried to ignore her frustration and guilt by telling herself she would deal with Will after she could confirm her mentor and Marcus were safe.

For a while, she stood at the bottom of the path leading to the tavern and attempted to muster the courage to enter. Every second made her worry about what she would find inside more, for the setting disgusted her. The strong stench of livestock mixed with ale and sweat turned her stomach, and the drunks and beggars parading themselves around kept her from approaching lest she be forced to interact with them. She had no clue how anybody could stand to be near the place for so long.

And this is just the outside...

After her senses adjusted, Coura prepared to approach from the main road until a glint of light nearby caught her attention. She paused, slid herself into the shadow of the last shop on the path, and waited. The shine came from a soldier's suit of armor as a pair of guards lingered under the streetlamp across from her hiding spot. One laughed when the other shushed him, and she strained her ears to catch their conversation.

"You crack me up. Why would an assistant general lie to us?" the first man asked a little too loudly for his comrade's comfort.

"Will you keep it down? All I'm saying is, *our* orders come straight from the capital. He might be able to restrain our target, but I'd rather not risk losing this opportunity to get promoted."

The first soldier produced an ugly snort. "You think too much. I don't care whether we follow the kid's orders or not. I also don't care about promotions and the like. Let's just arrest the mage, confiscate those papers, and be done with it."

Coura felt on edge from the moment they mentioned Marcus; when they concluded their conversation and strolled away, her heart pounded in her chest. *Arrest a mage? Could they mean Byron? Why would they arrest a messenger? Something isn't right here. I better warn Byron and see if I can find Marcus.*

With the questions as motivation, she slipped onto the road and moved toward the tavern at a hurried walk.

The Seer's Prediction

Although Byron wasn't one to stop at taverns while traveling for business, he always cherished his visits to Fester for the chance to return to the particular place he currently occupied. He spent all afternoon sharing drinks and catching up with some familiar faces.

When he first arrived, he recognized a farmer he became acquainted with several years earlier. The man's youngest son accidentally set their barn on fire after discovering his ability to wield dark magic and didn't tell anybody. That had been the example Byron used for Coura when the two left the academy and she needed to understand when to avoid casting spells based on the dilemma. Symon ordered him to take the boy to the MAA, easing the burden on the family and allowing a professional to explain the situation. In their case, the farmer and his wife had three other sons, so their fear shifted to excitement upon learning how one of their children would become a mage once he could control his power.

When Byron joined the man that afternoon, he heard the four sons had turned into five with a younger sister and received an update on the boy's position as a mage stationed in Fester. Soon enough, three of the sons, including the recruit he recognized from years ago, joined them.

By the time the men left for supper, he felt ready to eat too. A barmaid brought him the tavern's special stew, fresh bread, and ale before chatting with him about the area's prosperity. Even though she claimed not to gossip much, the woman seemed to possess a talent for collecting tidbits of information in her position. Byron recognized several names and memorized many more during their conversation. Overall, Fester remained stable, but rumors circled of livestock being spooked by creatures in the woods.

"That's why the soldiers are out at night now. One or two worked before, but now at least six patrol the area," she concluded at a lower volume. "I haven't seen the beasts myself, but I'm always in here. You should try asking the guards when they arrive."

He thanked her after and ate his meal alone. *I would rather avoid soldiers at the moment. After all, my first task is to return those documents to Symon. There's a potential for trouble if too many people learn we're in Fester. Besides, I'd hate to raise suspicion with Marcus.*

That morning, he and the assistant general got up together and ate before the young man requested they remain an additional day. Luckily, Byron felt the same, yet he asked for a reason.

"I intend to meet some friends stationed here, soldiers I trained and who trained alongside me. I believe it's important for them to hear why we stopped. Don't worry, I won't go into detail. I plan on telling them we did this as a precaution in case anybody trailed us, that's all. Their testimonies should protect us if we do run into an issue and are blamed for what we can't necessarily control."

I do like him, Byron reflected as he cleared his bowl. *He'll grow into an honest man and a skilled commander if he continues down that path.*

Later that evening, after sharing a few drinks with new and old friends, he made his way to the back of the building as the main area filled. What he neglected to share with the others in his company was his second reason for visiting Fester specifically.

Half the common room held tables and benches with the bar at one end while a third of the remaining space stayed open for musicians and performers to entertain. That evening, a band consisting of various string and wind instruments could barely be heard over the chatter, laughter, and attempts at singing over the music. It felt like the perfect time for Byron to consult with one of the tavern's famous ladies.

Several women adorned with makeup, jewelry, and fine clothing offered their time in reserved spaces for the right price. Guests paid beforehand for some privacy, meaning they told the ladies what they didn't want repeated beyond the closed doors. Despite this, he hoped he would be able to gather intel from a reliable source.

He knocked on the final door in the row while the other women gave him looks of mock sadness at his rejection. Byron offered a polite smile and waited. The entrance painted with a gold star at its center opened a minute later, and he couldn't keep from grinning as his old friend's jaw dropped.

"It's been too long!" she exclaimed with a mixture of disbelief and joy.

"It has, Cintra."

As she ushered him inside, he caught her nod to the others, who understood her silent request to leave them alone. When the door closed, his longtime friend turned with arms wide open so the two could share an embrace before he accepted a seat in one of two empty chairs. The space felt rather confined compared to the inn's room and contained a bed with a heavy canopy, a table holding burning incense, various, decorative accessories, and a pitcher of water.

Cintra spread herself out on the mattress, lying on her side and eyeing him with nothing except admiration. Whenever he visited, Byron couldn't help but be enthralled by her appearance, especially when she wore silk and tied her lengthy, blonde hair partially up to leave a trail down her back. While she wore too much makeup for his liking, it made her sapphire eyes stand out, her cheeks look flushed, and her lips shade a brighter scarlet, even in the dimly lit room. As he always noticed, her low-cut dress exposed plenty of skin with the skirt positioned to show part of her legs.

Despite her presence, the woman showed no desire to seduce him, which was exactly how he liked their relationship. He didn't approve of her profession as an entertainer, mainly because of his own, protective feelings that blossomed from their years together in Fester, yet she became more well known for another service.

Cintra carried a unique ability from her light-blooded lineage, one that made her an incredibly valuable asset: Her power showed her visions of possible futures. Byron had heard of such a spell but didn't know anybody able to use it as clearly, including the master light mages at the academy. Many also frowned upon the magic because of its regular inconsistencies and tendency to frighten the user.

This happened to his friend after she began experiencing visions when they were just children. The spell scared her, but he promised to help. The premonitions would come true, and that part terrified her almost too much to bear; however, Byron remained at her side until he was forced to deal with his own developing power.

He urged her to join him in East Hoover on multiple occasions, yet she always refused.

"If anybody found out, I could be taken away or forced to serve for the rest of my life," she had argued. "I would rather cope with these visions than become someone's slave."

Years later, Byron learned of her position at the tavern. When he first visited, she taught herself to control her magic by channeling it into a source. The first time she showed him, she brought a violet gemstone and focused on that. He sensed the energy at work, and she successfully predicted a brief part of his future. Every now and then, she accepted payment for reading guests' futures, earning her title 'Cintra the Visionary.'

"What brings the famous master mage to me?" she asked with narrowed eyes.

Byron feigned innocence. "I can't come to visit without suspicion?"

Cintra laughed, a rich sound compared to the grumbling and singing in the common room. "If that's all this is, I would love to catch up."

He welcomed the invitation to talk for a while, so the two traded stories of events at the academy, in Fester, and across the region.

"I'm told a rising number of creatures are lurking in the woods," Byron brought up after a while, when matters turned more serious.

His friend nodded slowly. "It's true, though the citizens act tough about it. I'll be honest, it worries me."

"Have you…"

This time, she shook her head. "I tried looking ahead, but I only see darkness. I'm frightened. I've never not been able to get visions. Whatever this is, I can only think of a couple possibilities."

"I'm worried too, but I have faith in your ability," he offered in a reassuring manner. "I hope you know that."

A little light returned to her eyes. "Of course."

"What do you think is happening?"

With a sigh, Cintra shifted into a sitting position. "Dark energy is involved for sure, perhaps enough to cloud my foresight, and I can't make sense of it. Either that or my light magic won't be able to look past it."

"And the other reason?"

"I believe it's more likely the future is too muddled at this point. Remember those times when I couldn't make heads or tails of what I saw? It might be similar, just on a grander scale. I don't know how else to explain it."

"I think I get the idea."

"I can try again. Maybe I'll pick up something else with you present."

"I'm up for it if you are," he answered and gave her a hopeful gaze.

Cintra bent forward to slide a sack out from underneath the bed. From it, she removed a crystal orb and some jewelry. She told him once how the metal and stones enhanced details, and he couldn't find any reason to doubt her. After putting the items on, she held the orb and took one of his hands.

Byron instantly sensed her light energy at work; its frailness reminded him of a spider weaving a fragile web. The feeling ended a minute later as Cintra released his hand and rubbed her temples.

He tried to be patient while she relaxed and failed. "What did you see?"

Her weary eyes slid to the floor. "It's still hazy, but I caught a few scenes surrounding you, a castle, and an army."

"An army?"

"Their silver bodies shined in the sunlight," she confirmed before lowering her voice into a whisper. "There was also an angel."

Alarm struck Byron. "An angel? What do you mean?"

"Exactly that. A person with wings flying through the sky. I focused on just one, but there may have been more."

"An angel," he repeated in a mumble, unable to comprehend Cintra's vision. Before he could question the appearance of a Yeluthian, his friend continued.

"You were covered in blood too." She shuddered to reflect her inner turmoil.

At that, he went to sit beside her on the bed and put an arm around her shoulders. "I know it must worry you, but thank you for trying."

She smiled at him, leaned over to kiss his cheek, then placed a hand on it. "Of course. I can't stand to watch harm befall those I care about."

"You and me both."

They remained close together and simply savored each other's company until Cintra rose, moved to the door, and exited. She returned shortly after with a jug of wine.

"The business is out of the way, so why don't we enjoy ourselves a bit?"

Byron returned her resulting grin. "I'd like that."

***

The inside of Wilken's Tavern proved to be utter chaos to Coura, who felt like she'd began drowning in a sea of people, noise, and smoke. In the back of her mind, she hoped Will stayed at the inn and wouldn't follow; she could barely tolerate the atmosphere, let alone keep track of him in it.

First thing's first. I need to blend in and figure out where Byron could be.

Barmaids weaved through the traffic while balancing trays of drinks, so she stole a mug when one became engaged in a conversation with an older man. Try as she might, Coura couldn't avoid staring at the faces around her. Plenty of soldiers in Asteom's crimson uniform put her on edge, though they all seemed to be in a casual, joking mood and paid her no mind. She couldn't imagine how anybody heard themselves or their companions in such a loud environment as she wandered around the space while trying to locate her mentor.

When she reached the farthest end containing an open area for dancing, she recognized Marcus mingling with a group of soldiers. Some held their partners in their arms as they chatted, though others attempted to dance. To her, the latter individuals appeared to be flailing around or swaying out of sync, yet they succeeded in becoming a diversion. She abandoned her mug and moved beside the assistant general without drawing attention to herself and grabbed his arm.

"What are you doing here?" she began when he glanced over to stare at her. "We were supposed to meet up hours ago."

"I'm glad you're here," Marcus replied, though he didn't appear to be fully sober. "Let me introduce you."

He placed a hand on her back to guide her forward before she knew how to respond. The unexpected gesture spurred a blush, as did the gazes of the men and women who noticed her.

"Look who's got himself a girl!" one of the younger soldiers announced and pointed his mug at them, prompting laughs, controlled cheers, and winks.

Coura's face burned from the resulting heat in her cheeks; however, Marcus removed his hand and joined in by chuckling. The noise settled a few seconds later, then the space returned to its normal level of volume and activity. Movement from the assistant general after had her turning to catch him leaning closer.

"Would you like a drink?" he asked and met her eyes with a hopeful gaze. "We can find somewhere quieter to talk, if you want."

The offer surprised her, especially since he sounded sincerely interested. Still, Coura recalled the earlier conversation she overheard and decided to take the necessary precautions when her anxiety returned. "We need to go."

"Why? It's not that late."

"The guards are going to arrest Byron, and I can't find him."

Marcus' relaxed expression tightened into one reflecting confusion before he voiced his doubt. "Who's going to arrest him?"

"A pair of soldiers outside mentioned-"

"Nobody has the authority to do that," he interrupted and scoffed to dismiss her plea. "Don't worry. I already informed them about my assignment."

"They won't listen. I-"

"Quit worrying. Let me get us a couple drinks to calm down."

Coura's patience ran out at that point, and she spun on her heel to head for the exit.

I can't focus right now, she admitted and ignored Marcus as he called her name. *He can stay here for all I care. Once I clear my head, I'll look somewhere else for Byron.*

She kept her eyes down while attempting to work through her mixed emotions. The exit came into view a minute later, and she slowed enough to chance a final scan of the room. Nothing appeared to have changed since she entered except the assistant general decided to follow. That gave her an idea.

Perhaps I can get him outside where we can discuss what to do. If anything, he might want to return to the inn and can keep Will company. With the thought in mind, she waited for him to push his way over.

Unfortunately, he paused to collect a pair of mugs from a barmaid before strolling toward her.

"Would you like to sneak out?" he asked while offering one of the drinks. His optimism hadn't waned, which left Coura wondering if he genuinely wished to spend time together.

Don't get distracted, she told herself after accepting the mug. *We're in trouble if Byron is arrested, even though Marcus doesn't believe me.*

Without a word, she moved toward the door and exited with the assistant general right behind. Her goal became to lead him farther along the main road, which worked until he seemed to realize her intent to abandon the lively tavern.

Marcus halted and glanced back toward the noise. "Where are you going?"

She refrained from releasing a sigh as she faced him again. "We should return to the inn. Will's waiting for us, and Byron's missing."

"You're still concerned about that?"

"Aren't you?" she snapped to show her repressed frustration with the situation. "He could be in danger."

The soldier narrowed his eyes and frowned. "The guards wouldn't let anything happen to a master mage. They should let me know if they sense an issue."

"I don't trust them."

"Why not?"

Coura bit her tongue to keep from losing her temper at his response, allowing him to step closer while continuing.

"You're overreacting, and if you plan on behaving irrationally, then I suggest you go back by yourself."

The assistant general paused to wait for her reaction, yet she refused to waste additional time by trying to convince him of what she heard. A sense of despair seeped through her irritation when she considered his position and who remained in the tavern.

His friends might ask about me, and I doubt he'll keep his mouth shut. I shouldn't let him go back...

"Marcus," she started and reached for his arm when he turned around.

Her hand seized his bicep for less than a second before he tugged it away, shot a glare at her, and readjusted his coat. The motion, as well as her growing certainty he would share the encounter with the other soldiers, pushed her into acting. She gripped the mug harder and raised it as soon as Marcus looked away to crack the wood against the side of his head. The blow knocked him to the ground with a thud, and what ale they both carried splashed onto them and the dirt.

Coura's head swung from side to side as she expected a witness or two, yet nobody had been near enough to observe the strike. She tossed the empty mug aside and paused for a few deep breaths in order to quell her shaking limbs.

I can't believe I just attacked a soldier. If anyone finds us, I'll be the one who's locked away.

Upon attempting to lift the limp body, she found she was too weak to do much except shift him around, though she managed to get him into a sitting position. His grumbles let her know she hadn't seriously injured his head despite a short gash on his temple.

"Marcus, can you stand?" she decided to ask when his eyes opened slightly after he repeatedly blinked.

He didn't offer an answer, so Coura put one of his arms around her shoulders as a bit of guidance and attempted to rise. After three tries, he mindlessly caught on, pushed himself to his feet with her help, then leaned against her for support, causing her to grunt and mutter a curse.

At least we're getting somewhere, she admitted before pulling him forward.

The soldier's feet dragged along the ground, but he managed a couple steps. To her dismay, he stopped and glanced around the road.

"What are we… Coura? You…you *hit* me!"

"I'll apologize later," she promised while continuing to struggle against his unevenly displaced weight.

About halfway down the main road, she saw a figure hurrying toward them and felt herself panicking until she recognized the silhouette as Will. The herbalist appeared frantic and carried his packs.

Now what, she grumbled in her mind after recalling how the two parted earlier that evening.

He paused nearby before approaching, seemingly after recognizing her and Marcus. Coura's curiosity piqued when he addressed her at a hushed volume.

"There you are!"

"What's going on?" she demanded while he caught his breath. "Why do you have your bags?"

He opened his mouth to reply until Marcus groaned weakly, then his attention shifted to the assistant general. "Is he all right?"

She ignored the question. "Will, what are you doing here?"

A sense of urgency took hold of his features after he mentally backtracked, showcased by scrunched eyebrows and a deep frown. "I returned to our room when you left to find Byron and sat there for a little while, then I decided I should go too. As soon as I went near the exit, I spotted the innkeeper talking with a man wearing a cloak. She mentioned Byron's name, a tavern, and that she didn't know when he'd be back. The stranger asked about the documents from the king's council next, but she couldn't remember seeing them. I hurried to the room again since I figured someone would eventually find the papers. With you, Byron, and Marcus gone, I decided it would be better to abandon the inn than risk the stranger coming after us. I can only carry this much, but the innkeeper didn't notice me slip out." He continued sharing his concerns before voicing his regret at neglecting to search for Byron earlier.

Meanwhile, Coura's head ached from the unraveling problem they faced. She also began to feel the unknown presence ever since she moved away from the tavern, albeit faintly.

If Byron and Marcus would have kept their word in the first place, we'd all be together. Still, I can't dwell on the past. What I heard matches with Will's story, so the city guards should be searching for us.

As if sensing her train of thought, the soldier mumbled about returning to the busy building instead of worrying.

"Be quiet," she snapped at them both.

Luckily, they obeyed.

"It's too risky to stay at the inn again. I caught a pair of guards mention they plan on arresting Byron, probably because we left the route or they intend to take the documents. It would be smarter to camp outside Fester."

"Aren't we avoiding the woods?" Will countered. "Besides, we're not certain they're going to apprehend him. If we explain our situation, they would listen."

Coura paused to consider that alternative; however, Marcus halfheartedly shook his head before joining the conversation.

"How would anybody here know about us already? We left a few days ago. They'll listen to me."

His head drooped after those words before he leaned into her body, and she struggled to support him.

"Wake up, Marcus!" she ordered while pushing him upright. "Someone told them about the documents and Byron's assignment. I don't have any idea who was at the inn either."

He continued to ignore her but adjusted more weight onto his own legs, which proved to be enough for the moment.

She glanced at Will next to get his opinion, yet he appeared clueless.

We don't have time to stand around and argue, she decided and looked around the empty area. *The cloaked stranger he saw knows we're staying at the inn, and I would bet the innkeeper would inform the guards if they asked. The presence from the forest isn't an issue now, so I would rather avoid causing trouble here.*

"Even if nothing happens overnight, we'd need to leave in the morning anyway," she began and addressed Will. "Let's set up a camp at the edge of Fester in case we need to return. I'll stay up and keep watch too."

Her companion hesitantly agreed to the plan, which proved to be enough to satisfy her at the moment.

Together, they hauled Marcus north along the nearest side road until they emerged from the surrounding buildings and into the clearing beyond. Wilken's Tavern glowed in the distance as they crossed the open area and entered the surrounding trees at the start of the woods. To their relief, a space wide enough for the four appeared in a matter of minutes, even in the dim light of the moon.

"This will do," she declared before motioning for them to set the assistant general down. Then, they surveyed the area once Will dropped his bags.

"What do we do now?" he asked without concealing his nerves.

Coura responded by grabbing him by the elbow and heading in the direction of the city.

"What are you doing?" her companion protested, though he didn't attempt to pry himself free. "We can't just leave him!"

As soon as they entered the open field beyond the trees, she released her grip, faced him, and put both hands on his shoulders to emphasize her next instructions. "I need you to return to the inn, pack the rest of our bags, and bring them to where we put Marcus. Load Byron's first, then Marcus'. My belongings won't be missed, but the documents should remain our priority."

"What will you do?"

"I'm going to find Byron. The guards might be searching for him already."

"This late?"

She nodded before urging him to hurry. Without another word, they parted for the second time that evening.

The Danger Angels Bring

s she searched Wilken's Tavern for her mentor yet again, Coura forced herself to breathe and keep moving lest she abandon the effort altogether. The stress of the unknown threatened to overwhelm her sense of responsibility despite the issue revolving around somebody else.

Where could he be? I doubt Byron would leave, but I suppose Will can find me if he returns to the inn. What if the soldiers already caught him? The news would spread among the people here, right?

The hour grew late, but nearly as many people remained as when she led Marcus out, and they all seemed to be as active. She realized after a lap around the room that the master mage wasn't in the common room and decided to head farther inside where several doors at the opposite end of the building caught her eye. When she recognized the women lingering in that space, she immediately halted.

Byron wouldn't go in there... Would he? I checked everywhere else, so I guess I have no choice.

Six of the ten doors had women standing in front of them. After waiting a while, three of the rooms emptied, leaving the one on the end. Before she could consider how to sneak inside, a pair of men near the musicians began roughhousing to draw everybody's attention, allowing her to hurry to the last room and try the knob. By some fortune, it hadn't been locked. She slipped into the doorway before closing it behind her.

Immediately, her eyes darted around to take in as much as she could of the cramped, heavily scented space before they landed on the enormous bed. There, her mentor lied on his stomach without a shirt on while one of the attractive women rubbed his back. Coura coughed at the incense filling the air without considering the noise, which startled the stranger.

"Who are you?" the stranger squealed while rising. "What are you doing in here?"

Instead of giving in to her desire to blow up at the questions, Coura glared and replied in as steady a tone as she could manage. "I'm here for him, so you can just stay away and be quiet until we're gone."

"No!" The woman stepped closer to Byron and instinctively placed a hand on his shoulder.

He groaned and lifted his head to glance at her with a sleepy expression. "Cintra, what's wrong?"

She ignored him. "I won't let you hurt Byron. If you come any closer, I'll scream."

Coura scoffed. "Hurt him? I'm here to *help* him!"

The master mage turned onto his side and rubbed his eyes. "Coura?"

"We need to go," she replied and moved to grab him.

Unfortunately, the stranger still didn't budge, even going so far as to reach out and push her away.

I don't have time for this.

Instead of fighting back, she used her shorter size to duck under the stranger's outstretched arm and slide behind. Then, she twisted around to kick the woman's backside, causing her target to fall forward onto the floor with a gasp. This allowed Coura to take one of Byron's arms and heave him into a sitting position.

"We need to go," she repeated with more urgency.

"What are you doing here?" he halfheartedly demanded, though he let her pull him to his feet after.

She decided to avoid answering and located his shirt on the table next to several, strange pieces of jewelry. He began chastising her for the interruption yet made no attempt to keep her away as she forcefully dressed him. Once he looked decent, she prepared to lead him toward the door when they heard a soft whimper.

"Byron," the woman cried in a gentle, wavering voice from where she remained on the floor.

He seemed to notice her then and attempted to go beside her; however, his body wouldn't cooperate, so he ended up wobbling before clutching onto Coura. She growled in response yet restrained herself from snapping venomous insults at his behavior. When she directed him toward the door again, the woman rose to block them from leaving.

"Move," Coura ordered with the last of her patience.

"I won't!"

"Are you all right?" Byron asked through a grumble, prompting another whimper from the stranger.

A curt knock on the door interrupted their argument and made Coura jump. The woman reached for the doorknob, paused, then glanced at her without hiding a sense of suspicion.

"Please," Coura begged after deciding to abandon her aggressive approach for a more helpless, honest one. "Don't tell them we're here."

The stranger's expression softened before she nodded and opened the door. As she did so, Coura shoved Byron by the bed and out of the doorway's line of sight into the room.

"What're you doing here?" he asked again and began to mumble nonsense until she shushed him.

Because of the limited view, she couldn't see who stood at the room's entrance nor hear the resulting conversation over the noise in the common room. It took less than a minute for the woman to dismiss the individual, close the door, and address Coura.

"Why are the city's guards looking for Byron?"

It became evident by the sincere concern in her voice that she had some sort of personal connection to the master mage, meaning Coura could trust her for the moment.

"It's a long story."

"I know what you must be thinking. Byron and I grew up together in Fester, so he's a dear friend of mine. He came to visit me, that's all."

Although Coura could tell the woman wanted to hide the details, she didn't doubt the reasoning. "We're heading to the Magical Arts Academy deliver important documents from Verona. An unnatural presence followed us through the woods, so we decided to spend time here and take a road back to East Hoover. The guards believe Byron is committing treason by abandoning the route. At least, that's what I overheard a pair mention."

"I understand," the woman answered with widening eyes. "The soldiers were probably ordered to keep him here and make it seem like he abandoned his assignment."

Whatever Coura was about to say slipped away at the words. *I didn't even consider them framing him. Byron said he didn't leave on friendly terms with the council, and I wouldn't put it past Hernan to sneak around either.*

The woman took advantage of the pause to move to Byron's other side and shake his shoulders. "I might have given him a little too much wine. You two can escape through the back door so they don't see you. What do you plan on doing once you… Actually, never mind. It's better I don't know where he goes."

With a groan, Byron raised his head and complained about Coura's arrival again before they moved him toward the wall opposite the bed. The woman drew the heavy curtain covering its entirety to reveal another door.

"This is a hidden exit used during an emergency or for fresh air," she explained while removing the master mage's arm and transferring his weight. "Since I'm at the end of the row, it won't be that far of a walk. Turn right, then follow the hallway until you reach the rear of the tavern."

"Thank you," Coura found herself saying.

The woman smiled before glancing at Byron with an unreadable gaze. "By the way, my name is Cintra. Please, take care of him. He's a kind man."

"I know. I'm his student."

Cintra's mouth fell open a bit, as if she realized a forgotten fact, though she said nothing more as she ushered them into the hallway beyond and noiselessly shut the door.

Once alone, Coura dragged Byron to the right, as Cintra instructed. The space didn't possess any lamps, so she kept a hand on the nearest wall and followed it through touch. As promised, they reached the exit a minute later. She turned the knob, kicked the door open, and emerged with haste. The crisp, night air felt refreshing on her body, so she paused for a deep breath before moving on. After being stuffed inside the tavern, she appreciated being alone with her thoughts, even though her mentor's continuous grumbling soon transformed into him scolding her for entering the place. Coura knew better than to argue with him in that state, so she continually apologized while pulling him along.

Since they came out through the back of the tavern, all she noticed were storage barrels, wagons, and various supplies for the kitchen. They also wound up a lot closer to the woods where she left Marcus, which became the most important location at the moment. Coura strained her eyes to scan the open field surrounding Wilken's Tavern and hoped to spot Will; however, the space looked empty.

He should have had enough time to return with the rest of our packs. I'm exhausted, but if I need to help him, I guess I must.

The two reached the trees after an agonizing amount of time due to Byron's stumbling. She shoved aside what branches got in their way until they entered the clearing where three bedrolls had been set up in a sloppy manner. Once the master mage saw his, he pushed away from Coura, nearly knocking her over in the process, and dropped onto it. She rolled her shoulders in order to ease some of the tension in her muscles while vowing not to lug anybody else around that evening. Marcus snoozed where she and Will left him, and after fumbling through the darkness, she located each of the four packs loaded with all their belongings. Most importantly, she found the documents in Byron's bag still sealed in their wrapping; her resulting sense of relief caused her body to tremble.

Thank goodness!

"Will, where are you?" she whispered into the night.

When she didn't receive a response, she wondered if he returned to the inn, and the reminder had her considering the innkeeper's willingness to share what the woman knew about their group. A groan escaped her then since she desired nothing more than to lie down, yet her conscience would not rest until all her companions were together. With that in mind, she trekked through the brush and departed from the woods to stand before the field and Fester beyond. Most lights in the city had gone out except for what lanterns illuminated the main street.

A glance at the sky told Coura it became closer to morning than she liked. With a reluctant sigh, she stepped toward the buildings with the intent to sneak toward the inn.

In the next instant, an overwhelming sense of magic, the same presence they had been trying to avoid, struck her numb. Her legs gave way after, leading her to sink to her knees. She couldn't mistake the sensation as anything different because of how terribly close it felt; that knowledge alone terrified her, and the dark energy flowing through her veins hummed in response.

Despair clouded her mind when she considered what she could possibly do. *I can't go after the source alone, I can't move both Byron and Marcus in time, and Byron's in no shape to fight. Neither is Marcus, and Will...*

She spun around to face the woods where she sensed the mage or creature lurking. *What if it got Will? What if it comes for Byron and Marcus next? I have to find out, then maybe I can lead it away from them. That's my only chance until Byron wakes up.*

With shaky legs, she got to her feet, took a few deep breaths to calm her mind, then entered the forest again. She returned to their camp and found their belongings just as she left them, yet before she turned toward the source of the unnerving presence, her eyes lingered on Marcus' sword. A second later, she decided going armed with a weapon would be safer than relying only on magic and procured it for herself. Her body started to ache from the stress, so she hurried toward their enemy without making too much noise. In the quiet of the night, the insects and nocturnal creatures covered her tracks, though they could only do so much.

The presence proved to be farther into the woods than where Byron and Marcus slept, which eased part of her anxiety. As Coura continued, she began to hear distant voices cutting through the stillness: one male and the other female. They remained too faint for her to understand, but a clear cry did carry over the distance a minute later.

"I don't know!"

She froze midstep. *That's Will's voice. They found him after all. Now what do I do?*

Even as she attempted to process the situation, her body involuntarily moved closer to the voices.

Why am I still walking? I need to figure out a plan or get help instead!

Despite screaming at herself for ignoring logic, her legs would not obey. What was worse, the trembling sensation from the clashing energies became nearly unbearable until her center steadied the imbalance. Coura instantly stopped shaking and focused with what she could only describe as anticipation. Meanwhile, her heart drummed away and threatened to suffocate her.

At long last, she noiselessly peeled away a branch and stopped in a crouch to observe the owners of the voices huddled over Will. He shrank away from the two with his arms wrapped around himself and tears streaming down his cheeks. Spots of blood splattered his clothes, and his nose looked bruised and swollen.

"P-please, I t-told you," he begged.

From the low position, Coura could see Will better once her eyes adjusted to the darkness. It also helped they wound up in another, open part of the woods, so moonlight shined on the landscape. Unfortunately, she didn't see the strangers' faces nor their bodies because of the bulky, white packs spanning the length of their backs.

"Why do you lie to us?" the woman cooed. She knelt in front of Will, who tried to shy away when she brushed his face with a hand. "We saw you and the mages together. Tell us where they are, and we will let you go. I would hate to cause such a cute boy more trouble."

Will remained silent.

"So stubborn," the man teased in a sarcastic tone.

"Why do you protect them?" the first asked after as she stood. What kindness she displayed vanished from her voice.

Still, Will did not answer.

Coura studied the strangers' with interest, particularly how the white bulks on their backs seemed to move with their movements. *It's almost like they're adjusting themselves. Could they be a special weapon? I can't fight these two if they have the upper hand. Who are they?*

In a sudden motion, the man reached down to grab her companion by the hair. Will yelped in alarm before his hands flew to the stranger's grip in an attempt to claw himself free; however, he was pulled to his feet.

"Where are they?" the man demanded in a deathly grim manner.

"Please," Will whimpered in response, a sound that broke Coura's heart.

From his other hand, the stranger called forth a flame large enough to brighten the entire space. She glanced away momentarily to let her eyes adjust again, and when she returned to the scene in front of her, every thought fled her mind as she tried to process what the light revealed.

The wrapped bundles on the man and woman's backs, what she assumed were packs, proved to be something else entirely. White feathers fluttered to life, as if the spell awoke them from a deep slumber.

Coura heard her breath catch at the sight as a sense of awe overwhelmed her. *They're wings... Actual wings! That must mean these people are angels. This can't be. Nobody has seen one of their kind in decades. Wait, why would they be after Byron? Could they be affiliated with another country? They're supposed to be Asteom's allies. If that's the case, why would they hurt Will?*

Amid the frantic questions, a voice rang out in her mind, more dominating than any other thought.

{*They are evil.*}

The claim made her uncertain. *How can an angel be evil?*
{There's no time. Act now, or let your friend die.}
Just then, Will cried out as the flame came closer his face.

"Unless you want your eyes burned out of your skull, you will tell us what you know," the male angel shouted ferociously.

Before Coura knew what to do, she found herself entering the clearing to approach the strangers.

"Stop!" she ordered with surprising firmness, like the voice didn't belong to her. "Let him go."

The angels cast her suspicious glares when she emerged, then they looked at each other before the one who seized Will released him. While her companion dropped to the ground, the male continued holding his flame.

"And who might you be?" he asked with no small amount of irritation.

"It doesn't matter," Coura heard herself announce. "Neither of us is worth your time. Let him go, and we can be on our way."

What am I saying? I shouldn't be so easygoing with them. They're still within distance to harm Will. I'm not strong enough to fight an angel, let alone two!

Her fear threatened to swallow her until the voice returned, hot with anger.

{Enough! Quit cowering and fight!}

Any emotions became snuffed out by an unseen force and replaced by a sickening sense of eagerness. Coura drew her sword and forced a challenging smile.

The female stepped forward before glancing at her partner. "Shall I, Brother?"

He nodded. "Of course, Elsa. Make sure to keep this one alive, though. I am rather interested in interrogating her once she has been beaten into submission."

The first angel drew a slim, shiny blade and strolled across the clearing.

"Who are you looking for?" Coura ventured to ask while hoping to stall for time.

She began studying every feature of her opponent during their response. Like in every tale about the Yeluthians, the female possessed hair so blonde it looked white, and she guessed the pair had deep blue eyes as well. The angel wore leather padding that covered her torso and thighs instead of armor. Her so-called brother showcased similar attributes. For some reason, Coura felt certain he wouldn't interfere unless it became necessary.

Her limbs are exposed. Maybe I should work on tiring her out before injuring them. Otherwise, the wings are an option. The vision of crimson staining the unmarred feathers seemed blasphemous, yet she knew it might save her life, and Will's. *No matter the consequences, I'll need to give it my all.*

"We are looking for a dark mage named Byron Rinod. He was last seen leaving Verona and heading toward the Magical Arts Academy in East Hoover." The angel paused, as if waiting for Coura to respond, then raised her sword. "We have been told to find him through any means necessary, so your cooperation would not go unappreciated, to say the least."

Coura shook her head before flashing a sympathetic smile. "I'm sorry to disappoint you, but I don't know anything about him."

"Then leave."

"Not as long as you're going to torture him," she replied and jerked her chin at Will, who watched with a look that reflected a silent plea for her to flee.

"So be it, intruder."

Wings of Destiny

Will could look on hopelessly as Coura stayed to defend him by fighting the female angel named Elsa. His head spun because of the male introduced as Devan, who nearly knocked him unconscious after punching him twice in the nose. He was sure it broke during the second blow, yet he became too distracted to consider such trivial concerns. Silently, he begged his friend to escape; he knew she saw his expression and dismissed it. Until that moment, he had been skeptical Coura would be the type of person to risk her life for someone she just met.

Still, she was definitely not one to back down from a fight.

The angel leapt forward and, with a push of her wings, covered the distance between herself and Coura in seconds. Swords clashed, and the sound rang through the otherwise-silent woods. In the dark, and with his face throbbing, Will couldn't comprehend much of what happened, but he did notice Elsa moved faster. *Much* faster. Coura blocked each swing, which sometimes sent sparks into the air, yet she couldn't attack.

Will bit his lip and sent up a silent prayer. *What should I do? She looks tired. She can't keep this up. I don't think I can get away, at least not with him here.*

He shifted his gaze to the other angel standing over him, like a wolf guarding its injured prey. The male's face remained impassive, though his eyes followed every motion. Will struggled to catch their movements again while contemplating how he could help.

It occurred to him then that Coura hadn't used magic yet.

She's a mage like Byron, so why doesn't she use spells? That's right, she said she didn't know me. Maybe they would realize the connection, or at least assume she knows Byron. This isn't good...

He jumped when Coura released a cry as the angel's blade swept across a spot on her left arm. While she staggered back and grabbed her bicep, the female laughed, a sound equally charming and sinister.

"Do you give up yet? I mentioned this earlier, but if you tell us where the mage is, we will let you both go."

"Keep him out of this," Coura shouted. "He's got nothing to do with me!"

Elsa quieted for a moment before holding a single-note whistle and glancing in Will's direction, causing him to instinctively freeze. "I remember now. Do you, Devan?"

"I did not think you would, Sister."

"Remember what?" Coura snapped.

"How foolish of me," the female angel continued. "Our leader informed us the dark mage traveled with a medicine boy and provided details on his behavior."

A shiver slid down Will's spine. *Leader? How could they possibly have heard about me when I traveled with Byron for such a brief amount of time? Unless... It has to be somebody in the palace.*

He forced the revelation aside to listen as she went on.

"He also said a young woman accompanied them, but that had been the only detail." She admired her blade and waited for a reply.

Although Will couldn't see Coura's reaction to the news, he expected it to be similar to his own. A lack of confidence tainted the denial in her next words.

"I don't know what you're talking about."

The angels laughed together in response.

***

How did they hear about us? Could they be bluffing, or is there an individual in the capital city with other intentions? Coura tried unsuccessfully to recall the servants, soldiers, and nobility in the palace, but her memories became drowned out by the angels' harmonious amusement, leading her to ground her teeth in frustration. *This is a problem. I'm at my limit just blocking her attacks. I've never fought anyone so swift. There's no hope of keeping up with her long enough to wear her down.*

The angel didn't seem to have even broken a sweat while Coura stood panting. She removed her bloodied hand from where it rested on her left bicep, certain the stranger sliced through at least a quarter of her arm, and braced herself for another attack when the two quieted.

"In that case, we shall continue until you do remember," the female concluded before charging once more.

Here she comes!

Again, Coura raised her sword to meet the other's blow for blow; however, this time, the strikes came slower yet with additional strength behind them. It worked to her opponent's advantage since her speed began decreasing far too soon. She guarded against the strikes without worrying too much about them landing, but the force behind each pushed her back.

I just...need to keep...going...

The fear that retreated minutes ago started creeping up on her as her mental fortitude chipped away. Somehow, Coura was able to stop the woman's blade during a vertical slice and hold the metal above her head, keeping the angel still. Her opponent savored the pause by leaning closer until their faces almost touched.

"Last chance," the angel cooed.

With a grunt, Coura shoved the other's weapon to the side and stepped backward to prepare a horizontal swipe at the female's exposed mid-section. To her utter disbelief, she lost her balance.

What's going on?

As her foot moved, it hit an above-ground root belonging to the nearest tree, causing her to stumble and slam her back against the trunk directly behind her. Then, it became too late to escape. She had been caught off guard, and her sword lowered as she fell. This gave her opponent the perfect opening.

Instead of striking with the blade, the angel rushed forward, reached across the space, and grabbed Coura by the throat, pressing her against the tree. In the next instant, Coura let go of her weapon in an attempt to claw herself free with both hands until the stranger dug the sharp fingernails into her skin. She felt a trickle of warm blood drip down her shirt before stars blotted her vision.

"How about now?" her opponent pressed in the sweet voice. "Will you answer our questions?"

"I…don't know…" was all Coura managed to spit out. After that, her body stopped responding, and the grip on her throat tightened.

"Fine, have it your way."

That's it then. She's going to choke me to death. I can't…

"Elsa, hurry up!" Coura heard the second angel yell, though she couldn't see him through the dazzling stars.

Just when she felt about ready to lose consciousness, a sharp pain in her chest made her body scream, then the pressure on her throat released. She tried gasping for air only to find herself coughing up blood in the process. After, her sight returned enough for her to glance down in horror at the blade sticking out from the middle of her chest.

Coura's opponent spun around to return to where her partner and Will waited a second later. The female angel had pinned her to the trunk with the sword, letting her bleed out while knowing she couldn't free herself nor produce a sound.

Her body ached from the sensation and her pity for Will, for how she hadn't been able to rescue him. *How…could I…*

Both hands weakly tugging on the hilt of the weapon before finally dropping to her sides. The strength in her neck went next, so she hung her head, which forced her to stare at the pool of blood forming like a shadow along the base of the tree. She closed her eyes to hide the sight and wheezed while she fought a losing battle to stay alive.

Somewhere in the night, the voices continued as though nothing had happened.

*

Coura found herself floating amid a gray space, looking at the emptiness above. She didn't see a ground in this place, nor clouds, nor anything distinguishable. She also couldn't feel pain, so

131

she relaxed and closed her eyes in a content manner. Her mind seemed at peace, but she couldn't remember what brought her there.

After a moment, she sensed another presence. Her body curled into a sitting position in order to face a shadow standing at eye level with her.

"So, you're finally here," said a feminine voice teeming with delight.

"Where are we?" Coura asked while glancing around. For some reason, she wasn't afraid of the figure.

"This is your *chi-alve*."

"*Chi-alve*?"

The shadow nodded. "It translates to 'soul space.' All creatures have one. It's the center of your being where your consciousness resides, though you should only be able to enter through a meditation of sorts."

"Why am I here?" she asked next against a fear penetrating her relaxed mentality.

Although the shadow had no mouth to frown, Coura could hear its disapproval. "Because you are weak. You allowed yourself to lose, thus sacrificing your body and forcing your soul to recoil as a last resort. Most mortals experience this before they die."

"I'm going to die?"

The figure shook its head. "Not as long as you allow me to help you."

At the mention of death, Coura wished to be saved so badly her chest ached, yet she wondered why this other person stood in *her* soul space. "Who are you?"

"I can't tell you now, but you must decide. Will you die or let me bring your body back from destruction?"

***

If Will had been scared before, he felt petrified once he witnessed what the female angel did. He understood Coura didn't stand a chance against a Yeluthian's speed and strength, and he let her fight. *I should have told them about Byron. I should have tried to run. At least I would be doing something other than sit here uselessly.*

132

Tears streamed down his cheeks through eyes glued to Coura's limp body as it hung from a tree trunk. Somewhere in the recesses of his sane frame of mind, he was grateful it remained too dark for him to see her in detail, or else he would vomit.

"It really is a shame she did not possess much stamina," Elsa commented as she strolled over to rejoin them. "Not many humans can hold their own for that long. I was beginning to think she would be entertaining."

"It is a shame humans are not tougher beings," her companion added to echo her disappointment.

After hearing their insults, Will's temper slipped. "Shut up."

Both angels turned to stare at him.

"Oh, now he talks!" the female exclaimed while shaking her head.

"I said, shut up!"

Will squeezed his eyes closed as he became unable to bear their presence. He wanted to scream and crawl to Coura's side until the hiss of a sword being drawn had his eyes shooting open and darting to Devan. A moment later, the metal tip of the blade touched Will's throat. His anger melted away, leaving him gazing at the pair, who lost all hint of amusement.

"Now then, enough of that. Dawn will be upon us in a couple hours, so I would rather not drag this out. If you do not tell us where the mage is, you shall share the same fate as your friend. Actually, it will be worse since I like to keep my enemies alive much longer than Elsa."

Will swallowed despite his mouth and throat going dry, but no sound came from lips, which worked in an attempt to form words. He prayed again before realizing his death would be imminent because beneath the fear, weakness, and pain, his commitment to Byron remained. He refused to sacrifice his freedom for Byron's life, not for the life of anyone dear to him.

Anyone except Coura...

He looked up into the handsome face and hoped to convey his resolve. It must have worked, for the angel appeared confused at first, then resigned.

"Pathetic," the being mumbled and raised his sword.

A sort of contentment settled over Will in that moment, as if accepting his fate brought satisfaction during his final breaths. He shut his eyes and prayed one last time for his death to not be in vain.

Seconds ticked by, extending what he expected to be a brief execution. When he opened his eyes, he found both angels' attention elsewhere. They appeared to study the tree where Coura hung with an air of suspicion. Suddenly, the female charged toward it while lightning sparked around her fists to illuminate the area.

"Elsa, wait!" her partner cried and reached for her to display how the unexpected action startled him.

Will couldn't understand what bothered the two until the lightning brightened the farthest part of the clearing. Then, his jaw dropped. Coura's hands were not only on the hilt of the sword in her body, but the blade steadily slid out of her chest.

It can't be... She already lost so much blood. How could she survive an injury like that, let alone have the strength to keep going?

With a sickening gush audible even at a distance, the weapon came free. Coura stumbled a bit yet somehow managed to stay on her feet. Will gasped as she did so and was shocked to find the air so humid he barely felt like he breathed in any at all.

What's happening? It's the middle of the night, so why is the air this heavy. Unless this is magic. Could the change be caused by the angel's lightning?

Will doubted that, which made him anxious. At the moment, he felt more concerned with the figure rushing at Coura who wielded a spell as lethal as a weapon and poised it to strike. He tried yelling a warning to his friend, but his voice broke on her name. The shout became lost in the crackling bolts anyway, leaving him to look on as the angel reached her.

What none of them had seen yet, or were expecting, was Coura's magic. The angel's lightning struck a wall of glittering, violet energy and produced a sound similar to metal scraping against metal. Will covered his ears as the sheer blockage of the female angel's magic pushed her backward. Then, she lost control of the rest of her lightning, sending sparks and bolts shooting around the area. Thankfully, none came close to her companion or Will, but one landed on the canopy of a nearby tree to set the wood on fire. Within a frightening amount of time, the fallen branches transferred their flames to two other trees, illuminating their space in an eerie, red-and-orange glow.

I need to get out of here, Will acknowledged in a panic as smoke rose around them. *This may be my only chance.*

Still, he wouldn't abandon Coura. Without a glance at the angels, he scrambled to his feet, turned on his heel, and sprinted as fast as he could into the bushes behind. Once hidden, he ducked behind the widest trunk he could find, and from there, he saw the entire clearing just fine, wasn't in the way, and could easily retreat.

The shield in front of his friend dispersed to catch his eye, allowing him to spot a shadow behind her back solidifying in the dim lighting.

Those kind of look like wings...

He squinted against the still-rising smoke in order to make her figure out better, and when she stepped closer, Will's heart stopped. A pair of wings definitely rested behind her, except they were colored black. Unlike the angels' feathers, which appeared soft to touch, these prickled with what he thought to be disdain.

Elsa snarled before unleashing another blast of lightning. It reached Coura, but she sidestepped just as the bolt would have struck her, causing it to crash into the tree behind her instead. Three more times, the angel fired her spells; each instance, Coura dodged with ease while creeping forward. When the female began retracing her steps with the obvious intent to reach her companion, Will caught a glint in the firelight and realized his friend held the other's blade, still covered with her own blood.

"Who are you?" the male shouted, startling Will. He attempted to draw her attention, but she remained fixated on his partner. When he addressed her again and received the same lack of response, he decided to draw his sword.

As it slid halfway out of its scabbard, Coura struck.

Elsa glanced at her companion in shock for a second when he yelled. When she faced forward, Coura leapt into the air, spread the dark wings like an aviary predator, and pounced with new speed. The angel's hands rose too late to do much except try to block the weapon, except she didn't use her weapon first. With her left hand, she seized the female's forearm and yanked it downward before her opponent knew what she intended to do. Only then did Coura bring the blade up to the angel's exposed throat and slice, cutting off a scream.

Will instinctively looked away and focused on his breathing so as to not faint at the sight of the blonde head rolling on the ground. Still, he forced himself to continue watching sooner than he would have liked in order to catch what happened next.

The remaining angel screamed his companion's name, mourning the loss of what Will believed to be a deeply personal relationship. Coura finally faced him, and indirectly Will, after, as if the death meant nothing. Although she appeared the same, her presence terrified him. The unnatural wings loomed over the rest of her body in a menacing manner, and her clothes had been ripped in multiple places with only scarlet showing underneath. Her dark, unbound hair waved in the slight breeze, which blew the smoke away, though the sapphire eyes that always seemed so bright had dulled into quite the opposite.

As she stared at her next target, Will admitted he'd grown more horrified than earlier. He had never in all his life heard of a human using wings, let alone ones not colored white. Coura's seemed to be the same size and shape as the angels', but their demeanor changed. Instead of the peaceful, divine nature the stories described, which had been what Will thought of when he first encountered the pair without knowing them, the black wings and Coura's appearance seemed wicked, wrong, and wholly evil in his eyes.

A demon. That's the opposite of an angel. Has she been possessed? Is she even human anymore? What happens to a person when they can't control their actions?

Will's knowledge about demons and their work never amounted to much since it wasn't a popular topic of conversation, and for good reason. In fact, in most towns he regularly frequented, bringing up demons led to either punishments or curses upon your descendants.

He wondered if the remaining angel reached the same conclusion because he stood unmoving while Coura stalked toward him with the blade hanging at her side, letting what fresh blood coated it soak into ground.

They faced each other then, as still as statues. He couldn't predict how Devan would strike, what he would do, or what he even could do to Coura; however, Will did notice the male's fingers curl and relax on the hilt of his sword, the only sign the being hadn't turned to stone. A minute later, he understood what actually went on between the two.

The angel didn't spend time planning an attack; he was considering the best escape route.

As sudden as the flashes of lightning, Devan leapt straight up into the air, pumped his wings to gain some height, then tightened them against his back. Coura followed a hair's breadth later, angling her body to meet him in the sky. Her sword swung for his neck, but he raised his own to block with one hand while shooting a ball of fire at her with the other. The flames hit her square in the stomach, though Will didn't believe she even noticed. One swing followed another, then another as their blades clashed in the graying sky. She kept the angel's focus on defending himself in order to avoid letting him fly away, yet Will didn't see him prepare the next fireball. It just appeared to strike Coura right in the face. He heard her growl while she jerked her head to the side, which allowed her target to climb higher into the air.

In response, she shot toward him after and managed to seize his ankle. He beat his wings while attempting to free his leg, but the effort proved futile. With a precise swing of her sword, she sliced his foot clean off and tossed it into the woods. Her victim howled in pain yet remained composed enough not to let the injury stop him from escaping. He launched himself higher into the sky and soon disappeared past the treetop.

Will fully expected Coura to pursue, yet she remained suspended in the air, pumping the black wings and looking after the angel as he flew away.

Who to Trust

ill wondered what he should do. A minute passed by, then two, and still Coura scanned the sky. He hadn't noticed how tense he became until his fingers cramped from grasping the tree trunk he cowered behind. As quietly as he could, he pried himself from the wood and took a couple steps back. He stopped again when his friend's body descended to the ground. Once her feet touched the grass, the wings dispersed into fragments that shimmered in the firelight before fading away. Then, she collapsed and remained unmoving.

What do I do?

Will repeated the thought in his exhausted mind as he waited for her to get up, for the wings to form again, or something else to attack.

Maybe she really is dead this time...

Although more tears threatened to rise, he felt too weary to even consider breaking down. His limbs went numb, and the aching in his face returned.

I...should get back...

It took him a while, especially with smoke from the dying flames hindering his vision, but Will managed to figure out which direction led to Fester from the approaching sunrise. Every step was a burden. His chest hurt from frantic heartbeats, though he breathed easier once he moved far enough away to not see any of the firelight. The air returned to normal, and he even heard insects hesitantly chirping.

After what seemed like an eternity, he pushed the final branch to the side to reveal their camp, complete with Byron and Marcus' snoring, as if nothing disturbing had happened. He took a seat against his rolled sleeping bag and stayed that way until dawn.

***

Byron covered his eyes as sunlight threatened to blind him, then he remained motionless until his thirst finally got the better of him. Groaning, he pushed himself up before pausing to settle his stomach. His head hurt worse, but the stomach pain came in a close second. With a mind too muddled to process much, he naturally started looking for water. He fumbled through the bags for far too long until he grabbed a waterskin and chugged every last drop. In the morning fog, he heard snoring and saw Marcus next to him. That was all he could take in before passing out on his bedroll.

Later in the day, he woke feeling a little more alive. Getting to his feet became easier on his body, and he relieved himself in the woods, drank more water, and located their food. A majority of the fruit, cheeses, and pastries made his stomach turn, but he found plain bread and nibbled on it.

What happened last night? He remembered spending the day at the tavern and bonding with Cintra. They caught up on each other's lives before she found another bottle of a delicious wine. *Leave it to her to get me like this. I haven't been drunk in months.*

With something in his gut, Byron could function better. He winced as he glanced at the sky to see it was early afternoon. *Great. I slept through most of the day. It looks like we'll need to head out now then. Wait a minute... What are we doing in the woods? What about our room at the inn?*

His eyes darted to the trees, then their camp, which didn't appear to be much of one. Will sat against his bedroll, facing the forest, while Marcus still slept. His head spun in protest, and he cursed himself for looking around so fast.

"Will?"

The herbalist didn't move, so Byron assumed he wasn't awake either. He didn't see Coura in the area, but he knew she couldn't stand by idly and wait for them to stir. He made a note to mentally prepare himself for a lecture from her when she returned, though.

With his foot, Byron nudged the soldier across from him. Marcus groaned and cracked an eye open.

"It's time for us to get going."

Their guard sat up, stretched, then went to relieve himself elsewhere, stumbling as he did so.

I see I'm not the only one who enjoyed Fester, Byron thought with a rueful smile.

Overall, it turned out to be a pleasant visit and an enjoyable break from their journey; however, while he wandered nearby for a water source, he remembered their goal and vowed they would focus on getting back to East Hoover. A stream appeared farther than he liked, but he took his time washing away his drunkenness and filling the empty waterskins before returning to the others. He would need to expend the energy to boil it later in order to purify it for drinking.

"There's a stream some distance that way," he informed Marcus once he reentered the camp.

"Good," the soldier replied and rubbed his eyes. "I feel terrible."

As he passed by, Byron noticed dried blood on the side of his companion's head. "What happened?"

"Hmm?"

"Your head." He pointed to Marcus' temple. "You've got a cut and nasty bruise there."

"I'm not sure. I need to clean up." With that, the assistant general disappeared into the woods.

Byron prepared to repack his bedroll until he spotted Will in the same position and decided to go over. "You up yet?"

He laid a hand on the herbalist's shoulder and was startled to see the young man flinch. In response, he knelt beside Will, who trembled while watching the trees with red-rimmed eyes.

"What's wrong?" he urged and began shaking Will's shoulder gently. "Talk to me."

The tired eyes peeled away from the forest before he blinked several times. "Byron? You're awake?"

"I'm managing. What's the matter? You look like you haven't slept all night."

"I couldn't…not when she's there…" His voice trailed off into mumbles before he stared into the woods again.

Until that moment, Byron hadn't noticed how bruised the young man's face was nor how he faintly smelled of smoke. "Who's there? What are you talking about?"

Perhaps this is why we're outside Fester. Depending on what took place, and the unknown presence, we might need to go back. I don't sense the foreign energy anymore. Could that have something to do with our current situation?

"Tell me about last night," he ordered after deciding to start over instead of asking questions.

"I spent the day like you suggested," Will began in a whisper. "When I returned to the inn, we…we went…to get you…"

"You and Coura?"

The herbalist nodded, but the memory touched a nerve. In a split second, he crumbled into a mess of tears, dropping his head into his hands.

The unexpected reaction concerned Byron. "I need you to explain what happened. I can't help unless I understand the problem."

Will shook his head. "I-I-I t-t-tried to k-keep them away…"

"Who? Keep who away?"

"Then, C-C-Coura came…" More sobbing.

"What's going on?" Marcus inquired as he returned from the opposite end of their camp.

"We need to leave," Byron replied.

"Why?"

He cast the soldier a serious look to let the assistant general know something was wrong.

Fortunately, Marcus read the message clearly. "I'll start packing."

With one companion taking care of the camp, Byron focused his attention on putting Will together. "Where's Coura?" he asked in a soft voice. Whatever took place the previous night, he needed to make sure she wasn't the cause.

After another minute, Will seemed to have cried himself out for the moment and could speak without breaking down.

"Where is Coura?" Byron repeated.

With a shaky hand, Will pointed into the trees straight ahead. "I…she's still…"

"Let's go for a walk then," he pressed and helped the herbalist to his feet before informing Marcus they would return.

Over the years, his ventures brought him face to face with people who suffered through traumatic experiences. Fires, raiders, sickness, and more caused ordinary townsfolk to react in unpredictable ways. Some lost their personality and closed themselves off from the world. Others were frantic with anger or sadness, worse than Will had been. Still, most recovered through attention and comfort, and they were able to accept what happened and move on. The memories still hurt or haunted them, but only time could heal unseen scars. Byron also assisted a small percentage of people who suppressed their past experiences in order to work toward a better future.

Coura had been one example. When Byron brought her to the academy, she remembered fragments of the attack on her hometown, though they didn't help him or Symon any. Without her memory, it was a relief she healed at all, and the details were forgotten in a few weeks, which Byron figured was for the best. She showed no interest in her past life, which spared him from informing her of when people returned weeks later and how no one claimed her as their child.

In Will's case, as they walked and talked, the young man came back to life, recalling pieces from the previous night. Byron put together that the guards were looking to arrest him, so Will and Coura had moved them into the woods for safety. It seemed harmless, yet the young man couldn't continue.

He's stumbling on his words, is barely mentioning names, and falls silent whenever he tries to tell me more. I can smell smoke now. We must be quite a distance from Fester.

Not long after, Will stopped and started his tale over again for about the tenth time. Halfway through, he paused his account and pushed a thin branch out of their way. Beyond, Byron could see a clearing where smoke rose from fallen trees.

"Is there danger?" he asked at a lower volume and prepared for the worst as his body instinctively grew tense.

"I…don't think so. I don't know."

"Wait here," he whispered while proceeding to exit the brush. Try as he might, he couldn't keep from making quite a lot of noise. With each crunch of a twig or swish of leaves, he cursed himself for letting his hangover affect his body so much. Once he could observe the entire clearing, he froze. No creatures or people were in sight, but he could make out plenty of blood and charred earth.

A fight took place here last night, he realized with a sinking sensation.

As his eyes glanced over the fire and broken trees, he spotted a body on the ground at the other end. He recognized it as Coura, and she wasn't moving.

Although he longed to go straight to her, Byron knew better than to burst out into the open. Carefully, he emerged and held himself to a steady pace. Once he learned no traps or an ambush waited, he sprinted over and knelt beside his student. He turned her onto her back and nearly wept at the rips in her shirt and drying blood covering her torso.

"Come on, Coura!" he growled while shaking her shoulders.

She didn't respond.

Despite the filth, he pressed an ear to her chest. This time, he did let out a sigh of relief when he heard her heartbeat, and tears stung his eyes. He composed himself enough to call out to Will, who observed his behavior from the edge of the clearing.

"I need your help. She's breathing, but I can't assess her injuries like this."

"She's dead," the young man replied just loud enough for him to hear.

"No, she's not. We need to hurry or else…"

The words fled his mind as he glanced at Will and saw the young man's eyes lingering elsewhere. Byron followed his gaze to where the body of another woman lied nearby, and he noticed her head beside it. The sight and Will's emotional reaction clicked together in his mind a second later.

He was here last night. He saw that woman die and Coura get hurt. No wonder he's in shock!

He looked between the two thrice before deciding he wouldn't get anywhere without the latter, so he set his student down. Once he rose, he went to Will, placed a hand on the herbalist's back, and led the young man into the trees so they couldn't view the remains.

"It's safe," he shared before pulling Will into his arms.

The embrace seemed to be a cue for his companion to snap, for Will broke down again. He held the other as he would a child, only letting go when the herbalist threatened to vomit; then he politely looked away when the young man did throw up. He had seen death in many forms over the years. Decapitation remained one of the worst and most uncommon, giving him nightmares for weeks.

Once Will finished, he returned and stared at the ground while holding his stomach. "I'm better," he said to answer Byron's unspoken question. The young man still trembled, but this time with a sort of ease.

"I know it's hard for you, but I need your help," Byron began in his most respectful tone. "Do you think you can find a stream or pool of water?"

Will nodded and turned to explore the woods surrounding them. Meanwhile, Byron hurried into the clearing.

That's one problem solved for now.

Coura remained unconscious, though he wouldn't be able to tend to her wounds without washing the blood away; however, before going to her to try and stop the bleeding, he needed to take care of two other issues.

First, he dragged the headless woman behind a tree and out of sight. He avoided looking at her face for too long as he reunited the head with its body, yet he noted the fearful expression stuck on it. Next, he tapped into his center of power and cast a controlled ice storm to put out the rest of the flames. They managed to be contained to a portion of the area, which felt like a blessing in and of itself.

Will returned then, appearing more alive than he acted all morning, and announced the location of a stream close by. His eyes wandered over to where the lifeless body had been, and he showed relief upon learning of the corpse's disappearance.

Byron checked Coura's breathing once again in preparation to move her. Its steady pace seemed normal, as though she were merely sleeping, so he lifted her in his arms with some effort before proceeding to follow his companion. It didn't take them more than a few minutes to reach the aforementioned stream, which stretched to look like more of a thin river.

While Will watched from the bank, Byron climbed into the water up to his waist before lowering his student's body. The stream carried away most of the mess, shading the water a reddish purple for a short period of time, and he rubbed the rest off her chest. From the amount of blood, he assumed the worst injury had been there, yet only unmarred skin remained underneath. As a precaution, he inspected the rest of her torso, midsection, arms, legs, and back, but didn't find a scratch on her body. Once he sufficiently inspected her, he brought Coura back to the shore where the young man paced.

Byron set her in the grass then analyzed her breathing again. Its continued regularity confused him immensely.

"Is she going to be okay?" Will asked in an impatient manner with his arms crossed.

"I think so. We won't know for certain until she wakes up. Her body is unharmed, though I can't check for internal damage."

"What?" The herbalist spun around and threw himself down beside Byron. His hands went straight to the center of her chest as he did the same evaluation, except he vocalized his disbelief. "That's impossible!"

"What's wrong?"

"How can she not be hurt?"

"Perhaps that wasn't her blood." Byron also considered whether Coura expended all her energy, or what mages referred to as draining their reserves, causing her body to shut down temporarily in order to recover. She had never done that before, so

146

it seemed like a plausible reason to him, especially since this had been her first, real fight away from the academy.

To his dismay, Will disagreed.

"No, no, no! I saw it all. She got stabbed right here." He pointed to the center of her chest.

Byron raised his eyebrows. "I think it's about time you tell me what happened after you two dragged me out of Fester."

After some hesitation, Will began with what Byron already picked up on. He and Coura met in their room at sundown, as they had been instructed to do. When neither Byron nor Marcus returned, they left to find the rest of their group but discovered the guards preparing to arrest Byron and possibly frame him for desertion. That part didn't surprise him as much as the idea of Marcus' comrades going behind their superior's back by disobeying his order to stand down.

Will found Coura helping the assistant general, and they decided to camp in the woods. While he made multiple trips to the inn to pack and retrieve their belongings, she returned to the tavern to get their final companion. The muddled memories came back to Byron once he remembered being hauled from Cintra's room.

"When I brought the last of our bags and set up a decent camp, I worried about how late it grew since she left to search for you. I headed for the tavern again, but a woman approached me in the field between and begged me to find a friend who ran off into the woods. I've been warned about such temptresses robbing a man blind by luring him away from the roads before knocking him over the head, so I refused. When I tried to escape, she drew her sword and used it to force me into the trees. I remained aware of where we were, though. She didn't figure out you two and our belongings had been in an area nearby. Once we entered that clearing, a man appeared. Then, they started asking about you."

Byron stayed diligent during Will's explanation to capture every word until the young man hesitantly looked at him with tear-filled eyes.

"I didn't tell them anything, I promise! They hit me in the face a couple times and threatened to burn my eyes, but I kept quiet."

His earnest expression warmed Byron's heart despite the nightmare taking place, and he offered a genuine smile. "I believe you. It wasn't fair for you to be put in such a horrible situation, so it means a lot that you stood up for me."

The young man's cheeks turned pink before he continued. "I knew I had to. Anyway, they tried to burn my face when Coura appeared and told them to stop."

"What is it?" Byron urged when Will paused.

"I didn't mention this, but the man and woman were angels."

"Angels?" he repeated in disbelief. "You mean Yeluthians? Are you sure?"

"I've never been surer in my life! They tried sweet-talking me by saying they were my friends, and a friend of Verona wouldn't deny their request."

"I never imagined their people would threaten someone," Byron interrupted.

"My thoughts exactly. You should have seen their wings, though. Their feathers looked soft and magical."

"Did the woman have them when she first found you?"

Will shook his head. "No, not until we were alone. They seemed to cast them, like they did with the fire."

Byron made note of that. *It's been a while since anybody has seen or heard from a Yeluthian. I don't ever recall them manifesting wings like I would a spell.* His thoughts were cut short when the young man went on.

He explained Coura's attempt to save him and how the female angel pinned her against a tree with a sword. What scared Byron the most were Will's descriptions, which sounded accurate enough to create the scene in detail. He had been admirably brave for not only surviving such an encounter, but also for forcing himself to memorize and recall such graphic information.

"So, that's why you said it's odd she has no wounds," Byron muttered.

"I was sure she bled to death, but somehow she pulled the sword out of her chest and…" A haunted look came over his face as his eyes fell on Coura. "She had them too."

"Had what?"

"Wings. I wasn't sure at first until she came closer. They seemed like the angels', except black in color."

Byron found himself speechless but didn't dare interrupt this time.

"I've never seen anything like it. Her eyes looked different too. She sprang off the tree, dodged the first angel's lightning bolts, and…removed her head. Then, she almost stopped the other from escaping by slicing off his foot in the air. When he got away, Coura watched him before falling to the ground, and the wings disappeared. That's when I left."

Byron inquired about specific aspects, such as her appearance and behavior, but he didn't know where to begin processing the story. *Will mentioned the angels can manifest wings without effort, then they can cast lightning and fire spells. Only highly trained light mages are able to manipulate their energy into an elemental form, which is rare since I believe it requires an understanding of dark magic.*

He cast a look of concern at his unconscious student.

Coura, I don't know what to do with you. I've never heard of someone possessing wings besides the Yeluthians. What Will described sounds close to demonic possession, but not many who see or experience it live. None ever produced wings before. I guess we'll just need to wait for you to wake up and tell us.

Her body remained still except for her chest, which rose slightly to show her breathing. Normally, a person having anything to do with demons was cast away or executed, even if the intentions had been just or results hadn't been intended. Most cities and towns did not tolerate demonic energy, which became normal since it brought unforetold troubles.

"Let's head back to the camp," Byron said at last.

"But, what should we do about-"

"Speak of this to no one," he warned before rising and taking Coura in his arms.

"You're bringing her with us? Aren't you worried about what could happen with a demon around?"

Byron faced Will without attempting to hide the pain his comment caused. It made the young man defensive, and he longed to lash out at such hateful behavior.

How suddenly he turned on Coura after mentioning demons. How can I blame him after all he's been through? Besides, I wasn't there to confirm one's energy. I have only his word to go on, for now.

"Stop," he ordered more firmly than he had ever spoken to the herbalist. "We must leave this place and go to the academy as soon as possible. If the angel you mentioned flew away, there's no doubt they'll be back. Not only for me, but for all of us. I won't condemn Coura until I can test her for demonic energy when she wakes."

"But she-"

"Enough," Byron interrupted and let his annoyance from a headache spurred by too much thinking show.

Will winced and ducked his head.

"I understand what you must be feeling," Byron continued in a calmer tone. "You were willing to sacrifice your life to keep us safe, and I thank you immensely for that, but I'm begging you. Don't mention this to anybody for now, not even Marcus. I sense more going on. I don't want word spreading about angels and demonic possessions until I can discuss it with my fellow master mages in East Hoover. I promise, I won't let something like that happen again."

The young man didn't answer yet appeared satisfied, so Byron began moving toward their camp, giving Will space to put together his own opinions as they returned together.

Finding Answers

At the camp, Marcus had the bags packed and ready to go. As soon as the assistant general saw Coura hanging from Byron's arms, he jumped to his feet to ask the same questions Byron discussed with Will earlier.

Byron set his student down, inhaled enough food to last for the time being, and shouldered his pack while summarizing how Coura and Will moved them into the woods and why. He expected Marcus would be upset at their distrust of the guards, but the soldier only released a sigh.

"I can't believe they would betray my trust," he mumbled.

"I'm sure they were concerned about being punished for disobedience by whoever gave them those orders," Byron added they adjusted Coura onto his back. Once she seemed settled, he began leading them out of their camp in search of the road heading toward East Hoover.

"Perhaps, but I don't know who could give them orders that override mine."

He means to say someone outranking him wants me arrested and expects him to assume responsibility of delivering the documents. I wish I could believe him. It's still better to keep the situation simple for now.

"Then what happened to Coura and Will?" Marcus continued while glancing at Will, who trailed behind just far enough to give the two privacy.

"The mage who had been following us all this time made an appearance. Will accidentally encountered them in the woods, and they trapped him in a clearing north of our camp. Coura went to rescue him and drained herself protecting him."

Marcus shot Byron a confused look. "What do you mean?"

"It's fairly common for mages who aren't experienced in magical combat to use up all their energy. Actually, you can compare it to physical combat. When you work your muscles too hard and for too long, your body shuts down afterward in order to recover. From my experience with this, she should wake within a day or two. She'll be famished but unharmed."

The assistant general nodded at the comparison and fell silent for a while as they located the main road.

A greater amount of people passed in and out of Fester than he ever recalled, and most utilized a wagon or cart pulled by a horse, mule, or ox. This made it easy for their group to sneak away under the added cover. That road broke into three paths outside the city's limits heading west to Verona, north to East Hoover, and east across the plains to a line of towns and ultimately the Mintelian mountains. Their temporary company followed one of the other roads leading west or east. By then, the sun started setting, so Byron decided they should rest for the evening in the grass along the side of the trail. While Marcus and Will disagreed with his choice of location, he assured them the unknown presence wouldn't followed them thanks to Coura.

They rose before morning, all except his student, and began the last leg of their journey in a weary stupor. Marcus offered to carry her for the day, for which Byron and his sore back were grateful.

"We've got about another couple hours before we reach East Hoover," he announced when the trail forked for a final time. They shifted to move alone along the right side from that point on.

"I'm glad to hear it," the assistant general replied after a yawn.

Even Will felt well enough to make conversation after the update.

During their next break, Byron shared a helpful observation he learned since he knew that path better than anyone, which made sense given how often he traveled it lately. "Just past these ferns is a wild orchard. I usually stop here and pick a few apples to carry me the rest of the way. Why don't we go there for a bit to refresh ourselves?"

His young companions agreed and hurried toward the space containing about a dozen apple trees that were in season. Marcus propped Coura against one of the trunks in plain sight before climbing for the fruit near the top. Will followed, albeit less enthusiastically, while Byron felt content with what he could reach from the ground.

"I see something else," the herbalist announced from above and rushed down the tree, prompting Byron to hurry over in case he lost his footing. After descending, he went to the edge of the orchard to inspect a bush. "Look, gooseberries!"

The green, round fruits looked ripe enough to eat, so Will began harvesting them carefully to avoid pricking himself on their thorns.

"That's strange. I don't remember this being here," Byron muttered as he tasted a few and savored their tartness.

After the three helped themselves, he ordered the boys to fill the empty food pack with some of the produce before they left. This would not only keep them going, but he always tried to keep fresh fruit in his room; his companions didn't need to know that, though.

He waited while they did so and enjoyed the warm day until he heard a groan from where his student rested behind him. The sound had him spinning around before he went to her when she began to sit up. "Coura!"

She held her head in one hand and rubbed her eyes with the other. "Byron? Where are we?"

"How do you feel?"

"I don't… I asked first," she retorted in an unimpressed tone.

Just like her normal self, he reflected and relaxed a trifle.

"We left Fester yesterday afternoon and are just outside East Hoover. We should be back home in a couple hours."

Her eyes darted from left to right as she become more alert. "We're that close already? Wait, we've been on the road for a day?"

"Take it easy. You're still weak."

"Weak? What did I...?" Her voice trailed off, then she looked at the ground with a thoughtful expression. After a moment, her eyes widened, as though she recalled something, and her hand slid to her chest to rest on the exact spot Will previously pointed out.

"What is it?" he pressed with feigned curiosity.

"It's nothing. Where's Will?"

"He's fine, but we need to get going." He helped her to her feet while their companions returned carrying more than enough fruit.

"Coura, you're awake!" Marcus exclaimed with visible relief.

"How's your head?" she asked as she eyed the apples.

"I don't remember what happened, but I take it you do?"

Her lips curved into a slightly mischievous smirk before she snatched a piece of fruit from him. "No idea."

***

Coura tried her best to hide her confusion but needed to bite her tongue in order to avoid snapping at Byron for his continuous questioning. She felt both tired and frustrated and didn't want to talk about what took place two nights ago until she could put the memories together herself. Despite that, her companions' behavior grew worse.

Only an hour to go, then I can be alone, she told herself.

At the moment, she hoped to confirm Will hadn't been harmed and figure out what took place with the angels after the female stabbed her.

It wasn't a dream. I remember the slice in my arm, as well as the blade piercing my chest, but I don't see any wounds. No one mentioned that we stopped in town, so how could my wounds heal without a light mage? The angels wouldn't help me, but they didn't kill me either. I can't sense their presence at all, so now what? This doesn't make sense! Coura racked her brain to no avail and recalled nothing after the fight.

Byron wouldn't leave her side or let her talk to Will, who avoided looking her in the eye and trailed far behind. At first, Marcus doted over her, as though she couldn't handle herself. He offered a shoulder to lean on, then a hand when her legs were still stiff, but she shooed him away until he finally walked beside Will. The two talked quietly while casting glances at her from time to time. Meanwhile, her mentor passively demanded she tell him what happened two nights ago, so she made sure to go into as much detail as she could, especially when it pertained to his drunken state, which he didn't appreciate.

"I know I misbehaved," he admitted. "You haven't told me what you did after you dragged me into the woods."

She knit her brow in irritation. "I said I don't remember."

"Coura," he began in a tone she recognized. Byron often used it when she caused trouble in her classes, and that meant he was about to lecture her.

She cut him off with a wave of her hand before he could go any further, increasing the throbbing in her head. "I told you this twice. I'm done talking to you."

"We're not finished. Will shared more about that night."

"Then go bother him," she snapped in response.

Byron recognized he had pushed her enough for the moment and backed off. Even so, Coura couldn't bear to remain beside him, so she picked up her pace and put herself a few steps ahead, against the protesting muscles in her legs.

Did Will send the angels away or convince them to heal me? Obviously Byron and Marcus didn't make it in time to help. Who chased them off? Where did my injuries go? What does Will know that I don't?

***

Seeing the academy in the distance was a relief to everyone, especially Byron. He had just about lost his patience with Coura's stubborn attitude, which grew worse after she distanced herself from him. Will didn't seem pleased she woke already, though Marcus behaved in the opposite manner. He figured their guard had never saved anybody in distress and tried to be seen as chivalrous. This

155

led Byron to consider informing the soldier of how the feeling fades after actually participating in a rescue, but he would let the young man figure that out another time.

They made excellent time getting to East Hoover, though his next few hours would consist of reporting on Verona, the final decisions discussed at the palace, and somehow bringing up Coura and the Yeluthians in the midst of the faculty's predictably negative emotions.

This won't be easy, for me or Symon. Our discussion will chart the course for a rough future; however, I need to take care of these three first.

"Gather around," he ordered after halting in the road. "Marcus, Will, once we enter the academy, I would like for you to accompany me to the headmaster's office so we can assign you rooms. Marcus, you're free to relax afterward. I can even arrange for a tour if you're interested."

The assistant general responded with a curt nod. "I've been directed to observe your delivery of the documents and add additional pieces of information."

Byron avoided the urge to groan at the reply. *Sometimes I forget he's another soldier under King Hernan's thumb. Here I was starting to like him.*

"Fine, but that won't be until tomorrow at the soonest. I need to take care of Will, and the headmaster has to arrange for the instructors to meet. I'll make sure you're told when that is."

It hurt him to see the trust in Marcus's eyes while he lied. In actuality, he would need the assistant general out of the way when he confronted Symon so he could inform the man about their situation in private. In turn, his friend would brief the other master mages, and they'd prepare for the final discussion. Even then, he wasn't certain they would allow anybody else into that meeting.

"Will, we'll head straight to a healer to fix your nose before vouching for what we discussed."

The other young man voiced his agreement without any hostility. Byron knew that part would be simple, so he felt eager to follow through on his end.

Finally, he glanced at his student, who dug the toe of her boot into the dirt in a bored manner. His next question reflected his desire to keep her out of the picture while leaving the decision up to her. Instead of commanding her to remain in one place, he would let it be her choice, not his order. "What are you going to do, Coura?"

"I'm going to my room to unpack and find something to eat," she answered nonchalantly.

The answer satisfied Byron. "Let's get going then."

***

For the next five days, Coura tried her best to stay away from everybody while the MAA went wild from the news Byron brought. The new law King Hernan issued stated that once a student from the academy turned sixteen, they were to be transferred to Verona for additional training lasting three years. There, they would act as a part of Asteom's army and obey whatever orders their supervisors assigned, including being stationed around the country, if necessary. In addition to defending the capital, should the country go to war, they would fight on the battlefield. The trainees officially graduated after serving their time and are given the option to remain in that position or accept one as a guard somewhere most suited to them in various locations around Asteom.

Byron hadn't mentioned any of this to Coura during their travels, not that she minded, but he had been secretive for months. Either someone messed up by letting the information spread outside the meetings or the faculty purposely shared it to prepare the older trainees; based on how the instructors responded, she figured it was the former. They canceled their classes while the headmaster advised the students not to leave East Hoover until he settled the matter; however, being cooped up seemed to make the building's atmosphere tense.

Her classmates whispered under their breaths around her at lunch. Almost all feared the idea of being stationed for three years at a locations they wouldn't be suited for and with strangers who might not be familiar with magic.

"There's no way I'd let them put me on a battlefield," a girl named Bridgette grumbled to their table in the mess hall. "How could the master mages let a law like this be passed?"

"At least you have two years left until you're sixteen," another boy named Robin replied. His ink-colored hair became ruffled from combing through it with his fingers all day. "Next year, I will be old enough! What if we go to war with the northern country? I don't think I could stomach it."

"What about you, Coura?" Bridgette addressed her next. "You're already sixteen, aren't you?"

"We already learned how to wield weapons," she began in a dismissive tone. "We're suited to using magic in combat, so I doubt their generals are foolish enough to assign us positions where we would be wasted."

During the resulting pause, she continued eating her meal even though she barely tasted the food.

Robin was the first to respond. "Really? Are you sure?"

She nodded, swallowed the bland bite, and pushed her plate away. "The king requested additional mages for his army. Why would he be so reckless? That's not considering if this law even stands for long."

Those at the table visibly relaxed and started other conversations a minute later.

"You sounded just like Master Byron," Bridgette added after with a giggle.

Coura rolled her eyes and shrugged. "Trust me. No one here would allow us be put in harm's way if they felt we weren't ready."

That lunch happened three days ago when the trainees first began spreading the word. When nothing had been accepted fully or denied, uncertainty loomed over everybody like a dark cloud. It became so predominant she decided to bring meals to her room and focus on training alone.

She didn't hear from Byron or Marcus ever since their group separated upon arrival. At first, Will joined her in the mess hall in order to warm up to her acquaintances, but she noticed he still would not acknowledge her. This made her even more curious about what took place in the forest outside Fester, mainly the missing pieces of her memory. After a couple days, he found light mages interested in medicine, and she stopped seeing him.

As Coura relaxed on her bed to stare at the ceiling, she wondered what would happen next.

I can't stand it here, she realized after listening to the birds chirping casually outside her open window. *I've been away from the academy and seen the world. I don't believe I can learn any more from the master mages here except Byron. Maybe it is better if I'm sent to the capital. I never seriously spoke with a soldier before about combat, so who knows what I might pick up. If only those awful noblemen and ladies weren't trouncing around and the servants didn't spy on everybody every, single second. It could actually be a decent place to live.*

She considered returning to the sparring field for the second time that day but decided to visit one of the classrooms reserved for practicing spells instead; however, as she sat up and went to close the window, someone knocked on her door. She bolted the window shut before opening it to see Marcus wearing his most stoic expression.

"The headmaster, instructors, and I would like to speak with you."

Her following laugh echoed through the corridor while she pushed past him and began making her way to the chamber used for faculty meetings. "Why are you so serious?"

"What do you mean?" he asked from where he followed close behind.

"Come on, Marcus. We both know each other, so you can stop behaving like a general with the formal nonsense."

"I'm representing my position as an *assistant* general. I'd guess this is the first time many people here have seen a second-rank soldier too."

"Sure. You didn't mention what the point of this meeting is, by the way."

He paused then continued at a lower volume. "It's about the presence outside Fester."

"Oh, right."

She decided it would mean more to Marcus if he led her inside and slowed so he could move ahead. Soon after, they stood at the entrance to the meeting chamber where a lone chair sat. Her guide gestured to it as an offer, yet she remained standing and frowned.

"Am I not allowed inside?"

"Not yet. Will entered just before I left to get you. He's supposed to inform us of the attack since he remembers everything."

Marcus leaned against the opposite wall with his arms crossed. When he didn't move, she asked why he didn't go in the room.

"Byron requested I wait outside," he answered without hiding his displeasure.

"Why?"

He shook his head. "I don't know, but he promised to tell me once it's fully discussed. We agreed its considered the academy's business due to its magical nature."

"I guess that makes sense."

In the resulting silence, Coura accepted the chair, rested her elbows on her knees, and stared at the floor. She remained fixated on one spot for what felt like an hour while attempting to remember any memories from after she blacked out.

Still, the doors didn't open. The longer she sat, the more irritated she grew with herself, as well as with Byron for summoning her prematurely. When she couldn't stand it anymore, she rose and began to retreat down the corridor.

The movement caught Marcus off guard, and he hurried after her. "Where are you going?"

"You can tell Byron I'll be in the training field whenever they decide they need me."

"Coura, hold on!"

She believed going outside would be best since she needed to breathe fresh air and ease the dull headache that formed. Marcus's persistence went ignored as she chose to go to a secluded area where she and Byron usually practiced dark spells. To the assistant general's credit, he didn't attempt to pursue her far. Eventually, he hesitated, providing an opportunity for her to turn a few corners and lose him.

What is so important that they need Will for such a lengthy amount of time? What more could he remember, and why won't they let me in too?

The Cost of Revenge

he matching training grounds made up the eastern and western spaces outside the academic structure. The faculty reserved one side for physical combat, while the other was used for magic. This way, energies and spells could be contained, and students working with just weapons wouldn't be in danger from potential backlash. A wall standing nearly as tall as the building surrounded the entire area, and unlike the brick around the queen's garden at the palace, it would be impossible for somebody to climb over the smoothed logs.

A few items had been spread throughout the grounds, which were necessary for the trainees' sessions. A well in the middle always possessed fresh water, and metal bins spaced equally along the outer wall contained a medical kit, towels, and basic, steel weapons. Although students couldn't use them without permission, the instructors liked to test everyone from time to time by pretending to be an enemy. It acted realistic enough for classes to practice facing a non-mage fighter, and vice versa. Finally, benches had been scattered around since trainees tended to use a substantial portion of their power during lessons.

As Coura scanned her chosen field, she felt thankful only three students practiced together farther away. It seemed they were focusing on accuracy, as they attempted to strike a target positioned on a straw dummy with elemental spells. She continued moving toward Byron's preferred section near the rear and took a spot at one of the benches facing the wall. With the building out of sight, she forced herself to loosen her tense muscles as she watched the sky. No clouds drifted overhead, but many birds flew above, which became enough to occupy her eyes so her mind could wander.

I can't keep losing my temper like that, especially since Marcus is just doing what Byron asked. Maybe I am better off going to Verona. The thought crossed her mind several times over the past few days since she would be among the first students sent to the capital, whether she chose that path or not. *I don't mind continuing my training elsewhere, but I feel like I won't belong in a uniform group. Perhaps my problem stems down to how much I hate following orders from a superior I don't trust.*

The notion had her recalling Byron's lecture after the two departed from East Hoover. If someone like Marcus gave her an assignment without revealing the purpose or it happened to be a decision she disagreed with, she knew it would raise issues.

I suppose he's tolerable, but I doubt I would be reporting to him. I'll never understand how soldiers can stand being bossed around.

Coura expected the assistant general to find and drag her back inside at any moment, yet she still jumped when a hand fell on her shoulder, interrupting her reflection.

"I didn't even hear you," she admitted with a chuckle and turned to address the person she fully expected to be behind her.

To her surprise, a stranger stood with his hand on her instead of Marcus. He gazed at the birds with blue eyes that mirrored the clear sky.

"I'm sorry," she apologized when he didn't respond. "I thought you were somebody else."

"That is quite all right. A bird-watcher are you?"

"No, not really."

The following, uncomfortable silence stretched to amplify the other students' chattering, the chirping from above, and a cool breeze.

"May I join you?" he asked her suddenly.

Coura tilted her head at the question to reflect her uncertainty with the stranger's purpose. "I suppose, but I won't be here for long."

"That is fine. I plan on leaving soon anyway."

He removed his hand, slipped around to the front of the bench, and took a seat on the edge opposite her. She noted his handsome features highlighted by blond hair, which had been tied into a braid at the nape of his neck. For some reason, he continued staring straight ahead or at the sky instead of at her.

The lack of conversation, as well as his odd behavior, left her at a loss for words, so she prepared to excuse herself in order to find Marcus; however, as she opened her mouth, the man spoke in a neutral manner.

"Are you a dark mage?"

"I'm just a trainee."

"I see. You do not learn about light magic then."

Although his expression remained impassive, Coura sensed another motive beyond curiosity while she watched him. "We study both here."

Pain flashed in his eyes. "In that case, you must know no magic can reattach a part of the body when it is cut off, no matter how much energy is thrown into a healing spell."

She didn't answer. Something felt wrong, so she began to rise with the intent to leave the man to himself and warn an instructor.

As soon as she stood, his head snapped to her so their eyes could meet for the first time. He dipped his head after then glanced down at his feet, prompting her to follow his gaze. Her eyes widened at the sight of his right leg, which was missing the foot. The base of his resulting stump had been wrapped with bandages, but scarlet spots showed it had yet to heal.

In that moment, she recognized she had been the one who caused his injury.

When did I... I don't remember him, but I know I did that. He looks so familiar...

Seeing the severed leg brought back a flood of confusing memories and caused her head to ache worse than earlier. She recalled being covered in blood and spotting the bodiless head of a woman before the blond stranger tried to escape. Then, she grabbed his foot.

This man and Will were outside Fester. He's an…an angel…

Coura's heart beat faster as her mind swarmed with scenes appearing too frequently for her to make any sense of. Among them, the name Devan rang to identify the stranger. Her body froze at the idea of the same threat from that night sitting nearby. Her eyes darted to his, and she saw nothing except rage beneath his mask of indifference.

Why am I remembering this now? More importantly, what is he doing here? I need to find Byron!

As soon as she moved, the angel lunged for her before she could turn around. His fist appeared out of nowhere to connect with the side of her torso, resulting in a sharp pain by her ribs while the rest of her body was knocked sideways onto the grass beside the bench. Her years of combat experience left her with plenty of bruises and broken bones, so she didn't become completely stunned after the strike.

Compared to the composed individual from seconds ago, the angel acted like a crazed animal. His wide eyes remained filled with anger, and he snarled as he hobbled to where she sat on the ground with the assistance of the bench.

"Demon child," he growled. "You killed her and damaged me!"

True fear gripped Coura during her indecisiveness. *He's insane! With a single punch, he brought me down. I don't stand a chance alone in a brawl.*

"There you are," a voice interrupted, breaking through the noise in her head.

She glanced away from her attacker to where Marcus approached from the direction of the building. Through her expression alone, she hoped to convey the sense of danger they were in.

Meanwhile, Devan hesitated, looked between the two, then drew a sword hidden underneath his cloak. "Enough!"

I'm dead...

Coura recited the words over and over as he raised the weapon above his head. Out of instinct, she brought up an arm in a feeble attempt to hinder the strike, squeezed her eyes shut, and anticipated the pain.

Instead, the sound of clashing metal rang in her ears, causing her eyes to snap open. Marcus had predicted the movement and hurried between while drawing the sword at his waist to block the angel's blow, likely saving her life.

"Run!" he cried as he shoved Devan back.

I can't leave you, she hoped to reply, yet her voice wouldn't cooperate. She also longed to tell him what she remembered, about how she murdered the angel's companion in addition to her inexplicable powers.

Such a discussion would need to wait, though, for their current enemy prepared to throw himself at her again.

Get up and find help!

She continued yelling at herself until she was standing, then she began sprinting toward the building despite the pain in her side. Marcus defended her as she did so and kept the intruder occupied.

After crossing the area near one of three metal doors leading inside, she noticed the other trainees who worked with the dummy. They hurried to intercept her and projected their concern.

"Are you all right?" one asked.

"What's going on?" another demanded as the trio approached.

Coura slowed her pace before halting with the intent to request they follow her inside until a vaguely familiar voice rang in her mind.

{*Send them away. We are not finished here.*}

"Find the master mages in the faculty meeting room," she instructed, uncertain why she decided to obey the sudden order. "Tell them there's an intruder in the magic training ground, and mention Coura sent you."

Her stern, unwavering words were all the reassurance they needed before each nodded and passed through the nearby entrance. *I should stay,* she thought with a strange, new strength. *He's after me, so I can't risk anybody getting caught by an unexpected attack.*

Thankfully for those in the building, the eastern side only held the metal doors as no windows adorned the wall. If she could hold him where they were until help arrived, nobody else would be wrapped up in her mess. Still, she had no idea how to restrain the crazed angel.

He moves with less balance because of his missing foot, but Marcus is slower. I suppose I should aim to distract him.

The clashing blades echoed throughout the area, reminding her of her lack of a weapon. This led her to consider using dark magic; however, after observing the swordplay for a moment, she knew it would be impossible to time a spell so it wouldn't hit Marcus.

{*Use your sword.*}

Coura flinched at the internal voice. *I don't have a sword, but there should be weapons in a supply bin.*

She spotted one container near the barrier past Marcus and Devan and another across the field. After noting their locations, she decided to go for the farthest bin in order to avoid distracting her ally and perhaps lure the angel away.

It's my best shot.

Her lungs burned from the effort of charging in that direction, but she soon closed in on her goal. To her dismay, the intruder's cackling replaced the sounds of combat.

"It's useless!" he shouted, though she wondered if his words were meant for her, not Marcus.

Out of the corner of her eye, Coura caught a flash of crimson before hearing a warning cry from the soldier. She glanced over her shoulder just in time to spot a series of fireballs soaring in her direction. The sight prompted her to dive to the ground, which spurred a grunt as she landed on her bruised side, and a wave of heat blew by while she waited. After scrambling to her feet, she witnessed the damage the flames wrought: The angel had been aiming for the container, not her. As she approached the metal, she bit off a curse. His spell didn't damage its structure, yet the heat from the fire singed the lock. She decided against burning her hands trying to pry it open and focused on the second bin near the continued fighting.

The closer she moved toward the pair, the more nervous she grew since the combat favored Devan. Marcus' swings and stabs looked weaker, he panted from the effort of maintaining his position, and beads of sweat covered his forehead. Both noticed her approach, but the angel alone appeared pleased before stepping toward the container, intercepting her from acquiring a weapon.

What now?

{Use your sword.}

The feminine voice spoke with annoyance this time, though Coura ignored it and continued creeping forward.

"Who are you?" the assistant general shouted at the intruder during the break in their match.

His opponent scoffed before assuming the pretentious attitude she remembered.

"You may call me Devan, or whatever honorable title you humans deem appropriate. It is only fitting you select one to bring with you to the afterlife."

"What are you doing here?" Marcus continued without hesitation.

The angel frowned and pointed his sword at her. "I'm here to kill the demon-child who murdered my sister and took my foot."

"Coura wouldn't do such thing."

Marcus' immediate answer startled her.

Again, a hysterical laugh filled the area. "There is no reason for you to die too. I suggest you spare yourself the heroics and leave."

"I refuse to let you run rampant," the assistant general replied while assuming a new sense of authority.

A snarl replaced Devan's crazed grin. He glanced back and forth from Coura to Marcus, as if deciding which was worth attacking first. Then, he hurled another fireball at the remaining bin to his left; Coura's heart sank in response.

"If you wish to die here, I will oblige you," the terrifying being muttered loudly enough for her to hear.

She prepared to backtrack when he cast a third spell, filling a bolt of lightning with more energy than the previous flames. Instead of using it against either opponent, the angel shot it toward the building where it slammed against the nearest door the three trainees used earlier. From the sheer power and accuracy, she bet the metal warped or dented enough to prevent anybody from going in or out.

He's trapping us, Coura realized with a pang of fear.

"I can take my time now," Devan added after. In the blink of an eye, he manifested white wings in a similar manner to the elemental spells.

The change visibly shocked Marcus, and he mumbled to himself before raising his sword. Meanwhile, Coura recognized the angel's magical presence as that of the creature pursuing their group outside Fester. Before she could strategize based on their opponent's altered appearance, Devan charged forward.

Marcus raised his blade and blocked the initial blow, but the angel continued beating down on him from above. Coura chose to focus on magic since the soldier could only defend, sending scattered blasts of lightning at the sky around Devan. Her intent was not to hit the target but to distract him.

With each spell she released, another presence touched her mind, as though it begged her to shift her attention. She shook off the feeling while attempting to help, though none of the power she spent proved to be worth it.

Devan dodged each attack with an envious amount of grace and control while raining blows upon Marcus, who seemed ready to drop to his knees from exhaustion. Between her bolts, the angel soon landed a hit. He folded his wings inward to roll and miss her blast by a hair's breadth, then he dove behind the assistant general. Marcus had been expecting another strike from above and positioned his body to reflect that assumption.

Before Coura could shout a warning, their opponent sunk his blade into the center of the soldier's back until the steel tip protruded from the front of Marcus' tunic.

She screamed the assistant general's name a second later as Devan slowly pulled his sword free in order to savor the moment. Her companion fell forward onto his chest after, and the hole in his shirt grew dark from the fresh blood.

What should I do? she thought before the angel fixed his menacing gaze on her.

He wiped his blade clean on his shirt while wearing a sickening grin; the sight made her knees begin to tremble. She wanted nothing more than to crumple onto her hands and knees and wait for death to come.

In her defeated state of mind, the growing presence from earlier seemed to take hold of her body, settling her frantic heartbeat and quivering limbs.

{*Use your sword!*}

I don't have a sword, she replied without considering the stranger's identity.

Devan began stalking toward her, so she started to back up.

{*Fool! Remember the blade you used before?*}

A vision of the past returned to Coura as clear as day. She found herself pressed against a tree trunk with a sword jutting out from her chest. It had been the female angel's weapon, so she yanked on the hilt until the blade came free. Then, she let it fall to the ground while ignoring the irritating sensation of what blood trickled down her torso. A second sword, one comprised of demonic energy, appeared in her hand with a pair of wings settling on her shoulder blades. Both were black in color, and she summoned them as easily as snapping her fingers.

How did I do that? she wondered instead of questioning the memory.

{*Don't you know anything? Manifest it as though you're casting a spell.*}

She noticed a fluttering tendril of power flowing from deep inside her center, beneath what she imagined to be the bottom of her energy pool, and reached for it. The sensation felt intoxicating as the newfound strength hummed in her veins, like she could conquer whatever was thrown her way. Despite her opponent storming closer and amid a sudden pounding on the metal door, Coura closed her eyes.

As though I'm casting a spell...

With a clear mind, she reached for that power while imagining the energy shaping in her hands. She could picture the blade as the energy took a form, so when she opened her eyes, it didn't startle her to see the same sword from that night in her right hand.

At first, Devan halted and went wide-eyed in alarm. He bent a bit to rub his leg, which she figured reminded him of his missing foot, then he stood straight and glared at Coura.

"I sense an unnatural presence. Demonic energy does not belong in this world."

He spoke so seriously she became curious about his thoughts on the matter; however, she dismissed the idea and prepared to resume the fight until the voice in her mind interrupted.

{Don't expect to keep up without your wings.}

My... wings?

{You are so helpless. Yes, your wings.}

The utter lack of concern from the stranger made Coura interested in their identity, but another memory sprang upon her before she could question them.

This time, she flew above the ground and leapt on the female angel, watching as the head rolled off the being's shoulders. She turned to face Devan after and pumped her wings like an extra set of arms to push her body higher. Cool air blew on her face and through her wings, tickling the flesh beneath the feathers. As the scene ended, she longed for the sense of freedom her flight revealed.

{Do what you did with the weapon.}

She followed the voice's instruction and pulled from her center again, though without closing her eyes. Her opponent sensed the dark energy she prepared and retreated a couple steps.

"Demon!" he growled. With a beat of his wings, he charged while raising his sword.

Despite his approach, Coura didn't feel intimidated. She not only brought up her weapon to meet his, but she successfully manifested her wings as soon as their blades touched. The spell cost more energy than the blade, yet both fed from her pool of energy. Normally, she would sense when she grew weaker; however, in her current situation, the newfound power didn't seem to have an end. The resulting exhilaration prompted her to grin into her opponent's face.

"You die here," Devan stated in answer to her unexpected giddiness before jumping back and rising into the air.

She chased after him without allowing herself a moment to think about her next move, letting her wings carry her up to his level. The angel continued their bout by diving to strike, though she easily dodged it from below. After, the two fell into a pattern of matching blows and blocks. Coura managed to skirt away from or stop each of her opponent's swings and managed to scratch him across his chest, left forearm, and cheek, prompting him to curse each time. While she enjoyed floating in the sky, he grew frustrated.

Finally, after she nicked him on the chin, Devan descended to the ground and adjusted his strategy to launch fire spells at her. Unlike him, she wasn't used to aerial maneuvering, so his first ball of flame hit her left wing. She gasped from the unexpected pain, and the wing crumpled against her will. The injury forced her to move lower, yet the angel's spells struck her twice more, though with less of an impact than the first. Another tendril of energy flowed from her center to the spots where she took damage, but Coura became too distracted to look into what that power did.

Once the two were on the ground together, they continued their swordplay, as did the distant pounding on the academy's door.

"Where is the ferocity and mercilessness you demonstrated during our previous encounter?" Devan demanded before retreating a few paces to separate them for the moment. His heavy panting revealed his physical fatigue, and blood dripped into the grass from multiple cuts along his body.

Coura's left wing ached a bit; otherwise, she felt only a competitive thrill. When she didn't answer, he spat at her feet.

"Demons do not belong in this world," he commented with underlying resentment.

She returned the glare and raised her blade. "This is your last chance. Leave, or surrender and turn yourself in."

Her opponent wordlessly mirrored her position before limping toward her.

{We must finish this. Focus on your sword and put every ounce of strength into a final, killing motion.}

I can't do that, she replied. The thought of ending someone's life both horrified and sickened her, even if the being in front of her lost his mind.

{You're a mage. It is your responsibility to keep peace by any means necessary, right? Do you not believe it's justifiable to kill in order to defend yourself? The strong should not show mercy to the weak. That is the way the world works, Dear One. Besides, if you don't hurry, your friend over there is going to bleed to death.}

Although Coura wasn't sure exactly what the voice meant, she trusted it as much as she could, given the circumstances. The presence did steady her hands when Devan charged, and somehow her breathing slowed enough to help her mind clear again. When he reached her, she dismissed his weapon and swung hers horizontally at his waist without worrying about his blow. The angel didn't expect her to ignore his sword in favor of a direct attack, leading him to twist his blade in order to block instead of follow through with his own weapon. Still, his timing was off, and he moved too slow. She cut across his midsection in a single slice without any restraint, retreated, then waited for a counterstrike.

The angel wrapped his free arm around the bleeding wound and paused for a few seconds before falling onto his back, all while howling in pain. His wailing quieted into moans, then silence after he stopped moving.

When Coura felt certain he wouldn't rise, she approached his body. Instead of the relief or nausea she expected after such an experience, she shuddered in a euphoric state, taking pleasure in her strength until Marcus' coughing tore her away from those emotions.

She mumbled his name after recalling his injury and sprinted over to kneel beside him as dread and fear began to overwhelm her. When all the confidence she possessed moments ago fled, it left her shaking again.

He managed to flip himself onto his back and pressed his hands against the wound. Coura released the spell she held on her weapon, causing it to noiselessly shatter into glimmering shards of dark energy. Then, she placed her hands on top of his. His face had gone white, and he grimaced at the extra pressure.

"H-how did you…" he began in a weak voice.

"I don't know," she answered halfheartedly while keeping her attention on stopping the bleeding.

"What…happened to…"

"I don't know, now stop talking," she ordered as her mind raced. The world seemed to freeze around them, and she tried to think of what to do against a surge of tears.

I did this, she admitted to herself. *He wouldn't have been harmed if I didn't go outside. I shouldn't have left. I…I didn't mean to…for this to…*

Guilt wracked her then, enough to let several drops slip and roll down her cheeks. The presence in her mind didn't say anything, but she knew it was still there, watching and listening.

No Turning Back

$\mathfrak{A}$ loud clang from nearby startled Coura just as she began to give up hope. She heard the damaged, metal door leading into the academy creak until whoever was behind it managed to shove it off its hinges. Not only were Byron and the three trainees she sent inside present, but several instructors, the headmaster, and plenty of other students huddled behind.

As soon as the opening became clear, everyone froze at the sight of her and Marcus.

No, not Marcus...

That was when she realized she had yet to release the spell keeping her wings manifested, so they sat behind her for them to see. When no one moved, she figured they questioned whether or not to come forward and decided to call out.

"He needs a healer," Coura shouted, though her voice seemed ready to break. "Please, somebody help him!"

One of the light mage instructors named Sylvia shook her head, as if snapping out of a trance, and hurried ahead. Her movement became the signal for the others to react too. A pair of women she didn't recognize jogged over to join the master mage. Sylvia knelt on the opposite side of the assistant general and focused solely on him. Coura removed her blood-soaked hands so the light mage could replace them. Then, the remaining women placed theirs on top. Their collective energy swarmed around Marcus while a faint glow from the wound showcased the healing spell.

Meanwhile, Byron went to Coura's side but didn't kneel like the rest. When he eyed her, she bowed her head to avoid his gaze, opting to stare at the ground.

"Will he be all right?" her mentor asked Sylvia after.

"We'll see momentarily. It's a serious stab wound that literally put a hole in him, and he's lost a lot of blood. If it can be healed, we'll need to make sure that can be replaced. My students and I will handle this, if that's what you're wondering."

"Thank you."

Coura felt his eyes on her again and remembered the blood coating her feathers.

"I need another healer," he called to the group waiting by the door.

{Tell them not to bother. Your wounds are already mended.}

It startled her to hear such a claim, yet after tracing the tendrils of energy that stretched to those spots earlier, she found the new power repaired her injuries while she fought.

"I'm fine," she said loudly enough for Byron to catch before dismissing the spell on her wings. They broke into glistening shards before fading, just like her sword had done, to many gasps and mumbles farther away.

With everything that happened, Coura felt herself sinking into her confusion and worry. She probably would have continued to do so if Byron didn't grab her arm and haul her to her feet. As soon as she stood, he returned to the door while dragging her behind since she avoided meeting the onlookers' stares by keeping her eyes on the ground. Those near the opening either emerged to provide additional space or flattened themselves against the internal walls in order to create a path. Her mentor pulled her into the eerily quiet academy without a word.

Once they were safely in her room, he locked the door and slid the curtain over her window. Coura needed to sit since her legs seemed about ready to give out, so she dropped onto the edge of her bed. Her stare shifted from the floor to her hands, which remained covered in drying blood. She still couldn't meet his eyes; however, the uncomfortable silence grew to the point where she decided it would be in her best interest to speak first.

"Byron, I'm sorry. I should've stayed inside, but I just-"

He raised a hand in a gesture for her to stop talking. When she obeyed, he procured the chair from her desk, lowered himself into it, and knit his brow.

"I want to start from the beginning. Tell me about what happened after you brought me out of the tavern in Fester."

*

For the first time in her life, Coura felt exposed as she waited for her mentor to process the story she recounted for him. Although her memories were restored, that was the first time she followed them in order. The haunting images, descriptions of the demonic power, and horrific murders, intentional or not, bothered her terribly. In order to reveal her side of the story, she needed to distance herself from the person in her memories, to pretend it wasn't her but what she witnessed through someone else's perspective.

Worse still, she constantly sensed the strange presence observing them, like another set of eyes in the back of her mind.

She didn't know what else to say or do beyond explaining her experience, which she viewed as concrete facts about the past. Her thoughts raced to keep up and seemed completely lost at the same time, leaving her unable to examine her own feelings and form her own judgements about the situation. Because of this, Coura chose to avoid mentioning the voice who guided her through most of the fight with Devan.

Byron closed his eyes when she began in order to savor each word. They didn't open until well after she concluded with the moment he and the others were able to open the door to the training ground. Then, he became fixated on a spot across from him with an unreadable expression.

Outside, the sun started to set based on the dimming light from behind the curtain. With nothing else to do, she watched it fade while allowing her mind to settle until the room grew dark and the tension became too unbearable. She turned toward her mentor and prepared to ask for his opinion only to find him studying her.

"What?" she all but whispered.

Byron opened and closed his mouth twice before speaking. "I have many questions," he began slowly, as if each word required careful consideration. "The first I want to start with is, are you okay?"

Coura licked her lips and cleared her throat. "I don't know. I haven't had time to process any of this."

He nodded to show he expected that reply. "My next question is, what do you plan on doing now?"

A chill sent through her body at his unsympathetic seriousness. "What do you mean?"

Her mentor remained stiff, and his eyes reflected no familiarity toward her.

He's looking at me like I'm a complete stranger.

"I'm going to be honest with you," he picked up. "This is bad. *Very* bad. Demonic possession usually results in a death penalty. It's unpredictable, and the risks associated with harboring someone who might snap are high. If you're not killed for those reasons alone, there's the murder of two people. Two Yeluthians."

"I didn't-"

"Not everyone will believe what you told me about those situations being out of your control. We didn't know their motives, and we never will. Besides, there's the matter of the demonic power."

The master mage paused, as if waiting for Coura to respond, yet she couldn't come up with a rebuttal.

He's right. I can't defend myself when the country doesn't tolerate demons. There's no working around that fact and what everybody outside saw.

"I'll ask you again. What do you plan on doing next?"

***

Byron found it difficult to interrogate his student because he needed to dismiss the urge to do one of two things.

First, he wanted to wrap his arms around her and make sure she was physically unharmed and mentally sane. For her to be in danger on multiple occasions under his supervision hurt. He taught trainees in the past who found themselves in precarious predicaments too but none he spent as much time with as Coura. Throughout this part of her life, he acted as her guardian in addition to her mentor, especially since she couldn't remember her past. His second inclination involved placing guards nearby and transitioning her room into a prison of sorts until he felt certain she would be safe to keep around.

Based on his experience with demonic possessions, her explanation didn't add up. Few people who became possessed survived the initial reaction to how great the impact of unnatural energy is on the human body. Those who did survive lost their minds once they returned to a somewhat normal state. Each case he had ever heard of ended with death, whether caused by another, random surge of power or by order of the law. For Coura to live through such an ordeal more than once was nothing short of a miracle, yet the possibility of another outburst would always remain.

Thanks to her restored memories, though, he learned she barely knew what happened during the first encounter because she had passed out from blood loss. During the second incident, she could apparently control her actions. He had no idea how that was possible.

Finally, and most concerning, were those wings. Nobody ever recorded a demon acquiring the ability to manifest wings like the Yeluthians. It sounded blasphemous, but unfortunately Byron and too many others saw them with their own eyes.

Our most pressing decision now is what to do with her, he reminded himself.

The entire academy either witnessed the aftermath of what took place or would hear about it soon. The lone silver lining was that her story matched Will's completely. He considered all aspects of their predicament when she finished talking. Both sides of his heart conflicted, yet his nature favored impartiality, leading him to ask what she planned to do.

"You can remain in East Hoover under close supervision with the possibility of the death penalty. The faculty and I would question you tirelessly, and the whole academy would know. To put it simply, you'd become an outcast. Or, you can run away. I wouldn't stop you if you opened the window and fled, but just know you'd be hunted and presumed a traitor. You might have the best chance at surviving outside these walls. The choice is yours."

"It's not much of a choice," his student mumbled while lowering her gaze.

He kept quiet and continued to monitor her for any hint of movement or emotion that might set the demonic power off.

After a minute, she met his eyes and answered. "I'd like to stay here."

***

Coura understood her limited options before Byron even laid them out and spent the brief amount of time considering the consequences of her newly discovered power. Ultimately, she decided she would be better off cooperating under his supervision. If she could show some self-control with the energy, perhaps they wouldn't kill her after all.

The master mage released a sigh of relief after she stated her intent to remain at the academy, and his following look reflected familiarity again. "I'm glad, but it won't be easy. I don't just mean convincing everybody. We need to resolve the matter with the angels, which is going to be messy since you,

Will, and Marcus were the only ones who interacted with them."

"I understand. I'll try my best."

"I'm going to ask you for a lot, so please be patient. I might be the only individual on your side through this, and I don't want you acting irrationally. To be blunt, you're not exactly the most reasonable person to deal with under normal circumstances." The slight, upward curve of his lips let her know he still considered her worth protecting.

That realization drove her to reach another decision. "Byron, there's something else I need to tell you."

{*Don't.*}

At last, the lingering presence spoke up, albeit in a menacing tone, and a shadow crept over Coura.

I have to tell him, she argued despite the unspoken threat. *He's my mentor, and my friend.*

Byron sensed a shift in the conversation during the resulting silence and glanced at her without hiding his interest before shaking his head. "I don't want to hear it, not yet anyway. You gave me enough to contemplate and work with. Besides, if it were important, you would have shared it earlier, right."

She hesitantly nodded, which covered her own intrigue. "I should stay in my room then?"

"Let's just say you won't have much of a choice for now."

"Fine. I'll wait for updates, I guess."

"Good, and thank you. Don't be surprised if we assign people to guard your door and window. I'll arrange for somebody to bring meals here too."

"I know, I know." Despite her apprehension, Coura stood to stretch, prompting her mentor to do the same.

"When I learn more from Symon and the other instructors, I'll pass the news along."

He went to exit and opened the door to find three, armed trainees huddled together. His departure startled them into apologizing while attempting to peek into her room, but he ignored their words and closed the door before she could catch their expressions.

Once alone, Coura couldn't refrain from pacing in an uneasy manner until she paused to glance down at her trembling, blood-encrusted hands. *The last time I was by myself had been in the training ground before Devan came. I felt different than I do now. It reminds me of when I...that night with Will and the other angel...*

In that moment, she sensed the presence sneaking forward. *You, you're a demon, aren't you?*

A tickle of amusement came from the occupied area in her head.

{It's about time you started figuring this out.}

"Who are you?" Coura muttered and took a seat on her bed again.

{You have much to learn, Dear One.}

"That doesn't answer my question."

The creature fell silent for a minute, seemingly to consider what it would reveal.

{Ask me what you would like to know, and I will answer with what I want you to hear.}

"That's not fair," she grumbled in frustration before continuing with the thought on the forefront of her mind. "Am I possessed? You're still inside me but..."

{Are you a danger to others?}

Coura winced at the question she couldn't bear to vocalize.

{It all depends on you. The choices you make and how you use our power will shape your future.}

She adjusted to lie on her back in order to stare at the ceiling. "Does that mean I won't randomly transform into a monster?"

{Perhaps. If you don't let yourself get close to dying again, you should be fine.}

Coura could hear a grin behind the words. "What now? How do I convince everyone I'm not an evil being?"

The demon laughed in response, a crisp, clear sound in her mind.

{What to do? I suggest you start by learning how to use your new abilities. A human with power is both frightening and threatening; one with control over their magic is more reasonable to deal with. I will teach you.}

"How? Aren't you just a voice in my head?"

{You forget you're talking to a true demon. Remember how I guided you through the fight against that vile light-blooded? It should be similar to that. I am able to direct my energy and show you what to do.}

"I see. That makes sense." Coura paused for a minute to consider everything the creature said. "What should I call you? Can I speak with you through my thoughts? I'd look crazy talking to myself all the time."

{You've spoken with me before, idiot. I can sense what takes place in your mind and body too, and my name is Soirée.}

"Soirée…" The name felt wrong, like when she used a curse word for the first time knowing the sound meant more than what was on the surface.

{It seems we have quite some time to get acquainted in this sad, tiny room. Why don't we get started then?}

Coura reflected on the offer and recalled what she once heard about demons. *They're tricky, and they like to cause humans pain. She's right, though. I need to learn control, and she's the only person able to help.*

Amid the nerves and strain came a flicker of the thrill she experienced in the training ground and a sureness about what she was doing. A tremendous desire to recapture that primal pleasure flowed from Soirée, leading her to wonder if she made the right decision to trust the creature with her life.

Part Two

How to Heal a Scar

For the fifth time that week, Coura trudged out of a faculty meeting and hurried to her room before the trainees were dismissed for lunch, per the master mages' instruction. She managed to calm down along the way by taking several, deep breaths and mumbling her ferocious comments so nobody would overhear. Once she slipped inside without being noticed, a hunger pang struck beneath the emotions to distract her, and the sight of a tray brought in earlier by someone in the kitchen made her mouth water.

Even if they keep me here like a criminal, at least they feed me well, she thought absentmindedly as she tasted a savory pastry filled with sausage and herbs. Most of the time, she didn't eat enough to make a dent in the platter's contents.

Her appetite ebbed after a few more bites, so she selected a handful of grapes and sprawled out on her bed. For as frustrated as she became with repeating the same story, Soirée echoed her complaints constantly to hinder her focus.

{*Humans seem to possess brains as soft as the sweets you devour. How can they not remember your words after this long? Do they need you in that chamber so often?*}

"Will you be quiet already?" Coura demanded aloud. As usual, hearing the being's voice raised her temper. "I told you before, it never helps with you chatting away in my head."

{*Perhaps we should kill a few to scare them into acting more considerate.*}

When Soirée first joked about that after their initial interrogation, Coura worried the persistent bloodlust would be a problem; however, a few days of the same, sadistic threats made her realize the demon could only speak inside her mind. The being could not physically force her to do anything.

"Don't you have any better comments to offer instead of whining?"

{Don't you have a spell to practice? Show me the wings, and try to suppress your energy this time.}

*

After agreeing to let Soirée show her how to wield demonic energy, Coura put off the task because she'd been summoned to meet with the headmaster and faculty. The instructors, including Byron, ordered her to explain how she used the power, both in the woods outside Fester and when the remaining angel attacked her in the training ground. Then, they took turns asking a series of prepared questions, which raised more. Some aimed for a particular response, though the wording had been construed differently.

"How did these spells come about?"

"Did you attempt to contact a demon and command it to go to your location during either instance?"

"Would you say, in a moment of distress, you called to an unfamiliar presence?"

"Can you still access those abilities?"

"Is there any way you can hear or feel the creature or its energy?"

Not only did answering such similar prompts grow strenuous, but Coura decided not to tell them about Soirée. She danced around the idea of the demon's existence residing within her body, yet she knew they believed there was a reason for her dilemma. So, they indirectly urged her to reveal the secret through their meticulous interrogating.

If Soirée understood this, she didn't show it. The feminine voice complained in the back of her mind while the master mages spoke, which gave Coura a headache and annoyed her to no end. Worst of all, she became used to speaking out loud to the creature in the privacy of her room. In front of the faculty, she needed to monitor her words lest she slip up and begin inexplicably shouting at the clueless instructors. The effort became exhausting.

After the third meeting ran short and left her with a free afternoon, the demon suggested she begin practicing magic. Coura expressed her apprehension, leading to a reminder of the past through conjured images of her black blade slicing through the hostile angels.

{This is how everybody views you now. Unless you prove them wrong, they'll never trust you again and you'll be useless in a fight. Besides, I can tell you're having urges.}

The claim was true, but Coura hated to admit it. She often found herself itching to dive back into the abyss of energy and savor its seemingly endless pool with a sadistic sense of glee. Additionally, she felt a strange fondness for the moments when she took to the sky. The muscles in her upper back were sore since the extra weight strained that particular area, yet to fly with complete freedom from restraints had been worth the pain. Now that she experienced the exhilaration such an ability produced, she desired to return for more.

Soirée's first lesson had to do with the tendrils of energy and how they naturally found their way to the proper locations so Coura could manifest her sword and wings. It acted similar to the dark magic she grew up training except for its wild behavior, causing the power to hum or jitter if left unattended.

{What human mages use is a lesser amount we demons attract, though your bodies dull the effect. Your channels of energy go to where they are called. I was able to direct them before, but you'll learn to do this on your own from now on. Soon, it will become simple to manipulate, and you won't need to think about managing its path for more than a second. The next item is suppressing your magical presence.}

"I already know that," Coura interrupted. With Byron as her primary teacher, she studied under one of the few mages able to clearly detect energy. He discussed how to do so, as well as how to prevent an enemy from picking up on her own. "I just cut off the connection."

{You understand the basics. Nonetheless, what if you're already wielding your power on a spell? I'll demonstrate how to hide the energy without eliminating those ties.}

Soirée instructed her to begin by creating the path that would cast a controlled fireball within the palm of her hand. A thin stream of demonic energy stretched from her center to her right hand.

{Good. Now, watch.}

Coura held the power in place to halt the casting, and thus prevent anybody from sensing what they were doing, but an invisible force wrapped itself around the tendril like a bandage. It was as if someone willed her power into another form. She had never experienced such a sensation before and didn't know if she felt entirely comfortable with the lack of input.

Soirée ordered her to do the same while dissipating the cover. After a couple tries, she got the hang of the process, though her imaginary bandage of sorts filled with holes.

{That will do. Keep practicing, and we'll move on when you're able to do this without sparing a thought.}

The faculty let Coura out early the following two days, so she spent the rest of her time working in secret. To her amazement, the exercise tired her out faster than usual, forcing her to take breaks often. Once the demon seemed satisfied with several covers of varying sizes and strengths, Soirée encouraged her to continue.

{The next step is to fully cast a spell while maintaining the suppression. Summon a ball of flame while doing what you learned.}

Step by step, Coura led the energy to her hand and shaped it while shielding its presence until an apple-sized burst of fire appeared above her palm. When nobody came knocking down her door, she released a sigh. "I did it!"

{Yes, and you'll be repeating the process until this happens automatically when you dive into your center.}

This meant spending the rest of that day and the next two practicing, which began to frustrate Coura. She repeatedly asked

Soirée when she would be able to manifest the wings and sword again, as well as what other abilities she possessed, but to her dismay, the demon acted more stubborn than Byron and refused to answer. Finally, after Soirée denied the request in favor of repeating the technique, Coura rose and went to stand in front of the hanging mirror above her desk out of spite.

{*What are you doing?*}

She closed her eyes and tried to remember Soirée's words during her fight with the angel. *I cast them like an ordinary spell by reaching into the pool of dark energy. Then, I lead it to the shoulder blades.*

{*Coura, don't!*}

She ignored the demon's protests and moved forward with the spell while attempting to cover as much of the power as possible. Once she triggered the ability, the weight of her extra limbs settled on her back, causing her to waver from the adjustment. Her eyes flew open, and she glanced over each shoulder to observe the ink-colored wings before brushing a hand against them. Despite the sharp-looking edges, the feathers proved to be softer than she imagined. She tried extending them after, like stretching her arm or a leg, and they obeyed in a similar manner.

Before Coura could fully understand how they moved, her door swung open as someone burst into the room to cut her inspection short. She spun around to see Byron marching closer, prompting her to dismiss the manifestation spell.

"What's going on?" he demanded as she did so.

After a pause, she sheepishly admitted to testing her magic, which earned her a scornful glare and stern lecture.

"How could you even consider doing that? Don't you realize it's a danger to everybody here? What if someone else senses the demonic energy? I ran out of a meeting because I feared the worst. How am I going to explain to them what you did? What a stupid mistake, Coura!"

Since she couldn't give him a better reason for her actions, she dipped her head and accepted the verbal reprimanding.

Meanwhile, Soirée's amused laughter echoed in her mind, causing her face to flush from embarrassment.

*

That incident happened a week ago. The demon drilled her in several, minor spells, such as lightning sparks, ice shards, and shielding, before even hinting at trying the new abilities again. When Soirée suggested it, Coura shrugged and rose to stand in front of the mirror.

"If you believe I'm ready."

{Just start slow. Remember, it's the same method.}

She inhaled through her nose, exhaled a moment later to ease her nerves, and turned her focus inward. The pool of energy tingling with a demonic essence swirled in her center, and a strand soon parted from the rest, as if begging her to utilize it. She led that power to where it would be manifested into the wings on her back while weaving a cover along the way, preventing the dark presence from being detected.

The sensation of interacting with such a significant amount remained invigorating and sent a shiver down her spine. She concentrated on maintaining her hold until Soirée approved, then she finished casting the spell. The added weight of the wings on her shoulders and the accompanying aches were growing familiar. Coura took pride in summoning them without somebody knocking down her door, though she expected it to occur at any moment.

{Well done. Now for the matching sword.}

In the same manner, she focused on the source of their shared power, guided the energy to her right palm while masking its presence, and grabbed the hilt of the demonic blade when the weapon appeared on command. She paused to study the slim sword before recalling how it saved her and her previous companions on two, separate occasions. In her current state, she ignored what remorse arose for ending the lives of those who wished them harm, yet part of her longed to understand the angels' purpose in Asteom.

"Why do I feel different?" Coura wondered as she pushed the thought aside in order to analyze herself in the mirror.

Soirée didn't respond.

I just...don't feel human, if that's possible. My emotions are all mixed up. I was nervous and scared at first, but now I'm eager to wield this power. I never seemed bloodthirsty until these appeared either, and I don't pity anyone when I recall what took place, not even Will or Marcus.

{*That's enough for the moment.*}

She released the spells with ease then began questioning Soirée about the experience; however, the demon kept quiet and shut herself away. For the first time since the incident in the training ground, Coura was alone in her mind.

*****

Byron rose before the sun ever since he returned to the MAA, not because he didn't want to sleep, but because it became necessary so the academy could function. In order for his fellow instructors to both teach their classes and tend to their duties during the rest of the day, they all needed to meet prior to when the students had lessons, which started around mid-morning.

As he made his way to the faculty's room near Symon's office, he tried to lighten his gloomy mood by thinking positively. *I should be thankful we reached more standstills than arguments, especially when it comes to Coura. It'd be better to do nothing with her for now than to push that subject.*

The week after returning home turned a chaotic mess. He'd taken care of Will and Marcus first before delivering information about the king's new law, which forced the academy to surrender any eligible mages to the army. Before his associates could process their situation, his student became involved in an attack that injured the assistant general.

Marcus' near-fatal wound incapacitated him for the next six days while the healers tended to him. Luckily, he remained in one of the most gifted mage's hands, so Byron trusted Master Chara and her apprentices with the soldier's life. After the commotion, the faculty grew so riled up they wouldn't consider other issues until the appointed problem child had been dealt with, which frustrated Byron to no end.

"I don't see why we're even discussing this!" Master Gage exclaimed. He acted as another dark mage instructor second only to Byron, though the man often believed their roles were reversed. "One possessed by a demon cannot be trusted, especially in a place filled with magic."

The shrill voice of Master Leni, who taught Coura's spellcasting course over the last few months, expressed her agreement. "I knew something was wrong when I worked with her. She's a troublemaker!"

A woman's soprano laugh echoed throughout the meeting space. Master Eva, Byron's pick for the most talented light mage at the academy, looked Leni and Gage over with a cool, amused gaze. "First of all, we verified the trainee showed no symptoms of possession until after she left for Verona, based on the herbalist's account. Second, we have yet to interview the group's escort. Byron conversed with Coura and deems her safe enough to be around. I trust his judgement."

She met his eyes in a silent gesture of reassurance before glaring at the next speaker, another light mage named Celia. Despite being a quiet person and the youngest of the faculty members, her soft voice carried strength to emphasize her authority and intelligence. "I can only vouch for those opposed to keeping Coura here because of the rumors and superstitions."

"There is truth to those," Symon added from across the table. "However, the individuals who are familiar with the results of demonic energy should have their opinions observed first. Now, who among us has experience interacting with the creatures' power?"

Byron, along with Terra and Gage, raised their hands, prompting the headmaster to encourage the trio to present what they knew.

Terra began by describing the wounds she treated over the years caused by deformed, vicious animals transformed into beasts by the unnatural energy and the victims' autopsies. After, Byron recounted several incidents of possessed humans and his fights against demonic creatures. He had never heard of someone staying in control of their mind, if they didn't die right away, which was the primary reason he opted to keep Coura in his care. Finally, Gage claimed his encounters had been dangerous and harmful, specifically to a southern town, though the circumstances sounded similar.

Once the three finished, Symon motioned to adjourn the meeting as he assumed they needed time to digest the information before moving forward with a decision. Byron made sure to catch his friend's arm to prevent the man from exiting while the others departed.

"Can I have a word?"

"What now?" the headmaster muttered and rubbed his temples.

"We've been so distracted by Coura, I haven't had the chance to talk with you about Verona and King Hernan's decision."

"I know." Symon pressed a hand to his forehead in distress. "Forget the law; His Highness has given us an ultimatum!"

Byron didn't comment on the accuracy of his friend's statement.

"The other faculty members aren't sharing their input yet, though I haven't pushed for responses due to our current predicament. Perhaps it is time to do so."

"I'll keep my ears open for their opinions, as well as the students'," he added while turning to leave.

This time, Symon seized Byron's arm to prevent him from exiting.

"Wait a moment, please." The impassive gaze his friend upheld relaxed into a sympathetic expression befitting the man's natural personality.

"What is it?"

"I'm sorry about Coura. I understand how much she means to you and how painful it must be to sit through what could be the planning of her death sentence. What's worse, you have to listen to a friend encourage condemning her."

Although he tried, Byron couldn't manage to completely hide the negative emotions reflected in his voice. "I appreciate the apology. Our decision might wind up being for the greater good, even if it means losing her. Still, I won't back down without giving her a chance."

"What do you mean?"

"What I said before about Coura's control over her mind is true. This is no ordinary demonic possession causing mayhem. She killed the two Yeluthians who attacked Will and Marcus without harming the young men. When did you ever hear of a demon trying to rescue humans?"

Symon's eyes widened a bit. "Never. In that case, consider me in agreement with you. Not only for the sake of researching her case, but also because I wouldn't feel comfortable imprisoning or executing an innocent student."

The headmaster's reassuring smile and the hand Symon placed on Byron's shoulder after lifted his spirits more than his friend could ever imagine.

***

While the assigned healers worked their magic on Marcus, his mind wandered back to Coura. He wasn't really concerned about her necessarily but what she had become. Their time together before that incident with the angel, as well as his interactions with Byron and Will, were in the past and lingered behind his responsibilities.

The memories keep replaying in my head, as though my mind is warning me to be proactive about the threat. King Hernan and his council ordered me to be an escort first and foremost, then Father recommended I sit in on the master mages' meetings, confirm the passing of the proposed law and collect the signed documents. With the winged stranger appearing to attack this place, as well as what happened to Coura, I don't believe the law is most important. What else can-

A soft yet sudden prodding in his tender midsection interrupted his assessment and spurred a gasp before warmth numbed the area. In response, he glanced at the healer, a blonde woman with gentle eyes and high cheekbones, causing her to lift her hands off his body.

196

"I'm sorry," she apologized before pointing at the same spot. "Did you feel pain here?"

Marcus admitted the pressure merely startled him and encouraged her to continue before turning to his thoughts again. All the healers he spoke with during his recovery were in their teens or early twenties. Since he fit in the middle of their age range at eighteen, they either fussed over him more than necessary, batted their eyelashes in a flirtatious manner, or remained doe-eyed. In each case, he was careful not to seem ungrateful for their assistance, no matter how drawn out their sessions or following conversations became.

His predicament grew tiresome since their superior named Chara needed to approve of his condition before he could leave the station. The instructors' meetings continued without him, making him question what they discussed and when they would reach a decision. He wanted to be present yet felt dismissed.

Marcus closed his eyes in an attempt to ease the tension building behind them before reflecting on his attacker and Coura instead. *The way she behaved when I arrived is proof the Yeluthian's appearance had been unexpected, which was why I stepped in. From what I could observe after he stabbed me, she summoned darker wings and found a sword in order to fight him. Her attitude seemed different compared to when we sparred, and the angel mentioned demons. Could it all be connected? What does this mean for Coura and her position here?*

The healer must have sensed his agitation because she gently placed a hand on his forehead. "I'm sensing a mild fever. It seems we'll never get you well enough!"

Although he recognized her remark as a joke, the comment increased his bitterness. He offered a smile to hide his sour mood and mentioned how some rest might be the best medicine for a while. To his relief, she accepted that as a cue to leave. Once alone, he stared at the nearest wall until he admitted he became too wound up to sleep. A hint of guilt gnawed at his chest, preventing him from considering a new subject, and his hands balled into fists.

Given how Coura acted and Byron's discretion regarding the service law, I think it's safe to assume the academy will take precautions to avoid trouble with King Hernan and his council. I suppose the documentation will be reviewed and accepted soon, which solves that problem. The next issue revolves around the Yeluthian's attack. Coura showed she's skilled enough to hold her own against one of their kind, but what if more arrive in Asteom? The news shouldn't be kept within the academy. I need to find somebody to talk to and figure out what's happening now.

Although he never experienced an injury as serious as a stab wound, he knew from the experienced soldiers' accounts not to rush a recovery unless it proved absolutely necessary. He became lost in his thoughts before eventually drifting to sleep.

When he woke during the night, a mug of herbal tea and a bowl of soup were cooling on his bedside table. He drank it all before a healer entered for another visit. One mage saw him in the morning for a general cleanup, then a second for a session in the afternoon, and a checkup after dinner allowed a third to ask if he needed anything else. Once the woman finished her evaluation, he shifted into a sitting position despite the slightly sore muscles underneath the closed wound.

I'll be on my feet in another day or two at this rate. Perhaps I should keep a journal until then so I don't forget the details. Would the academy permit me to send messages to the palace? Even if they don't trust me, I still have to try.

When his healer arrived the next morning, Marcus requested paper and a writing utensil. He noticed the mage's interest, but she shared her appreciation for his pursuit of an activity to keep his mind occupied and went to fetch him a quill, ink bottle, and enough parchment for a dozen letters. He debated asking how the letters would be delivered in order to assess the reaction yet decided against it. His reluctance saved him from looking foolish when the healer shared she would bring them to a messenger that afternoon.

Once she slipped out into the hallway, he studied the blank sheet of paper for a few minutes until he organized what he wished to say and who to address the letter to. First, he planned to write to his father in Verona, though mainly for the king's council, because believed they needed to know about the Yeluthian's appearance and Coura's involvement. In his opinion, the power she possessed seemed too useful to ignore, especially if more attacks took place. Then, he would craft personal messages to Byron, Will, and Coura to share an update on his recovery and welcome visitors. He considered composing one for his mother or his closest friend but grew concerned too many messages would raise suspicion from the MAA.

The first draft for the council ended up crumpled and tossed aside; the second followed suit as he struggled to form a professional tone and include those involved, their motivations, and their actions without rambling. In the end, Marcus opted to write as a son to his father, not one soldier to his commander, with the hope that the general would focus on the important pieces. He detailed the trip and detour to Fester while making sure to emphasize the reasoning behind the change. After mentioning the group's arrival at the academy, he described his fight against the rage-filled angel, his injury, and what happened to Coura, including the wings. He made sure not to share any names except for Byron's throughout the entire letter since he wasn't certain his father knew who Coura or Will were based on their first visit to the palace.

Near the end, he found himself yawning more than writing and remembered how he planned to send three other letters too.

I will not be returning immediately due to my recovery. There's much to look into, including the service law documents and the individual I spoke of earlier.

Marcus was barely able to sign the parchment and seal it before drifting to sleep.

*

The same healer from that morning took his father's letter away after his nap, as promised. Meanwhile, he contemplated writing to Byron and what he would even say. No doubt the master mage had precious spare time; however, as much as he hated

199

burdening the man, he needed to know what took place between the faculty and headmaster. He scratched a note requesting the master mage visit when possible, specifying Byron should not make time for him but see him when an opportunity presented itself.

Regarding Will, Marcus didn't believe the herbalist would be too busy to stop by the medical station unless he found a library or similar space to continue his research. He added the jest in his message's conclusion, folded the paper, then set it beside the former.

Lastly, he thought about contacting Coura, and the idea caused him to frown. The entire memory of their fight in the training ground against the stranger played again in his mind. What he saw and heard remained vivid because he memorized the experience for the inevitable interrogation with the academy's headmaster, and potentially others. He would tell them the truth, that he had never met an angel before.

Did a demon actually create the wings and sword? I've only known tales about the beings possessing humans and the Yeluthians protecting Asteom. If demons are involved with Coura, then the angel had every reason to attack her. Still, he fought against me. It seemed like I became an enemy because I stood in his way, not because I defended her. On the other hand, demons are meant to cause destruction, and she didn't do that. She protected me, killed him as herself, knelt to cover my wound, and called for help. Would the headmaster condemn her for murder even if it had been a result of self-defense? Should I even bother with a message at this point?

When the next mage stopped by later that afternoon, Marcus handed her his letters to Byron and Will before telling her he no longer needed the supplies. With a conflicting heart and mind, he lied on his back to rest while the healer began her spell.

***

It took Coura six days of practicing before she felt confident casting the wings and sword while suppressing the demonic energy. Soon, Byron said the faculty members would no longer need to question her, though she had to remain in her room for the time being. She didn't the order mind. In fact, perfecting the new abilities spurred an eagerness she hadn't experienced in months. With both mornings and afternoons free, she could work with Soirée whenever she wanted. The demon remained silent for the most part, yet a twinge of satisfaction often came from that corner of her mind.

The issue they faced shifted to practicing wing stretches and movements to make fighting on the ground easier. Coura tried what she could manage given the space and improved in the short amount of time, but nothing could replace being outdoors.

She grew so accustomed to the solitude that a knock on the door caused her to jump. Thankfully, it happened during a break when she sat on the side of her bed, allowing her to call for whoever stood in the corridor to enter right away. As Byron stepped inside, shut the door, and trudged over to the desk chair, her mouth fell open.

"You look terrible," she told her mentor.

"I know," he grumbled in response and rubbed his tired, pink eyes. She had never seen him go so long without shaving, which resulted in the start of a charcoal-colored beard. Besides his weary gaze, it seemed physically apparent he missed out on at least one, proper night's sleep. His shoulders slumped forward and his chin dipped to touch his chest, as if keeping himself upright was a burden.

When she considered the cause of such distress, her heart sank at the thought of the instructors and headmaster reaching a decision regarding her presence. "What's wrong?"

Byron shook his head at her concerned tone and leaned back in a casual manner. "Don't worry. I'm here for a personal visit."

Coura crossed her arms. "You make me sound like a prisoner."

"Technically, you are, and before you mention it, we still haven't reached a verdict on what to do with you yet. I need to ask for a favor."

"A favor?"

They leaned forward at the same time, then he met her eyes and held them with a serious stare.

"Did you discuss what happened in the training ground to anyone outside our meetings?"

Coura shook her head. "Not a word. I never left my room except for those. Why? What's going on?"

"That's not good." Byron chewed on his bottom lip for a moment before continuing. "We're facing another problem at the moment. Word spread to Verona and King Hernan about the Yeluthian who attacked you and what unnatural powers you used against him. From their point of view, the headmaster possesses what they consider to be a weapon of sorts using demonic magic."

"You're joking!"

Before she could comprehend what this meant, he went on like she didn't make the outburst.

"On top of that, we still haven't figured out what to do about the proposal they're calling the Mage Service Law. King Hernan has us backed into a corner." Byron explained the ultimatum presented to the MAA, as well as the faculty's concern about Verona's citizens believing the academy would be betraying them by declining to allow additional mages to serve the capital city.

When he finished, Coura felt too upset to sit still and hopped off her bed to begin pacing. "That's ridiculous! How can they consider any of this your fault? Does having the freedom to choose what we do with our magic mean nothing? I can't-"

"Calm down."

She paused to glance at her mentor without hiding her surprise. "You're okay with this?"

"I most certainly am not," he answered while rising to stand in front of her. "In any case, I want what's best for everybody. If it means keeping the academy open and its residents safe, we'll need to comply."

"But..."

"That's also why I came to talk with you; I wanted you to know ahead of time what we plan to do. If the king and his council didn't learn about what took place before, or rather, you specifically, we could have kept it a secret."

The fact that she would be going to the capital city along with the eldest trainees dawned on her then. "I'm still being sent to Verona, aren't I?"

Byron nodded and put his hands on her shoulders, forcing her to look into his emerald eyes once more. The idea of being forced into serving the kingdom bothered her, yet she wasn't completely against leaving East Hoover.

"Why else did you come here?" she pressed to push the topic aside.

"I'd like to say I believe you told us the whole story, yet something tells me there's more you don't want to share in front of the other instructors. Now's your chance."

The invitation caught her off guard, and she fumbled for a reply. Soirée's presence instantly burned in the back of her head, reminding her of their most recent argument regarding the subject. Coura wasn't sure about revealing their connection so soon but trusted her mentor more than anybody. Meanwhile, the demon remained opposed to enlightening him and threatened various punishments if she did.

He'll understand. It may help him defend me against the rest of the master mages and the people in the palace.

{Or, he could change his mind about you. Would it make you more or less trustworthy if they knew you shared your soul with a demon?}

Although she didn't agree with Soirée's comment regarding Byron's integrity, Coura figured she could use some time to adjust and tucked the valuable piece of information about their connection away. With that settled, she shook her head.

Her mentor frowned in response, removed his hands to resume rubbing his eyes, then moved to exit. "Just remember, I'm ready to listen if there *is* anything you need to discuss."

"As long as you remember you can't function without sleep," she added while placing her hands on her hips.

He glanced over his shoulder at her with a startled expression before grinning. "Well, here I thought you didn't care about my health. How touching!"

Her sympathy turned bitter when she felt her cheeks growing hot at his playful tone. "You're delusional," she grumbled before pointing at the exit. "Go take a nap!"

Byron's resulting chuckle followed him out before the door closed behind him.

The Mage Service Law

Three days after Symon received a letter asking for a response regarding the proposed law, another arrived bearing King Hernan's signature, and the man demanded an answer on behalf of the MAA. Byron and his fellow master mages expected those in Verona to press for a decision; however, they were unable to figure out a way to decline the Mage Service Law without being branded as traitors. The headmaster replied with a request to update the requirements by suggesting the trainees most fit for combat be sent instead of every graduate. He intended to lighten the impact on their students by creating the perception that it would be an honor to go instead of a rule forcing them to serve against their will.

The attempt must have been too obvious, though. The king's final letter included a short timeframe for the academy to accept before his council would personally see to their cooperation. With no other options available, Symon documented his agreement, completed the necessary paperwork, and sent their messenger to Verona the following morning.

That afternoon, Byron went to visit his friend. The two became close over the years, so he could walk into the private office whenever he needed to, which didn't happen often. Jann wasn't in the front room, leading him to assume she'd been dismissed for the day. Everybody still seemed stressed about the incident in the training ground; their mindsets would worsen when news of the approved law circulated.

Based on his conclusion, he wasn't surprised when he found the headmaster alone at a desk with a half-empty bottle of wine. A sorrowful expression stretched his features, and he didn't raise his eyes at his guest, who remained standing in the open doorway.

"Read this," Symon ordered and held out a piece of paper for Byron, prompting him to enter, close and lock the door, then take the parchment before sitting in one of two empty chairs across from the desk.

He loves this place and has been here longer than most instructors. The students are like his own children, so I imagine he's blaming himself for this while picturing the worst scenarios. It's already difficult to cope with the loss of a trainee once they're in a position away from Easter Hoover. That pain will double when we, as their teachers, learn what we couldn't prepare them for during their new assignments, like a battle with the northerners. He must also be considering himself a failure by letting this happen, even though it is by no means his fault. What's frightening is no one knows if this will be a change for the better because it's never been done before.

True to Byron's observations, Symon buried his face in both hands while mumbling incoherent sentences. After skimming the letter, his friend's behavior made sense.

It had been signed by a general named Preston, a man he recognized from their many meetings at the capital. The commander already crafted a rough draft of the new recruits' combat training, an outline of how they will be divided among the generals' companies, and the two-week timeline for transitioning from the academy to the palace where they will live with the soldiers.

General Preston ended the message with two requests. First, Symon must send a copy of the documents containing the names and information for each year of mage trainees. This way, no one would be exempt from the new law, similar to how regular troops can't abandon their positions or summons. Second, the king's council needed a faculty member permanently relocated to act as the representative for the mage recruits. They already housed a master light mage who supervised the healers, but nobody else.

Byron got the impression the general grew impatient more than worried, making him wonder if trouble surrounded the capital city, northern border, or another location. He stopped himself from diving into the notion before it consumed him and reluctantly set the paper down. Symon hadn't moved, but the headmaster no longer mumbled.

The pair sat in silence until he decided it would do neither of them any good to voice their concerns at that point. Instead, he requested a drink from the well-stocked cabinet along the back wall, then the two shared their sorrows together.

***

As Marcus roamed the halls of the Magical Arts Academy for the first time in weeks, the building's atmosphere felt livelier than he remembered based on his arrival in East Hoover. That morning, Master Chara inspected his torso and instructed him to perform various exercises in order to test the previously damaged muscles. She deemed him healthy enough to be on his own again, so he spent no time lingering around the medical station.

He made his way to the mess hall, snatched a couple pieces of fresh fruit left out from lunch, and headed straight to the training ground reserved for physical combat since the healer permitted him to exercise as long as he didn't push himself. With her blessing, he practiced all afternoon with some trainees until his stomach growled enough to distract him. Then, he hurried to the busying dining area.

That was when he realized the occupants had been chatting wildly throughout the entire day while strolling in either an eager or nervous manner. When Marcus found Will and joined the herbalist's table, he learned the reason behind the odd behavior. His messy-haired, former companion appeared the same as during their travels, if not more energetic because of the surrounding group who looked suited for studying rather than fighting.

"It's a relief to see you up," Will greeted him with a genuine smile. "How are you feeling now that your injury healed?"

"Better than ever. Have you been adjusting?"

The herbalist nodded then proceeded to ramble about the experience while Marcus ate. Eventually, the others at the table emptied their plates and excused themselves, giving the two privacy. During the following pause, he sensed the same, anxious energy that filled the corridors earlier and inquired about the change.

"Is it obvious?" Will asked before releasing an awkward chuckle as his eyes wandered around the room.

Marcus mirrored the gaze. Each person's face appeared tightly controlled into an expressionless stare or melancholy frown, and most simply ate without conversing and went on their way. The negative mood had him considering Coura and the stranger who attacked them again. "What happened?"

"The king passed a new law yesterday," his companion began at a quieter volume. "No one knows what the future will be like, though I believe a lot of students regret coming to the academy." He went on to share the details of this service law, including how mage trainees would be forcibly stationed in the palace for additional training and as extra protection, presumably against Nim-Vala to the north. Every year, graduates would transfer to Verona and serve in the army for three years before becoming eligible to accept a position elsewhere. The instructors had openly shared details about the new policy when it passed, including their attempts to stop it.

All the while, Marcus kept his mouth shut. As an assistant general, he had been familiar with the proposal for months and didn't consider the emotional impact on those currently around him. Witnessing how poorly the mages felt toward King Hernan because of the decision, no matter the reasoning, made him wish for the time to pass sooner.

"They also heard about the murdered Yeluthian and what happened to Coura," Will added. "Somebody told me the king doesn't fully believe in the angel's existence while others are saying he blames the attack involving you on the headmaster. It sounds like his council is interested in Coura too. They requested she join the others traveling to the capital, and no one is pleased because she uses demonic energy. I guess that hinders the other mages' abilities, but I didn't quite understand the explanation."

Marcus tried not to gawk once he recalled the letter he sent to his father and superiors, which seemed to have had unforeseen implications. *It sounds like it was only a matter of time before the king's council put this law in place, but the headmaster and faculty didn't plan for them to learn of the angel or Coura, at least not right away. Were they leaving the reveal for another occasion, or were they dismissing the idea of sharing it altogether? Did the people here intend to keep the demonic power a secret from everybody outside East Hoover?*

When he didn't continue the conversation, Will rose, went over to the bins used for collecting dirty dishes, and left the hall without another word. Marcus pushed the remaining food around on his plate while contemplating his position until the kitchen staff started cleaning up for the night. He returned to his assigned room after, the one he hadn't used for some time, and laid down to rest his weary body. Whatever was destined to take place with the mages, including Coura, would happen no matter what he did, so his next goal focused on returning to the palace and speaking with his father about the future.

***

No visible surprise showed on any of Byron's colleagues' faces when he volunteered to be the representative in Verona for their graduating trainees. With another master mage already present to lead the healers, the logical option would be to send somebody experienced with dark energy in order to split the responsibilities. Gage and Leni seemed competent enough to take over his work and few students without issue, as they'd done for the last several months. His only concern had been that the faculty would oppose his sacrifice because he became too valuable to the MAA; however, they vouched for his professionalism when it came to dealing with the king's council and understood his unspoken desire to supervise those traveling to the capital.

Classes resumed immediately after the law's announcement. Those assigned to leave would copy their own paperwork and hand it over to Byron or the master light mage upon their arrival. Under Symon's orders, predetermined groups would depart each morning for ten days with Byron leading any stragglers the final morning. He assumed responsibility for this schedule since the headmaster dealt with notices and backlash from the students' families, who felt blindsided by the news.

Thankfully, a majority of the trainees didn't protest their decision, though the atmosphere in the main building remained solemn. No one smiled, conversations stayed brief, and classes he peeked in on appeared dreary. Never in all his life did he see his home so disheartened.

*

Just before sunrise on the first day of the transfer, those scheduled to travel ate breakfast then met Byron at the front gate with their belongings and paperwork. Since each person managed their own documentation, he only needed to glance over the papers for approval. Together with an appointed, trusted leader who received proper direction beforehand, the group of about a dozen students moved out.

According to the council's letter, once the mages arrived, they would be provided with a room, clothing for their training sessions, and a schedule listing their supervisor's name. Then, the trainees would go through interviews with the generals, their assistants, and the master mages in order to assign the newcomers to a division. When Byron finished the journey, he needed to double-check the placements and help organize the magic lessons he would manage. He expected it to take weeks for everybody to get used to the routine, but he felt certain the situation would look up afterward.

It must. No one can survive mentally or emotionally if it doesn't, though King Hernan is a smart, strategic man despite his attitude. It'll be interesting to see how he treats the new recruits, if he interacts with them at all.

At the end of the day, the single issue Byron still faced had to do with Coura. How the people in the capital found out about the demonic power was anybody's guess, yet his concern had been that they would punish her, not request her presence in the palace. He begged Symon to reconsider sending her by changing her age to prevent her from traveling with the others or releasing her from the academy in order to break the connection, but it became a hopeless effort. No matter how frequently he expressed his distaste, he knew their opportunity had passed.

"Where would she go if we send her away?" Symon argued, projecting his own worry during those moments. "The townsfolk who returned to Neston never claimed her, and from what you've said, she doesn't remember the place anyway. Besides, the king and his generals already know she's here and what she can do. Unless we arrange for somebody else to take her position and mimic the demonic energy, they won't be fooled. What you should be concerned about is how they seem to view her as a unique weapon of sorts. At least, that's how their messages described her. The best advice I can offer is not to try and hide *her* but the magic itself. Introduce her to the king's council, warn her about their intentions, and advise her to lay low."

Byron decided then to have Coura accompany him once the other groups set out. That way, he could keep a close eye on her outside the academy in case the unnatural power appeared again. He hadn't sensed more after the incident where she messed with the energy in her room, yet the chance of something going wrong didn't lessen. He and Symon restructured the groups to depart over nine days instead of ten, leaving the last for the pair and anybody else who did not leave prior, for whatever reason.

I'll need to find the time to visit Coura and share what Symon and I discussed. I doubt she learned more than what I've been informing her of. It doesn't help that she's confined to her room and the students don't want to go near her. I just can't predict what will happen when we arrive at the palace.

A number of possible conflicts flooded his mind, stemming from both her attitude and lack of understanding to the king's hubris and relationships in the capital. With a yawn, he shoved the paranoia aside and prepared for the toll the next couple weeks would take.

*

The evening after the first set of trainees departed, Byron ran into Will in a hallway on the way to his room. He avoided bothering

211

the young man more than he had to because of how the intense questioning brought up haunting memories, but it had been the herbalist who walked directly in his path to spark a conversation.

"How are you, Master Byron?"

"Fine, except for the amount of work I'm dealing with. Are you becoming familiar with East Hoover?"

Byron considered how bright Will's future looked if he remained at the MAA, or at the very least in the populated, northeastern area. Symon accepted the young man as a scholarly student as long as he followed a schedule like everyone else and informed the instructors of his experience and goals. The potential connections with light mages and the students focusing on academia would provide invaluable insight. That was also without mentioning the combat skills and knowledge necessary for safely living and traveling alone.

Will's next words thwarted such potential accomplishments. "I want to come to Verona with you and the other mages."

"What? Why?" Given how many surprises he received over the past few weeks, Byron couldn't keep from sharing his astonishment.

"I never could stay in one place. There's plenty out in the world I hope to explore, and I plan to document it all. Besides, the palace's texts contain rare information on medicines, potions, and botany, more than I managed to study last time."

"This isn't a friendly visit like the last trip," Byron said sternly. "I won't be present to watch over you, and to be frank, neither will anybody else."

"I understand. That's why I asked Marcus to help me."

Will shrank back a bit under Byron's resulting, questioning gaze.

"Did you now?"

"I need to continue training in order to face the rest of the world."

Byron tried to repress the smile creeping up on him and covered his mouth with a fist to hide it. *He has no reason to ask me about going to Verona, except to be considered a student so those in the palace won't turn him away. I suppose there's no harm in him not staying here if he wants to leave, though I'm honestly surprised Marcus agreed. I would think the assistant general has more important matters to attend to, but that's not my problem.*

"Fine. I can add you to one of the groups."

When he finally caved in and grinned, Will released a shaky sigh of relief.

"Thank you. I promise I won't cause trouble for you or the trainees moving to the capital city."

"I appreciate that," Byron concluded and began walking toward his room; however, Will hovered at his elbow. "Is there anything else?"

"I also wondered if you've been all right. A lot of rumors are in the air, and I can't imagine the stress from her."

Of course, he knew Will was referring to Coura, but the way the young man spat out the last word made him worry. *I never conversed with him after the council interviews. I'm not shocked he's been holding in his emotions about the incident outside Fester, especially after the state he wound up in. I suppose I expected there to be more fear instead of this hatred I sense.*

"What did you hear?" he inquired to flesh out the reasoning.

The herbalist rubbed his arm nervously and wouldn't meet Byron's eyes. "Everyone who saw the results of the fight shared enough to recreate the scene for those of us who weren't there. I never revealed what I went through because you and the other instructors asked me not to, but the incident sounded similar. I wasn't aware of how horrible that energy is and how it bothers light and dark mages. The more I hear, the less comfortable I feel supporting somebody who uses it."

They approached Byron's room and waited while a pair of whispering girls strolled by. Because of his age, status, and professional relationship with Coura, none of the trainees would go so far as to comment on her around him. He expected that and didn't care for gossip.

What did concern him was how twisted Will's perception of his student became. Anyone with an inkling of magical potential could feel the unpleasant sensation brought about by demonic energy, as it seemed to seep into a person and irritate whatever power it finds. Even Byron hadn't been immune when he experienced it in the past and around Coura after she cast the unnatural spells. Despite that, he grew familiar enough with her to trust it didn't muddle her judgement.

Will would have no reason to let that bother him physically, so he based his view of her on his experience with the Yeluthians, in addition to what others were saying.

"I appreciate how patient you're being," Byron began once they found themselves alone again.

"I hoped to avoid bothering you, considering all that's happening…"

"That's not what I mean. Ever since the four of us left Verona, we dealt with some unexpected events."

A twinge of fear flashed across the young man's face.

"I can handle it," Byron continued. "I did handle it in the past, and so has Marcus. He might not possess as much experience, but the generals are no pushovers. If you plan on traveling to the palace, lean on him and trust his training. Think of him as a friend and a source of comfort when you're discouraged. The most terrifying moments throughout my life left me with nightmares for weeks."

Will's silence and uneasiness told him they had that last part in common.

"It'll get better," he added with a reassuring smile. "I can offer you some advice to help to ease the shock."

"Yes, please."

Better for a senseless person to obediently follow sound advice until they're back on their feet than to sink deeper into fear and rumors.

"First, work harder and more diligently than ever. Your body and mind should be exhausted by the end of the day so your sleep is dreamless. Eventually, you'll overcome the nightmares, but it takes time to heal. Mind you, don't overstress yourself. It's necessary for a man to balance his responsibilities, both professionally and socially, which is why my second suggestion is to embrace the friendships you created. There should be plenty of opportunities to meet people once we're in the capital. Learn their stories, and listen to their comments. You just might find yourself sympathizing with their experiences."

Will had been nodding constantly to show he absorbed every word. "What is the third piece of advice?" he pressed as Byron turned to place a hand on the doorknob.

"I suggest you visit Coura before heading to Verona."

Even without glancing behind, he knew the idea bothered the young man based on the appalled tone of the resulting question.

"Why should I?"

"Remember what I just mentioned about getting to know other people? When we met you, that was her first venture away from East Hoover. She had been vulnerable to the dangers roaming Asteom. I see her as often as I can, and it seems like you two are a lot alike."

"What do you mean?" Will mumbled with less disgust, prompting Byron to look at the young man.

"Her fear is as real as yours, though I believe it's more severe because I can sense the energy resting inside her. You might not understand, but Coura is a victim of a demonic attack where the presence latched onto her center of power. Nobody fully comprehends what happened, not even her, yet she's being kept away from everyone except me. She's also being forced to transfer, doubling the strain."

"Why isn't she allowed to leave her room if what you say is true? Is she really safe to be around?"

"I believe so. You think ill of her because of what she did to the angels, but not once did she outright strike without reason, according to your reports. What were you afraid of when you saw her that night outside Fester? Was it the wings, the magic, or the blade? Do you believe she would have killed you too?"

Will didn't answer, but Byron didn't expect one right away.

"In any case, our interviews proved Coura is not dangerous as long as she isn't thrown into an immediate conflict," he went on while opening the door. "With the new law and what took place regarding the second attack, we as leaders of the Magical Arts Academy figure everyone needs space to adjust. Speak to her when you can, though not about that particular topic. Find something else to discuss. I think you'll understand what I mean and learn you could each use a friend."

***

Since she wasn't permitted outside to practice physical combat, Coura put extra effort into her magical training, which still left her sweaty and breathing harder. She pushed her body more than before, testing the duration of the wings' manifestation in order to build the muscles they put weight on. This lasted from the moment she rose until around the time she would be interrupted for supper. Although Soirée refused to give out praise, the demon sounded satisfied enough with her progress to leave her alone for the rest of the afternoon. Thankfully, the kitchen servers always knocked before slipping into the room, providing ample time for her to dismiss the spell. The last thing she needed was for Byron to burst through the door in an uproar again.

Over the past few days, the faculty became focused on other matters. Her mentor made an appearance a day earlier to inform her the eligible trainees were already being sent to the capital. From what she counted, they reached the sixth day of the transition, giving her three days to relax.

Coura wondered how the rest of the student body handled the changes and what their thoughts were on the new law. She assumed no one felt too excited considering the crunched timeframe for the transfer alongside the drama surrounding its proposal. Oddly enough, Soirée never brought up the subject. She asked for the demon's opinion several times when her mind wandered to the near future but received only vague answers before being told to continue working. This led her to put all her attention toward controlling and maintaining the pool of energy in her center instead of worrying about her classmates.

During a break, she closed her eyes and relaxed on the bed while remaining motionless and thoughtless in order to reach a near-sleep state until a knock at the door roused her. The time had her fully expecting an assistant from the kitchen, so she called for them to enter.

"I hope I'm not bothering you," came a timid yet familiar voice.

She opened her eyes, sat up, and spotted Will standing in the doorway. "What are you doing here?"

He accepted her response as an invitation to enter and slipped inside before closing the door noiselessly behind him. "I thought I would visit."

Coura rubbed the back of her neck then gestured to the desk chair. "You can have a seat, if you want."

It had been weeks since she interacted with somebody other than Byron and the instructors, so she didn't know what to say to begin the conversation. Additionally, Will had been a victim of the circumstances, so she worried what he thought about her.

Whatever his own concerns were, though, he behaved just as awkwardly. He never took his eyes off her as he pulled the chair over and sat on its edge with his hands folded in front of him.

She tilted her head at his posture. "Why so formal?"

He simply shrugged and continued staring with a hesitation she didn't see from him before. Will had always been the first person to find a topic to spark conversation, yet this time, they looked at each other without speaking until he revealed the reason a minute later.

"Byron said you're lonely."

The unexpected comment left Coura dumbfounded, and her cheeks heated a bit while she struggled to respond. Her expression must have been a funny sight because Will raised a hand to cover his mouth, but not before she caught the corners of his lips turning upward.

"Leave it to Byron to overexaggerate," she replied with a chuckle to hide her embarrassment.

Fortunately, that exchange lightened Will's attitude. He slouched forward and let his shoulders drop in a relaxed manner.

"You're not lonely? I remember you hated staying inside the shared space in the palace."

"Being alone has never been an issue. I was upset because we were forced into one spot without knowing why."

Coura readjusted her position so she could lean against the wall beside her bed and glanced at the ceiling before recalling their time in Verona. That had only taken place a couple months ago, yet her memories of the palace seemed so distant.

When neither of them continued, she decided to switch topics and inquire about the Mage Service Law. Of course, Byron informed her of the details from his perspective, yet she wondered what the students thought.

Will proved to be the perfect person to ask since he kept up with the news floating around the academy as attentively as the trainees who lived in East Hoover for years. The longer he spoke, the more his personality returned as well. He even referenced people Coura didn't know, mainly light mages and scholarly students. Based on their insight, a fine line had been established, separating those who accepted the transition and those who detested the idea of being pushed into the capital. Evidently, it was too late to argue with the decision.

An assistant from the kitchen made his appearance during the middle of their discussion and looked amazed to find somebody else in the room. The pair cleared the platter of food together before Will excused himself and departed with a promise to visit her tomorrow.

Part of her doubted he would stop by again, but Coura still felt touched by his sudden interest in her and hoped their developing friendship would last.

*

The herbalist kept his word, though he stopped by in the morning immediately after she rose and got dressed. His eyes wandered over the scraggly state of her hair and unmade bed from a night of tossing and turning before he dove straight into new information regarding the group who departed within the past hour. He knew three of the trainees from their shared meals, and all shared their concern about traveling to the capital since they hailed from less populated villages.

Coura recognized the names yet couldn't get a word in between Will's. *He's definitely acting normal today.*

{*It's normal for this boy to chat so much?*}

Soirée's presence slid to the front of Coura's mind to observe their interaction.

He talks more than anyone I've ever met, but it's nice to have company, especially when I've been stuck with you.

{*Hmm... I remember him.*}

You do?

When the demon assumed control over her unconscious body, Coura had no recollection of what transpired with the pair of angels. Pieces returned when the one named Devan pursued her, but the scenes proved too confusing for her to comprehend until Soirée described the events in chronological order. Some memories of the night outside Fester returned with accompanying headaches upon hearing the explanations.

{*He remained in the area, hiding behind a tree for cover. Based on his terrified expression, he didn't appear worth the effort to approach. The cursed light-blooded beings ignored him as well.*}

Coura went cold at the thought of Will observing the horrific events play out. The detailed descriptions were enough to send a chill down her spine, yet he had been present to witness it all.

While she contemplated how that affected his mentality, he said her name warily.

"Sorry," she apologized and smiled to mask the ill feeling inside. "I got lost in my thoughts for a moment."

The enthusiasm with which Will spoke faded, and he grew tense as he lowered his eyes to the floor. "You looked gloomy just now."

A second later, Soirée echoed what she steadily realized, though the demon's voice tingled with amusement instead of reflecting Coura's displeasure.

{*He's afraid of you, Dear One, and rightly so.*}

I was only trying to rescue him...

"It must have been my imagination," the herbalist added while rising to stand. Although he shook his head afterward, his strained expression showed the past still bothered him. "Anyway, I need to eat and find Marcus."

"Marcus?" Coura hadn't thought about the soldier in days, aside from recalling his injury and how she struggled to cover the bloody wound. The light mages were skilled enough for her to trust them with his life, but Byron didn't mention any details regarding his recovery. The reminder that Marcus probably disliked her as much as, if not more than, Will left a bitter taste in her mouth.

"I'm going to ask him to train me once we get to Verona."

"Wait, you're coming to the capital too?"

She heard Will's stomach growl faintly to interrupt their conversation, and he wrapped his arms around his waist while blushing.

"I can tell you more when I return around dinnertime," he promised, waved, then exited.

Not long after, the ever-punctual kitchen hand made an appearance just when she grew hungry. Coura had enough time for lunch and her dark spells with Soirée before Will returned.

"How did it go?" she inquired from where she stood by the window to observe the weather, which depicted a cloudy yet colorful transition into fall.

"Good, actually. Everybody seems less upset, and Marcus agreed to help. I'll be traveling with his group tomorrow."

"That soon?"

"I guess he needed his superior to request his presence given the extended stay was for medical reasons. The head healer sent a message stating he's fine to make the journey, and Marcus received a response yesterday. Byron placed him with the others leaving in the morning, though, so that's when I'm scheduled to go."

Coura stretched her arms upward to ease the tightness in her back that arose around the later part of the day. "Why the change from East Hoover to Verona? Surely they can find you space and supplies to do your research here."

This time, Will laughed in a bashful manner, which sounded like the most natural response she heard from him. "I have no doubt the academy would treat me well, but I've always been a traveler. Because of my interests, it doesn't make sense for me to stay in one place. Besides, I…"

"What is it?"

His lips curved into a frown. "It might be worthwhile to investigate what information the palace holds on Yeluthia. What happened with the angels is important for people to understand."

When he didn't continue, Coura figured he would keep the details a secret. She hadn't been expecting him to bring up the shared incident and felt guilty since it caused him to close himself off from her again.

{*What a child, hiding behind such simplistic emotions.*}

Shut up, Coura snapped at the demon's remark. *Now seems like the best opportunity to talk about your power.*

"Will, can I ask you something?" she began in a serious tone. "Are you afraid of me because of what happened?"

The herbalist shifted uncomfortably at the question. "Of course not…"

"Tell me the truth," she demanded when he hesitated.

This time, he paused to contemplate her request before answering again. "I'm not afraid of you. In fact, I enjoy being with you. We sat and talked for hours the past two days, and it brought back fun memories from our journey. When I was in danger, you stood against those angels without feeling scared either."

"I wouldn't say I wasn't scared," Coura added as she reflected on the moment. "Letting my fear show wouldn't have done any good."

"Even if that's true, you still risked your life to protect me, and Marcus the second time. I believe you care about people who are in trouble, but the magic you use to do it worries me, especially the wings. Demons are mysterious, wicked creatures, yet you wield their power. I never expected a Yeluthian to be so cruel. I don't know who to trust anymore. That's why I'm determined to learn about them for myself alongside the friends I made here."

Will's confident words took Coura back, though she felt pleased with his resolve, as well as how he admitted his view regarding her. Soirée's sweet giggling echoed in her head for some, unknown reason before they resumed talking about Marcus. The upper-level soldier healed fine and worked in the training ground when Will found him earlier. The update resulted in another sense of relief.

"He said I might be able to assist with the supply transfers, like blankets, clothing, and other items for the new rooms being put to use," the herbalist finished.

"I'm certain the palace will be bustling for a few days at least," Coura commented while crossing her arms and staring out the window.

"Are you going to be traveling with Byron?"

She nodded. "We're the only two scheduled to leave on the final day. I imagine nobody wants to be around me."

Will rose from the desk chair and went to the door. "Marcus and I can make sure everything is ready when you get there then."

As he exited, she silently wished the two a safe trek.

*

The next couple days passed in an uneventful fashion. Coura managed to fill two packs with her belongings while abandoning several, useless items of personal value she collected over the years. Byron explained how the palace would provide armor and weapons for them when necessary, so aside from clothing, not much else would be needed. She could also manifest the demonic blade with less than a thought, though she doubted anyone would allow her to do so without a valid reason.

During that time alone, Coura often found herself reflecting on Will's words. *He believes I'm brave because I rushed in to help him and Marcus when they were in danger. We haven't known each other for long, yet he has so much faith in me. I'd like to learn about this power so I can use it for that purpose; then, nobody needs to worry about me.*

{Valiant words, for a human.}

You mean a human with a demonic pet. Coura chuckled to herself when Soirée seethed at the nickname.

{You half-witted brat.}

Is that the best insult you can come up with?

Several curses followed her taunt and resulted in Soirée fading back to a corner of her mind, abruptly ending the magical exercises for the rest of the day.

*

The evening before her departure, Coura hardly slept, leaving her tired but not unprepared for the days ahead. Her nerves came alive from a mixture of excitement and anxiousness at the idea of returning to the capital city. Not only would she train with some of the finest soldiers in Asteom, but she would be assigned missions and given duties to fulfill. No more classes beneath her skill level or mindless work.

Being considered an adult capable of acting on her own felt invigorating; however, she knew better than to overestimate her freedom. With Byron and the dozens of trainees moving as well, the whole palace would soon figure out what made her different. There would be no shortage of eyes constantly watching and waiting for her to slip up.

I should be extra careful not to use demonic energy, or even speak of it. Who knows what could happen if I scare someone by accident.

{Simple. We silence them.}

Coura shuddered at the sudden bloodthirstiness in Soirée's voice. *Do you always have to listen to my thoughts?*

{A single body possessing two minds allows limited room for privacy, Dear One.}

"Why do I get the impression you're not really trying to give me any?" Coura grumbled in response.

A pair of footsteps approached the door before Byron entered without knocking. *Not him too! Why is it nobody can show a little respect?*

{Would you like me to go into detail?}

"It's about time," she said by way of greeting while brushing aside the demon's comment. "You look better than a few days ago."

"I've been able to sleep now that matters are settled and plans are going into action," he replied. "Are you ready?"

She hurried to don her cloak, grabbed and shouldered the bags, then glanced around the room for any missing items. Once satisfied she had packed everything, Coura turned to her mentor with an eager smile.

Byron raised an eyebrow. "Is that all you're bringing?"

"Do I need more?"

"Compared to some of the other students, particularly the girls, you're just traveling rather light."

"I don't exactly have a lot," Coura added before following him into the hallway where they moved toward the front gate. Along the way, several students cast her both glares and fearful glances, so she ignored them as well as she could and remembered what Will shared during his first visit.

Demonic energy isn't a power they can or should trust when it lingers in their home. Their hatred is for the best, I suppose.

Astonishingly, Soirée remained silent.

The fresh air that hit Coura's face as they went outside smelled like rain and chilled her to the bone, which wasn't surprising given the change of seasons. The slight scent of hay also tickled her nose until she noticed Headmaster Symon approaching with the reins for two mares in each hand.

Horses?

"You're right on time," Byron greeted the man before glancing over at her to explain. "I'm rather sick of walking everywhere, so I figured we could make better time and avoid spending more of it in this weather. Have you ever ridden before?"

Coura shook her head.

He grunted, as if expecting that answer, then stepped aside to speak with the headmaster.

As she stared at the ordinary-looking beasts, a memory too foggy to recall completely formed in the back of her mind.

She remembered being a child in an unfamiliar place with homes along a dirt path and evergreen trees everywhere past the buildings. A horse drank from the trough directly in front of her, and she heard herself giggling as she watched the animal intensely. Its owner appeared at the animal's side with a wide, toothy grin.

"You like my girl Sunkiss?"

Coura bobbed her head up and down without removing her eyes from the horse.

"I'll bet she'd appreciate a treat. Would you like to give her one?" the stranger asked while removing a carrot from his satchel.

In the memory, her heart pounded during the encounter with what she considered an exotic creature. She snatched the vegetable from the man's hand after.

Coura's head began to ache when she let the memory continue.

"Careful now, watch your fingers. The old girl likes to nibble!"

Oblivious to the traveler's words, she leaned on the water trough to raise the carrot to the animal's face. It sniffed its treat, started to take a hesitant bite, then did so. All the while, Coura swung her head from side to side in order to stare into its intelligent eyes. A sharp pain in her hand spurred a cry before she dropped the half-eaten vegetable into the water.

"It bit me!"

Like any child would do, she whimpered as silent tears slid down her cheeks. The man examined her hand and apologized for the resulting bruise, yet Coura scowled at the horse until her mother's familiar voice called her name...

The dull ache abruptly became a steady pounding, drawing her out of the scenario. She pressed the heel of one hand against her forehead and squeezed her eyes shut until the sensation vanished, along with the memory.

Soirée, what happened?

{*How should I know? I suggest you stop doing that, though; it hurts me too.*}

She removed the hand and stared at it, as it had been the one the horse bit. *Was that really from my childhood? It seemed to be so distant, but I don't remember anything from back then.*

Byron came nearer with both mares and handed her the reins belonging to the smaller of the two. "If the weather gets better, I'd like to take a slower pace for them. Right now, we can start with the basics."

He demonstrated how to tie the packs on first, then once their bags were secure, he helped her into the prepared saddle. The initial discomfort lessened as they began at a leisurely walk. When she grew somewhat used to the motions, Byron waved goodbye to Headmaster Symon, who watched them depart with a poorly concealed expression of concern.

A New Normal

The trip to Verona proved unfavorable for Coura this time around. Riding horseback hurt every part of her legs and back, but the journey did go by faster because they could travel farther in one day. Flying would also have accomplished the same, and she desired nothing more than to crawl off her horse, spread her raven wings, and soar above the treetop.

The rain finally came during the afternoon on the second day, soaking their clothes and chilling them even more. Because of the circumstances, Byron had them pick up the pace and avoid conversation. Several areas appeared where the rain didn't reach them under the canopy, so they pitched their tents, which the headmaster left on the animals. After tying the horses up where they would remain relatively dry with fresh grass, they prepared a fire to last through the night. Coura noticed how the master mage cast a spell instead of using flint stones and longed to comment on his decision, but she grew too exhausted to tease him. They ate a crude meal before sleeping, and he woke her at dawn to begin again.

This routine continued until the trees' spacing thinned to signal they were close to the castle.

"We'll be there tomorrow around midday at this rate, so there's no reason to stretch ourselves by rushing," Byron shared. "Besides, the rain is letting up."

Despite the clearer sky, the area remained too wet to build a fire. They ate the rest of their rations while his controlled magic kept them warm until he fell asleep. In the morning, the sun shined enough to lift their spirits, and Coura took pleasure in the trot through the edge of the forest and across the clearing to the south of the palace where Byron had them dismount. Its structure impressed her as much as it had when she first laid eyes on it.

As they approached the bridge before the entrance, he halted and gestured to her. "Come here."

"What is it?"

"There's something we need to discuss," he began in a serious manner, piquing her interest. "Once we enter, I have no doubt King Hernan will request to see you at some point. We're not going to hide your power from him or the other council members, but I order you not to wield magic unless I give you permission."

Coura opened her mouth to argue, but one look from Byron had her snapping it shut. "Why?" she asked after a moment.

"These people and their politics can be tricky. They'll use you as a tool once they find out what you're capable of, even if it isn't what you expect or agree with. Use me as an excuse to keep those abilities hidden. I also don't want to push you until everybody else settles in and the people here become familiar with dark magic. If there are problems, come directly to me. Don't take matters into your own hands."

"Fine."

He moved forward, waved to one of the guards posted in front, and shot her a reassuring smile. "Just remember, this is all to protect you."

Before she could address his final comment, they were greeted by three servants in tan tunics. Two took the reins and led the horses away while the last remained behind to guide the newcomers through the giant doors.

*

The first week of living in Verona passed by in a complete blur. Coura had been put into a room on the third floor near Byron's, which happened to be in the southwestern corner and provided at least double the space. She later found out the entire third and fourth floors of the palace acted as housing quarters for the soldiers who chose to stay there, and now the entirety of the transferred mages.

After dropping off their bags, a kitchen hand delivered items for lunch before she was whisked away to an introduction ceremony in the grand lobby. King Hernan loomed at the top of the main staircase to briefly welcome everybody in a warmer manner than Coura ever remembered from him and turned the speech over to his subordinate. She vaguely recalled the balding man who introduced himself as the high priest. His plump face gave him a friendly appearance, and he presented them all with the same, general schedule.

Each mage, with the exception of Coura, as she knew, would practice magic for two hours in the morning, get a break for lunch, then break apart for physical combat training or academic lessons in the afternoon, switching off every other day. This continued for six days, allowing for rest on the seventh. The specific groups and levels would be organized by Byron and his assigned assistants while the light mages worked with someone called Lady Emilea. It sounded reasonable considering its layout sounded identical to how the MAA functioned.

After the introduction, the king dismissed them for dinner in the mess hall, which remained open at all hours. Unfortunately, the palace didn't readily prepare for an additional mass of people to appear at once because the space crowded with mages and soldiers shoving their way to the front or impatiently waiting at the back. Coura decided to avoid the chaos by choosing to eat later but fell asleep before returning.

Byron stopped by the next morning with her special schedule that included studying in the morning instead of magic training, lunch, private combat lessons, and assigned work in the evening. He left in a hurry before she had a chance to complain about the amount of reading.

Once alone, she hurried to breakfast. After nearly picking a fight with a soldier who felt entitled enough to cut ahead of her in line, Coura ate, climbed the stairs, and found a servant carrying a stack of books standing at her door. A moment's glance revealed they weren't short nor entertaining texts. Nonetheless, she accepted the pile, dismissed the younger woman, and dumped the books onto her desk. Soirée tempted her to practice magic after, but Coura refused before diving into the first of two geography books. When she could no longer keep her eyes open without effort, she caved into Soirée's demands and hid her energy while they worked.

Lunch became a mixture of mostly unfamiliar faces and individuals she knew from the academy. The trainees she recognized cast her disapproving glances and muttered to each another, so she told herself not to care what they said. Her next task, the combat lesson, was what she had been looking forward to anyway.

She found Byron at the edge of the expansive training ground where a stone wall standing as tall as her shoulders surrounded the area and separated it from the forest beyond. Those nearest to them still kept fairly close to the palace.

"Why are you so far out?" she inquired upon arriving.

Instead of answering, her mentor handed over one of the two steel blades he held.

Coura raised her eyebrows as she accepted it. "Real swords?"

"What's wrong? We've worked with them before."

"I know, but it's been a while since our last lesson," she replied while weighing the weapon in each hand.

"It'll be a test to see how rusty we both are," Byron joked before initiating the sparring session.

After a few minutes, Coura got the impression he waited for that point in the day to take out some pent-up aggression. Not once did he hold back a blow, which left her with several, nasty cuts and bruises. She managed to defend herself from the most dangerous strikes and even nicked him a handful of times, but her heart wasn't in the seriousness of their fight. The clanging of metal on metal rang across the field as teacher and student danced in the controlled space. Meanwhile, Soirée observed and added comments on openings or missteps.

{It seems you two draw quite the crowd.}

During a pause between attacks, Coura let her eyes wander to the left where the castle stood and noticed a few dozen people inching closer to watch, including a group of trainees she recognized. They wore leather padding while the others must have been the soldiers supervising their progress. The onlookers' mouths moved as they shared their observations, though their voices remained inaudible from such a distance.

Byron followed her gaze before relaxing his stance. "It's time for a break," he announced and lowered the blade.

Coura did the same as they moved to where he kept a bag with waterskins in the shade and handed one to her. Together, they leaned against the warm stone and watched as the groups broke into their own sparring pairs.

"You didn't lose too much," she commented after a minute.

"I must say, I'm impressed. You've gotten slower."

"Hey!"

She elbowed him in the side as he began to take another drink, spilling water onto his tunic. This caused them both to laugh until they relaxed and enjoyed the cooling air and sunshine. The echoing whacks of the nearby, wooden weapons smacking against each other soon had them observing the soldiers instructing the trainees.

"It'll be a relief when they learn to trust the process," Byron shared before releasing a sigh.

"Is that why you've been stressed?"

He wiped his forehead to clear away the beads of sweat that formed earlier. "No, at least not entirely. I'm the only familiar figure of authority from East Hoover, so a lot come to me for private tutoring and comfort in their new surroundings. Sad to say, I'm busy enough organizing and teaching the more competent of the bunch to assist. It'll take me time to get used to delegating lesser tasks to my former students and, more nerve-racking, to servants and soldiers I don't know well."

"I don't blame you for not wanting to rely on people here, mainly because they backed you into a corner with the service law."

"Yes, but that's neither here nor there anymore. Hanging on to those impressions and emotions only hinders our progress and damages relationships. Speaking of which, how have you been transitioning?"

Coura considered lying but knew Byron was smart enough to understand what went on. He proved it by giving her a straight, sidelong look, which prompted a groan.

"I'm getting used to it. Honestly, I have enough on my mind to keep me from worrying about what others think."

{*Well, you do have twice as much in your head.*}

That means I can tolerate twice as much too, right?

{*I can sense you're losing interest in these humans and their approval. There's no reason to hide it from me.*}

"Coura?"

She had been too preoccupied with Soirée to hear Byron's previous question. "What did you say?"

Her mentor shook his head and pushed himself off the wall. "Never mind. You're just as careless as ever."

Once she joined him away from the stone barrier, he unexpectedly charged forward, initiating the second half of their session.

*

On the seventh day of their first week, the palace stayed relatively silent since everybody seemed to be resting or exploring the city. Coura planned to ignore her assigned readings and stared out the window while contemplating her recent interactions with Byron. He appeared more at ease during their lessons the past few days but would often raise uncomfortable questions regarding the demonic power.

"Do you ever feel a surge of energy, like you might lose control again?"

"Can you sense a connection or telepathic bond to a demon?"

"Would you guess the being's features are more human or monstrous?"

"If we tested your energy, could you contain it?"

"Did it hurt when the wings appeared? Are they an illusion?"

Coura continued to skirt around the truth in order to avoid revealing Soirée's presence or any indication she regularly used her magic in secret. It didn't help that the demon spoke over her thoughts until she ordered Soirée to be quiet.

On the outside, she feigned ignorance regarding the demon who possessed her and its dark energy. Even though he didn't rebuke her, Byron didn't appear or sound pleased with her answers. She knew he didn't fully believe her; however, at the moment, his lack of knowledge would benefit her the most.

She decided to wander through the halls of the upper floor out of boredom when she became unable to do much besides ponder the master mage's questions.

{*Why do you not tell him more?*}

You said you would kill me if I brought up your presence?

{*That was before when your life was on the line and you were untrained with the manifestation spells. There must be another reason for your secrecy.*}

I'm not ready to face what will happen, Coura replied with a heavy heart. *I can already picture his disappointed expression, and worst of all, we'll keep it a secret. I'm powerful enough to be a threat, and he knows it, which is why I stay away from the other mages. The last thing I want is to be ordered around and hidden like a gem only to be shown off when the time is right.*

{*That's not what you should worry about.*}

What do you mean?

{*You compare yourself to a gem when we're more of an eagle among mice.*}

Coura huffed a laugh as she completed taking another lap. *Leave it to a demon to think they're above every creature in this world.*

{*Although that's true, you should be concerned by this lack of freedom. With extraordinary power, not to mention the ability to fly, greedy humans will beg for your service. Given the position you're in, it wouldn't surprise me if you're forced to do so behind the public's back.*}

That's an interesting concept. Frankly, it troubled her more than she was willing to let on.

The sound of footsteps echoed from farther down the corridor to draw Coura's attention, and she peered ahead after spotting a familiar face, that of the assistant general. Marcus steadily approached before noticing her a second later, leading them both to slow to a stop.

"I haven't seen you in a while," he greeted her with a friendly smile. His clothes appeared as normal as anybody else's, preventing him from standing out among the hundreds of other soldiers.

"I'm sure you've been occupied."

"True. I'm not used to working with so many people at once, though I must admit your academy possessed talented combat instructors. A majority of the mages understand the basics, so their skills just need sharpening. I also educate them on the tactics of a fair fight. Hopefully, they don't resort to cheap tricks."

Marcus shrugged dramatically, causing Coura to roll her eyes before chuckling. He laughed at her reaction, as if nothing changed between them.

Speaking with someone who ignored the past warmed her heart, yet she couldn't resist being wary around him. *There's no way he already put the attack behind us.*

{Perhaps he might know how the information about your abilities leaked into the king's hands.}

You're right. His father is a general after all. Maybe I can ask when we get time alone.

He continued down the hallway without another word, prompting her to hurry and catch up.

"Where are you going?" she inquired in order to maintain the conversation.

"It's been a while since I wandered through Verona. I should get my mother a birthday present today."

"Do you mind if I come along? I've never been in the city."

"I wouldn't mind the company."

They descended the flights of stairs and strolled out the front gate together. A pair of guards posted there cast her dubious glances, yet one nod from Marcus had them diverting their eyes. Coura watched the entire process with a growing sense of uneasiness.

"Does everybody know?" she grumbled as they crossed the bridge leading to the main road.

"I don't believe so. Only the generals and their assistants are allowed to discuss it. Those two must have heard a rumor."

It comforted her to be able to speak openly with someone who, at least on the surface, didn't hate her for what she'd become. Instead of hiding what took place like she did with Will, she decided to be upfront about his feelings toward her. "Does being around me bother you too?"

She nearly ran into Marcus when he abruptly halted and faced her with a disquieted expression.

"Absolutely not. In fact, I never thanked you for saving my life."

"I should be the one thanking you," she replied bashfully. "If you hadn't been there, who knows what would have happened."

A long, uncomfortable pause stretched before he spoke again. "I asked Byron what took place in the training ground after I fell unconscious, and he mentioned you wielded demonic energy to manifest wings and a sword. I'm not about to claim I understand magic, but you fought the threat when I couldn't. The Yeluthians are supposed to be our allies and demons our enemies. I assume that's why there's distrust surrounding you; it's difficult to believe an angel would harm a human while somebody using forbidden power would protect the innocent. With that being said, I was present to witness what you did, which is why I'm not avoiding you or sharing the details. I still consider you a friend, and now a comrade. Because of how uncertain the situation is, it might be worthwhile to keep quiet and avoid causing trouble."

Coura stared at the soldier in amazement because of the long-winded yet honest insight and remembered what Will and Byron said after they began tolerating her circumstances. It made her realize Marcus wasn't just a muscle-bound fighter, prompting a fit of laughter at how incorrect her assumption had been.

"What's so funny?" he demanded with a faint blush.

She debated sharing her conclusion while savoring the mixture of emotions displayed on his face. Evidently, he figured she found what he admitted humorous and crossed his arms to reflect his frustration.

"I'm sorry," she responded before moving to his side, locking away his words, and cherishing his honesty in the process. "I didn't expect such a sincere explanation."

He scoffed at her answer. "I *am* a professional, you know. That's one characteristic of a general, so I must uphold it if I intend to get anywhere."

"That sounds restrictive. Maybe a career change would ease the burden of acting serious all the time."

She pretended to consider the idea as they moved down the road and grinned at him. Marcus frowned until he caught on to her teasing. Then, he shook his head with a slight smile.

"Perhaps if you were more demon-like I wouldn't need to try too hard. It's difficult to scorn a girl."

{*What does he mean "demon-like?" How ignorant! Tell him I am more beautiful and graceful than any human.*}

I can't really vouch for you when I've never seen you, Soirée.

{*If you don't believe me, you're as empty-headed as he is.*}

The assistant general raised an eyebrow when Coura giggled at the demon's bitterness. When she didn't elaborate, he led them into the busying city.

*

Verona proved to be easily three times the size of Fester with ten times the people, so Marcus laid out its composition in a way she could understand. The widest of three roads stretched to the palace and provided areas for vendors to post their tables and booths. Those spaces would be especially popular because of the soldiers', and now the mages', free day. Buildings also housed craft shops, bakers, butchers, smiths, and more. At the heart of the city, the path branched to the north and south but were named based on their relation to the main street.

The western road twisted south and straight out of Verona. Most of the wealthier citizens and nobility lived there since their expansive, elaborate homes could bear lavish gardens. The assistant general described it as a clean, desirable area because of its array of color throughout the year, sweet scents, and peaceful atmosphere.

He promised to take Coura down that path the following week so she could experience it during the fall.

"They love visitors and like to compete with each other over who owns the fanciest decorations or flowers," he explained while they continued west. "I don't know any details about their lives, but I can't imagine they do much if they have enough free time to spend on pampering their property."

The eastern road extended north and appeared to be similar to the main one with shops and back alleys. At the end, it held an enormous courtyard used for festivals and performances. An elevated platform wide enough for dozens of people would be added during those events to act as a stage, and another to the side remained reserved for the royal family. Farther away were the stables for soldiers to use, which provided space for the animals to graze. Cavalry training took place there while cleared trails ran through the woods beyond for casual horseback riding.

The main road spanned the entire city; however, the quality of the buildings deteriorated the farther it went from the palace. Animal farmers lived and worked along the outskirts without the pressure of the people's activity, and the prison loomed at the edge away from everything else.

As the pair wandered on, Coura found herself amazed by how fluid business in the city seemed. Each individual acted as though they belonged there and respected their practice, from the merchants to the musicians playing on the street. That, as well as the road's overall organization and the citizens' acceptance of color, music, and food, shaped Verona into the ideal location for somebody looking to begin a new life. She told Marcus as much.

"That's no coincidence. One of the royal families from decades ago, back when the Yeluthians were still around, loved the arts so much they decided to dedicate parts of the capital to it. Traders are welcome as long as they're honest, but reports of cheats and frauds are investigated and swiftly dealt with by General Dillon's company. Who would want to buy or sell their products in a city known for swindling? Additionally, festivals throughout the year welcome performers from across Asteom. Speaking of which, the Harvest Festival is coming up in a couple months."

The idea of such activities involving music and dancing spurred fuzzy memories from her younger years, but Coura became too distracted by the vendors around them to think about it further. She suggested they go together before he stopped at a booth showcasing various pieces of jewelry. Although she had no preference for owning such trinkets, she enjoyed the bright gems and polished types of metal.

They visited several after until he settled on an emerald necklace for his mother.

"What a wonderful choice for your lovely lady," the seller chimed to Marcus while she admired the man's products nearby.

"She's not my… I mean, we're only friends," the assistant general hurried to explain.

Coura pretended not to hear the comment, and the merchant apologized with a chuckle before handing over the wrapped gift.

{What an honest soldier. Smart too if he denies having anything to do with you.}

She frowned at the indirect insult. *That's funny coming from the disembodied demon confined to a human body.*

{That's what I meant; there's danger in befriending someone with your abilities. Did you think I was referring to your personality? I could point out your impatience or rude behavior, just to start.}

Enough, you nuisance.

"Did what he say bother you?" Marcus asked when the two began moving through the stream of people.

Coura realized she had been scowling because of Soirée and shook her head. "No, sorry. I just became lost in thought."

"Why don't we grab a bite to eat? I know a nice restaurant with the best sausages and stew."

Their next goal turned out to be on the eastern road and lived up to her expectations. Due to the amount of guests in the building, they settled for dining on the street where a pair of benches were placed. She scarfed down her meal in a few minutes, which tasted as delicious as Marcus claimed, and licked her fingers while he still worked on the second half of his order.

"You sure eat fast," he mumbled around a mouthful of bread dipped in the beef stew.

"It's not often I'm treated to a meal. I can't remember the last time I ate outside the academy, except when Byron, Will, and I visited the palace."

Marcus swallowed his bite before leaning against the wall to enjoy the sunlight. "You'll earn enough money to do this often, if you want. We soldiers are paid every other week on the fourth day, so I would imagine it's the same schedule for the mages."

"We get paid to be here?"

"Of course," he answered without hiding his astonishment at her question. "Whoever oversees your orientation should've explained that. If we didn't get compensated, most people wouldn't serve."

Coura dropped the subject since she figured nobody needed to know she stayed under Byron's supervision instead of being assigned to a company like the other recruits. For the moment, she was full, warm, and with pleasant company. Mentioning such news would spoil the mood during one of the best days she'd had in months.

Once he finished his meal, Marcus led her down the rest of the eastern road so she could observe the open courtyard. It appeared to be roughly double the size of the palace's grand hall, which made sense when she considered how it held hundreds of people, not to mention the platforms for performers and the royal family. They returned to the main street and the palace after since the sun began setting.

"I appreciate you letting me spend the day with you," she added once the pair returned. "I like Verona quite a bit."

"You're welcome, and me too. Now, if you'll excuse me, I've got a date tonight I can't miss."

After he strolled away, Coura wondered who the assistant general could be meeting as she returned to her room. There, she found herself unable to sit still with nothing except the books she'd been neglecting keeping her company. When she considered who else might be available that evening, an idea popped into her head, motivating her to hurry to Byron's room and knock on the door with the hope he wouldn't be busy. Heavy footsteps approached from the opposite side before the master mage opened it, and she noted his formal attire.

"Why are you dressed up?" she inquired while her mentor stepped out into the corridor.

"I get the pleasure of dining with the royal family as the MAA's representative," he replied with an eyeroll, which caused her to chuckle.

"I won't keep you from such an important event. Can you tell me where Will's room is?"

Byron informed her it was on the way, and since he didn't mind delaying his dinner plans, he took her to the eastern side of the palace. She thanked him once they reached her destination and knocked before the master mage left. Shuffling from inside grew louder before something fell to the floor with a thud, and more scurrying followed. The door cracked seconds later, then Will's face peeked out.

"Hello, how can I... Coura? I wasn't expecting a guest! Come in, but be careful. I meant to clean up. It got away from me..."

She entered the well-lit space reflecting what she expected based on the herbalist's personality. Piles of books were scattered everywhere, including on the bed and chairs, and candles dripping melted wax caught her eye before she noticed a set of empty lamps by the door. The wider room held two desks and chairs, a bed, and three bookshelves lining the walls around the pair of windows to avoid blocking any natural light.

While Coura inspected the furniture, Will attempted to pick up the books, plates, mugs, and clothes only to shove them into another spot with an apology. Of course, she didn't mind at all and found it amusing.

"I haven't seen you in days," he began once he cleared the bed enough so Coura could sit comfortably. He dropped into an empty chair after, brushed a strand of hair away from his eyes, and removed his glasses to polish them with a spare cloth. As usual, his behavior and expression revealed how he felt.

She told him about the uneventful week and the afternoon spent with Marcus. For the most part, the conversation focused on the city's layout and unique characteristics. He only responded with grunts or short responses when she explained the places yet perked up when she mentioned the jewelry vendors and restaurant.

"You went to dinner together, like a date?" Will muttered without looking at her.

"Kind of. When we returned to the entrance hall, he said he had one to go to." Coura shrugged to show her disinterest in Marcus' reason for leaving.

They talked well into the evening, sharing their studies until he wasn't able to keep his eyes open. Amid Will's protests, she moved the remaining items on the bed to the floor before shoving him onto his mattress and departing.

*

In the silence of the hallways, Coura hummed to express her contentment with the free day. Nobody else wandered because of the late hour, so when she heard footsteps near the south side of the floor, she ended the tune. A woman she thought she had seen before walked toward her from the other direction, wearing a loose, amber-colored dress and sporting blonde hair pinned into a neat bun. She expected the stranger was a mage, not only by the appearance, but by the powerful energy radiating from the figure. Although she tried to avert her eyes afterward, she noticed the woman making an effort to shoot a nasty glare her way.

{*It's only natural for a light-blooded human to be disgusted by its opposite.*}

Even though Soirée's comment sounded like the truth, Coura still grew uncomfortable.

She focused on looking forward and ignoring the stare until they passed one another. A few steps later, she paused to glance behind and found the stranger doing the same; however, as the blue eyes studied her with the same, putrid stare, she noticed an underlying emotion mixed with the hate. It seemed defensive, almost like she expected Coura to attack.

Then, without a word, the woman broke their eye contact and went away, leaving her fumbling for an answer.

She sensed the demonic energy, of that I'm sure, but her eyes reminded me of... I'm not sure. Do you know, Soirée?

{*I've seen that defiant stare dozens of times throughout my explorations. It's as if she were preparing to protect something, or someone, from our power. I wouldn't care about one mage's pathetic attempt to appear formidable if I were you.*}

The ruthless, unconcerned side of the demon bothered Coura enough not to question what the demon meant. Instead, she contemplated the rest of their observations.

Protecting a loved one... Like a parent or child? Maybe I've seen that gaze before? Not from Byron or any of the instructors at the academy.

A pair of deep, sapphire eyes came to mind, accompanied by a dull headache. She tried recalling every light mage she knew, but no one stuck out as much.

Suddenly, a cry rang in her mind.

"Coura, get behind me!"

A hand grabbed her arm and hauled her back, behind the owner's massive body. She peered from side to side, but it grew too dark for her to see anything clearly. A reddish light appeared in the trees, followed by several more after. They were the torches of the people coming to save her and the man.

From what, she wasn't certain.

A snarl close ahead caused her to gasp, and a pair of violet eyes gleamed as the shadow beyond watched them.

"We'll need to wait it out," the deep voice rumbled.

Fear gripped her young self to the point where she couldn't move or breathe. She was no match for the demonic creature lurking in the darkness.

The headache's increased pulsing caused her vision to blur for a moment, so Coura stretched a hand to place it on the cool wall before shutting both eyes. A moment later, she leaned against the stone and pressed the other hand to her forehead when she couldn't stop herself from diving deeper into the memory.

> *The man had been knocked to the ground where he coughed and swung his sword blindly through the air. Thankfully, the torchlights were close enough to illuminate the area. That's when she saw the creature.*
>
> *It seemed like a giant, elongated cat with fangs too large to keep in its mouth and claws which dug into the earth. At the sight of fire, the beast hissed once more at them before leaping away into the bushes.*
>
> *Only when she saw the townsfolk making their way toward her did she breathe again. While most people went to her protector, one shoved his way directly to her and picked her up in his arms. He squeezed her tightly then looked her over with deep, blue eyes...*

{Stop it, Coura!}

She whimpered as the pounding blossomed into stabbing pain. Her legs trembled, so she sank to the floor and dropped her head into her hands until she finally let go of the images. Tears stung her eyes during the incident as well, so she paused to wipe them away.

After a few, shaky breaths, she stood and made her way back to her room where she fell into bed and calmed down, yet the scenes vanished.

{Can we please not do that again?}

Sorry...

Sleep took her then, but she remained restless all night and woke feeling exhausted.

Yeluthia's Ambassador

No more stray memories overtook Coura during the following weeks while they passed in a casual routine. Eventually, the stares and dirty looks from the mages declined too. Byron let her begin sparring with some of the soldiers and Marcus once he became convinced she wasn't going to lose control of her power. Those oblivious to her abilities acted friendly, so everybody got along. She ate meals with Will and whoever wanted to join them, or could tolerate her, and life seemed normal, aside from hiding Soirée.

However, a letter soon arrived from Yeluthia to throw the whole kingdom into an uproar.

Coura learned of it from Byron when he gathered her, Will, and Marcus into his quarters one evening. The room looked to be the complete opposite of the herbalist's: neat, orderly, and containing enough space for the four of them to sit comfortably on the bed or in a pair of chairs.

"Yeluthia, the city of angels?" she asked her mentor without hiding her awe.

"Yes. It's quite a surprise since Asteom hasn't heard from their people in years, according to His Highness. Apparently, they wish to rekindle our old relationship, starting by sending an envoy. The message didn't hint at if they knew about the angels you three encountered or any demons. They just claimed an ambassador would be at the palace within the next two weeks."

"I take it you summoned us because of the two strays," Marcus stated as they processed the information.

"Are we in trouble?" Will asked next.

Byron shook his head. "Nobody else knows I called you here to talk. Obviously, I don't want you discussing those situations or what took place as a result."

He purposefully shot Coura a suspicious stare during the following pause.

"I won't say anything," she protested.

"It's what you might *do* that concerns me."

She crossed her arms and stuck her chin up. "Well, I'll be careful."

"As for the ambassador's entrance, King Hernan is preparing a ceremonious welcome and introduction, which will be open to the public," Byron continued. "I recommend we all go together to note the guest's appearance."

They conversed about what the event might entail before Coura, Marcus, and Will were excused. The idea of an angel living in the palace concerned her, especially when she needed to keep her energy hidden. On the other hand, the possibility of a reestablished alliance was positive news for the kingdom, so she grew nervous about remaining in the shadows in order to avoid conflict.

Oddly enough, Soirée seemed passive on the subject, only agreeing they stay far away from the envoy but not seething with rage as Coura expected.

*

On their next day off, Marcus took her into Verona at her request. As he mentioned during their previous endeavor, the king compensated each mage with silver coins, which proved to be more money than she had ever collected at one time. The students at the MAA didn't need money except to spend when traveling or looking for a meal in East Hoover.

They explored the western road and admired the clean-cut shrubbery, flowers, fences, and lawn decorations. The first home was too tucked away to see because four willow trees dangled their branches in front, as if waving to those on the other side of the property's silver gate. A couple gargoyle statues guarded the entrance and had been polished until they shone an ebony color. Next door, that owner arranged the lawn into sections of various flower gardens with a fountain in the center of one and a pair of wooden benches in the other. A cobbled, stone path connected each area, reminding Coura of the queen's gardens she snuck into during her initial visit to the palace.

About three dozen houses lined both sides of the street in the same, extravagant manner with their own, unique designs. It took her and Marcus most of the day to walk to the end and back, then they hurried to the eastern road for a snack at a bakery and ate as they made their way to the castle before sundown.

"It's nice to get a day off," she commented when they approached the bridge. "I don't think I'll ever get used to living here."

The assistant general shrugged and shoved the rest of his jam-filled pastry into his mouth. "I could use a drink," he added afterward.

"Do you want to visit the kitchen? I wouldn't mind a glass of the fruit tea the cooks leave out."

"I can't. I've got another date tonight. If I'm late, they'll be kept waiting." He shot her a sympathetic smile, as if to emphasize his loyalty to the individual.

Coura couldn't think of a response, so she wished him well and turned to leave; however, as she began heading toward the main staircase, Marcus called for her to wait. When she stopped to glance behind, he looked her over while appearing to contemplate his next words.

"What is it?" she decided to ask.

The assistant general nodded to himself a moment later and gestured for her to follow him. "Come on. I want you to meet somebody."

He led her to the third floor then near the north side of the palace. That was when she realized he planned to include her in his personal gathering.

"Marcus, I don't want to interrupt…"

He merely waved a hand to dismiss her concern.

Soon, they approached a room at that corner of the building where he placed a hand on the knob, grinned at her, then pushed the door open.

Inside, the space seemed unexpectedly warm and possessed an earthy scent. It stayed dimly lit since light only entered from two windows facing away from the setting sun. Banners of the kingdom in red and gold hung on the walls, and paintings of various animals were scattered around the room. Like Will and Byron's rooms, Marcus had a set of desks, plenty of bookshelves, a bed, and a nightstand.

Coura felt at home in the cozy atmosphere after she entered until she noticed a person leaning against the wall to stare out the window at the training ground below.

"It's about time," the young man said before focusing his attention on them. He prepared to add more but paused with a slightly alarmed expression when he saw her with Marcus.

"Hey, Aaron," her escort began while pointing a thumb at her. "The masculinity in here has been suffocating, so I brought a friend."

She took a moment to recall her original encounter with the prince, who was no doubt the figure in front of them. If the slim, gold band sitting on his head didn't act as an indication of his royal status, he most definitely appeared to be his father's son. The men shared a similar facial structure and physique that made Aaron almost like a younger version of the current king.

As they awkwardly shifted on their feet, she decided to break the silence. "It's been a while, Your Highness."

"Do you know each other?" Marcus inquired from where he remained at her side.

Aaron stepped closer and adjusted his lips into a controlled smile. "We met before, but I wouldn't claim we know each other."

The assistant general visibly relaxed before crossing the room to drop onto his bed. "This'll make the introductions easier. Coura, this is Aaron. Aaron, this is Coura."

To her surprise, the prince bowed, spurring a blush that had Marcus chuckling.

"Quit being so formal," the latter ordered and threw one of his boots at Aaron, who caught and tossed it away. Their behavior was all she needed to observe in order to understand the pair's friendly relationship.

"So, this is your special date, Marcus?" she teased while covering her embarrassment.

The prince huffed a laugh before crossing his arms. "Date? Are we really *that* close?"

He shot Marcus an incredulous look before ducking when the other boy threw a second boot at his head. The pair laughed together after, which helped Coura to feel less uptight, and she made herself comfortable in one of the open chairs.

"How did you two meet?" she asked before Aaron went to a bag on the desk, removed a wine jug, and offered it to her.

Meanwhile, Marcus sat up and raised his eyes to the ceiling. "We've been friends ever since we were kids. With my father acting as a general, I always stayed in the palace to train for the position."

"Every member of the royal family must learn at least the basics of combat," the prince added. "Unfortunately, I didn't get the greatest teacher…"

The assistant general snickered in response before accepting the bottle Coura handed over.

"If it's who I think it is, you're right," she told Aaron. "I beat Marcus when I was still a student."

The soldier nearly spit out his mouthful of wine while the prince didn't hide his amusement. His laugh proved to be a wonderful sound, one she didn't expect from a royal figure, and especially not from King Hernan's child.

"You cheated!" Marcus argued. "Besides, it happened a couple months ago, so you weren't truly a student anymore."

"I'll be the judge of that," Aaron interjected before looking them over and requesting they share the story.

As a result, Coura and Marcus pieced together their own sides in a construed mess, which worsened when she decided to exaggerate certain details for fun. Marcus, the ever-honest soldier, scolded her for stretching the truth but soon realized she did so on purpose.

"You're hopeless," he mumbled with mock disdain when they finished.

She felt a twinge of pity and decided to test Aaron's tolerance for jokes next. "Should I be more polite in the presence of royalty?" she countered and slid a sly glance at the prince.

For some reason, her question caused him to blush. "Please, not in here. I get enough of that during the day. It gets tiresome always using proper manners and addressing everyone as "Lady so-so" or "Lord Who's-it-now.""

"Whatever you say, Your Highness," she replied with a partial bow from her chair.

Aaron frowned a little to show his annoyance before addressing Marcus. "She sure knows how to fit in with us."

"That's why I invited her."

"Now I must endure being picked on by two people," Aaron continued in a dramatic tone and raised a hand to his head as a display of pretend fatigue.

His reaction spurred laughter, and the rest of the evening became filled with such humor until they transitioned into mundane yet interesting discussions.

*

The next day, Coura went to the mess hall during suppertime, but Marcus surprised her there and requested she follow him.

"Where are we going?"

"To my room. It's time for our dinner date."

"Do you two meet every day?" She could hardly believe it when he nodded.

"As you probably noticed, it gets crowded in the mess hall. Aaron is usually supposed to eat with his family and the nobility in the royal dining hall too. We decided meals would be less stressful with just the two of us in a private setting, so we've been doing this for years. One of the chefs in the kitchen got tired of us requesting

249

food to sneak back to my room, so she started sending a helper. It's not out of the way either since a lot of upper soldiers and scholars who live here eat in their rooms regularly."

They met Aaron in the hallway and moved into their designated space before people noticed the prince. Coura caught him send Marcus a look, as though he wondered why she joined again, but their time together afterward felt as normal as the previous day.

A servant brought dinner once most of the soldiers and mages came through the mess hall, so the trio didn't eat until later, which seemed fair. The woman entered bearing two trays with seared meats, potatoes, and vegetables and raised an eyebrow at Coura's appearance, yet a few days of the same routine lessened the surprise of a newcomer. She soon understood there would be another mouth to feed and loaded more food onto the trays.

Coura found herself getting along well with Marcus and Aaron, leading her to often forget their statuses; however, Aaron never scolded her for it or appeared the slightest bit upset. In fact, he acted like he enjoyed the presence of another person who didn't grovel at his feet, especially since she learned the women he encountered on a daily basis did just that.

*

The three of them met every day from then on, and dinner became an event Coura eagerly looked forward to. She never had close friends to joke or have serious discussions with, yet in Marcus' room, they abandoned their roles outside those walls. The weeks passed smoothly, including her seventeenth birthday, and from what she could tell, the recruits from the academy melded into their new lives.

All seemed well, except the ambassador from Yeluthia was expected to arrive the next afternoon, much later than the initial letter led those in Asteom to believe.

"We won't be meeting here tomorrow, just so you're aware," Marcus told her while they finished their meal the evening prior.

Coura swallowed a mouthful of savory, cooked carrots before responding. "Because of the welcome ceremony?"

The two nodded before Aaron picked up the conversation. "I have to be with my family to greet and dine with the Yeluthian, and Marcus will be on guard duty with the other assistant generals. There's going to be a feast in the grand hall for the soldiers and mages as part of the ceremony."

Marcus appeared hesitant to say more, so Coura figured she could try lightening their moods.

"Don't worry about me," she began and waved a hand at them. "I'm sure I can find a way to keep myself occupied. Byron's been harping on me about my studies too. The sooner I can get out of the hall, the better."

That must have been what the two hoped to hear, for both visibly relaxed.

They're probably worried about another situation with the angel. I don't blame them, especially Marcus. Who knows how powerful the ambassador is and what their full intentions for being here are.

The next morning, Coura donned the single dress in her possession, which she selected in Verona specifically for the event. The rose-colored material felt thin enough to keep her cool despite it covering her arms and shoulders, and the skirt flowed straight to touch the floor. It wasn't fancy, but it would allow her to blend in with the sea of reds, golds, whites, and blues. She threw her hair up into a bun before heading to meet Byron in the corridor.

Her mentor greeted her while eyeing her appearance, as if assessing whether she met the formal code or not, then they hurried down the hallway. He wore in the traditional, cobalt robe of the dark mages, making him appear years older and wiser. She had only seen him in that outfit once during a funeral at the academy months after she first arrived.

"I bought this dress in town," she commented with no small hint of pride to spark a conversation.

"Really," he mumbled while giving her half his attention.

Coura knew his thoughts were on other matters at the moment but couldn't help herself from bragging. "I spotted a shop that dyes fabric and hangs handfuls of gowns in the windows. Of course, there were more elaborate ones, but I figured you wouldn't care for the colors or cuts."

"That's nice." He continued straight to Will's room and firmly knocked thrice.

She swayed and marveled at how fluid the fabric moved as they waited until she decided to pry. "Why are you so concerned about the ceremony?"

"You aren't?" he asked and sighed when she shook her head. "Our country is making history today. To witness the angels and humans coming together to reestablish peace between our peoples is positive news for the future. I'm nervous because I can never trust everything to go as planned."

Coura rolled her eyes and began fingering a strand of loose hair. "You worry too much."

"Better to care too much than not at all," he retorted before brushing down his robe.

{*You're all fools for relying on such an abominable race.*}

"You're crazy," she muttered to both Soirée and Byron before Will opened the door.

Like her, he belonged to no uniformed group, so he improvised with the outfit he wore during their first visit to the palace: black boots and pants, a white shirt, and an emerald-colored vest. His scraggly, brown hair had been combed, and his glasses shone in the lamps' light.

Byron looked the herbalist over like he did with Coura before nodding and ushering them to the nearest set of stairs. "Marcus is meeting us down there. We'll be standing where he's stationed by the far wall on the north side."

The grand hall had been adorned with hanging, scarlet banners showcasing the kingdom's crest: a golden horse in front of a castle. Half a dozen servants rolled out a matching carpet stretching from the entrance to the staircase. From what Coura understood, their guest would be invited to join Hernan at the top, then he would offer a proper greeting and a statement about unity. Together, the two would lead the way to the dining hall, an honor only extended by the royal family. Marcus, Aaron, and Byron were required to be present for that part, leaving Coura and Will to eat with the others.

The ceremony began whenever the Yeluthian arrived, which the king's council expected to be around midday thanks to the watchmen posted around the city. Because of this, everybody had been warned to meet in the grand hall late in the morning. By the time midday approached, the hall grew so crowded Coura couldn't move even if she wanted to, which became more confined because soldiers lined the walls, as they were instructed to do. Marcus wore the same, crimson coat, save for an additional badge on its left side. With their hair combed, faces cleanly shaved, and clothing spotless and unwrinkled, she found Marcus, Will, and Byron handsome enough to allow her to fade into the background.

The light mages wore their white robes possessing gold trimmings and whispered excitedly to each other while the dark mages had blue robes similar to Byron's yet not as decorated. Since Coura never officially graduated like the others in her class due to Soirée's intervention, she never received one. Not that she particularly cared about such novelties, but the pink dress made her stand out. Having Will nearby in his contrasting green did provide some comfort, though.

In front of the mages and soldiers stood citizens from Verona, mainly the nobility who made an effort to be seen as much as possible. Gazing upon their flamboyant colors and jewelry hurt her eyes, yet it became obvious to everybody who had money and who simply wound up lucky enough to find a spot.

The time ticked by, and still people managed to squeeze into the space.

Perhaps it was Soirée's curiosity and seething hatred flowing through her veins, but Coura grew tense at the thought of facing another angel. She reflected on how beautiful yet vicious the female proved to be; the male hadn't been any better. No one knew what to expect.

Before she could consider the situation further, Marcus sidled next to her while Byron and Will talked to the mages around them.

"You look nice," he commented in a polite manner.

"I'm surprised you can see me at all with so much light shining off you," she teased and poked at the golden buttons on his uniform to relieve her unease.

He gently slapped her hand before holding it in both of his when she tried to touch them again. "Stop it. I just had them polished yesterday."

"You sound like a prissy, old woman," she added, causing him to frown.

The noise steadily died down once everybody realized the royal family had entered the hall from a doorway at the top of the staircase. A pair of older servants and the bald priest in his glorious, white-and-gold robe trailed them. Coura glanced at Aaron, who continued to reflect her impression of him as the spitting image of the king. Both dressed similarly to the soldiers, yet a greater amount of gold weaved into the clothing to signal their status and no badges rested on the breast. King Hernan also wore a scarlet cape and held a sword in the holster at his waist.

Despite their demand for attention, the queen was by far the most stunning woman in the room. Her face, like Aaron's, appeared rounder than her husband's chiseled features and had been painted with various kinds of flattering makeup. Instead of pinning up or adorning her hair, the chestnut locks fell down her back in waves. Her ink-colored gown seemed unconventional, but the designer embroidered the fabric with crimson and gold, revealing patterns of horses and angels, which glittered in the light as she moved. It reminded Coura of a painting, far surpassing the beauty of every dress she'd ever laid eyes on.

Her eyes returned to the prince after a moment. He somehow noticed and mirrored the stare before shooting her an encouraging wink that prompted a smile. Then, Hernan stepped forward.

***

Aaron grew familiar with ceremonies and speeches from his father over the years thanks to his upbringing in the public eye. While the king preached about their country's pride, honor, and

254

service while thanking each group for their contributions to keeping peace in Asteom, he avoided the urge to yawn.

Despite his boredom, he always found himself admiring his father's ability to speak about the same topics so fluently that they were never the same presentations. *I can't imagine when I'll do that. All the more reason for my father to remain in charge for as long as possible. I have so much to learn.*

He continued masking his true emotions with a civil face and let his gaze wander around the room. Many of the young women were studying him, and he tried his best to send a polite smile to each, but his eyes continually returned to the group huddled along the northern wall. Aaron longed to stand by his friends and disappear into the crowd instead of being displayed as the center of attention.

Marcus leaned over and whispered to Coura, who nodded in response. Her stare never left his father throughout the speech. When he and his parents entered the hall earlier, he caught the two chatting, then Marcus held her hand in his while she laughed. For some reason, Aaron became inexplicably upset and longed to find out what was so funny; however, he felt a little better when he met Coura's gaze after and shot her a wink. Her resulting smile made his heart jump.

"It is with my deepest gratitude and honor as king of Asteom to welcome the envoy from Yeluthia."

His father's words brought his mind back to the present. As if rehearsed, a couple soldiers at the opposite end of the space pushed the oversized doors open. Sunlight from outside nearly blinded him, and dozens of people below shielded their faces from the unexpected brightness. Everybody watched eagerly as a handful of figures came into view. A minute later, Aaron worried his eyes were deceiving him.

Four escorts led the way across the crimson carpet while a girl followed behind. She was definitely a girl, he guessed around eleven or twelve years old, wearing a simple, white dress as blonde hair trailing down her back in a braid. Aaron wondered if she had been made aware of how grand the palace intended this event to be. Despite her lackluster appearance, she carried herself as his mother did with her chin held high and eyes looking straight ahead while murmuring sounded from the crowd.

Against his better judgement, Aaron took a brief moment to glance at his father. The king's face appeared calm, but the tightness of his lips revealed his displeasure.

Is this a joke? Why would they send a child to act as an envoy? Do they not think us worthy to host a fully-fledged Yeluthian?

Those questions and more ran through his mind until her escorts approached the bottom of the staircase. Behind them, the girl paused, turned her head to the left, and scanned the nervous onlookers. She showed no emotion, but Aaron sensed she was searching for something, or someone.

I've heard rumors about a special mage among the new recruits from the Magical Arts Academy. I wonder if they share similar abilities with the Yeluthian. He possessed no light or dark powers, so the topic had always been foreign to him. Still, with how composed the girl behaved, he assumed she wouldn't look away without reason.

His father spoke again to draw her attention, and his booming voice startled Aaron enough to jump.

"My people, let us welcome our Yeluthian envoy!"

The crowd overcame their initial surprise faster than he did, for their cheers and clapping filled the space while the girl climbed the steps to approach those at the top. In these situations, as he became well experienced with, they greeted the guest in order of importance. First, his father bowed, took one of her hands in his, then addressed her. Aaron couldn't make out his words because of the noise below, but his mother soon moved forward and curtsied before High Priest Hendal shuffled over.

When it was his turn, Aaron approached her. "We are honored to have you staying here in Asteom, my lady," he offered with as low a bow as he could manage.

"The honor is mine," she replied in a high-pitched, soft voice and with the same sort of controlled expression.

Once the greetings concluded, the high priest went forward to close the first part of the ceremony in an eager manner. Hendal always acted kind toward Aaron on a strictly professional level and had been beyond excited to hear from the city of angels.

"My beloved citizens, I am pleased and humbled to welcome a Yeluthian into our kingdom. For decades, our peoples were divided by circumstance. We developed our nations with the hope that one day we could be united again. Today begins the process. Today, we celebrate the arrival of Yeluthia's ambassador, Lady Grace Zelnar!"

The resulting cheers became so deafening, Aaron found himself genuinely smiling at the celebration. Hendal's words cued the servants, who began bringing out trays of food for the feast, and musicians at the bottom of the staircase started playing. Meanwhile, Aaron and his parents would lead the way to the dining hall where a private, more civilized meal would be served.

He followed his father and mother through the nearest door and into the next corridor before finding himself walking beside the girl, Grace. She seemed relieved to be out of the immediate spotlight yet upheld a regal appearance.

"If you're going to take a breath, I'd do it now," he leaned over and whispered.

She stared at him with an uncertain expression. "Why is that?"

"You won't be standing in front of anyone, but I guarantee you'll need to converse with a few lords and ladies. They can be unbearable unless you get them going on about themselves. I always make it a game by seeing how long they talk before I get a word in."

Her shy smile lifted his spirits before they faced forward again. As they approached the entrance to the dining hall where the doors already swung wide open upon their arrival, he heard a tiny, "Thank you."

*

Dinner tasted delicious, as usual, yet the meal felt similar to every other evening. Despite the special guest, most of the ladies flocked over to him at one point or another. His mother eyed their flirty behavior with a sense of approval while his father discussed business items with the lords. Grace sat next to the king on his other side, yet Aaron's father never spoke a word to her.

I bet he's still upset at the surprise, he thought and recalled his own, initial shock.

The young Yeluthian took Aaron's advice, though he sympathized with her because she couldn't get enough to eat between those who wished to introduce themselves and ask questions. When they inquired about Yeluthia's businesses, crops, or other topics related to the mysterious kingdom, she answered with a general remark before shifting the inquiry to Asteom. This set the lord or lady off on a prideful monologue that inflated their status and wealth but gave her time to sneak bites of food.

Music began right after dinner, so Aaron excused himself before anybody could request a dance. To his amazement, his father followed closely behind.

"You don't plan to entertain the lovelies?" the king commented with a knowing smile.

"I've had my share of this lot." At that point in his life, he'd been introduced to each woman in the dining hall multiple times, both publicly and in private.

Hernan chuckled and slapped him on the back. "That's my son. I remember being your age and ladies throwing themselves at me. It gets tiring."

"Without a doubt. You didn't want to stay?"

His father's pleasant mood shifted to annoyance in an instant. "And sit next to that child for another second? The least those people could do is warn us beforehand. I refuse to believe she's anything more than what I've seen so far, which is a pawn. How can I preach unity with an equally powerful kingdom when they can't be respectable enough to send someone decent?"

The mumbled venting continued until they reached his parents' chamber at the rear of the first floor. There, they parted ways, so he roamed through the corridors until he returned to his own room.

*

"How was babysitting?" Marcus asked in lieu of a welcome. Both his friend and Coura were already together when Aaron entered their shared space the following evening.

"Strange," he replied and took his spot. "I don't think anybody expected that."

"No kidding! I imagined an adult, or at least some sort of show. How could *she* be their best option?" Marcus shook his head before analyzing their guest, just as Aaron's father did the night before.

All the while, Coura remained silent and stared down at her hands.

"You're awfully quiet," he added during a pause to bring her into the discussion. "I wanted to ask what a mage thought about the Yeluthian. Can you sense her power?"

She only shrugged before raising her eyes and looking out the window.

Aaron turned to raise an eyebrow at Marcus but found his friend watching Coura with a strange expression. "Is there something going on?" he inquired while glancing between the two.

"No, I just got lost in thought," she replied, shook her head, then met his eyes for the first time that day. "I can tell by her energy she has potential but nothing drastically different from most of the light mages I trained with."

"Really? Then why send her?"

"I don't know." She left it at that.

While the trio ate, Marcus filled Aaron in on some of the drama that took place in the private dining hall after he exited with his father. Before they finished their meal, Coura excused herself for the evening.

"What's wrong with her?" Aaron wondered aloud when they were alone.

Marcus fidgeted. "I don't know if I can say."

"Why not?"

"Because it's not my business. Besides, I wouldn't want to hurt her any more than I might have already."

"Tell me what's going on. I thought the three of us are friends now."

For a while, Marcus stared at him while contemplating the request before caving in. "I'll explain because you should hear the truth, but you must promise not to speak of this to anyone."

Aaron's curiosity piqued. "Sure. What is it?"

"I'm serious. Not a peep or else I could get in trouble and something might happen to her."

He held a fist over his heart. "You have my word on my family's name."

A True Test of Courage

Coura groaned with dismay as Byron set three books on her desk right after she let him into her room. "Is this really necessary? I have other work to do," she whined and pressed her forehead against the nearest wall.

"Stop acting so childish," he responded to scold her. "Besides, you don't have anything else except our combat session in the afternoon."

"If you'd let me practice magic…"

"Absolutely not."

She threw up her hands in defeat and sat down at the desk. "Fine. Don't hurt yourself getting worked up."

He grunted at her remark before turning to exit.

After resigning to her fate, Coura opened the book on top, began reading the introduction, then noticed her mentor standing in the doorway.

"Is that it?" she asked when he didn't move.

"How would you like to come with me on a visit to a friend's house? He lives just outside the capital, and it might be nice for you to clear your head."

"How long has it been since we got here?"

Byron paused to count the weeks. "We arrived at the end of summer. The Harvest Festival is in ten days, so it's been nearly three months."

"That long?" After a moment, she realized he was waiting for her reply. "I wouldn't mind going along. That is, as long as you old men don't bore me with stories the entire time."

"We'll make sure to tell the most exciting ones," he added before leaving her to the texts.

She returned her eyes to the pages yet couldn't focus on the words. Her thoughts drifted to the few items she'd been attempting to dismiss, the most prominent being the Yeluthian ambassador. When the doors to the grand hall opened, Coura expected somebody like the two angels she faced and defeated in combat. To see a child enter caught her completely off guard, as well as every other witness. Aside from the obvious issues and complaints she heard multiple times over the following days, she didn't doubt the girl sensed Soirée's presence.

She glanced in my direction during the procession. I couldn't tell if she noticed me in particular, but I would wager she knows a human possesses demonic energy. If the rest of her kind learns about it and pieces together how two of their own were already killed, they might come after me.

The possibility of fighting another angel, let alone more than one at a time, terrified her; the idea of doing so against a child was worse. Not to mention, the balance between the kingdoms hindered on reestablishing their alliance.

So many concerns arose in her head that Soirée's venomous voice took her back.

{You're pathetic. Frightened of a child? I'm ashamed to share such glorious power with a coward.}

Whether you like it or not, I will fight for this country and its allies.

{Will you be preaching that when they find out what you are? What about when the light-blooded raise their weapons to you?}

I won't be part of any plot endangering the potential peace. Even as Coura projected the comment in her mind, she felt her own hesitation, which Soirée pounced on.

{*Peace is a pitiful notion. When will you realize what you are and accept the way things have to be?*}

With a mental shove like nothing she ever dared to do before, Coura forced the demon's presence out of the forefront. She expected curses, insults, or pain, yet nothing happened. Instead, Soirée remained at a distance and said no more.

Coura stared around her room in an attempt to calm herself. *I haven't seen the Yeluthian since the ceremony. It's been three days since then, so as long as I stay away and keep myself under control, I should be safe.*

After trying and failing to refocus on the books, she moved to her feet and decided to check if Will or Marcus were available. She opted to eat with the former in the mess hall the previous evening since he often read in the library or worked alongside the light mages who delved into his field of research, thus preventing her from visiting him often. He would fill her in on what he learned as well. Although the information proved too confusing for her to understand, she enjoyed the company over being alone with Soirée in her head.

She knocked a few times on Will's door but received no response, so she crossed the floor to head toward Marcus' room. Most of the people she passed were going for the stairs and ignored her; however, when she turned the final corner near her goal, she spotted Aaron standing alone and called to him. At the sight of her, his expression abruptly shifted into one reflecting indifference, and he stretched his lips into a fake smile.

"What's wrong?" she asked after approaching.

"I was looking for Marcus, but he must still be outside. I won't be joining him for dinner again tonight. Could you pass that message on for me?" He sidestepped around her without waiting for an answer.

"Wait, are you–"

"I'd love to stay," he interrupted. "I just have other plans."

Coura could only think of a single reason why he acted so impersonal toward her. Once she acknowledged it, a wave of dread washed over her. "You heard about me."

His steps stopped. "Yes, I did," he replied at a lower volume. The hurt in his voice betrayed the unconcerned expression. *"When will you realize what you are and accept the way things have to be?"*

Without another word, she spun around to hurry in the opposite direction at a brisk walk until a scuffle of feet and a hand on her arm prompted her to glance behind. Aaron held her firmly in place, not that she made an effort to escape his grip.

"I understand you barely know me," she said instinctively without meeting his eyes. "On top of that, you're royalty. If it wasn't for Marcus, we never would have met again. Maybe we weren't ever supposed to. I wouldn't associate with someone like me either."

"I'm sorry." The façade dropped before he released her arm.

She rubbed the spot and remained where she stood. "For what?"

"Marcus told me about the angel who attacked you two and how you saved his life. That explains why you were acting uncomfortable after the Yeluthian arrived."

"That's only half of it," Coura muttered.

"I heard about your powers too. As unnatural as they are, I believe Master Byron and the academy's headmaster wouldn't send you here if they didn't trust you. If they do, then why should I doubt their judgement? Now, if Marcus didn't mention the situation before the transfer, there might be concern regarding Yeluthia and your magic. The proper precautions are in place now. I promise you that."

"What do you mean 'before the transfer?'" she countered with rising suspicion despite Aaron's genuine effort to reassure her. "What did Marcus say?"

"He shared the details in a letter to his father. Didn't he tell you?"

Coura shook her head and listened while he described how the assistant general reported what took place with her demonic abilities to the general and members of the king's council. No one learned it was her specifically until Hernan ordered Byron to reveal that information upon his arrival. Even so, she recalled the ultimatum Aaron's father used and figured her power fit somewhere into the demand.

Marcus told them about me. Nobody in the palace would have suspected I was involved, and I wouldn't have been forced here. Why would he do that without asking me?

{*It's obvious they intend to use you as a weapon. What better opportunity to rise in status than to act as a reliable informant?*}

Would he actually trade me away like that?

{*Why not? It's not as if you two have known each other for long.*}

The resulting sense of betrayal lit a fire under Coura. She thanked the prince for his time before moving down the hall while ignoring his following call.

By the time she reached the training ground where Marcus worked with the mage recruits, her anger had doubled. The lost possibilities and current problems she faced, as well as what Byron and the academy endured, swirled in her head. The significance of the angels' merciless behavior dwindled in comparison to the news of a human wielding demonic magic, and Coura worried the citizens would consider the Yeluthians justified. Soirée's additional comments fueled such negativity.

The assistant general's group appeared to be breaking apart for the noon meal, so she marched in his direction. One look at her serious expression must have been enough for him to come closer in order to investigate the issue. As he opened his mouth to question her sudden appearance, she cut him off at a lower volume akin to a growl in a vicious tone.

"How could you tell the generals about me?"

At first, he seemed confused before evidently recalling the letter. "I didn't mean to… Where did you hear-"

"It doesn't matter," she interjected. "I know you did, and I want to know why! Is my life just a means for you to earn favor with Hernan? I thought you were different, but I suppose you view me as a tool for you and your soldiers to use. What about the angel who confronted us? Wasn't he more of a problem to emphasize instead of me?"

Marcus tried to butt in several times during her rant, yet Coura spoke over him until she worked herself up to the point where no answer would suffice. Surprisingly, it was Soirée who intervened.

{*Hold your temper, Dear One. There's no reason to draw extra attention to this.*}

Out of everybody, I least expected you to be so passive, she spat.

{*Grow up. What's done is done, so shut your mouth and calm down before you do something stupid.*}

She ground her teeth while Marcus continued to stare at her, dumbfounded and at a loss for what to say. Since she couldn't let go of her emotions, she stormed away.

That evening, she ate with Will in the mess hall and informed him of Marcus' letter. He didn't seem nearly as upset, yet he understood her reaction. The two went their separate ways after the meal, and it took her a long time to fall asleep because images of the day kept spinning in her head.

*

Byron's knocking woke Coura late the next morning. Her mentor wasn't pleased to find her still in her nightgown and showcasing messy hair, prompting him to order her to get ready before heading down the corridor. With a final yawn, she prepared for the day, went to the mess hall, and found him grabbing a bite to eat with Will.

"We were supposed to get there around noon," Byron grumbled as he impatiently led them through the entrance hall.

"How far is this place we're going to?" she inquired.

"His house is just outside Verona's eastern road. It's remote enough in the woods to take all morning."

Hiking away from the capital city proved to be a shorter journey than she imagined. Soon, rows of trees surrounded the trio and lined the road.

"Are you sure we'll make it by sundown?" Will asked. The weariness in his voice revealed how he hadn't been expecting so much walking that day.

"We're almost there, though I might ask to spend the night. They have spare rooms, so don't worry about space."

"You never mentioned who these people are," Coura added.

"Didn't I? Since you transitioned to the palace, have you heard of a man who goes by Clearshot?"

Both she and Will shook their heads, which made Byron smile.

"That should deflate his ego."

Will cast the master mage a dubious glance. "Is his name really Clearshot?"

"It's just a nickname. He's a soldier, one of the best archers in Asteom. We used to train together when I was stationed here years ago. Recently, we were able to catch up. That's when he invited us to his home. I believe you'll like him and his family."

As promised, they reached their destination a few minutes later. The house and yard space appeared equal to the mansions along the eastern road in the city, except without the additional decor. Woods circled the brick building, a wide stretch of open area beyond, and a pond peeking around the back. Out of the corner of her eye, Coura caught a pair of smaller figures running into the trees while giggling to each other.

"Those are his children, Mace and Lexie," her mentor shared before knocking on the front door.

Even with it closed, they heard a man's voice from inside. "It's rude to keep such hospitable company waiting!"

"Then hurry up and let us in," Byron yelled in response.

The door flung open to reveal a lean, middle-aged man wearing a brilliant grin. His dusty hair had been trimmed short, and his face looked as chiseled as his arms. The old friends clasped hands and greeted one another before the master mage introduced Will and Coura.

Clearshot's head bobbed while he analyzed them through brown eyes spotted gray at their rims. The personality he presented seemed carefree yet observant. "Let's head to the table. Emilea's preparing dinner."

The home smelled of freshly baked bread and stayed heated by a lit fireplace at the center of a sitting room off to the left. The dining room opened directly ahead as they entered, a doorway led into the kitchen, and a staircase loomed farther back.

"Emilea, Byron and his students are here," their host announced before inviting the three to take a seat. Then, he disappeared into the kitchen.

Coura remained standing with her mentor as Will sank into a chair to rest his legs. Through the nearest window, she watched the sun fall beneath the tree line and listened to the man and his wife in the next room.

"I'm glad they made it before dark. Now, bring these dishes over, please. Have you seen Mace and Lexie?"

Clearshot emerged first carrying a steaming, copper pot and set it on the table.

"We'll help as well," Byron offered yet hesitated when the woman hurried out with a tray of rolls.

Coura froze as well when she recognized the woman as the spite-filled light mage she encountered weeks ago in a hallway on the third floor. Unlike that occasion, her facial features smoothed into a kind expression, and nothing brought about painful memories.

Emilea glanced at Byron first with matching amazement. "Master Byron? I had no idea you would be here."

He recovered in seconds and smiled while responding. "Please, it's just Byron. I suppose it's my fault for not getting to know the leader of the palace's mages. Although, I'm not familiar with many Emilea's, and somebody could have warned us both."

His eyes simultaneously narrowed and shot toward Clearshot, who snuck into the kitchen with an amused expression.

The light mage shook her head but relaxed and continued setting the table. "Well, now we have the chance for a proper introduction."

"Let me start with these two," Byron began and gestured toward Will and Coura. "This is Will. He's interested in medicinal herbology and potions. From what I hear, he's been involved with those in the medical stations, including your light mages. Coura is a former student of mine who arrived with the…"

His words faded into silence when he noticed Emilea's complete attention fixated on Coura. The woman glared as vehemently as before, which was to be expected.

"What is a being possessing demonic energy doing in my house?" she accused in a venomous tone.

Can she sense you? Coura asked Soirée when she became suddenly alarmed by the notion. She figured the master light mage would react poorly, but if the woman became aware of the creature's presence, that would cause more trouble.

{*Perhaps. I'd rather not stay to find out. After all, she isn't the only one experiencing a negative reaction.*}

Coura had grown tense too, which reminded her of the journey with Byron, Will, and Marcus to Fester. The feeling of restlessness and being watched seemed identical.

Clearshot made an appearance with a stack of plates and a handful of utensils during the pause. "Didn't I tell you we were having special guests?" he reassured his wife in a calmer manner as he placed the dishes without looking at anybody.

Emilea shifted her glare between Byron, who looked persistently impassive, and her husband. Will remained perceptive enough to keep quiet and help set the table.

{*I bet she feels the same way you do. Our energies are opposites clashing in one meeting. It will take time for them to adjust, as you have been doing with the others who carry light energy.*}

Coura found herself becoming accustomed to the negativity and tried to ignore it. In order to ease the tension, she decided on a dismissive approach, a tactic she used ever since she acquired the demonic power. In her mind, if she acted normally, the light mage might realize how dramatic such antagonistic behavior was and ease up.

"Maybe it would be better if I give you a moment," she added in as neutral a tone as she could manage and to nobody in particular.

Byron said her name as a warning when she opened the front door.

"I'll be right out here getting some fresh air. The food smells delicious by the way."

Once outside, she breathed easier. Soirée bristled with a predatory instinct while Emilea's strength intimidated Coura. What was worse, she could still hear their discussion beyond the door.

"I will not welcome someone like that into my home!"

"I'm sure you heard the rumors, and that's all they are."

"A wolf in sheep's skin is what I see, and if the rest of you aren't smart enough to notice, I'll be the responsible adult."

One of the men said something too quietly for her to make out, but she felt restless enough not to stay and eavesdrop. She imagined a stroll would help her body relax before the forest grew too dark, so she wandered around the house until a worn path caught her eye. After confirming it was indeed a trail, she followed the dirt walkway for a while, enjoying the sounds of insects buzzing and chirping, birds settling in for the night, and bats catching their meals. Soon, Coura figured she needed to return or risk fumbling through darkness.

I'd hate to worry Byron and Will too. They probably feel terrible about this.

A loud, shrill cry in the distance halted her steps.

{*That was no normal creature.*}

Immediately after came a girl's high-pitched scream.

Before she understood what was happening, Coura sprinted off the trail and into the twilight-filled woods in the general direction of the sound. *Where did it come from?*

{*Over to the left. Use your senses.*}

Soirée was right, though she mistook the demon's impatience for urgency. She opened her mind and found two hosts of a twisted, dark energy nearby. Within the next minute, she burst through a pair of bushes and into a clearing at the bottom of a hill. Another, much closer scream sounded, and her eyes shot toward the source.

On the far end of the clearing, two children, presumably the ones she caught exploring when she arrived at Clearshot's home, huddled together. The girl sat on the ground while the boy stood in front of her with both hands clenching a hunting knife. Their eyes were locked on the creatures stalking them.

When Coura appeared, the beasts she assumed were demonic creatures swiveled their heads with glowing, violet eyes to target the person who disturbed their hunt. Their wolf-like bodies stretched about double her height, and their black fur shimmered in the dying light. Everything, from their appearance to their movements, reminded her of a memory she couldn't fully recall, sending a shiver down her spine. They growled before the larger of the two crept toward her.

As Coura's heart pounded, Soirée's presence remained unaffected. The demon spoke without a hint of fear or concern, which steadied her mind and body.

{What will you do now?}

Her initial idea was to summon the demonic blade, prompting her to reach inward for the necessary power.

{You sure are careless. If someone caught you wielding magic, specifically the children, they would surely report such a phenomenon to those in charge of you. How well do you think that will go over with the master light mage? Not to mention what they might assume once they learn you were around demonic creatures to begin with.}

Coura's heart sank once she realized this, which sparked amusement from Soirée.

I'll distract them so the children can escape.

{Good luck. These predators divide their attention between prey, which makes sense since they don't need to eat. Demonic creatures entertain themselves before slaughtering. What a mess you've gotten yourself into.}

Is there anything useful you can tell me? Coura snapped before forcing Soirée's observations aside. *Without magic, I'll need to find a weapon and get to the children first.*

Although her instincts urged her to run, she steadied her legs and forced herself to circle around the closest creature at a methodical pace. It sidestepped away while observing her moves intently. Being so careful strained her muscles, especially when the beast could pounce at any point, yet neither attempted an attack.

She soon stood between them and the victims, who finally noticed her. The girl let out a whimper as Coura began backing up in order to reach the helpless pair. To her dismay, the sound triggered a reaction from the second creature, the one that remained still after she arrived. She spun on her heel as soon as it lunged forward in an effort to go to the children and found them scrambling toward her.

"No!" she shouted and gestured for them to stop.

They slid to a halt with panicked cries, allowing Coura to look at the beasts. In a startling display, the larger of the two towered over the second while bearing its teeth. This caused the smaller creature to lower its head in a submissive fashion before snapping its jaws, as if issuing a challenge.

The one that lunged interrupted the other's stalking. Even if they assume the appearance of wolves, they don't seem to share the animals' sense of cooperation.

Whatever the case, their bickering provided enough of a distraction for her to approach the girl and her brother. They came forward and clung onto her legs until she pulled them off and addressed the boy.

"Give me the knife," she ordered with whatever confidence she could muster.

They stepped away and directed their fear at her before the boy held out the weapon. Coura swiped it from him as she faced the creatures in a single motion.

The beasts' eyes flared to reflect their rage while they growled.

Great, now what?

Before she could consider a plan, the smaller one charged again.

"Run!" she screamed at the children, leaned forward, and prepared to stab at the charging beast.

As she expected, it leapt into the air, so she rolled underneath its belly to dodge the attack. The action placed her between the creatures, though the first twisted around to strike before she had time to recover. Its claws swiped across her left thigh, causing her to gasp and retaliate by thrusting the knife toward its head. The short blade sank into its right eye before she yanked it free while it shrieked.

Meanwhile, the second creature approached. Coura held her position until it lunged, then she jumped to the side so it flew past her and into its partner. This sparked another bout of snapping jaws and growls while she tumbled away; however, as soon as she rose to her feet, a surge of pain stemming from her thigh dropped her to one knee.

I've been severely cut before, yet this burning sensation seems worse.

{Hadn't you noticed their claws are dripping with venom? Our healing magic is stronger, but I wouldn't rely on it for too many injuries.}

Even as Soirée spoke, the discomfort ceased enough for Coura to stand.

Meanwhile, the wounded creature rubbed its face with a paw and backed off, and the other glanced between her and its original, vulnerable prey cowering nearby. When it averted its eyes, she snuck in a couple steps to close the distance between herself and the children. Unfortunately, they became so frightened she couldn't catch their attention. Their behavior prompted her to make a break for their location since the movement would draw the creature away and keep it focused on her instead.

She burst into a sprint, attracting its eyes before it noticed the direction she headed in. Although she ground her teeth and forced her legs to go faster, no interruption hindered her progress.

The girl spotted her first, yelled an indiscernible message, then began creeping away from her brother. Before Coura could order her not to continue, the creature crouched in preparation for another lunge at the slower target. She extended her arms upon reaching the pair and shoved each child backward with the intent to whirl around with the knife poised. Unfortunately, the ground stook as the creature landed right behind her, rose onto its hind legs, then swiped at her with its front paws.

This time, she couldn't dodge. The claws swept diagonally across her back one after the other from shoulder to hip. Although the healing began immediately, the resulting stinging made her dizzy enough to fall onto her hands and knees. In response, the children screamed, yet she focused on gripping the weapon, her only chance at survival.

The creature pounced after, slamming her face-first into the ground before adjusting its stance to hover over her. Coura responded by rolling onto her back in order to look up at it, though the way her open flesh rubbed into the dirt caused her to involuntarily hiss.

Being so close to such an abomination disgusted her. The oily fur smelled rotten, its unnaturally gray teeth dripped a dark liquid when it snarled, and the violet eyes gazed down at her. When it opened its mouth to bite at her throat, Coura held up her arms for protection. The oversized jaws clamped down on her right forearm, producing a sickening crunch and splattering warm blood onto her chest. She tried kicking the beast in an attempt to free herself to no avail.

Afraid and nearly out of options, she remembered the knife. Using her left hand, she pried the weapon from her clenched, right one and hacked at the creature's exposed neck. Black blood poured all over her, but the grip on her arm released.

The beast recoiled off her body with a gurgling noise while more liquid dripped out of the wound. Like its partner, this creature rubbed at its injury, as if unsure of what was wrong. It backtracked until it stood against the trees where it disappeared into the woods.

Sharing Secrets

Coura pushed herself up from the ground and waited, holding the knife in her left hand while her right arm and torso throbbed. Her whole body shook violently. The darkness made it impossible to see more than the shadows around them, so she opened her mind and sensed just one of the creatures' presence far enough away to no longer be a threat. The trembling subsided, and she rested her head against her knees while catching her breath.

What happened?

{*You're beginning to get the hang of killing.*}

The pride in Soirée's voice was haunting, so Coura ignored the sickening feeling it arose. "We need to get back," she muttered before getting to her feet.

Farther behind her were the children, who watched the area the creature disappeared through. *They're okay. Thank goodness!*

Coura released a sigh of relief and approached them. "We should be safe now. Those beasts are gone."

They stared at her without responding, presumably uncertain whether to trust her or not. To remedy this, she knelt despite the effort, dropped the knife, then extended her left hand to them.

"Come on," she urged reproachfully. "I won't hurt you."

Slowly, the children wrapped their arms around her neck and began sobbing. She didn't say anything until they finished, even though the added pressure bothered her shoulders. After making sure they could manage the upcoming trek, she stood.

"We'd better get you home."

"W-W-We don't even kn-know where we are," the boy stuttered while wiping his nose on his shirt.

"Don't worry about that. Just hold onto me."

Coura opened her mind and located two powerful sources of energy beyond the clearing. *Byron and Emilea...*

Each child took one of the hands she offered before following her lead. Her back no longer throbbed and only a slight ache came from her right arm, but she felt exhausted. It became apparent when they moved through the trees that the girl couldn't keep up without tripping over the foliage in the dark. Coura decided to carry the younger sibling on her back to save them time while the boy tightly grip her hand.

For what seemed like the entire night, they hiked through the forest. The insects' noise soon filled their ears instead of silence, and the sound of voices began blending in with the nightlife.

"Mother?" the boy cried hopefully before trying to hurry ahead.

Coura held him in place. "Not yet. Wait until we get closer."

After a minute, they could discern the calls as names.

"Mace? Lexie?"

"Here we are!" the children yelled in response, yet they didn't attempt to push their pace.

Lights through the trees brought them to the front of the brick house where Clearshot, Emilea, Byron, and Will huddled with their cloaks on, as though they were about to head out for a search. Once the group spotted the three figures, Emilea and Clearshot rushed forward.

"Mace! Lexie! Where have you been?" the former exclaimed.

This time, Coura didn't stop the boy, Mace, from dashing into his parents' open arms after they dropped to their knees in the grass. His sister, Lexie, wiggled on her back until she lowered herself and let the girl down, allowing the child to join the reunion. Emilea questioned the two on their whereabouts while Byron started doing the same to Coura. When she stepped closer they all fell silent, reminding her of how horrifying she appeared in the tattered, blood-soaked clothing.

Lexie gasped dramatically and tugged on her mother's cloak. "The beasts hurt her! You need to heal her!"

"Their claws and teeth were like knives," Mace threw in.

While the children rambled on about the creatures and how Coura fought them off, injuring herself in the process, the rest of the group gaped in disbelief. Emilea still glared at her with the same hatred, yet it softened, either due to surprise or gratitude.

As the story continued, she began to feel incredibly weary, both physically and mentally, and realized she would need to clarify details about the incident later. She rubbed the back of her neck before remembering the pond around the opposite side of the house; the thought of its cool water on her dirty skin became enticing enough to drive her in that direction.

"Where are you going?" Byron asked with an edge to his voice.

"I'll wash up and be inside shortly," she answered without glancing behind.

*

The impromptu bath seemed to be exactly what Coura needed. There wasn't much left of her shirt to salvage, so she tore it off and tossed it aside, along with every other article of clothing. Then, she slipped into the water. The crusted blood, both hers and the demonic creature's, disappeared as she scrubbed, leaving her to marvel at the flawless skin underneath.

While she studied her right arm in particular, a pair of footsteps approached in the grass.

"Are you actually hurt?"

Hearing Emilea's voice shocked Coura, though the resentment beneath the question told her the woman still didn't think highly of her. "Not anymore," she replied and listened as the steps went away.

It's not a warm welcome, but hopefully she'll let me inside.

When she crawled onto the grass, she discovered the light mage left her a towel and a new set of clothes. She dressed in the brisk evening and grew exhausted from the effort.

I must have done more than I thought.

{Remember when I recommended you don't exert our power for healing? Our core of energy is strong and full, but that spell puts a strain on your physical body. You can't replace flesh by using magic without tiring yourself, and you are certainly not used to that.}

How come you never told me this before?

{I like to believe we're capable enough to avoid major injuries.}

Coura yawned and entered through the nearest door leading to the hallway in front of the kitchen. The others already began eating and made conversation at the table while Clearshot hung up their cloaks. Although a seat remained open between Will and Byron, she felt more worn out than hungry, driving her to snatch a couple rolls off the table and drop into an armchair near the fire in the sitting area. She appreciated that no one stopped the meal to speak with her since she desired nothing aside from relaxing and collecting her thoughts. The bread proved to be just enough to settle her stomach, and the heat from the fireplace lulled her to sleep within minutes.

***

Emilea's cooking didn't compare to the chefs' in the palace, yet Byron found the company much more tolerable. He buried his personal questions and suspicions regarding Coura and the demonic creatures the children described and instead focused on a light-hearted meal. Everybody else did the same, though Will snuck several glances at his friend, who dozed by the fireplace. Mace and Lexie also grew fatigued from the excitement after their parents' lecture about sneaking off by themselves, which led to the girl almost lowering her head into her food.

"It's time for bed," Emilea announced while rising to carry her daughter away.

"Will, help me with the dishes," Byron ordered before he stood and stretched. He figured the young man needed something to do besides keep an eye on Coura.

They cleared the table, washed the plates, utensils, and mugs, then began snuffing out a majority of the lamps. Mace joined his sister upstairs when they finished as Clearshot brought out a couple mugs filled to the brim with ale and set one in front of Byron.

"Excuse me," Will chimed once the men returned to the table. "Where will we be staying? I'm about ready to fall over."

"I'll show you to your rooms," Emilea offered with a candle in hand.

Byron caught her eyes slide to the armchair after and moved to rouse Coura. As soon as he touched his student's shoulder, she jolted upright and rubbed her eyes.

"What's wrong?" she grumbled while blinking without really seeing him.

"Let's get you to bed."

Emilea and Will already went up the stairs, so he helped her to her feet and followed behind. The second story held the master and children's bedrooms, as well as an additional four guest rooms and other spaces with the doors closed. Each spare bedroom contained the same items as those in the palace without any decorations to set them apart.

Will excused himself after thanking Emilea for the meal. She seemed flattered and wished him pleasant dreams with a smile that disappeared when she turned to Byron.

"You can put her in the next room over. I already lit the candle inside for you to use."

He already figured Emilea was sensitive to the demonic energy, like everybody else, so it made sense why she acted hostile toward Coura. In some ways, he didn't blame the light mage; on the other hand, her behavior made him wonder how such negativity affected his student's mindset and attitude.

After nodding, he pulled Coura into the designated room where she immediately climbed into the bed. He took the candle, closed the door, then returned to the dining area where Emilea kissed her husband on the cheek before leaving them alone.

Byron and Clearshot silently sipped at their drinks for a few minutes until the latter cleared his throat.

"Are you going to tell me about her?"

"Who?"

Clearshot grinned from behind his mug. "That's the one, right? The dark mage everyone's talking about who uses demonic power?"

Byron rubbed his temple. "She's more of a headache than anything else."

His friend and comrade had always been straight to the point ever since they met. The man hadn't been born into a noble household and avoided the pretty words and politics, which he appreciated after dealing with worse in the palace.

"You've got to give me more than that!"

"I'm just as clueless about it as you are."

Clearshot glanced over at the staircase for a moment before continuing at a lower volume. "Nobody's telling the soldiers what's going on anymore, no matter our experience. It's obvious King Hernan's furious over the ambassador, and everyone's saying he hasn't heard from Yeluthia since. To the north, there's conflict in Nim-Vala, but the generals won't release the information. Now, we've got a mage they're labeling as a weapon who wields forbidden magic. I just don't know who to trust, and it's bothering me."

"I know just as little as you do about Yeluthia and Nim-Vala, but it seems too soon to expect a response out of either country, if you ask me."

The soldier downed the remainder of his drink and wiped his lips on his sleeve. "Your student saved my children's lives; I can't hate her for that. In fact, the way I view it, I'm indebted to her. I can't say the same for Emilea, though."

"I imagine she'll have a harder time," Byron added, nodded, and finished his ale.

"You might not know this since it's your first time out here, but demonic creatures are wandering through the denser parts of these woods. They keep multiplying into savage beasts every year. I'm worried something's nurturing them, or possibly controlling them."

"Really?" Byron thought back to his previous encounters with demonic creatures over the years. They always acted like any predator would, even in Coura's case.

"All I'm saying is, I'd like to know what's happening. Emilea too, but she hates that type of magic. I trust you as my friend, as well as one of the strongest mages around."

"I'm flattered, and I promise to share what I learn with you and Emilea. Keep an eye on this area, though. Perhaps you might consider moving into Verona, just to be safe."

Clearshot huffed a laugh. "I'd rather live with the threats in these woods than near the dangerous creatures wandering around that city. The flocking and flaunting of wealth are enough to make a man sick!"

He launched into a story containing various topics for them to discuss, filling the space with jokes and reminiscing before they decided to call it a night.

"I'm glad you could visit," the soldier added when they rose and tiptoed upstairs.

"Anything to catch a break. I swear they'll work me until I'm gray-haired within the next few years."

Byron selected one of the remaining vacant rooms and prepared to enter when he heard Clearshot whisper his name. "What is it?"

"Make sure to tell me if you hear more about what we talked about earlier, okay? I want to be able to protect my family. I could have lost them tonight if it wasn't for…"

"I will," he replied firmly into the surrounding darkness.

***

A beam of light escaped through a crack in the curtain to land directly on Coura's eyes and wake her. With a groan, she rolled over while covering her head with one of the soft pillows in an attempt to rest longer. Unfortunately, she became alert enough to avoid slipping into sleep again, though she desired a day in bed.

Her first movements reminded her of Soirée's recent note about the healing ability. Her arms, legs, and back ached, as if she spent the whole morning exercising and being beaten up in the process. Her stomach eventually drove her out of the comfortable sheets in search of breakfast until she spotted a plain, gray dress with an attached note from Emilea telling her to keep the clothing. With the light mage's blessing, she threw it on before heading downstairs and straight into the kitchen.

When she entered, Clearshot addressed her, as cheerful as a lark. "It's about time the hero makes her entrance!"

"There's no need for that," she commented while observing the assortment of fresh sandwiches on the counter.

"Fair enough. Now, eat up! It's just after noon, and Byron's itching to return to the palace."

"After noon?" Coura repeated in disbelief.

I slept through half the day!

"Don't worry," came Byron's voice from behind before he placed his hands on her shoulders. "There will be plenty of time to catch up on your readings."

"I think experience is the real lesson," she replied while sneaking out of his hold to grab a sandwich in each hand.

"I agree," Clearshot added with a proud smile. "You are beyond your years, Coura. Leave the books to the scholars, not the fighters."

Byron rolled his eyes and pointed an accusing finger. "Don't encourage her!"

Their host responded with a hearty, contagious laugh that had Coura giggling, and even Byron grinned at his friend's lax attitude. She moved into the dining area, sat, and dove into the food. Her mentor joined her a minute later.

"How are you feeling?" he asked.

She shrugged. "Tired. A little sore."

"Emilea told me she discovered more than just blood on your clothes," he added with a touch of seriousness. "She identified it as a potent venom. Were you aware of this?"

After nodding, she had to glance away from his shaken reaction.

"We'll discuss this later," he decided when they heard the front door opening.

Will entered and went into the kitchen with a wave at them, then the children slipped inside. Lexie pranced toward the table carrying a handful of flowers and startled Coura by shoving them in her face.

"Look what we found," the girl announced.

"They smell lovely," Coura commented despite their pollen tickling her nose. "What are they?"

"Pansies. Mother says they have the sweetest smelling petals, and that's why you can bake with them." Lexie pulled the bouquet away, plucked a yellow flower out, and held it in front of Coura, who gingerly accepted the offering.

She thanked the child and inhaled the floral aroma to savor the scent while Lexie continued into the kitchen where they heard Clearshot's overdramatic amazement upon seeing the flowers.

Mace waited for his sister to leave before jumping into the chair at Coura's left and dumping a collection of pebbles on the table, creating tiny thumps. The stones were lightly colored, smooth, and circular.

"What's this?" she inquired when he didn't explain.

"I look for stones to use in my slingshot. The ones that are too flat can be skipped in the pond. Mother says I'm still too young for a bow and arrows."

Coura and Byron finished their lunch as Mace elaborated on his interest in the rocks and the ways he utilized whatever he found. All the while the boy kept his eyes down and filed through the pebbles, organizing them by what he saw and touched.

When he began picking them up, Coura got the impression he expected her to comment on his hobby. "Thank you for showing me. You have a well-trained eye for spotting the ones you need.

That's a useful trait for somebody who wants to do archery, and I think your father would agree."

Mace's eyes widened a bit and his cheeks blushed, but he nodded and took his collection into the sitting room. She watched him go as she reflected on the children's behavior toward her and their enthusiasm for the world around them. When she faced forward again, Byron studied her while wearing an amused expression.

"What?"

"It looks like you earned a pair of admirers," he mumbled loudly enough for her to hear.

Coura shook her head and stared out the window. "It's just a phase."

She felt a sense of relief when Byron stood to join Clearshot and Will in the kitchen instead of pestering her more.

{*Don't pretend you don't like the attention.*}

Like I said, they're just grateful I saved their lives.

{*The children respect you now that they saw how you defended them.*}

For a moment, the demon's seemingly positive attitude confused Coura. *I thought you didn't care if they died?*

{*I wouldn't have, but since you saved them, it's refreshing for ones so young to idolize their rescuer. Just imagine when the older humans recognize our power.*}

Coura frowned. *Of course that's what you're imagining. Why would I assume anything different?*

The trio from the kitchen shuffled out to linger around the table and talk, and Emilea eventually joined after appearing from the hallway farther back. As expected, the master light mage became unnerved around Coura yet avoided staring daggers her way.

Clearshot wrapped his arms around his wife once the current conversation ended. "My, what a crowd we gathered in our humble home!"

"Too bad it can't last," Byron responded and gestured to the front door. "We'd best be on our way if I'm ever going to get my work done while the sun is up."

The soldier mentioned his upcoming travel plans to Byron, so Will helped Emilea grab what bags they brought. Coura shifted her legs to stand only to find Lexie at her side.

"You're leaving?"

She smiled sympathetically and patted the blonde head. "I'm afraid so. Don't worry, I'm sure-"

"You can't," the girl interrupted with a pout. "I didn't even get a chance to show you my magic."

"You can use magic?" She didn't expect the child to be older than seven or eight.

Lexie's face brightened as she grinned and bobbed her head. Upon hearing the outburst, everybody glanced over. "I can wield light magic, just like Mother."

"I can use dark magic," Mace called from the other side of the room with his own sense of self-importance.

"Both children possess magical potential," Byron muttered and shook his head in disbelief. It wasn't unheard of for siblings to share the ability to manipulate energy, but more than one in a family had always been rare.

Clearshot jabbed his thumb to his chest. "Of course! Whose children do you think these are anyway?"

"Why, Lady Emilea's of course," Will answered nonchalantly. His following smirk prompted a chuckle out of Byron and Coura, and even Emilea smiled before putting a reassuring hand on her husband's back.

"There's no need to be so rude," Clearshot mumbled in a deflated tone.

Byron shouldered his bag and moved to the front door. "Come on you two; let's get going."

Despite the order, Lexie remained in Coura's path, forcing her to address the child. "I'll be here again to see your magic before you know it. Both of you."

"Fine," the girl murmured without attempting to hide her displeasure.

Coura glanced between Lexie and Mace and contemplated leaving the subject at that; however, they looked disappointed enough to bother her. "How about this: If you behave, I'll show you my magic too."

She winked to emphasize the surprise, spurring interest from the children. While Mace and Lexie eagerly agreed to the deal, the others in the room didn't appear as enthusiastic.

*

Since the trio didn't plan on staying with Clearshot and his family for another evening, they needed to hurry in order to reach Verona before it grew dark. They set off on the road an hour after noon, meaning they would arrive at the palace just as the sun set. Byron kept conversation sparse while Coura watched the trees around them out of habit due to the first time the three ventured through the area.

The environment seemed peaceful until Will gasped loud enough to alarm his companions.

"What is it?" Byron demanded, but the herbalist already jogged ahead and stripped off his bag in the process.

"Is this what I think… The dragon-berry flower!" he exclaimed while bending over a patch of cherry-colored flowers.

Their leader calmed down, and Coura groaned at Will's overenthusiasm. He turned and apologized for scaring them after.

"Just hurry and take your samples," Byron urged.

With vials and a notebook in hand, the researcher wasted no time gathering the plants. Some had grown underneath a bush, so he crawled off the path to retrieve them.

"Why are some silly flowers worth fawning over?" Coura muttered as she observed the rustling leaves.

During the resulting pause, her mentor quietly said her name.

"What is it?" Even though she inquired, she had an inkling it related to what took place at Clearshot and Emilea's home.

"When you fought off those demonic creatures last night, did they injure you?" His emerald eyes never left Will's position as he spoke.

She sighed before answering despite sensing Soirée inching forward to eavesdrop. "Yes. It happened exactly how the children described."

"If that's true, you should have serious wounds on your leg, back, and arm."

"And?"

Byron glanced at her, narrowed his eyes, and tightened his lips to show the severity of the situation. She understood what he was expecting to hear but wouldn't directly ask.

{*Don't mention the healing.*}

That won't help. He already suspects I can do so because of your power.

Soirée only repeated herself and lingered like a head on Coura's shoulder.

Her mentor continued to wait for a response, so she shrugged off her pack and removed the tiny blade she always brought along for typical camping and cooking needs. Byron raised an eyebrow at that yet remained cross-armed and patient.

{*Stop it!*}

While the demon hissed in her mind, Coura placed the sharp edge along the palm of her hand and slashed her skin in a single jerk. After the damage from the previous night, she hardly noticed the pain; however, blood dripped onto the ground to form a tiny puddle.

They studied the cut in a stretch of silence broken by Will, who shouted that he was almost finished. There came a tingling sensation as a tendril of energy spread from her center and through her arm. The damaged area began mending, and the magic faded to reveal her unmarred palm underneath drying blood. To emphasize the spell's potency, she opened and closed her hand before returning the knife to her bag and rubbing most of the blood onto the clothes inside.

Byron didn't comment on the process, and Will returned as Coura picked up her pack.

"I can't imagine how you keep your supplies in order," she told the herbalist. "After all, your room is such a mess. I'd lose my shoes if I didn't wear them in there."

"I hope I didn't take too long," he offered to her, then Byron.

When the master mage didn't respond and continued staring at where Will had disappeared within the brush, Coura thought perhaps Soirée was right about revealing the secret. Fortunately, the demon became too upset with her to intrude again.

"Are you ill, Master Byron?" Will asked hesitantly. "You look pale. I might be able to mix a potion with the items I gathered this morning."

As he prepared to remove his bag, their leader snapped out of the trance.

"Thank you, but that won't be necessary. We lost enough daylight already."

Will bought Byron's faint smile and casual tone, but Coura knew better than to assume he moved on from what she showed him. The realization that he now viewed her differently filled her with despair.

Soirée's, "I told you so," afterward made her feel worse as they continued on.

Widening the Circle

lthough Coura met with Byron over the next five days for their combat sessions, he kept their discussions strictly professional and never raised any concerns regarding their recent adventure. The questions relating to demonic energy and her abilities stopped, yet a sense of unease stretched between the two and was never addressed.

She remained heated with Marcus and avoided their shared dinners, instead opting for meals with Will in the mess hall. He seemed to be her only friend and appeared excited to spend time together, though her presence drove away the mages around him. Despite that, Coura found she enjoyed Will's company quite a bit, even if all he talked about were his studies and research. It comforted her to hear such mundane topics from somebody so passionate about their work.

On her next free day, she focused on independent sword techniques at the far end of the training ground. She didn't expect many to be people outside, yet at least three dozen soldiers fought in a mock battle using actual helmets, armor, and metal blades. Nearby, ten mages worked in their own circle. She paused to observe them as they practiced wielding spells in tandem. While four light mages created a center shield by combining their energy to form a transparent, shimmering wall with a silver hue, the dark mages took turns firing minor lightning bolts, fireballs, and ice shards in multiple directions in an attempt to strike the others' location. This forced the light mages to unite under a single leader and shift the balance of power.

How long has it been since I cast a spell?

Coura closed her hands into fists when her fingers began twitching. The sensation of releasing her pent-up energy and the image of freedom above the ground caused her back to itch. Soirée pounced on that feeling after to remind her of their magical potential through elaborate scenarios and enticing descriptions.

It wasn't until one of the mages behind the shield spotted her that Coura realized she still stared at the group. She recognized the young man from one of her lectures at the academy but couldn't remember a name. Obviously, she didn't make enough of a positive impression for him to overlook the rumors because he glared in response. His friends noticed, mirrored his gaze, and gave her the same treatment before continuing with their session. It stung, but like the physical cuts and bruises, the sensation grew numb as time passed.

She dismissed their behavior and turned away from the mages in order to move toward the stable where she returned her wooden blade. When she took a few steps in the direction of the palace after, she heard someone call her name. The soldiers sparred to her left except for a lone figure who jogged over to meet her. Coura didn't recognize them with the helmet and padding on, so she waited until they stopped in front of her.

"We haven't seen you in a few days," said a familiar voice. "Aaron and I miss having another person to put us in our place." Marcus slid the helmet off, held it under one arm, and wiped away the sweat decorating his forehead with his free hand.

"I have nothing to say to you," she snapped as she recalled the last time she'd seen them. Marcus knew she remained upset with him, but she wondered what Aaron thought after she left him fumbling in the corridor.

I don't belong around... I'm not safe around somebody as important as a prince. That applies to Marcus, Will, and Byron too. The realization spurred a sadness that gripped her chest.

While she started to wallow in self-pity, Marcus smiled, albeit with a wince. "I'm sorry about that letter and its consequences. I had no intention of hurting you or causing problems for East Hoover. I can't undo the results, but please don't hold a grudge for a mistake in the past."

Before she could consider a response, he continued in a lax manner.

"I'll make it up to you somehow, someday. For now, let's try moving on. Can we expect you for our dinner date tonight?"

"You're terrible at apologies," Coura replied in lieu of an answer.

The negative emotions eased; however, she didn't feel like being outside anymore or by the assistant general. Without another word, she spun around to head inside where she returned to her room and focused on her studies for the first time in weeks.

*

Will knocked on her door later that afternoon so they could go down to the mess hall together. "Are you sick?" he asked after entering her room. "I see open books. That's not like you."

A laugh escaped Coura as she marked her page in *The Geography and Geology of Asteom* and closed the text before shooing him into the hallway. "I'm starving is what I am," she announced while closing the door behind them.

Once they reached the nearest staircase, Will started to descend, but Coura paused at the top. She couldn't help herself from glancing farther to her left where the corner turned, leading to Marcus' room.

Are they actually expecting me? she wondered with an odd, nagging sensation. As she considered their shared meals, an idea formed in her mind, one driven partly by her frustration.

"Are you coming, Coura?"

"How attached are you to the mess hall?" she asked Will, who shot her a confused look.

"Not much, I suppose. It's usually just us eating-"

"Perfect," she interrupted and went to where he lingered. After grabbing his arm, she pulled him back up the stairs and through the hallway.

"Ouch, that hurts! Where are we going?"

"We've got a dinner date."

"A…what? A date?"

She chuckled when his cheeks flushed while he began mumbling to himself. As they approached Marcus' room, Coura let go of Will to knock.

"Whose room is this?" Will whispered in the most flustered manner she'd ever experienced from him.

The door opened before she could reply, and the soldier offered a polite smile as he assessed the pair. At first, he appeared relieved to see her, then his eyes slid to the herbalist.

"Can I help you, Will?"

"I didn't…"

"He's going to join us," Coura stated while sticking up her chin a bit and pushing Will forward.

The unexpected gesture and additional guest visibly startled Marcus, though he presumably understood how rude it would be to turn a friend away and said nothing. She followed close behind Will and shoved him into the nearest chair before he could faint; he came close to doing so when he noticed Aaron sitting at the desk with a wine bottle in hand and a dumbstruck expression.

Coura savored the satisfaction of catching not one, not two, but all *three* of the boys off guard. A mischievous smirk stretched across her face as she curtsied. "Your Highness, I would like you to meet my friend, Will."

The prince cleared his throat. "I wasn't expecting-"

"It's an honor, Your Highness!" Will interrupted before jumping to his feet and offering a proper bow.

Aaron shot Coura an irritated glare and set the bottle aside when the comments from the newcomer continued. Meanwhile, Marcus lingered by the open door, as if expecting somebody to leave soon.

"What are you waiting for?" Coura finally asked him as Will rambled on.

"I guess nothing," he replied in a voice teeming with disapproval and closed the door.

They didn't sit in an awkward silence since her friend, true to his talkative nature, threw compliments at Aaron and apologized a dozen or so times for the intrusion. Every sentence either began or ended with "Your Highness" directed toward the prince.

"Please, there's no need to be so formal," Aaron snuck in between breaths. His annoyance seemed to melt into exhaustion as he pleaded.

At some point, a servant entered bearing the usual tray of food, yet that didn't stop Will from finding more to discuss. Coura nibbled on one of the pastries when nobody moved and found both Marcus and Aaron scowling at her.

Perhaps I've tortured them all enough.
{I quite enjoy this.}
You're twisted, that's why.

Soirée took her comment as a compliment before fading away.

The herbalist was in the middle of a sentence when she set a hand on his back and handed him the wine that found its way to her. "You can stop now."

He stared at her for a moment before accepting the bottle. While he drank, he couldn't speak, so she used the opportunity to apologize. Although she directed the words at Will, Marcus and Aaron relaxed as well.

"I'm sorry for throwing you in here like this. It was cruel of me to not warn you, and worse to let you remain the center of attention."

"It's fine," he responded a bit sheepishly.

"Grab some food while I introduce you."

Everybody else had finished their meal, allowing Will to eat without feeling pressured.

"That lackluster man over there is Aaron. When we're in here, it's just Aaron, not "Prince" or "Your Highness." Got it?"

Though he appeared hesitant about the order, her friend nodded.

"You already know the idiot over there," she added and pointed indifferently at Marcus, who lounged on his bed.

The soldier frowned. "Don't be rude."

"We eat dinner together almost every day. In here, we can be ourselves, talk about whatever we want to, and not worry about being alone."

By that point, Will calmed down enough to offer a timid smile. "I like that, especially the part about not being alone."

"Why?" she prompted.

This time, the explanation of his travels and observations on the road felt natural. He told them about his hometown, which Coura and Marcus heard about before, and some of his studies on the herbs and plants he frequently tested.

When he finished, Aaron picked up on the last topic. "My mother loves flowers. She keeps a garden in back of the palace. I'd love to hear more about their medicinal properties since the ones she has are only for decoration."

The two discussed the idea while Coura and Marcus listened. Their conversation lasted well into the night until the four started to nod off.

*

The next day at dinner, she brought Will again and found the prince eager to talk more about his mother's garden.

"I informed her of the properties those flowers might have, so she wants to plant herbs for the chefs and healers now. Can you believe they never kept a garden of their own? Apparently, most people have been growing plants indoors or purchasing what they need in the city. This could be the perfect opportunity for you to educate them."

Will blushed. "Thank you, Your Highness."

Coura reached over to pinch his arm as a reminder about their view on titles, causing him to yelp and rub the spot.

"Sorry. Thank you, Aaron."

"You sure care about your mother's garden," she chimed in after.

The prince stared at her with an unreadable expression. "Well, of course. It's one of a few activities she's passionate about. She always hoped to learn more about the plants."

Soirée usually disappeared when Coura ate with her friends since the demon grew too bored to bother with them. For the first time that day, she could think for herself and considered what her own parents' interests used to be.

"What does your mother do?" she asked Marcus, who didn't seem as irritable as the previous evening.

"My mother? She lives in Verona with my older sister."

"You have an older sister?"

"What does it matter?" he countered.

"I haven't heard you mention much about your family is all, and we've been through Verona twice."

He shrugged and stared up at the ceiling. "With my father living here as a general, my mother doesn't need to work. She enjoys being around my sister and her two granddaughters while they mend clothes for some old man's business. I can't remember the name, but it's off the main road. I visit them when I'm free, though I would rather be in the palace. Besides, my father is the person I interact with the most."

"Besides us," Aaron threw in.

"I guess."

Will released a sigh. "I wish I had siblings."

"Me too," the prince added at a lowered volume.

Coura sensed a point to his reply, but Marcus addressed her before she could question it.

"What about you?"

"Mother, when will I get a little brother or sister to play with?"

She closed her eyes and focused on the child's voice that came to mind before shaking her head. "None I'm aware of. I don't remember anything from before I came to the academy."

The three stared at her incredulously, though Will was the one to press the subject.

"Really? I thought you were only there for a few years?"

Coura shifted her gaze to the bookcase across from where she sat and tried recalling her distant past while the boys watched with interest. "I don't know what my life was like before Byron brought me there."

The room fell silent until Marcus sparked another, more comfortable topic to discuss. While they chatted, she contemplated the unexpected voice in her head.

Who was that? Mace and Lexie are the only children I encountered recently. Maybe... Is it another lost memory of mine?

Soirée's voice echoed from a distance.

{Remember what happened the last time you ventured into forgotten places. Don't embarrass yourself by recklessly poking around again.}

You're right, she decided and reluctantly closed off her curiosity.

As the demon's presence disappeared, Coura realized the room fell silent and glanced at the other three, who seemed to be expecting her to speak.

"What?"

"Will mentioned you both went with Byron to visit Clearshot," Marcus repeated. "I asked for your impression of him and Lady Emilea."

This time, she jumped into the conversation and explained their experience while omitting a few details.

***

Byron paced around his quarters in anticipation for yet another meeting with the king's council. Because of the Yeluthian ambassador's arrival and the upcoming Harvest Festival, he managed to prolong that a bit. The latter event meant the entire palace and city would celebrate and spend the following morning recovering, except for the vendors who wished to market their wares, servants from the kitchens, and soldiers who volunteered for guard duty. King Hernan needed to approve each aspect, such as the performers, rules about selling merchandise, and the numbers, positions, and schedules for the soldiers, so he didn't have time until just before the festival.

The letter Byron received with the king's seal explained that and more, including what he already assumed.

They want to hear about Coura. I'm not sure what details exactly, but I would imagine they'll be interested in learning how she can heal from otherwise fatal wounds.

Upon reading the message hours earlier, he became conflicted about what he should reveal. To tell them she was a skilled fighter, if not better than most soldiers, would give them confidence; to admit she was nearly as magically gifted as himself but hasn't used the demonic power in months would make them impatient.

If I mention any injury mends itself, who knows what they'll do. They could care more about her training, though. Depending on what Clearshot said, if trouble is brewing, the council might decide to rely on her healing instead of her skills.

Eventually, he needed to get going and came to a conclusion that satisfied him the most.

I will not risk her life on assumptions without her consent. Just because she showed me the trick with her hand and the children included it in their stories does not mean I received all the answers. Until I can talk with Coura, the healing should remain a secret.

*

The meeting chamber was located in the center of the palace on the second floor where it stayed far enough out of the way to be secure but not secluded because of its frequent use. Byron had been in the room dozens of times over the past year and memorized the route. Soldiers walking by, and he waved to the regular guards stationed outside the space before heading inside.

Windowless, stone walls blocked natural sunlight yet kept the area at a cool temperature, so mounted lamps provided as much light and projected a warmth to counter the chill. The chamber's wide design could hold at least fifty people, as showcased by the additional seats remaining around a circular table placed near the front. A semi-formal throne loomed along the eastern wall on a raised patch of flooring to overlook those present, including the generals, a pair of wealthy noblemen in charge of the palace's finances, and the high priest.

King Hernan assumed his position above the council and gestured for him to enter. "Please, join us."

In front of the throne stood Emilea. She looked at Byron when he stepped beside her but didn't speak. Since the master mages were only required to report at the meeting, they felt no need to seat themselves like the rest of the participants.

"Why don't we get this particular discussion started," one of the generals named Preston began with an amused smirk. "We've been hearing some interesting stories about your pupil, Master Byron."

"Oh?"

He caught Emilea's eye before she turned away. If the light mage already brought up the assumption Coura could heal herself, he would need to find a way to refute it. Although he prayed that wouldn't be the case, the king's next words dashed his hopes.

"Managing a combative dark mage impervious to injury should prove rather effective," King Hernan commented nonchalantly.

"Or disastrous," Hendal piped from the table. Unlike Emilea, Byron sensed no light energy from the devoted high priest. He figured the man's dislike of demonic power stemmed directly from its blasphemy against most gods' teachings, or something along those lines.

"We seem to be in disagreement," another general named Casner chimed from his seat.

Hendal nodded, put his hands together, and leaned forward. His expression appeared almost desperate as he addressed Byron. "Please, share her progress with us. We have other matters to discuss afterward."

As carefully as he could, Byron weaved a report that included both Coura's physical and magical abilities without exaggerating or hiding any details. His tightened jaw remained the only sign he let show of his frustration. "Her combat skills are a match with mine and most of her sparring partners'. She has always been fluent with a weapon, especially when it comes to sword work."

"So, she could fit in as a soldier," one of the noblemen commented.

"I wouldn't say the same about her magic since I haven't been able to observe it since the transfer."

"Have there been any instances of demonic activity?" another general named Dillon interjected.

From their previous encounters, Byron got the impression Dillon was the type of person to make sacrifices for the betterment of the kingdom. *A loyal man indeed*, he thought while shaking his head in response.

"To avoid suspicion, I ordered Coura not to wield magic. If she did, either I or Emilea would have sensed it."

Dillon crossed his arms. "What about the healing?"

Byron paused to stare at Emilea.

"I told them what took place involving my children and their explanation of the demonic creatures," she elaborated in an unbothered manner.

"What about Coura?" he mumbled, though it proved difficult to avoid letting his emotions seep into his voice.

The light mage shrugged indifferently. "She returned without a scratch and covered in blood, and she later told me she had been injured, as my children described. When I discarded her clothing, a substance was mixed with the blood. It's a venom often secreted by the beasts through the pads on their feet or in their saliva. I've treated a handful of similar wounds and know it causes an extreme burning sensation and can lead to death if not treated immediately. Based on the evidence, I would say the most plausible conclusion is she can heal herself. At the bare minimum, she can heal from wounds caused by demonic creatures."

For a moment, Byron considered how much Emilea actually knew about his student and realized his advantage. *Only I saw her healing up close. The children couldn't focus on it during the attack, and the rest of us weren't there.*

"From what you shared and my own experience, I can't say for certain if it's a healing power or not," he replied.

"She could be hiding something," one of the men at the table growled.

"Why don't we see for ourselves?" Dillon commented, spurring a reaction from the high priest.

"There will be no blood shed in the name of promoting demonic activity!"

Byron and Emilea watched as the council erupted into a debate with several points of interest.

"The Nim-Valan soldiers are moving south to reinforce the border. We need protection on our side."

"What can one person do? We'd have to send an army to match what the scouts reported."

"What about the Yeluthian?"

"Why bring the child into this? As far as I am concerned, she's nothing more than a show animal. I suggest we send the angels a message."

"You're right. If they provide soldiers, we'll actually consider an alliance between us."

"Do you really think they would help?"

"What a joke! We don't have time to waste on possibilities. I say we focus on what we've been doing so far and organize who we station there."

"I concur. With one hundred mages, we can make more of a dent than with regular soldiers."

"Are you saying my troops aren't as strong? They possess years of training and experience over some fancy magic."

"Quiet!" King Hernan ordered above the noise.

With a single word, he silenced the argument, and those whose tempers drove them to rise to their feet returned to their seats.

I know the king can be stubborn, but I cannot deny the respect he earned from his subordinates, Byron reflected as their leader continued.

"Now then, we troubled our master mages enough for one day. Does anybody else have any questions for Master Byron?"

The men at the table grumbled to themselves before falling silent or shaking their heads.

Meanwhile, the high priest hesitantly raised a hand. "Forgive me, my memory from our previous meeting is failing me. Is it true your student can actually manifest black wings, like an angel's?"

All eyes slid to Byron, and he inhaled a deep breath before answering. "It did occur on two, separate occasions. I wasn't present for the first, but I did see that exact description the second time."

"With those, she fought off a pair of Yeluthians?" Hendal asked next. His expression remained unreadable.

"Again, I wasn't present during the first incident; however, based on the academy's interrogations, two angels appeared outside Fester. Coura killed the female in self-defense and let the other escape. The one who fled attacked her and Assistant General Marcus in the training ground at the Magical Arts Academy about a week later. I reached them after she defeated the Yeluthian using that same power. We concluded she had been possessed by a demon on the first evening, and the results are lingering. How the creature is able to copy the wings' manifestation spell is unknown."

The council began buzzing again before the high priest revealed his final question.

"Can you, as a master mage, vouch for Coura's sanity after such traumatic events?"

Though the request startled him, Byron remained resolute. "Yes. In my experience with demonic possessions, it's obvious when a person loses their mind and body and cannot regain them. Her case is inexplicably unusual, and I believe it requires time to observe. She's smart and loyal to those she cares about, which drives her to be protective instead of cynical."

"I see." Hendal put his hands together and knit his brows.

"Anyone else?" King Hernan asked. When nobody pressed the subject, he dismissed the master mages.

While Emilea tried hurrying away, Byron caught her arm in the corridor. "I'd like a word with you," he said before releasing his hold.

She reluctantly faced him with her hands on her hips. "Make it quick, please. I am rather busy today."

"You had no right to share what happened outside your home."

Emilea huffed a laugh. "Do you realize how foolish you sound? What takes place on my property involving my children is my business."

"I know, but… I'm trying to protect Coura," he admitted with a frown.

"Why?" she countered, though in a less abrasive manner. "Why protect a person hosting such destructive and evil potential?"

"Because she deserves to have someone fighting for her humanity. What I said during the meeting about demonic possession is true. I'm sure you've noticed from your work how nobody has ever survived the experience. Not only did Coura survive, but the only time she used that power was to fight the angels who threatened her and her friends. Until I see more, until I know we're beyond hope, I will protect my student as a master mage should."

A little light shined in Emilea's eyes at his determination. "Byron, we're not adversaries, except for our opposing energies. I value your contributions to this kingdom and your friendship with my husband, I really do. But if it comes down to protecting Asteom and my family, I need to think logically. My senses find your student repulsive and seething with demonic power that might hinder the peace. Even my subordinates are uncomfortable around her. You're not the only one who cares about their students' well-being."

Every concern Emilea raised resonated with Byron. She sounded honest about her feelings and sensible when it came to Coura, which he appreciated.

"Fine," he replied after a moment. "I don't expect you to want to help her, and I can't blame you, given your position; however, leave her as my responsibility."

"I can't," the light mage began before Byron cut her off.

"Yes, you can. Though we're not opposites, we are equals, in status and power. Don't overestimate my judgement and mistake what I'm asking. I'm not foolish enough to assume I can bring her back if she does lose herself, and I know what needs to be done at that point. I've taken care of others in the same situation before. I'm requesting you leave Coura and any information about her to me."

As he spoke, Emilea's eyes widened to show her understanding. When he finished, she dipped her head.

"I will agree to that."

He thanked her before they parted ways, leaving him feeling much more comfortable with his acquaintance.

***

Since the most anticipated festival was two days away, the palace became so hectic Coura avoided being inside by opting to study at the far end of the training ground where she normally sparred with Byron.

He would be proud of me, she thought while opening one of several texts she brought down.

From what Marcus and Aaron explained the night before, festivals in Verona were public affairs that welcomed all citizens, regardless of status or wealth. Poorer people emerged from the shadows because of this yet couldn't afford the snacks vendors offered. A past king sympathized with them and decided it would be the royal family's responsibility to provide an assortment of food to those who could not make or purchase their own meals. These treats were offered just outside the palace and under the guards' careful supervision in order to prevent trouble.

The chefs organized a system to prepare the items during the week of the event, giving them enough time and space to monitor the mess hall too. Meanwhile, soldiers and citizens volunteered to hang decorations around Verona and set up the stage on the east side of town where Marcus once brought her.

By mid-afternoon, Coura found herself imagining what the city would look like and how the participants chose to dress, which distracted her from reading. She lounged in the grass and enjoyed the sunlight instead.

I wonder what I should wear? Perhaps I'll ask Marcus and Aaron what's appropriate...unless that's too silly.

{Your excitement sickens me. Why celebrate the growing of crops done every year?}

She became amused by the disdainful demon, who couldn't seem to understand such merriment. *Because, there's never a bad time to commemorate the season.*

{What about the slaughter of an entire town, or a plague wiping out hundreds of humans?}

Well, other events throughout Asteom revolve around previous wars and hardships. They allow us to look at the brighter side of life and honor the past. Most people are farmers, merchants, craftsmen, even soldiers and mages, but we live routine lives. What's the worth of working if you aren't able to take a break and appreciate the world around you every once in a while?

{There are far more important matters to be concerned with.}

What does a demon have to worry about?

{Being stuck inside a disgustingly optimistic child, to name one. Another would be the appearance of foul light-blooded being bent on destroying us, or did you forgot about that like everything else?}

Coura frowned. *I'm safe here. The mages and soldiers, including Byron and Marcus, would help me if it ever came to a war. I'm not alone.*

{That's only true if you're all on the same side.}

What do you mean? Even as she asked, Coura knew what Soirée implied.

{In the hundreds of years I've dealt with humans, they act primitive. Power is enticing and frightening. They want more for whatever ridiculous reason; pride, money, status, it doesn't matter.

It's so tempting they'll start wars to gain control. If you still don't believe me, look at what you're doing in the palace.}

Coura sat upright after suddenly growing uncomfortable with lying in the open.

{You see? Such a desire can only lead to death and despair. It is no justification for these humans to throw celebrations.}

"I get the point," she muttered aloud to the demon. Her anticipation for the festival melted into disappointment and annoyance aimed at Soirée.

{Don't be delusional enough to deny the truth of my words. Enjoy the music and food built on a history of violence.}

With a sigh, she reached over and pulled the topmost book onto her lap. *Byron would be grateful to you since you know how to keep my head out of the clouds.*

As the demon laughed in her sickly sweet manner, Coura returned to reading after her excitement deflated.

An overcast blocked the sunlight later in the afternoon and dropped the temperature. She grew cold, which distracted her from studying but helped her realize how close it crept to dinnertime. With a huff, she pushed herself to her feet, grabbed the stack of books in both arms, and began walking toward the palace. As she approached the door, she heard the faint ringing of a church bell signaling the time and silently counted the chimes.

Four…five…six. It's six o'clock? I'm already late!

Once inside, Coura decided to use a shortcut she found while exploring. Instead of crossing the first floor and passing the crowded mess hall to reach the staircase closer to her room, she chose to climb the nearest set, leaping two steps at a time. On the palace's upper floors, the eastern and western walls were built with a segment that jutted out, like a balcony with windows not protected by glass. She imagined they had been built centuries ago for archers and mages to utilize during combat should the castle ever be attacked. At the moment, one would allow her to bypass the winding corridors making up the bedrooms on the third floor.

A wooden door separated the outside hallway from those inside, so she adjusted the books to free a hand, twisted the knob, and kicked it open; however, she found she wasn't alone.

An Asteom Welcome

For a thirteen-year-old girl in a new and strange country with a looming presence threatening her sanity, Grace managed not to break down after the first few days she arrived in Asteom. She tired herself out by maintaining her composure and acting polite to the well-dressed men and women who talked to her about their lives during meals. Worse still, the royal family made it apparent they were displeased with her acting as an envoy and ignored her despite her magical gift.

She remained in her quarters for most of the day and read what books had been left on the room's shelves. As a Yeluthian used to an open sky above her, the windowless space felt like a prison, though she wondered what those with the ability to summon wings would think of such accommodations.

The evening meals were the only times she left the space, yet she hated every minute of them. It would be rude to excuse herself from a private dinner, yet she never ate her fill because so many gossip-hungry noblemen and ladies approached. Grace pretended to show interest in them and refused to choose sides on the outside; on the inside, she cried for them to leave her alone until she returned to her room and collapsed into bed. After all, that level of feigned control was what she had been raised to perfect.

The loneliness felt terrible, but the judgement of the people with their curious glances and fake personalities made life nearly unbearable. Guards escorted her everywhere, and she wasn't allowed to leave the castle. Her single solace had been discovering a spot on the upper floor, which allowed her to remain in the palace yet experience the outdoors.

A strange balcony had been carved into the building, like a stone hallway where the windows were always open. Some held plants and herbs on their sills while others remained clear so the humans could lean on them and directly breathe fresh air. After the private dinners, she would sneak there to do just that until the night wore on.

In the silence of the lingering twilight that day, Grace wished her goddess gift allowed her mind to reach Yeluthia where she could speak to her parents.

"I suppose I better return," she told herself while reluctant to do so.

Right after those words, the door nearest to her opened with a loud bang that had her recoiling in alarm. She immediately sensed who the stranger carrying an armful of books in front of her was, and a slight pang of fear caused her heart to skip a beat. An instinctive glance down the corridor revealed the two were alone as well.

"I'm sorry," the woman apologized as she stepped forward and kicked the door shut behind her. "I didn't mean to startle you."

Trapped... I am trapped, Grace realized in a panic, though she managed to maintain an annoyed expression on the outside.

As an envoy, her people sent her to Asteom for a number of reasons. One in particular involved investigating the rising population of demonic creatures, as reported by King Hernan.

I had no idea until I first arrived that this horrific power stems from a single human. She appears normal, but I sense a strong, dark presence. What is she?

The stranger decided to come closer, and Grace avoided the urge to flee. Instead, she slowly reached for the dagger she always kept buckled at her waist. With a huff, the woman dropped the books on the sill one window over and leaned against its frame while panting.

What should I do? Her hand gripped the hilt of the weapon before she silently slid the blade from its sheath.

"And this is what he considers light reading," the human grumbled and gazed up at the sky. She paid no attention to Grace, who continued to consider using the weapon.

Do it now, she repeated over and over to herself. *She is exposed. I need to end this wicked presence!*

"Your name is Grace, right?"

She froze and couldn't help herself from stuttering a reply. "H-How do you know?"

When the stranger turned to look at her, she slipped the dagger behind her back.

"They announced it at the welcome ceremony, remember?"

"Yes. Of course."

The woman returned to staring out the window as stars began twinkling above. Every aspect of her appearance and behavior seemed genuine.

I refuse to harm an innocent human, yet I cannot leave without learning what this sensation is.

"What are the stars like in Yeluthia?"

"What kind of question is that?" Grace wanted to snap in response.

Instead, she opted for the polite approach. "They are a bit brighter in my opinion, but otherwise just as beautiful." Her gut clenched when the stranger looked over to assess her.

"Do you miss your home?"

"I do," Grace answered before she could stop herself. "More than anything."

A strange sadness softened the woman's gaze. "When I first transferred, I struggled to get along with people. I locked myself inside or focused on training because I didn't have much else to do." She paused, as if waiting for Grace to comment, before admiring the darkening sky again. "Did you make any friends yet?"

Grace longed to scream at the stranger for such random questions while her heart raced. *I have never seen any being like this before. She is human, an actual person, but filled with such wrongness. Show me what you are so I can kill you! Stop trying to be nice when you possess a demon's energy!*

Unfortunately for her resolve, she was still young and inexperienced. She never needed to use a weapon before and didn't feel certain she could harm another living creature. It had also been years since someone spoke to her like an ordinary child, not a political figure's daughter. Because of her sheltered life in Yeluthia, and currently in Asteom, nobody ever bothered to get to know her. Her spirit and the hate motivating her to draw the dagger chipped away until all that remained was a vulnerable, tired girl.

"No," she choked out.

While the woman studied her, Grace realized how pathetic she sounded and lowered her eyes to the floor in an attempt to mask her embarrassment. She expected disciplining or mocking at first since that usually followed a mistake; however, upon remembering where she stayed and the stranger in front of her with the demonic presence, she prepared for vicious insults or a physical strike. At the moment, she didn't care.

The stranger's next words were the last she ever expected to hear.

"My name is Coura. I'll be your first friend here in Asteom."

Grace's jaw dropped before she recalled her title as a political representative and regained her professional expression. After clearing her throat, she felt more composed. "Thank you, but that is not necessary."

The woman, Coura, didn't seem to notice the flustered behavior, or if she did, she didn't show it. "Too late. I already offered. Now, tell me about what you've been doing. I'm sure you eat meals with the royal family every day. What do you think of this place? Have you been into the city yet?"

Grace answered the questions as generally as she could, like she did during the previous hours when she dined with the king, queen, and nobility. By doing so, she prepared to switch her mentality in order to fit the previous, pompous characters she conversed with earlier.

This is not the same situation though, she realized while Coura told her about Verona. *It is just as I thought. She is sincerely interested in learning about me, not like the lords and ladies who gossip for their own gain. Can I trust her behavior?*

A slight breeze blew through the window they stood in front of, making Grace shiver. Even the human shuddered and wrapped her arms around herself before commenting.

"I didn't expect it to be so chilly."

Grace watched as Coura opened her mouth to say more then abruptly closed it and looked away. "What is it?" she pressed as her curiosity got the better of her.

"How would you feel about meeting more people tonight?"

Her first thought was of being shoved into another stuffy room with dozens of new faces who saw her as a potential ally. "I am not sure…"

Apparently, Coura didn't accept an indecisive response. She gathered the books and began moving down the hallway. "Don't worry, they're three friends of mine. I wouldn't suggest it unless I believed you would feel comfortable."

Grace remained where she stood, unsure whether or not to willingly follow the seemingly kind source of such malicious energy. At the reminder of her empty, suffocating room, she decided it would be worthwhile to take the risk and returned the dagger to its place on her belt.

If she causes trouble, I have a weapon and can call for help. Her hands are also full, so I essentially have an advantage.

"Hurry up," her new friend called from the other end of the hallway. "I can't open this door by myself!"

***

When Coura found the ambassador, she wasn't surprised when their clashing energies left them both fumbling through their introductions. She had been so preoccupied with hurrying to meet for dinner she ignored the Yeluthian's growing presence until they came face to face in the upper, outdoor corridor. Thankfully, she had enough sense not to cause a scene that would send the girl searching for the evening guards. The last thing she needed was to create even more tension between herself and the angelic race, as well as raise suspicion from those in the capital.

Similar to her previous journey with Byron, Will, and Marcus, being in a Yeluthian's presence made Coura squirm, like she were loosely bound by invisible rope. If she didn't figure out the danger, Soirée's ranting in her mind painted a clear reminder of their relationship. Similar to an aggressive feline, the demon prickled and hissed insults and curses directed toward the ambassador and her kind. She even went so far as to try convincing Coura to slit the girl's throat.

The pressure in her mind and the temptation to give in were enormous.

She gave up on arguing with Soirée and opted to ignore the demon as best she could. When that didn't seem possible, she turned Soirée's rage against them by deciding to befriend the Yeluthian out of spite. It succeeded in angering the demon on another level towering over any amusement Coura found.

While she led Grace to Marcus' room, her head pounded from the strain of keeping a hold on her mind and body. Yelling at Soirée to stop only provoked the creature to aim that natural hatred at her. Eventually, they reached the door, and she readjusted the books so she could knock.

"It's about time," she heard Marcus announce before he opened the door. "We were going to finish the-" When he saw who accompanied Coura, his mouth hung open before he glanced between the two of them.

Coura forced a smile. "Aren't you going to let us inside?"

"S-Sure. Come in."

Luckily for Grace, Coura learned her lesson about proper introductions a few days ago with Will. She entered first, dropped the books nearby, and gestured for their guest to follow all while the pounding morphed into a ringing in her ears. Aaron and Will looked startled as well, and the latter opened his mouth to presumably bumble a respectful greeting, but she spoke before any of them could.

"Grace, I'd like you to meet Aaron, Will, and that's Marcus who let us in and is impolitely standing by the door."

Marcus caught the message and returned to his spot on the bed while Coura dragged over the empty chair and instructed the Yeluthian to sit. She then went to the far window and opened it wide. Since no breeze blew from that direction, the weather did not chill the room drastically.

I've only flown twice, yet I can imagine how confined you must feel in a stone castle, she thought beneath Soirée's overwhelming hatred.

During the awkward pause as everybody watched her, she snatched the half-empty bottle off the desk, returned to Grace, and lowered herself to the floor at the girl's feet. Still, no one spoke. She took a swig and hoped the wine would muddle some of the demon's presence before breaking the silence.

"The four of us almost always meet for dinner because we prefer each other's company over the mess hall or private dining area. In here, we are who I introduced us as." She pointed to each person as she repeated their names. "You met Aaron already. Marcus is a general…"

"Assistant general," he corrected from his spot.

"Will is an herbalist and researcher," Coura continued, glanced at Grace, then pointed to herself from the floor. "And I'm Coura."

To her relief, the Yeluthian seemed to relax and bowed while remaining seated. "It is nice to meet you, Prince Aaron, Assistant General Marcus, and Sir Will."

The latter boy blushed. "Sir?"

"The formalities aren't necessary," Aaron gently chided.

Coura leaned back on her hands and closed her eyes. "In here, it's just Aaron, Marcus, Will, and Coura. Oh, and Grace too. Remember, this is sort of like our escape from the outside world. You can be yourself among friends without the burden of a title."

"I understand," the ambassador responded and offered a timid smile.

The gesture was acceptable enough for Coura. Her mind felt suffocated from the wine and Soirée's ever-looming presence, so she lied on the floor with her arms behind her head.

"*General* Marcus. I like the sound of that," the soldier mused afterward.

Coura groaned dramatically. "This is why we don't use titles. Everybody gets a big head!"

"I beg your pardon, but I hear 'Prince' and 'Your Highness' all the time," Aaron chimed from his seat. "I think I'm pretty modest."

"I've never been called 'Sir Will' before," the herbalist added with his own, inflated sense of pride. "I'm on Marcus' side."

"You're both just as vain as the lords and ladies," Aaron muttered and shook his head, prompting them to chuckle.

After a minute, the conversation continued well enough to ease Coura's worries. Soirée settled down and quieted for the most part but stayed attentive while the boys asked Grace about Yeluthia. It seemed obvious the girl hid the important details, at least to Coura, yet the topics revolved around her people's culture.

"What's your favorite part about Asteom so far?" the prince inquired when Grace finished explaining the city's architecture.

"The food, without a doubt," she replied in a pleasant tone. "I have never eaten such juicy, tender meats. Even though the meals are dull, forgive me for saying so, every bite is delicious."

"Why do you think I don't eat dinner there? I can get the same food with better company here."

A yawn from Marcus drew their attention. "I hate to be the bearer of bad news, but I'm afraid I'm going to have to kick you all out if I'm going to sleep before the sun rises."

Will and Aaron excused themselves, and Coura walked with Grace to the girl's room, against the demon's protests. Once they reached the opposite end of the third floor, the Yeluthian approached the center-most room before waving in a hesitant manner.

"I'll stop by tomorrow," she promised before Grace went inside.

*

The day before the Harvest Festival, Coura spent most of her time reading in order to catch up to where Byron assigned her to be, then she ventured through the busy halls. She felt significantly more energy than normal in and around the palace since everybody either prepared for the next morning or finished what additional work they needed to squeeze in; this included exercising.

Visiting the training ground had been her first idea to occupy herself, but it became so crowded she couldn't find a spot to practice alone. She then decided to eat a late lunch. It took her all of a few minutes to grab a plate, load it with whatever sat within reach, and head upstairs. Once she hit the third floor, she remembered Grace lived close by and moved in that direction.

Her decision prompted Soirée to spring to the front of her mind, along with the negative emotions.

You should calm down, Coura told the demon as she found the correct room and knocked.

{*If you wouldn't test my patience, my rage would still slumber.*}

After a moment, the door opened, and Grace stood in a lovely, cream-colored gown. When the girl saw who disturbed her, the serene gaze showed alarm before settling into a more normal expression. "Coura, how can I help you?"

"You can invite me in and tell me why you're already dressed up."

The Yeluthian glanced behind her, revealing some uncertainty, yet she agreed and opened the door wider.

As she entered and set the plate on the bedside table, Coura grew disgusted by the cramped room. An itching sensation tickled her shoulder blades as well, but she ignored it. Even Soirée, with all her hatred for the angels, commented on how claustrophobic the space felt.

"This is unbearable," she couldn't stop herself from commenting with a hint of frustration.

Grace lowered her eyes to the floor. "I know."

Coura made a mental note to speak with Aaron about moving the ambassador before forcing herself to focus and accept a seat in one of two chairs. "Anyway, what's the gown for?"

"I wanted to try it on before tomorrow," Grace replied. She lifted the skirt and waved the fabric from side to side with a slight smile. "A servant delivered this on behalf of the royal family for the festival."

"It's beautiful," Coura added while admiring the bodice, which had been covered by glass beads.

"Yes, but I wish I did not need to attend."

The girl's openness startled her, given how defensive the Yeluthian behaved the evening prior. "Why not? It's supposed to be the grandest event in the country."

"As a political representative, I am not allowed to explore without an escort, and there is no fun in being watched wherever you go. Besides, I must uphold myself as a public figure and act accordingly."

Coura met the sapphire eyes and mustered what sympathy she could. "I understand what it's like to worry about how people view you and know they'll wait for you to mess up. Still, just because you need to keep an image doesn't mean you should hide your personality or ignore what you want to do. If you feel like dancing, you dance. If you want to close your eyes and listen to the music, no one can stop you. If you feel like dragging your escort around to buy you sweets and shoving the treats in your face, who cares!"

The scenario prompted a giggle from Grace, reminding her just how young the Yeluthian actually was.

"I suppose you are right," the girl replied seconds later.

"What you choose to do is up to you, though nobody knows what your people are like. They might find your outgoing personality contagious, or see your shy behavior as arrogance; I did at first."

"You thought I was arrogant?"

Coura nodded, to Grace's visible shame. "It's not a problem now because I'm learning more about who you are. For the citizens of Verona and the soldiers and mages in the palace, though, it might be beneficial to talk with them. Be kind and honest, but not overly optimistic or naive."

While she began nibbling on the food from her plate, the Yeluthian took a moment to consider her words.

{*Your charity makes me want to strangle you.*}

She ignored the demon's comment and the suppressed fury that brought about a ringing in her ears.

"Thank you," the girl added and curtsied before meeting her eyes again with a natural, pretty smile. "I think I will take your advice."

That evening at dinner, Grace seemed like a completely different person. Her overly-courteous behavior and reserved mannerisms adjusted to be more casual and outgoing. Several times throughout the meal, the boys shot Coura sideways glances when the ambassador wasn't looking, as if to ask what happened over the course of a single day. She would just shrug and drink more wine to block out Soirée's spiteful insults.

Harvest Festival Adventures

endors began opening their booths at sunrise, thus marking the start of the Harvest Festival. The night before, Coura, Marcus, and Will decided they would go together since Aaron and Grace remained with the king, queen, high priest, and reputable councilors of various committees. Organizing their day proved to be a struggle as performances took place in the afternoon with dancing in the evening. This meant they would need to wander through the shops and along the main road during the morning in order to find a spot before the crowd took up most of the space.

At dawn, Coura woke with a surprising amount of anticipation for the event. She decided to wear an emerald-colored dress that didn't look too formal and possessed sleeves that covered her arms, then she pulled her hair into a neat bun and tied it using a pair of ribbons. After a general review in the mirror, she selected a matching shawl and hurried out the door.

It's not as if anybody will be paying attention to me.

{Hopefully, they won't.}

Were you always this bitter?

The entrance hall held dozens of soldiers in uniform and plainly dressed mages who mingled while servers began arranging platters with fruits and breakfast pastries. Coura heard someone berating a group of boys for snatching pieces of food as she located Marcus. At his side stood Grace. The Yeluthian's lighter dress distinguished her from the others, like a dove among the rainbow of colors.

"I thought you couldn't be alone," she said by way of greeting the girl.

The assistant general grinned in response. "She's not alone."

While Coura glanced between them without comprehending, Grace beamed and answered her unspoken question. "Marcus volunteered to be my escort for the day."

He shrugged indifferently. "Her assigned guards were more than willing to relinquish the job."

"Besides, it's not like you're working when you're among friends," Coura added.

While they waited for the final member of their party, her eyes roamed the hall. Most of the remaining people took notice of her interaction with Grace, and nearly all the mages threw subtle glares her way.

{*It's taboo for a demon and a light-blooded to interact peacefully. Your behavior sickens me.*}

I'm not a demon.

After what seemed like an hour later, Will appeared wearing his black boots, pants, a red shirt, and a black vest, which felt odd because he blended in with the soldiers.

"It's about time," Marcus called as their friend jogged over.

Will apologized and tried to hide his rosy cheeks, but Grace inched toward the door before he could be chastised further.

"Never mind," the girl said in the process. "Let us go!"

*

If Coura thought a normal day in the streets of Verona seemed crowded, she wasn't prepared for the business of a festival. The main roads were tightly packed with more people than ever and lined with tables for vendor booths. Every shop propped their doors open too, allowing potential customers to wander inside at their leisure. In between the buildings or at whatever corners became available, individual or multiple musicians, jugglers, dancers, singers, and other types of entertainers accepted donations for their performances. The movement, sights, and smells became too much for Soirée, so she shirked away and left Coura alone.

Fortunately for their small group, Grace's elaborate appearance had onlookers parting to let them through with smiles and respectful glances at her and Marcus. Some even did the same to Will as they mistook him for a soldier, much to his embarrassment. Coura felt content with trailing behind and catching glimpses at the items on display.

The four scoped out the main road for most of the morning, stopping only to purchase treats and souvenirs. The young Yeluthian in particular revealed an unsatiable sweet tooth. At first, she would glance longingly at certain booths before politely requesting Marcus stop for her. By midday, she resorted to tugging on his arm like he was her older sibling.

"You just finished a pack of roasted nuts not even five minutes ago," her escort complained. "Aren't you getting full?"

Grace shook her head in an innocent manner without taking her eyes off her next target.

With a begrudged sigh, Marcus let her lead him away. "Don't blame me if you get a stomachache!"

Will and Coura laughed at their banter and followed the pair. With the money she brought, Coura bought a fried pastry for breakfast as soon as they entered the city then gave some to a street magician who tricked an older man with his deck of cards. At the moment, the remaining coins jingled in the pouch at her waist, as if begging to be spent.

While Grace observed each of the sweets at her chosen booth, Coura wandered around until she noticed one farther back next to two, female dancers. On the table were dozens of shining metals and jewels molded and shaped in ways she had never seen before.

"You don't recognize Mintelian metalwork, do you?"

She glanced up to meet a pair of gray eyes belonging to the silver-haired, dark-skinned man behind the booth. "Mintelian? I've never even heard of it," she replied honestly before returning her attention to the pieces.

"Oh-ho!" the man chuckled. "I'm a fifth-generation jeweler on my mother's side, and she'd roll in her grave if I didn't share our talents with the younger folk like yourself."

Will approached from behind her to assess the merchant's wares too. "If I'm remembering correctly, Mintelians are from the Ghurun Mountains out east. I always thought they were secretive about their traditions."

"Yes, sir." The man nodded and extended a hand. "Call me Steiner."

Her friend accepted the handshake. "It's a pleasure to meet you, though I'm curious why you and your dancers are in Verona. I assumed Mintelians don't mingle with people other than their own."

Steiner shrugged and looked them both over before continuing. "It's not that we don't like other people; most of us would rather stay in place than travel is all. I happen to be one of them, but on this day, it's a family tradition for the jewelers to pass along our work."

"Why?" Coura pressed while still assessing the assorted pins, necklaces, rings, and various, glimmering pieces. When he didn't respond, she looked up again and saw the Mintelian's eyes steadily analyzing the crowd of men and women who gathered to watch the dancers.

It wasn't difficult to figure out why the group stayed entranced given how exotic the two ladies appeared. Their brown skin color became common in Asteom since their ancestors traced back to immigrants from across the Ghurun Mountains, yet the limited amount of clothing showed more than people in the capital were accustomed to. Each showcased voluptuous, brunette hair, gold bands around their ankles, wrists, and necks, and a strip of brightly colored silk around the upper half of their chests, exposing their midsections. Their loose-flowing pants were the same color and material as well. As they danced, the metal chimed to create a melody of their own and compensate for a lack of music.

Not only did they prove to be physically attractive, but their movements were unlike anything Coura had ever witnessed. They kept their arms extended and shoulders still while sweeping their hips in all directions. Their legs remained planted until the pattern changed. Then, the women bounced, spun their arms in tight circles, and stomped their feet in a random yet entertaining pattern. All the while, they flashed delighted smiles at the crowd with white teeth that seemed to glow against their darker complexions.

Coura found herself enticed until Steiner spoke.

"Let me show you what my business is," he said at a lower volume before shooing them away from the front of his booth. Marcus and Grace, who savored another pastry, joined the two after and listened while Will summarized the Mintelian's introduction.

Without a word, Steiner caught one of the dancers' attention, and they shared an unspoken message. She nodded a moment later before approaching a middle-aged man, who studied her closely, looping her arm around his, and pulling him toward the table.

"I see you've taken a fancy to Griselda," the merchant announced loudly enough for those around them to hear.

The stranger blushed and stuttered an apology the Mintelian waved away.

"None of that, sir! Our ladies enjoy the praise. Still, you seem as though you prefer another?"

"How did you-"

"I have a way with people. It's how I craft my wares. Go on then, take a look! There's one for every type."

The man didn't bother to hide his skepticism, yet he inspected each item until a piece caught his eye. From what Coura could tell, he selected an ebony-colored ring and held it up into the sunlight.

"Aha! So, you're a fan of onyx then? Excellent taste, if I do say so myself. You know, that's half of a pair."

"It is?"

Steiner nodded enthusiastically. "Onyx is a lonely metal. Only those with strongly connected hearts can wear them together."

What the Mintelian proclaimed must have resonated with the man, for he began mumbling to shift the discussion into a private conversation.

"Do you think it's a hoax?" Marcus leaned closer to ask Coura while he pretended not to stare.

"It can't be," Will interjected before she could respond. "What I read on the Mintelians says they forge a connection to the planet and the souls of its people."

"I sense no magical energy from him," Grace added between licking her sticky fingers clean.

Coura shrugged. "Maybe it really is all from experience."

The man laid several coins on the table while Steiner wrapped another, matching ring, handed it over, and waved as his customer hurried away. As soon as he stood alone, the Mintelian gestured for her and Will to return.

"Who was he?" the herbalist inquired.

"Somebody who needed reassurance in himself and his relationship with the woman he deeply cares about," Steiner explained in a wise manner.

Marcus and Grace approached the items for the first time, and the former casually picked up a gold ring embedded with a ruby. "So, you guess what jewelry a person should buy based on their life story?"

"Quite the contrary. Who am I to claim what's best for them? Who knows oneself better than they do? I let them find the piece that most satisfies their self, just like you're doing now, young man."

Marcus' eyes widened, and he self-consciously set the ring down, causing the merchant to laugh.

"Gold and ruby stimulate creativity, courage, and self-esteem. Excellent qualities for an upper-class soldier."

"How do you know my position?"

Steiner tapped on his chest to mirror the location of the badges on Marcus' uniform, much to the assistant general's chagrin.

Suddenly, Grace clapped her hands together with a startling amount of eagerness. "We should take turns choosing a piece!"

"I don't know," Will started, but it was too late.

The Mintelian took advantage of their hesitation to direct everybody except Marcus away from the table.

When the private discussion at the booth began, Coura glanced at where the main road branched off farther ahead. "We really don't have time for this."

"I apologize. I did not realize it grew so late already."

A minute later, the soldier returned to their group, so Coura gave the Yeluthian a gentle shove.

"You volunteered us, so you might as well hurry."

"What did he say?" Will asked Marcus while Grace scampered to the merchant. The three continued to keep an eye in her direction because of their shared duty as her guards for the day.

"Nothing really," the assistant general answered while fingered the new ring on his right hand. "I didn't have much to tell him, so he gave me some advice, and that was that."

"What kind of advice?"

Coura reached over to pinch Will's arm. "Leave him alone."

"Ouch! I'm only trying to learn what their people are like. There's not a ton of information, other than how spiritual and mysterious they are."

"Maybe that's all they *want* you to know," she added pointedly.

Grace and Steiner spoke for a long time before she chose what appeared to be a necklace and thanked him.

"You're up, Will," Marcus said when the girl returned. "Go ask him your dozens of questions."

As the third member of their group went toward the booth, the young Yeluthian held up her prize. Coura's eyebrows raised at the sight of such a gaudy necklace. The thick, silver chain had been encircled with pink quartz all around, and an oval opal surrounded by more decorative metalwork rested in the center.

"It's a bit…flashy," the soldier commented, obviously just as amazed as Coura.

Grace ignored their awestruck expressions and clipped the jewelry around her neck. Against the white dress, the gems shined brighter, making her smile in a proud manner. "Steiner mentioned he has not encountered a Yeluthian in years. When I selected this, he told me opal is a favorite of my people. He explained how silver signifies elegance and sophistication, and the rose quartz symbolizes an unconditional love."

That's why she's so excited. The necklace reminds her of home, Coura realized before asking what the opal represented.

The girl relaxed before glancing at the jewel. "It represents faithfulness and balances emotion. I believe I…I could use that now while in Asteom."

Marcus and Coura didn't pry any more. In the midst of the surrounding noise, Steiner's humor-filled voice boomed to draw their attention again.

"I knew it! I knew you were a scholar. No wonder you're so curious!"

Coura smiled to herself and, despite her impatience with hoping to experience the rest of the event, found herself apprehensive. She wondered what sort of characteristics he could identify and what advice he would offer, as opposed to feeling excited about purchasing his products.

"Why don't you two go on ahead and find us a spot," she told Marcus and Grace.

"Are you sure?" the Yeluthian asked.

"The longer we stand around, the less room will be available. That's what you said earlier, Marcus."

He agreed, so they went off toward the eastern road after promising to save extra space. They followed the stream of citizens heading in that direction before disappearing down the street.

Will's conversation with Steiner continued to the point where Coura decided to intervene. When she did, she found they were discussing the metals and gems mined in the Ghurun mountain range.

"Excuse me," she interrupted. "I'd like to enjoy the rest of the festival, if you don't mind."

Her friend gasped. "Sorry, I forgot about… I mean, look what I chose."

What Will held out was not something she expected because it hadn't been one of the items she remembered spotting on the table. It appeared to be a thin sheet of metal, rectangular in shape and colored orange with warped circles. A string of colored beads on a chain had been welded onto an edge, leaving it hanging off.

"What is it?"

"It's a bookmark. I've never seen one so well-crafted."

"That's because it's not a piece I typically make," the merchant stated. "It's not often I run into a scholar, and when I do, there's a chance they won't need it."

"I don't own any," Will admitted. "It's made of copper, which helps your memory and mental flexibility, and the gems are amethyst."

Coura tilted her head. "What do those do?"

He paused for a moment, seemingly unsure if he wanted to share, then he glanced at Steiner. The Mintelian turned the palms of his hands upward in a reassuring gesture.

"Amethyst helps with anger."

"Anger? Why would you need to monitor that?"

"It's hard to believe I can get upset because I'm so passive," he replied with a sad smile. "I hate considering the moments when I am, though, because I stop thinking rationally and act with my emotions instead of my head. Unless it's addressed, I continue to roll an issue over in my mind until I feel like I'm going insane. This is a problem I've dealt with my entire life."

Coura tried to recall an instance where he had been in that state and stumbled upon a memory from just after they left Fester. *I forgot. He had been attacked by those angels, and I changed right in front of him. He avoided me and only visited when Byron coerced him. Even when we did see each other again, I could tell he acted strange. Looking back, I'm sure his anger arose because of me, or what I became.*

They stood in an awkward silence until Will looked up from the bookmark and over her shoulder. "Where are Marcus and Grace?"

"They went to save us a spot before it grew too crowded on that side of the city. You can head there now, if you want."

"Would you mind?"

Coura shook her head. "I'm sure I won't take as long as you."

He thanked her, bowed to the Mintelian, and hurried off.

"Curious one, isn't he," Steiner commented before facing his next customer.

After a moment, she realized he was waiting for her to choose from the remaining pieces. She took her time analyzing each and even picked up a few to inspect closer. There was no doubt they had been crafted by a master jeweler; however, by the last item, she found none she desired to wear.

"I'm sorry," she began with a hint of disappointment. "They're all beautiful, but none stand out in the way you described."

The Mintelian didn't even hesitate to lean down and snatch a cloth sack resting at his feet. "Not a problem, my dear! Your last friend had the same mindset. Usually, it means I don't encounter your type of personality often, so these beauties have no need to be on display."

"My kind of personality," Coura muttered while Steiner laid out the additional necklaces, bracelets, and rings.

"When selecting a piece, people show certain characteristics more prominently than others. Some are fairly obvious and make up the whole of a person. For example, that young Yeluthian is proud of her country and needed a reminder since she's away from home. Others, like Will and the first young man, Marcus, are plagued by underlying thoughts or self-doubt, which bring about hints of change. Our experiences and relationships shape who we are. The wonderful characteristic about humans is, we have the ability to change in many ways, especially in our personalities. That's also pretty good for business!"

Once each piece of jewelry sat in front of her, Coura took her time looking at them. Again, she sifted through the items and shook her head with a deflated mentality. "They're still stunning, but I wouldn't feel right about accepting one. I was never interested in jewelry to begin with, so maybe that's why. Your skill is impeccable, though."

A lengthy pause followed her response where Steiner simply stared at her, his face set into an impassive mask. When she contemplated speaking, the Mintelian shifted his eyes upward and tugged on his silver beard.

"It's been a while since I ran into this issue," he mumbled.

"What issue?"

"As I explained, personalities can be similar to each other in various ways, yet new patterns are always rising since the world is constantly changing. You seem to be one of those special cases."

"What does that mean?"

Steiner released a heavy sigh and extended his arms in a defeated posture. "It means, I'm afraid I don't have a piece that suits you."

Even though the news disheartened Coura, she couldn't help but feel worse for the expert metalworker, who carefully returned the additional jewelry to his bag before setting it down and covering his face with both hands.

"I'm sorry," she apologized after.

The man removed his hands and chuckled. "There's nothing to be sorry for, my dear. In fact, I would like you to come back next year."

"Next year?"

"Yes," he said with growing enthusiasm. "You will return to this festival in one year, and I will have crafted the perfect item for you. You shall become my motivation from this point forward, a new challenge!"

Coura gaped at the merchant and his eager attitude before shaking her head and turning away. "Good luck, I suppose," she offered and waved.

To her embarrassment, he shouted a final farewell loudly enough for the people around them to begin staring.

*

The eastern square appeared full of citizens invested in one singer's rendition of a merry tune. That song must have been the final part of his set, for he left the stage following the applause, prompting a break. Coura took the opportunity to search for her

328

friends while people were moving around. No chairs or benches crowded the area, leaving only the cobblestone court, the stage, and a raised seating area reserved for the royal family and those important enough to be with them. At the moment, nobody occupied the upper space.

"Coura!"

She searched in the direction of the high-pitched voice until two children hurried over to her. "Mace? Lexie?"

"We're glad to see you," the girl squealed and wrapped her arms around Coura's waist.

"I'm glad to see you too. Where are your parents?"

Mace pointed behind to where Clearshot was approaching, and Emilea, in the same dress and cloak she wore the night Coura saw her in the upstairs corridor, watched from a distance.

"Hey there! Long time no see," Clearshot greeted her and placed a hand on her head to rub it in a slightly demeaning yet friendly manner.

She ducked away from his hand and grinned. "You're going to mess up my hair."

The children giggled, then Lexie let go to push her father back. Then, Mace ordered his father to stop bothering Coura, which made her laugh.

Clearshot feigned a shocked expression, wrapped his daughter in his arms, and lifted her to kiss her cheek. "You would turn on your own father? How heartbreaking!"

"How's your day been going?" Coura asked when the children settled down.

For a few minutes, Mace, Lexie, and Clearshot discussed their morning and enjoyment with the previous performances. She prepared to bring up Byron, Will, Marcus, or Grace until Emilea came to stand beside her husband.

"Mother, it's Coura!" Lexie announced.

"I can see that," her mother responded in an unamused tone before addressing Coura. "If you're looking for Byron, he's near the front of the raised seating area. Those benches are reserved for the master mages and our guests."

"Thank you. I'll head over there now."

After a brief goodbye, she found her teacher, along with Marcus, Grace, and Will, seated exactly where Emilea directed her. Byron already procured a bottle of alcohol, which he held in one hand while waving her over with the other. Although his face looked flushed, he seemed about normal otherwise.

"You made it. These three were just filling me in on their new souvenirs from the Mintelian."

"What did you choose?" Grace inquired.

Coura rubbed the back of her neck and struggled to admit it didn't matter that she hadn't received a special piece. The Mintelian's inability to decipher her personality bothered her enough to dismiss the subject. "I'll tell you later."

"Why?"

Another musician began playing a lively melody on his sitar as Grace posed the question, signaling the end of the interlude.

"Because, it's time to watch the performances," she answered and squeezed between Byron and Marcus while silently thanking her timing.

At the next break, nobody mentioned Steiner or her experience again. She talked with the assistant general, and he explained how more benches would be placed around the area for older audience members who could not stand for long periods of time; once the dancing began, they would be available to anyone. Eventually, the royal family made an appearance, so he escorted Grace to the raised seating where they viewed the rest of the performances. By sunset, Coura had seen several musicians on various instruments, a family of jugglers, acrobats and tumblers, dancers, and plenty of singers. Merchants advertised juice, wine, ale, and portable snacks like roasted nuts, fruit, and meat pies for sale, which kept her satisfied. As the afternoon crept into evening, she found herself joking with Byron and Will while admiring the captivating acts.

After sunset, the guards on duty took to lighting the street lamps, and the area somehow became more crowded. People began shuffling away from the stage once the current show, a dramatic theatre troupe, bowed and exited.

"Is that it for the performances?" Coura asked Byron, who reached a content state of drunkenness some time ago.

"Of the acts to watch. The rest of the festival is for dancing."

As if on cue, a string quartet started a tune apparently familiar to the populace because the center area immediately filled with pairs of people.

"I don't remember the last time I danced," she mused aloud while they observed the moving figures and twirling skirts.

Will hopped off the bench and extended a hand toward her. "Do you want to be my partner?" he asked without any hint of his usual timidness. He consumed his fair share of alcohol earlier, with Byron's encouragement, and seemed just as carefree as the master mage.

"I'm not very good," she admitted.

Still, he gestured for her to stand. "Neither am I."

As she contemplated the offer, Byron slapped her on the back, causing her to jump to her feet from the sting, turn around, and glare at him.

"Go on," he urged impatiently yet with a wink.

Before Coura could stick out her tongue, Will grabbed her arm before leading her into the open space.

During their time together, she felt glad she had not been asked to be anybody else's partner. The herbalist offered instructions for the basic steps, taking each movement slow and with enough room between their bodies for Coura to look at her feet. After a few songs, she got the hang of that dance and glanced at the ground less.

The pair relished the melodic music and exercise until they grew warm in the crisp, fall weather. Finally, a panting Will separated himself from her and begged to return to their seats. Coura obliged with a giggle, reminding her of how energetic she felt when she sparred in the training ground. Once they neared Byron, they were surprised to find Grace and Marcus on the bench again.

"Had enough of the royal seating?" she asked the Yeluthian.

"My legs grew stiff."

"What she means is, you seem to be having a lot of fun down here," Marcus chimed in. "She's right, though. Even Aaron can never stand observing the event with the king and queen."

He gestured to the crowd with his chin before they spotted the prince and his partner: a young woman whose dress puffed out three times as wide as her waist. He kept a polite smile on his face while expertly executing the movements, and Coura silently commended him for not tripping all over the excess fabric.

Before she could claim a seat after Will, Marcus extended a hand. "How about a dance?"

Although she wasn't confident in her skills, the energy from earlier hadn't worn off completely. "I'm not very good," she repeated yet accepted the offer.

When she danced with Will, it had been a friendly proposal, so she could mess up as she learned the steps. Something about accompanying the soldier made Coura nervous. She mirrored his form with her right hand on the other's shoulder as the opposite hands came together in an identical manner to the pairs around them. The closed space between the two steadily broke apart when she caved in to her instinct to stare at her feet. His calm expression didn't put her at ease either, especially when she stepped on his foot several times. He would wince but never comment on the mistake.

"I told you I was a bad dancer," she grumbled after doing so again.

"You didn't say you were bad; you just claim to not be very good, which is different."

His following wink had Coura glancing away as her cheeks heated into a blush. When she faced Marcus after a moment, he studied her while wearing a cool smile.

"What?" she asked after sensing a need to break the silence.

He shrugged. "It's a perfect night for the festival."

Another song ended, and she longed to rest with the others in their group; however, before she could initiate the break, Marcus proposed an unanticipated question.

"Do you hate me?"

"Why would I hate you?" she countered to reflect her surprise.

"I worried you would because of the letter I wrote to my father about the academy, and about you." His tone and expression remained neutral.

Coura remembered the initial incident, the demon's insight, and how she berated him in front of his comrades. A sense of frustration stirred in her chest, but the flame had died down considerably since then. "I don't hate you."

"But you're still mad?"

Of course I am! You practically sold me to your superiors in order to gain their favor, and now I'm another tool for them to use, whether I like it or not. She was tempted to throw those words in his face, yet the sense of betrayal she experienced subsided. Coura realized then what that lack of emotion meant.

Over the weeks we spent together, I've been able to see what kind of person Marcus is. He's not somebody who would sacrifice others for his own benefit. If anything, I get the impression he would do the opposite.

"I don't hate you for what happened, and I'm not upset anymore," she explained while meeting his eyes. "I just don't think I can trust you. At least, not right away. No matter the purpose, you told the council about me, about that secret, without my permission or without speaking to Byron and the other instructors. If no one else knew, I wouldn't have been forced to come here and risk my life obeying their orders."

"Do you regret moving to Verona?"

Coura shook her head. "I don't know. It's too soon to tell, but I never got a choice. I'm practically a prisoner with powers the king and his generals can manipulate like a new weapon."

The sting of her words showed in Marcus' eyes, yet a sense of understanding remained present as well. Before she could step away to separate the pair, he leaned forward until their cheeks touched to whisper into her ear. The unexpected sensation of his breath on her skin sent a shiver up her spine.

"I'm sorry for hurting you and for what others may think. I became so attached to my responsibilities I was inconsiderate of what you might want. If I can earn your trust, I promise to try. You're becoming one of my closest friends, and I don't regret meeting you and fighting alongside you as an ally." He lingered for a moment before moving his head back.

After the confession, Coura desperately desired a break and spotted Grace, Will, and Byron farther behind from over Marcus' shoulder. She smiled and released his hand. "I'm tired."

"One more dance?" he practically pleaded.

"Sorry, but I might be done for the night. You should ask Grace. She seems interested."

When they circled around minutes earlier, Coura noticed the Yeluthian girl watching the dancers with a longing in her eyes. Marcus apparently had not since he stared at her with a raised eyebrow before the two returned to the bench.

"You looked like you were having fun," Will commented and flashed Coura a smirk before she plopped down into the spot at his left.

"Shut up," she mumbled as she leaned forward to relax her upper body.

Meanwhile, Marcus extended his hand toward Grace. "Would you like to be my next partner?"

"Me?" she squeaked before accepting. Together, the current pair strolled into the flowing crowd. After an introductory lesson, Grace picked up on the steps much faster than Coura and appeared to be enjoying herself in no time.

Behind them, Coura noticed the prince dancing with another woman while wearing the same, polite smile. "Does Aaron ever get a break?" she wondered aloud.

"I doubt it," Byron answered in a lazy tone. "You're forgetting he's royalty, so most of the women in Asteom will try to make a positive impression on him."

She rolled her eyes and chose to focus on the music instead. After a few songs, Marcus and Grace returned, as did Will's energy. He and their Yeluthian friend moved into the populated area while

Marcus recovered, though he assistant general said nothing since they all seemed to be savoring the lively atmosphere.

A few minutes later, an older man in a soldier's uniform stumbled to Byron's other side and initiated a conversation. She learned they previously worked together when her mentor had been in the army, and she grew bored listening to them. A young woman approached Marcus soon after to request a dance, glancing in Coura's direction in the process. He accepted her offer, and the two left.

Nobody appeared to be in a hurry to rejoin those on the bench, so Coura decided to return to the palace despite the ongoing festivities. She rose, bid Byron a good night while he continued reminiscing with the soldier, and started walking away just as the previous song ended and another began.

"Coura, wait!"

She spun around at the call to find Aaron sneaking past the couples to make his way over.

"You're not leaving yet, are you?" Already, she noticed more life in his expression when he spoke to her than with anybody he had been partnered with that evening.

"I was just about to head back," she admitted.

"How about one more dance before you retire?"

The eagerness he projected became too much for her to decline. He took her hand, led her to an open space, and began the most tense experience of the night. Like with Marcus, Coura couldn't keep her eyes on her feet and ended up stepping on his often. She tried glancing down when possible, but it didn't help any. All the while, they received curious or jealous looks from the other participants.

Aaron ignored the missteps as he told her about his day, which consisted of wandering around the city with his parents and their escorts and sitting above to observe every performance. When it was her turn, she struggled to speak between the movements. By their third song as a duo, he grew annoyed with her.

"You need to relax," he complained right as she glanced down again. "You're too tense. Don't focus so much on your feet."

The comment hindered her already thin concentration. "I can't do both."

Aaron decided he'd had enough of her attempts. Before she knew what was happening, he released her hands in order to put his around her waist and pull them into a tight embrace. This left no other option but to wrap her arms around his neck, bringing her face so close to his that she felt the heat radiating from him. Because they abandoned the traditional and much less personal form, Coura completely forgot about the steps in the process and followed his lead as they swayed in a leisurely manner.

"Your cheeks are turning red," he commented before offering one of his genuine smiles.

"Is it?"

For a while, they remained silent. She ignored the glares they received by opting to relax the tighter muscles, as well as her pounding heart, instead. Two songs later, she felt at ease enough to converse.

"You're going to make the ladies jealous if you spend your time with me."

"*I'm* going to make them jealous? You're the most beautiful woman here; that's why they're staring."

She huffed a laugh. "Right."

"I've been waiting all night to get a break from them."

"The burden of being royalty, I suppose." Coura chuckled as the music ended and gently pushed herself away from him to roll her shoulders. "Dancing so close together hurts my shoulders."

"I'd rather not have you stepping on my feet."

In that moment, Coura realized how weary she'd grown and thanked Aaron for keeping her around a bit longer.

He frowned after her words. "You're leaving?"

"Yes. Honestly, I don't know where you get the energy to stay up so late."

"It comes with the title."

From across the courtyard, she caught Grace's gown under the lamplight as the girl sat alone next to Byron, who continued to entertain somebody else at his other side. A strange guilt tugged at her, and she prepared to bid farewell to the prince until a slim woman grabbed Aaron's arm.

"Prince Aaron, you haven't danced with me in ages!"

The impassive mask appeared again. "Forgive me, Lady Hilda. I've quite lost track of the time."

"You are forgiven, Your Highness. As long as you make it up to me by-"

"Sorry, but he's promised one more dance," Coura interrupted.

While the lady shot her a filthy glare, Aaron raised an eyebrow with a little hopefulness. She stared at where Grace waited and silently thanked him for catching on to what she attempted to do.

"That's right!" he exclaimed and removed his arm from the woman's grasp. "I did promise Lady Grace a dance during the event. I'd hate to keep the Yeluthian ambassador awake later than she's used to. You understand, Lady Hilda?"

At the mention of Yeluthia, the woman's eyes went wide. "Of course, of course! I-I don't want to be rude to our guest," she stammered before backing away.

Aaron released a sigh then faced Coura one, last time. "Have a wonderful evening," he said and began heading in Grace's direction.

*

Everywhere except the eastern main road emptied during the late hours with couples or drunks wandering on their own business and yawning guards patrolling the city. Coura hummed one of the tunes she liked as she wandered toward the palace alone. Her body felt rather warm despite the chilly air as she reflected on the day spent with friends, especially her time relearning to dance.

I can't believe how far I've come in a few months. Verona really is an amazing city...

{*So, this is what it's like to be blissfully ignorant of the world. My, how simple it must be to be human.*}

Soirée's voice startled Coura out of her pleasant thoughts. *I figured you would be gone throughout the festival.*

{Now that it's quiet around here, I can tolerate the evening, though I could do better without your naive feelings.}

Naive feelings?

{Do you honestly believe any of your so-called friends actually care about you?}

While the demon laughed wickedly in her mind, Coura became irritated and snapped back. *I get it. You believe all humans are pathetic, and having friendships and feelings toward each other are pathetic. I don't need to hear this from you, not now.*

{This is the perfect time for you to hear it, while you are so light-headed from the euphoria taking place.}

Like I said, I don't care what you think about humans.

{Oh, but I'm not talking about humans, Dear One. I'm talking about you.}

Me?

{You house foolish notions that need to be snuffed, lest your little 'friendships' wreck our rising power.}

She stopped on the bridge leading into the palace and leaned on its wooden guard rail to stare up at the stars as her hands subconsciously clenched into fists. *The only problem I'm having is you. Give it a rest already.*

{Do you see the way they look at you when they believe you're not paying attention?}

She couldn't stop herself from remembering the nasty and frightened stares from the recruits.

{Those were mostly mages. What makes you think the light-blooded brat is any different? You know your history. How many leaders were assassinated by their closest friends or relatives?}

"Grace wouldn't do that," Coura whispered aloud when she became too aggravated with the voice in her mind to keep the words as a thought.

{Why wouldn't she? You just met her a few days ago.}

"The Yeluthians are our allies."

{Weren't they the humans' allies for decades? Where have they been then? Why would two attack you?}

Coura couldn't consider a response fast enough.

{What of your teacher? He has no reason to keep monitoring you unless he has been instructed to do so. He will hide our power until it's convenient for him and those he serves.}

"Don't talk about Byron like that," she growled.

{I know you've noticed how he behaves around you. He doesn't trust your control, that much is obvious.}

Again, she knew Soirée was right; Byron had been keeping a closer eye on her than normal.

{Then, there are the others. Three young men. All different... All suspicious of you.}

"They *are* my friends."

{Two of them nearly died because of you, or did you forget? It's awfully difficult for anybody to ignore.}

Coura let out a "tsk" before pushing off the rail and continuing inside. *Say whatever you want, but it won't change my opinions of them. We'll continue to be friends, whether you like it or not.*

She expected a retort from Soirée or hoped the demon would drop the subject altogether and disappear for the night. The last thing she wanted to hear was snickering, yet the sound rang in her mind.

{How selfish of you. This whole time you thought I was attacking them?}

You sure know how to run your mouth. Why don't you give up this pointless argument? Coura felt exhausted, but Soirée seemed active and ready to poke fun in a condescending tone.

{As I said earlier, your attitude is growing too optimistic for my liking. It's strange, especially since you wear blood on your hands like gloves and hold the weight of so many lives on your shoulders.}

Although she knew she shouldn't ask, that doing so would be an invitation for Soirée to elaborate, she did. *What do you mean?*

{You really are stupid. You're a murderer, or did you forget the light-blooded beings? We didn't even know their stories or why they were sent looking for your group. They could have been innocent soldiers, like those you train with. Consider how you would react if a scared, young human murdered one of your friends.}

Coura didn't get a chance to offer a rebuttal as the demon continued.

{It's also your fault the mages were sent here. Without your little outburst, there could have been a chance to avoid sending as many. You just had to demonstrate how powerful a magic user can be, let alone your unique abilities. I've witnessed their fear. So many mages afraid of fighting, of a war on the horizon with a faceless enemy. What do you suppose would happen if they went up against trained soldiers?}

Soirée conjured images of bloodshed, including numerous figures in the white and blue robes being slaughtered by suits of armor.

Stop it! Coura cried before hurrying toward her room. Her physical and mental exhaustion kept her from pushing away the demon's words.

{Do you believe your friends don't know how dangerous you are? If they chose to abandon you, what would stop you from killing them? You are a true monster holding them hostage with your relationship.}

She couldn't stop her eyes from watering with unshed tears while Soirée continued hurling insults at her.

{How could anybody care about an abomination like you? You're a mistake to the natural order and shouldn't exist. No one wants you here. You'll never be accepted by these people because of what you are.}

If the demon was trying to break her morale, it nearly worked until Coura fell asleep at some point. She woke groggy and depressed from last night's verbal abuse as echoes of the words repeated in her mind. Meanwhile, Soirée returned to her normal attitude and didn't provide an explanation as to why she decided to say what she did.

A Cruel Assignment

Winter came and went over the course of three months. Since Verona and East Hoover were located in the northern half of the country, Coura and those new to the city felt relieved to know they would receive only the few inches of snow they became accustomed to.

Byron continued to mention training her dark magic but never followed through with any comments, so she and Soirée practiced in her room while suppressing the demonic energy. The physical training expanded to include unfamiliar soldiers, which tested her focus and skill against experienced opponents. In the meantime, Coura, Marcus, Aaron, Will, and Grace met for evening meals regularly. She sincerely believed each of them grew closer, much to Soirée's disapproval. The demon began insulting her more often than usual because of that, leaving them both in sour moods throughout the day. More than anything, she longed to tell somebody about Soirée, if only to rest easier; however, she understood how dangerous it would be for her to mention she shared her mind and soul with the creature.

Thankfully, with the arrival of spring, everyone was in better spirits. Will brought the warmer weather up that evening and encouraged the group to hike with him on their next day off in search of a special type of fungi growing during that time of the year. They all enthusiastically agreed, especially Grace, who longed to leave the palace again. The girl's blossoming personality brightened Coura previous concern. Ever since she introduced the Yeluthian to their friends, Grace's fun-loving personality flourished, and she found the motivation to spend less time in uncomfortable situations, such as the stuffy private meals. Aaron even convinced a housekeeper to move her belongings to an empty corner room with windows.

While they ate together, Grace tossed tiny, round tomatoes to Marcus, and he attempted to catch them in his mouth from various spots around the space. The others chuckled when he missed one when lying on his back. Instead of landing in his open mouth, it bounced off his forehead and rolled away, causing the group to howl with laughter.

"You need better aim," the assistant general chided and pointed at the Yeluthian as she popped a tomato in her mouth.

"Maybe you just need a smaller forehead," Coura added with a grin.

"Hey!"

{*You're one to talk about appearances. No wonder none of them find you attractive. Now, if I had my body...*}

If your physical appearance is anything like your personality, I can imagine how ugly you must truly be.

Soirée growled viciously, to Coura's satisfaction.

"There you go again," she heard Will say after.

When no one responded, she pulled her eyes away from the wall she had been staring at and found the four watching her. "What?"

Will shook his head. "I hope you know you always do that."

"Do what?"

"Somebody asks you a question, and you don't listen, or you're ignoring us. I wouldn't bring it up, except it becomes tiresome having to repeat myself."

Coura rolled her eyes. "I was just thinking. Why is it such a problem?"

Will didn't answer, but he also didn't appear convinced.

Instead, Grace changed the subject, startling everyone in the process. "If you want, I can peek inside her mind to find out what is so distracting," the girl said in a mischievous.

The rest of the group looked at her with bewildered expressions.

"What do you mean?" Will was the first to ask.

The Yeluthian smiled proudly. "It is my goddess gift."

A pause followed her reply before Marcus voiced the next question. "What's a goddess gift?"

"You...do not know?"

They shook their heads.

Grace sighed. "I would have thought your people were aware of a Yeluthian's strongest ability." When no one spoke, she continued with a hint of impatience. "It was written in legend when the goddess of light, whose name has been lost to time, sent her people to this planet, she bestowed on them special abilities. Only Yeluthians with a strong connection to their light energy can use it, which varies among my people. For some, they can manifest the elemental powers, like fire, lightning, and ice, while others like me are able to speak mind-to-mind with living creatures. There have even been Yeluthians who bond with animals or plants, create portals to another location, or manifest physical illusions, but I have not heard of any in the recent decade."

"Can you try it on us?" Aaron asked slowly.

Grace giggled at their baffled stares and nodded.

{*I'm quite intrigued.*}

Coura winced to herself and regretted how the demon learned about the angels' secret ability. *What if she senses you?*

Soirée didn't respond, though it was too late to find out, for the next words they heard were Grace's but didn't come from the girl's mouth.

{*If you really do not mind.*}

For once, Coura felt grateful for her familiarity with the sensation of hearing another voice in her mind because the others didn't take it well. Aaron nearly fell over in his chair, Marcus gasped, and Will went pale and looked like he might pass out. She eyed Grace and suspected the Yeluthian could sense Soirée at any moment, but her friend merely beamed after experiencing their reactions.

"H-How did you…" Marcus began, yet Grace put a finger to her lips to silence him and pointed to her left temple.

{If you think at me, I can pick up your words telepathically.}

With scrunched eyebrows, all three boys must have sent their thoughts because the girl's smile widened.

{Excellent, but do not try so hard. It tickles my head!}

She paused while listening to what they were saying.

{I can only hear one of you at a time, though I can project my words to more than one person. It takes more energy than I am used to. Still, it is helpful.}

Grace glanced over at Coura, who rose to stand by the window.

{You did not try sending me your thoughts.}

Instead of continuing the game, Coura shook her head. "I prefer not to be kept in the dark about what everybody else says."

"Why didn't you mention this when you arrived?" Aaron interjected in an enthusiastic manner.

"I did," the Yeluthian replied while tilting her head.

"I mean, before now."

"I did," she repeated with a puzzled expression. "My king sent a formal letter the week before I left explaining why he chose me specifically and what my ability is."

In the resulting pause, everyone stared at the prince.

"We never received such a letter," he admitted, switching the carefree atmosphere into a serious discussion.

"Could somebody have intercepted it?" Marcus asked.

"I don't know. If we heard about this sooner, my father would not have been upset. He figured Yeluthia sent a child because they think poorly of Asteom and consider the alliance a trivial matter. He hasn't taken any actions to reach out to them yet, and we didn't receive messages from your people either. It makes me suspicious of where the missing letter went. If it was intercepted, there might be somebody out there who doesn't want this alliance."

They began to consider the implications of both an enemy seeking to sabotage Asteom's relationship with the angelic city and what they could do now that Grace shared her goddess gift with the prince. When no one picked up the conversation, Aaron stood and bowed before their Yeluthian friend.

"Grace, I'm sorry you've been treated like a child instead of a representative up until now. I appreciate you explaining your ability, and if you don't mind, I'm going to let my father know about this immediately."

She nodded to show her understanding and thanked him.

*

The following free day, Coura and the others agreed to meet in the morning and set out into the southern woods to look for Will's mushrooms. She rose early to bathe and eat beforehand, then she hurried into the entrance hall. Once there, she saw Aaron, who already had his cloak on with the hood covering his face, and Marcus in his uniform. Shortly after, Grace appeared in a green sundress.

"Of course Will is the last person here!" the assistant general exclaimed and threw his hands up dramatically as the leader of the expedition arrived, dragging three packs behind.

"Can someone please help?" the herbalist begged.

"What's all this for?" Coura inquired when Marcus and Aaron hurried to shoulder the extra bags while Will did the same with his own.

"We need jars to keep the samples in, and the medical station supervisor asked me to look for plants to restock their supplies. Plus, I need the books in this bag to identify the right fungi before dissecting it to ensure its properties are what I'm looking for."

"I don't know what you're talking about, but if we're going to finish this by dinner, I say we get moving."

Will stumbled forward, followed closely by a curious Grace; however, before they reached the front gate, they heard a familiar voice calling for them to wait. From the nearest door along the left side of the room entered Byron, who jogged to where they stopped.

"What is it?" Aaron demanded in a concerned voice, making Coura wonder if he told anybody where he intended to go.

The master mage took a few seconds to catch his breath, then he greeted them and addressed her. "I've been looking everywhere for you. We need to talk."

"About what?"

He shook his head apologetically. "I'm afraid we've been invited to a meeting that may take the entire morning. I tried finding you sooner, but-"

"It's my day off," she interrupted to show her annoyance. "Can't this wait?"

"It's with King Hernan," Byron replied at a lower volume, prompting Aaron to step forward.

"Why would my father suddenly request this?"

Coura prepared to ask the same thing, and also tell him Hernan had no right to force her to work on a free day, but her mentor shot her a look that told Coura the man wouldn't wait.

She stifled her frustration before putting her hands on her hips. "What's the expression they use here? A soldier is never off duty?"

Her friends looked on without hiding their concern, obviously aware of her situation.

She turned to them and waved with as much of a reassuring smile as she could muster. "Don't wait for me. I'll be out there as soon as I can."

Byron apologized to them before gesturing for her to follow him. They walked at a brisk pace toward the main staircase and used it to get on the second floor.

"So, what's this about?" Coura grumbled as they hurried down the winding hallways.

"I don't know. A servant brought me a letter not long ago requesting us to meet the king in the council's meeting room immediately. You weren't in your room, so I ran around everywhere trying to find you."

She didn't comment any further and compelled herself to relax as her mind raced through several possibilities for their summons. None led to positive outcomes.

*

The meeting room sat at the center of the second floor and consisted of nothing but a round table, enough chairs to seat over a dozen people, and a throne positioned a head higher than the rest of the space. As Byron and Coura entered, they caught Emilea standing alone, then the king seated on his throne.

"I need to think of a more fitting term than 'immediately' to request your presence since you two like to take your time," Hernan's deep voice rumbled throughout the enclosed area.

You could have given a proper timeframe for this meeting, or don't hold it on our day off, Coura considered arguing.

Instead, she tightened her lips while Byron apologized on their behalf. Before they entered the chamber, he had grabbed her arm and warned her not to be disrespectful.

As if a man with this much power cares what we say anyway.

"Now then, let us begin," the king continued. "The reason I called you three here is because I believe we might have a spy among our ranks who intends to sabotage our potential alliances with Yeluthia and Nim-Vala."

Coura went a bit cold at the unexpected discussion topic.

"What do you mean, Your Highness?" Emilea asked with no small hint of surprise.

"We have reason to believe communications with these nations are being severed and possibly manipulated by a mage. I called you three here to see if there's a method for tracing magical energy if it is in fact involved."

While the master mages conversed about the issue with each other, Coura stood stunned and useless.

I'm not in trouble? He actually brought me here to help? For once, I feel more like a student and not a trained recruit. The idea amazed her, and she regretted being so pessimistic as the initial ire melted away, leaving her wondering if she could keep up with their plotting.

After a fair amount of questioning, Byron and Emilea evidently reached the same conclusion.

"Without our contact and intervention between the energies used for manipulating the evidence, we can't pinpoint where the source would be. Also, it's too difficult for us to constantly search for interference since many magic wielders live in the area," the light mage summarized.

"I hoped for a better answer," Hernan muttered before rubbing the side of his head.

None of the three mages seemed to know what to say to help the situation, so they waited for the king to make up his mind. Finally, he sat straighter.

"This leaves me no choice but to postpone the matter until we find proof that something is being tampered with. In this case, we will move forward with the generals' and my decisions. I would like both master mage positions to become permanent members of the king's council from this moment forth. Emilea, you will continue to be stationed here in order to continue training your students, as well as to gather information about what we discussed should the opportunity arise. Byron, I'm assigning you and your student to our southernmost base in Dala."

"Dala?" Byron repeated without attempting to hide his surprise.

"Yes, Dala," Hernan growled in response to the outburst. "You mentioned how it would place a burden on the mages to train her here, so perhaps we can compromise. More importantly, the base requested we send some of our new recruits south. It would be best to have you inspect the facilities before we send them away."

At first, the order to move from the capital left Coura numb; however, her mind caught up a moment later, and she realized she started scowling. The idea of traveling didn't bother her too much, but sending Byron along and forcing the mages who were beginning to make a life in Verona seemed harsh. She desired to voice as much yet tightened her jaw to keep her tongue behind clenched teeth. Of course, her mentor agreed to the proposal, though she noticed the displeasure in his voice and downward curve of his mouth when he did so. Even Emilea cast a startled glance at him.

Hernan continued in a bored manner, despite their reactions. "Bring along whomever you wish to accompany you. You'll have three days to prepare and delegate your normal duties. On the morning of the fourth, someone shall see you off."

Byron asked a few more questions regarding the towns they would need to be in and who to contact at the base, but Hernan acted unconcerned and impatient. His attitude shifted from a pretentious ruler to a man too preoccupied with his own desires to care about his subordinates. The disrespect drove Coura mad.

Soirée said nothing, though she had been listening in on the conversation.

"Anything else?" the king requested at last.

When nothing else was said, he gestured to the door with one hand. Coura held in a sigh of relief upon hearing their dismissal and prepared to turn away until Hernan caught her eye.

"Master Byron and Master Emilea, you are both excused," he said calmly while holding her gaze.

The two glanced at one another, then Byron cleared his throat. "Your Highness?"

"That will be all."

As the pair bowed and reluctantly made their exit, Coura's doubts returned two-fold. She became rigid once the door closed behind the master mages, and the guards scuffled outside once more. Still, she refused to be the first to break their eye contact.

What did I do this time? Why keep me here alone? What can't he tell me in front of anybody else?

Hernan adjusted his position to rest an elbow on the throne's arm and lean on it with an unreadable expression. The two continued staring at each other in silence until Coura crossed her arms to avoid fidgeting, even though she knew it would be seen as impolite.

The man appeared more attentive when she moved, and a faint smile danced on his lips. "You're not a patient person, are you?"

She didn't respond, so Hernan took that as an invitation to keep going.

"I can also tell you don't like me, do you?"

"You're a king. My opinion should be of little concern," Coura couldn't help herself from saying.

"I am a king? Not *your* king?" he asked with an edge to his voice that made her flinch.

"You are the king of Asteom, and I am a mage under your law, so I suppose you could say you're my king." The words poured forth solely from her anxiousness, and she cursed her inability to speak fluently under such pressure.

Hernan's head shook ever so slightly as his eyes narrowed, then his expression changed. "Do you know why you're here, Coura Galdwin?" he began in a softer tone.

A shiver slid along her spine when he said her name, but she managed to shake her head.

"You're here because I allow you to be. Demons are horrible beings. I've ordered the execution of cult leaders who worship those creatures and try to bring them back by offering their own lives, as well as ordinary citizens' who become possessed even though they did nothing wrong. I'm sure that's not surprising for you to hear. If I wanted to, I could have you killed for what took place at the Magical Arts Academy, but I see a benefit in letting you live. Besides, what would my son or the Yeluthian ambassador think if I had you executed? For some reason, they've taken a liking to you. It would be a shame to get them involved in this business of demons."

At the mention of Aaron and Grace, Coura's heart stopped. She became frightened of what the man could do to them, and probably Will, Marcus, Byron, or anyone else who associated with her too. The previous frustration returned as well to give her the strength to speak. "So, either I behave and do what you command or you'll kill me or use my friends against me. Is that what you needed me to hear? Why the dramatics then?"

Hernan sighed, almost sympathetically. Something unpleasant stood out about his expression, and a glimmer of vexation rose in his eyes. "Since you seem to only grasp half of what I am trying to explain, I'll make it simple. You are neither a mage nor a soldier but a tool to serve this kingdom, unable to act unless I give you an order. Your life means so little that one false move, one wrong word, and you will be executed. My son, the Yeluthian ambassador, and your other friends are excellent sources of information. No matter what you may think, any relationship you build in this kingdom will bend to my authority, especially when it's for the betterment of our nation. You obey, and you live. You are nothing and nobody. Is *that* easier to understand?"

His gaze never let up as he spoke, and the words burrowed under Coura's skin. Her anxiety from addressing Asteom's king and her fear of the consequences he could bestow subsided while her resentment grew after the belittling. Even Soirée started simmering.

Lest her tongue betray her, she nodded once before pivoting to exit.

From the throne, Hernan let out an "ahem" to get her attention. "You forget you're in the presence of royalty," he reminded her with the same, heated expression.

Beneath her anger, Coura wondered why the man seemed to become more irritated with her. She recalled how Byron and Emilea bowed before leaving the chamber and did the same. As she straightened and hoped the gesture would be the end of his lecture, her head pounded with the strain of holding her temper in check. Unfortunately, Hernan kept talking.

"Try again. In your position, I expect better."

The thought of staying just to entertain the king enraged her, yet she bit her tongue, clenched her hands into fists, and continued to tell herself to remain obedient, if not for her sake then for those associated with her. With as much dignity as she could manage, Coura placed her right hand over her heart, lowered herself onto one knee, and bowed her head. Each motion burned her pride away, melting it into pure rage directed at Hernan and supported by Soirée. She counted to five before rising and masking those feelings behind a disinterested expression, which almost slipped once she saw his amused smile.

{*What an infuriating coward to hide behind something as worthless as a bloodline!*}

The demon's venomous voice continued as she insulted the king, and Coura felt the energy in her center humming in response to the high level of stress. By that point, her mind was in such an icy state she couldn't think clearly as she departed from the room.

The master mages had been waiting outside, and Byron slid to her side with Emilea close behind as she stormed down the hallway.

"What happened?" he pressed once they were away from the guards; however, one look at her face told him she wasn't in the mood for questions.

She refused to direct her attention at anyone or anything until she could safely release the pent up power, lest it overwhelm her in a violent outburst. The master mages trailed behind in silence while she made her way to the busy training ground. After reaching the outer wall, she climbed over the stone structure to trek through the woods beyond. Her mentor called to her before deciding to follow, and Soirée continued venting until they were deeper inside the northern forest.

{*Are you running away? Don't be foolish.*}

Tell me when we're far enough for nobody to notice us.

Soirée instantly understood the message and her intentions and let her know when they were safe from any prying eyes or mages able to sense the demonic energy.

Byron and Emilea still lagged behind, so Coura held up a hand, gesturing for them to halt at a distance. Their footsteps did stop, so she approached her chosen target: a tree whose trunk proved to be as wide as three of her arms' length put together.

Soirée, make sure nothing slips through, she ordered.

A grip seized around the stream of active power flowing from her center, preventing anyone from sensing it. That was all she remembered for a while as she manifested her blade and took her pent-up emotions out on the wood with wild swings meant only to wear her out.

*

When she could keep track of herself once more, tears streaked down her face, and tiny sparks flew off the backs of both hands where the energy chose to exit against her control. Coura stood panting before striking the stable tree three, additional times.

Why did this happen to me? she begged as the pain seemed to catch up to her. *Why does everybody treat me like a mad dog? I have friends... I have a life here... I'm still human!*

Another surge of anger swelled, so she threw her sword to the side and began punching the tree with all her remaining strength. Her knuckles split open and healed again and again, each time causing less pain. Though blood splattered onto the bark, she wasn't nearly strong enough to do damage, and eventually, her hits grew weaker. Once she noticed how scarlet her knuckles became, though they displayed no open cuts, she gave up and put her palms against the tree to lean on it while her body cooled down. After another minute, she wiped off her sweat and tears when a pair of footsteps came closer, reminding her of the two onlookers.

"Come on. Let's go back." Byron's voice sounded calm and steady as he directed her, which somehow left her feeling worse about leading them away.

She nodded, turned around, and hung her head. Now that her energy waned, Coura felt how weary and hungry she was. Her legs wobbled, but she stayed behind her mentor with a pale-faced Emilea keeping to the rear.

During the heat of the moment, she had not realized how far she took them into the forest. When they returned to the training ground, it looked to be well into the afternoon, but Byron didn't bring them inside. Instead, he asked Emilea to fetch water and ordered Coura to sit on the grass against the stone wall. The light mage returned carrying a waterskin and handed it to her. She drank nearly the entire amount at once.

"Tell us what happened," her mentor ordered when she could look him in the eye.

She raised an eyebrow at Emilea, who appeared somewhat uncertain about being included, but told them what Hernan said. Reciting the comments hurt, but she remained too fatigued to cling on to any emotions that would raise another tantrum. For a long while after, both master mages avoided the other's eyes, opting to contemplate what transpired on their own.

At last, Byron cleared his throat. "Out in the woods, how did you hide the demonic presence from us?"

Without mentioning Soirée, Coura sheepishly admitted to practicing her magic behind his back.

He rolled his eyes in response, though he didn't appear surprised or upset. "You nearly made us faint with that secret of yours. As for what took place in the meeting room, don't let it concern you. What King Hernan said was out of line, but he's right about where your loyalty should lie. Keep behaving, and you'll rid yourself of the image he has of you, especially if you don't dart off and behave like what I just witnessed. It's irresponsible and reckless, and you should know better than to do that when you lose your temper."

She anticipated as much from Byron, who never seemed subjective about anything, and dipped her head submissively. What did startle her was Emilea's unexpected outburst after.

"How could you be so passive?"

He stared at the woman with eyes wide in astonishment, allowing her to elaborate.

"His Highness may have his reasons for speaking to Coura alone, but such a lecture is unacceptable! You and I both know we *never* tell our students they're tools for their superiors to use. I would think you'd understand that since most of the academy's mages thought the same when they arrived. How could you be so heartless, and to your own student?"

Emilea never looked at Coura when she spoke but gave Byron a stern gaze while continuing in that manner. Then, she made him swear to not take the situation so carelessly before claiming she had other business to attend to.

Coura couldn't stop herself from chuckling after noticing Byron's blank expression and crimson cheeks as the woman strolled toward the palace.

"And here I thought Emilea didn't like me," she mused.

On the Road Again

That night at dinner, Coura informed her friends of the reassignment without mentioning details about the meeting. No one felt like eating afterward.

"Do you think Byron would let me come?" Will asked to break the lingering silence.

"I don't see why not," she answered truthfully.

Marcus sat straighter. "I'll request to join too."

"I want to come," Grace added next; however, she understood her place was in Verona.

Coura placed a reassuring hand on the girl's shoulder. "Don't worry. With your ability, we can keep in contact, right?"

The Yeluthian perked up a bit. "I think so. It might be too far, but I promise to try."

*

The next morning, Byron agreed to let Will and Marcus accompany them, along with Clearshot. The evening before their departure, Coura bid Aaron and Grace goodbye. When she returned to her room, she found a package on her desk and a note.

A gift from King Hernan at his request. He hopes you will wear it with pride.

"What now?" she muttered before sighing and tearing away the paper wrapping. Inside, she discovered a set of matching, black clothes and a pair of shined boots at the bottom.

"A soldier's uniform," she whispered in an astounded breath.

Despite her suspicion, she grew eager to try on the outfit and changed immediately. The pants had been crafted using a strange material, one as soft as silk yet durable and stretchy enough to move around in. Although the boots looked as though they would be tight, she was again pleasantly surprised to find them comfortable with extra padding against the cold.

So far, so good, she thought and picked up the shirt and crimson coat. *I don't think I've ever worn such conspicuous clothing before.*

When she finished donning the sleeveless top, Coura expected the outfit to make her appear older and muscular, like Marcus did in his uniform. Once in front of the mirror, she became a sight to behold. It looked different than his, yet she felt just as important. From the waist down, the uniform proved to be sliming. The pants appeared formal enough without revealing how flexible they actually were, and the shirt acted similarly. She also admired the polish of her boots and hoped the sheen would last through the trip, and then some.

Finally, she procured the coat, put it on, and closed it using the gold buttons before observing the results. While Marcus' coat broadened his shoulders, hers accentuated her hips and chest by resting along her curves, though her upper body did appear sturdier as well. She figured it was fitting for a female soldier because it kept her professional, demonstrated her physicality, and still managed to be modest.

While she marveled at the material, Coura noticed what had her feeling uncertain about the uniform. *It's the buttons. Marcus' coat is adorned with more gold, like on the shoulder and breast. Mine just has the buttons and...*

She reached up to brush her fingers along the badge resting over her heart with a mixture of awe and disapproval. Where her friend and the other soldiers showcased sewn badges, such as stars or swords in gold to represent their status, hers displayed a pair of wings in silver thread.

{*What a sense of humor they have.*}

Coura's bitterness matched Soirée's once she realized what the badge meant. *He's trying to label me again. 'Not a soldier or a mage.' Well, I'm not this either.*

With a tug, she broke the stitching keeping the rectangular piece sewn onto her coat. After a few yanks, the patch came off. She held the crimson cloth for a moment to admire the meticulous detail in the threaded wings. Once her eyes started drooping, she tossed the badge into her nightstand's drawer and closed it.

*

Coura rolled in bed all night with unpleasant dreams she could not remember until she fell into a comfortable sleep. When the light of dawn woke her, she didn't feel well rested, but she rubbed her eyes and dragged herself out of bed anyway.

It didn't take long to pack her belongings into a single bag. The other base where they would be living would provide most of the necessary items, just as the palace had done, so she only brought what she needed for the journey. Once finished, she stood staring at where she discarded her uniform the night before until she started pacing the room and chewing on her bottom lip while contemplating what to do. Then, she noticed the amount of sunlight outside, indicating it was nearly time for their group to depart. She approached the window, opened it halfway, and gauged the temperature to find it warmer than normal.

"That does it," she told herself with a curt nod as she grabbed the crimson coat and shoved it into her pack. Without wasting additional time, she dressed in the rest of the uniform and proceeded to the main gate.

Byron, Marcus, and Will were waiting in front of the palace beside their own bags while Clearshot chatted with a servant. The latter two seemed more awake than the rest, and their laughter echoed throughout the area in the otherwise peaceful morning.

"You're late," Byron called as soon as she stepped beyond the doorway.

"You're even worse than Will," Marcus chimed after.

Coura shrugged off the comments. As she approached their group, Marcus' eyebrows rose once he recognized the uniform. He wore his own version while Byron and Will had on travel-appropriate outfits. Clearshot also dressed in the full soldier's clothing with a single, gold arrow and star patched on the left breast of the crimson coat.

Byron apparently expected her to be given the outfit, for he frowned and pointed out what she neglected. "You're missing the jacket."

"I have it," she replied while turning her head to gesture at the pack. "It's too warm for that."

She expected him to scold her since he appeared displeased with her lack of pride in the gift, but it was Marcus who spoke up.

"The entire uniform is a signal displaying who we are to the citizens of Asteom. Even in the worst weather or event, we're expected to remain approachable in case anybody is in need."

"Let's continue this along the way," Byron interrupted as the servant returned to the palace and Clearshot merged to join them.

*

They set off down the main road leading west before it branched south. Many other people moved on all sides of them, some riding horses or leading carts pulled by various animals. Knowing they would not need to fend for themselves and were safer on a busy path comforted Coura.

"What were you saying about the uniform?" she asked to spark a conversation when Marcus walked beside her.

As ever the respectable soldier, he cleared his throat and resumed the lecture. "There's really not much to it. Every soldier is expected to wear their uniform when on duty because citizens don't often recognize us without it. It's the same with mages, I would think; no one can tell you're a mage unless you wear a robe. Even the colors don't seem to matter since a lot of people aren't familiar with magic around here."

She considered her own coat's lack of gold next. "What do the buttons and badges mean?"

This time, Clearshot slipped over to Coura's other side to add to the explanation.

358

"Each soldier is categorized into a specific grouping, which helps the generals keep track of their own or assign ones they're not familiar with." He pointed to his own badge: an arrow sewn using gold thread and stitched just as finely as the wings on hers. "See, I'm an archer. This makes it pretty obvious what my specialty is. Marcus' is a sword, so he's a close-combat soldier."

"There are close-combat soldiers, distance-combat fighters, including archers, and defense specialists," Marcus interjected while counting the groups on his fingers. "The last category's badges are circular."

"What do the stars mean?" she inquired and pointed to his uniform. Next to the sword were a pair of gold stars.

"Oh, those? They just show our ranking. Generals wear three stars, assistant generals have two, outstanding soldiers who are experienced on the battlefield under the generals but who aren't their assistants have one, like Clearshot, and common soldiers don't wear any."

Coura glanced back and forth between them, comparing the groupings against her own, unique badge. "Yours are both in gold," was all she thought to add.

"That's another categorizing system," Clearshot replied in an amused tone. "Gold means you are top ranked in your classification. Marcus and I are both accomplished combatants, so we earned the right to possess gold badges. It's a matter of how much experience you have, as well as how skilled you are. This way, anybody not familiar with us can see we're go-to soldiers in a time of crisis, and we can be trusted to lead or fight when necessary. Common soldiers who are still in training or those who don't belong on the battlefield unless needed, like the healers, get white badges. They're meant to follow orders, not necessarily give them. Lastly, badges with silver thread indicate a soldier's ability to wield magic. It's not common since most soldiers who start with silver thread usually make their way to gold or step down to become dark or light mages once they get older. I believe that's the path Byron took."

"Yes," their aforementioned leader confirmed while slowing his pace to speak with them. "I was a close-combat soldier wielding dark magic. It didn't take me long to realize if I kept it up, my body wouldn't be useful later on."

"They're specifically helpful in certain strategies," Marcus shared before Clearshot continued.

"You bet! With a mage who can fight, it's easy to cover any distance and create shields. I imagine your badge is silver, isn't it, Coura?"

She nodded and contemplated mentioning the wings but decided against it.

Before lunch, they neared the next closest city.

*

Coura had been somewhat familiar with the layout of their journey yet listened as Byron explained it to the rest of their group. Since Dala served as a high-traffic area leading to the southernmost cities and towns in Asteom, they would be able to take the main roads passing through less populated cities instead of camping in the woods. The king provided each of them with an extra allowance to pay for inns, food, and provisions, which she learned when her mentor tossed her a pouch with several silver coins in it.

"The first city this road goes through is called Sindaly. We should reach our inn for the night later, so make sure you eat enough to last all day."

Once in the smaller version of Verona, they spent no time inspecting the environment because a bakery worker noticed the crimson uniforms and ushered them inside his establishment.

"Best wishes to you all!" he greeted the group in a cheerful manner and led them around the crowded front area toward a round table. On it, toasted sandwiches filled with some sort of meat and cheese had been laid out. They appeared to be straight out of the oven, and Coura's mouth began watering at the smell of fresh bread.

While the baker began wrapping the items on the plate, he chirped to Marcus and Clearshot, startling her a bit since she became accustomed to Byron handling the interactions.

"Best wishes indeed! I hoped a soldier or two would stop by. Lots of rumors are coming down from the capital city." He stopped, glanced from side to side, then went on at a hushed volume. "Is it true we've got a *real* angel in Asteom? That their kind is looking to rekindle old ties, if you catch my drift?"

Clearshot remained silent while Marcus spoke with the man as professionally as ever.

"It's true. The Yeluthians sent an ambassador to begin reforging our alliance."

The joy on the man's face coupled by his already plump appearance and rosy cheeks made Coura smile.

"Bless us all!" He raised his eyes to the ceiling before shaking his head and resumed wrapping their meals. "Forgive a man for hoping, but it's been too long since we got positive news around here, what with talk of monsters and demons and the like. First, mages are being recruited from the east, then angels. It's enough to make us hope for the better."

The baker prattled on about gossip from around the area for a couple more minutes until the sandwiches were prepared and tucked away into their packs.

"I'll be grabbing fresh ones now. Just you wait," the man informed the group before disappearing into the kitchen beyond.

By that point, Coura's stomach rumbled, and she felt ready to move on. Her impatience doubled when she saw the man return with a woman around the same age who clutched her apron to display her nerves. He handed them hot sandwiches and mumbled about her being his sister and wanting to ask them a few questions. After he begged their pardon numerous times, her temper finally snapped.

"Get on with it already," she muttered loudly enough for the pair to hear before digging into her meal and ignoring the glares of her companions.

Fortunately, they showed no indication her words offended them. The sister must have been more comfortable speaking to another woman, for she stepped forward to address Coura instead of the others.

"My lady, the rumors and all are good, except I heard about soldiers to the north and an evil weapon of sorts in the palace."

Coura swallowed her mouthful of food and paused to stare at the woman. "Evil weapon?"

Marcus instantly retook the reins on their conversation. "There are soldiers heading south in Nim-Vala; however, as of this moment, they're no threat to the northern border. In any case, we are prepared with troops and mages of our own. I wouldn't worry too much."

Although he offered a reassuring smile, the woman and her brother didn't appear convinced. They conversed with each other before facing the assistant general again.

"And the weapon?" the baker urged.

King Hernan's words repeated in Coura's mind, and she turned away while Marcus fumbled for a response. When he couldn't come up with one, he glanced at Byron.

The master mage cleared his throat before stepping forward and introducing himself with his formal title. "Please, share with us what you heard," he said after.

The two sets of eyes grew wide as they became captivated by a real mage. Coura caught them shrinking back, though the man mustered the courage to approach the topic. In that moment, he seemed to be regretting bringing it up.

"From what we heard, there's some sort of demonic creature with wings as black as the night. It flies and summons the creatures that have been roaming around. They say it's King Hernan who controls it, though we doubt that part. Why would he be letting the creatures hurt us innocent folk?"

"Who told you these things?" Byron asked as Coura chuckled to herself and finished her sandwich. Unfortunately, the food sat like a lump in her stomach.

"My sister heard it from the smith's wife, and her from the tavern owner when they stopped in. Old Warner's the one who speaks to the soldiers, and now the mages, when they come into town."

"It was a mage!" his sister interrupted. "Warner knew because their group wore the robes."

Coura knew she needed to stay inconspicuous, and not necessarily be proud of the rumors, yet the idea of being controlled by Hernan left a bitter taste in her mouth. *If other mages are spreading lies, I might as well add my own twist.*

She released a dramatic sigh to get their attention before pretending to act as uninterested in the discussion as possible. "Well, I've heard more rumors than that. The creature also seems to be one of the most powerful magic users in Asteom. That's why Hernan had to beg them not to attack the palace."

The pair's faces fell and blanched; the sister in particular went as white as a sheet.

Byron interjected to remind them those were only rumors, and Marcus began to make similar, reassuring comments at the same time.

{Now, this is fun! Tell them we held a blade to his throat until he cried for mercy.}

Though Coura opened her mouth to voice the twisted lie, the siblings' attention shifted to Byron once he thanked them for their time and the meal. He reached into his pouch to pluck out a couple coins, but the baker only accepted one.

After, the man grinned at her without masking his fear. "It's been a long time since we heard such ferocious tales coming from the capital. My sister and folk around here don't appreciate the darker bits, yet I find they hold value, especially if they lead to more."

Once their business concluded, he hastily ushered the group back toward the road. They continued until they were outside Sindaly, then Coura earned herself an earful from Byron, Marcus, and Clearshot about the senseless gossiping.

"Why tell them anything if you don't want them knowing the truth?" she was finally able to blurt out when the three settled down.

Her mentor released a frustrated groan. "First of all, what you said isn't the whole truth. Second of all, it's part of our duty to the kingdom to recognize false rumors and put them to rest. It's easy to do this by finding people like that man and his sister who are familiar in this city. Their words hold weight, and they'll pass along the information."

"If that's true, how did they hear about me? I thought my abilities are supposed to be a secret."

"My thoughts exactly," Will added, which startled everyone since he had been quiet for most of the day. "Why would mages from the palace be allowed to share it? Surely they're aware it's meant to be kept behind closed lips."

Byron rubbed his eyes and shrugged. "I'm sorry, but no matter how respectful we tell others to be, sometimes tongues slip. It shouldn't be surprising considering we've been in the capital for nearly a year. Our advantage is that no one outside the academy should know it's Coura. I plan on keeping that secret for as long as possible."

***

Grace tossed and turned in bed until the sheets became too stifling. With a tiny grunt, she pushed the covers off, went to the window, and threw it open. A warm breeze greeted her against the setting sun, leading her to appreciate the fact that spring was nearly upon the capital.

Coura, Marcus, and Will left that morning, leaving her on her own again. She spent the peaceful day reading in the palace's main library before returning to her quarters for a nap. Then, she changed into more appropriate clothing for dinner. Although she liked Aaron a lot, they began eating meals in the private hall again, which meant mingling with the unbearably flamboyant, gossiping lords and ladies.

She dressed in a lavender gown before hurrying toward the dining hall. *I must have been resting longer than I thought! The meal has started for sure, but hopefully I can sneak in.*

Grace made her way down the nearby staircase to the second floor, moving soundlessly lest anybody notice and keep her even later. As she passed a closed door at the center of the building, a man's deep outburst caused her to jump in alarm.

"I tell you when to go!" he yelled and slammed something down.

She froze when she couldn't recognize the voice. After glancing around, she found herself alone in the hallway. *They must all be at dinner.*

The stranger continued at a lower volume. His grumbling tempted Grace enough to pique her curiosity, so she tiptoed to the door and eavesdropped. Her heart beat painfully against her chest as she pressed an ear on the crack.

"…leave tonight under the cover of darkness."

"You are sure he will depart tonight?"

"Do you question my sources?" the deeper voice snapped in response.

"What about the royal family?" a tenor asked impassively.

Another pounding noise startled her.

"Your main concern for now is the base! You have your orders and a leader."

Silence.

"We understand," the tenor replied after the pause.

"Good. Now, get out of my sight."

Upon hearing the dismissal, Grace moved away and retraced her steps as her heart still beat frantically from a mixture of excitement and anxiousness. *Who are these men? What are they planning?*

The mentioning of targets and a base left her mind racing and her stomach in knots. She made it to the hall without drawing attention, though Aaron noticed something was wrong. He signaled to her during the remainder of the meal for a dance once the music began.

To her amazement, and at the moment, her displeasure, King Hernan spoke with her for most of the evening. His whole demeanor changed from what she believed to be arrogance into sincerity. He explained what she already knew about the missing letter from Yeluthia, though she pretended to be shocked, and apologized for treating her dismissively. Seeing such a powerful man be humbled reminded her of the better qualities of the humans in Asteom.

"My son also told me you wish to use your goddess gift for our kingdom. I will accept only if it is safe and you consent. Do not feel obliged, especially after how you've been disrespected up until now."

"Thank you, but I offer my services as a representative of Yeluthia," she responded politely.

King Hernan nodded, flashed a genuine smile, then leaned closer. "As a king, I appreciate your cooperation. As a father, please don't push yourself. Forgive me for thinking of you as a child, but if you need anything while you are here, do not hesitate to ask."

Grace's cheeks blushed at the man's kind words. After their conversation, she felt more welcome than she had since meeting Coura and their friends. Not long after, Aaron took her to dance, and her mood sobered once she told him about what she overheard in the hall just before the meal.

"A base?" he repeated, projecting just as much confusion as she felt.

"I am not sure what any of it means either, but I figured I would share it with you since they mentioned the royal family."

He fell silent. After the song, the prince thanked her for the dance and the information before going to his father.

With her purpose fulfilled, Grace went to the outer hallway along the southern side of the building to enjoy the crisp, evening air. A few minutes later, the sound of hoofbeats below caught her attention. She saw three people, all in the crimson uniform, on horses that impatiently shifted in place. A servant in a white tunic approached carrying a pack he handed to the nearest man.

She recognized Aaron in the lead a moment later because his golden hair brightened in the twilight. They talked for a moment before the riders threw on their cloaks, covered their heads with the hoods, and took off into Verona. Grace watched them go while wondering why the prince was traveling into the city. In the next instant, she remembered what the mysterious voice had said.

The stranger mentioned somebody leaving tonight. Could they have meant the prince?

Darkness crept over the land in the moonless night, making her sleepy despite her worry. She became conflicted about what to do and decided against acting until tomorrow when she could find help, perhaps from King Hernan, High Priest Hendal, or one of the generals.

Just as she straightened and prepared to turn away, a patch of gray slid across the sky, like a lone cloud in the otherwise clear sky. She squinted at it and noticed how the steady pace seemed unnaturally consistent yet familiar. After a moment, her body went rigid as she discerned multiple parts forming the shape.

Those are wings, at least four pairs. I would know the sight anywhere, but I am sure they are flying too high for anyone else to identify. I thought I was the only Yeluthian sent here? Are there others with light blood strong enough to perform the manifestation spell?

Grace followed the figures as far as she could see while panic gripped her chest. They were heading south.

Memories of the Past

yron had been right about their travels for the rest of the first day. As the group moved from Sindaly to the next town called Umbridge, they relied on lamps from others and light from the buildings to continue ahead. The amount of travelers occupying the road impressed Coura, yet she felt grateful for their company.

Throughout the late afternoon, most strangers recognized the soldiers' uniforms, prompting them to start conversations with Marcus and Clearshot. Once somebody mentioned Byron's abilities, more people turned their attention to him. Will even found a woman interested in his specific field of research to befriend during the journey. They were in high spirits as they approached Umbridge despite the ominous darkness from the moonless sky.

While everyone became occupied with their own business, Coura used the time alone to consider what the baker told them. *I can't believe they think I'm controlling the demonic creatures.*

{It only makes sense. They associate all demon-like beings with one another.}

Are they not connected? She didn't know what relationships the creatures had with each another, but Soirée scoffed, as if offended by the question.

{Of course not. Are humans in control of what another does? Demons rarely associate with each other since we hate sharing power or possessions; however, we can release our energy to other living beings, such as humans and animals.}

So, you don't control the demonic beasts?

{*Most of the time not directly. That kind of manipulation has effects on the individual controlling the power. I believe that is superstitious information you humans spread around. You see, a demon releases energy to attract mindless animals or those foolish enough to desire the power, yet it still belongs to us.*}

Why bother losing energy by giving it away?

Soirée giggled in her wicked manner.

{*That's the trick; we don't lose any. When a human or light-blooded uses their energy, it fades into the world once more. Since demons are creatures of the planet, our power does not leave us. Instead, it constantly cycles in and out of our bodies. By sharing it with other beings, we can only increase our reserves by making their energy part of ours.*}

The thought of being attached to Soirée suddenly seemed repulsive. *You bonded with my soul and steal my energy to get stronger?*

When the demon didn't respond, Coura prepared to pursue the subject until a second presence appeared in her mind.

{*Coura?*}

Grace's voice acted like a bright bell, causing her to forget about the explanation.

Grace? You found me! Although she kept the words in her mind, it took some effort to focus on walking without stumbling.

{*I am glad I can still reach you! Please, you must listen to me before I grow too weak to hold the connection.*}

What is it?

{*I overheard some men plotting in the palace tonight. They sent at least four people south to attack a base and kill certain targets.*}

Hearing such news from the Yeluthian worried Coura, and she halted her steps in order to focus on the message. *Who did you overhear? What base?*

{*Sorry, I did not catch any details. I did see Aaron leave the palace on horseback with two guards not too long ago. They went into Verona.*}

Coura tried flinging additional questions at the girl, but she could tell Grace was growing tired by how the mental voice faded in and out. Meanwhile, Marcus had been the first to notice her lagging behind in the middle of the road and staring back at where she imagined the capital was.

"Coura, what's wrong?" she heard him ask.

{*There is one more thing. The four sent south used wings to fly.*}

Every muscle in her body went tense at the image as her mind filled with questions that demanded answers. Fortunately, she had enough sense not to overreact. *You don't know those angels, do you?*

{*I did not see them up close, but I can assure you, to my knowledge, I am the only Yeluthian in Asteom.*}

She forced herself to breathe before sending her gratitude and breaking the connection. By that point, the rest of her group returned to where she remained standing. Onlookers gave her odd stares but said nothing as well.

"Coura?" Byron began before she faced them.

"I'm sorry," she apologized and continued forward. "I got distracted."

Soirée reappeared right after, teeming with curiosity.

{*You're not going to tell them?*}

She considered discussing the subject on the way to Umbridge but ultimately opted to keep the matter to herself in order to avoid setting them off course. *No, not yet. I imagine they'll ask the same questions I did and not get enough answers. I would rather wait for Grace to find out more than make assumptions.*

If Soirée disagreed with her intentions, the demon didn't mention it.

By the time the group reached the inn they planned to stay at in the center of town, everybody was ready for a hearty supper and their beds.

***

Byron stretched his legs out in front of the fire conveniently located next to their table in the dining area. Since their party contained a pair of official soldiers, the innkeeper became more than willing to provide the best spot in the public space, as well as better rooms. In addition to the seating, the woman also brought fresh bowls of stew and warm bread just as they settled down.

As he ate, he appreciated how they entered at the end of the dinner rush since the only patrons remaining were burly men with mugs in their hands who created a ruckus with drunken songs and loud stories. It became enough of a distraction to keep them awake for their meal yet not so obnoxious it wouldn't allow for private conversing.

He could tell Marcus relished the attention, and he knew from experience how Clearshot loved being recognized. Will appeared content with listening, for the most part. In fact, everybody besides Coura seemed to be enjoying the atmosphere.

Byron studied his student while she sipped her food without removing her eyes from the stew. "Something must be pretty captivating in that bowl," he commented in a lighthearted manner before raising his own to his lips and slurping down the rest.

"It's no use," Will added from his other side while waving a spoon at Coura. "She likes to get deep in thought about stuff. It happens all the time; just ask Marcus."

Byron raised an eyebrow at the assistant general, who in turn shrugged and resumed his conversation with Clearshot about weapon materials.

"I don't know why I have to be the one to talk."

Hearing Coura's voice surprised him after how silent she'd been throughout a majority of the day. *Perhaps I scolded her too harshly*, he wondered and recalled Emilea's lecture.

"You don't need to, but you seem distant today. Would you like to talk about it?" he offered at a quieter volume meant only for her ears.

She broke her stare to glance around the room with a hint of concern before replying. "Maybe later."

He didn't press further yet kept an eye on his pupil. *I'm fortunate I know her well enough to tell when something's wrong. I'd hate to consider what she would be like on her own right now.*

As he reminisced on the many instances when he reached out and got through to Coura during the times when she tried to keep her problems bottled up, the room steadily grew louder. Soon, he wasn't able to think as the men's voices and slamming of mugs on the table caught his attention. Marcus and Clearshot pretended to ignore the noise, but soon they stopped conversing. Byron and Will didn't even try to hide their interest once their fellow patrons began growling at each other.

"How are we supposed to get any work done around here when beasts make us come into town before sundown?"

"Take it up with the demon conjurer in the palace," a younger man said after raising his mug to his lips.

"The…what?"

"How could you believe that's real?" an older farmer argued and shook his head, letting his gray beard sway against his chest.

The first individual slapped the table again and continued. "There's no way a king like Hernan would let a demon roam wild and turn the animals into monsters!"

"Like I said," the younger man chimed, obviously in a drunken stupor. "I heard from the capital itself they've got some sort of angel with demon powers on our side."

"Wasn't there one from the city in the clouds staying in Verona?"

"He's controlling the demons forcing us inside?"

"That's what I assume, though I don't think so myself."

Another mug slammed down. "Why trust somebody like that? We shouldn't have to live in fear for our families and livestock."

The group cheered and discussed what they considered a threat while Marcus began to rise from his seat; however, before he could fully stand, Clearshot grabbed the assistant general's arm.

"I'm not going to let them spread foolish rumors," Marcus argued with a glare at his comrade.

"They're high on life at the moment. It's probably not the best time to try talking sense into them," Byron's friend cautioned.

Eventually, Marcus realized Clearshot was right and dropped down. They all avoided glancing Coura's way until the chatter quieted. When Byron finally did look, he saw nothing had changed; she merely stared at her empty bowl while twirling the wooden spoon between her fingers.

I can't imagine what she's thinking. So many lies surrounding her, and none sound positive. Perhaps we do need to talk tonight.

"I believe it's time for us to retire," he announced to the table. "I'll wake you in the morning to get ready."

The rest of his party rose to depart for their temporary quarters in unison.

The innkeeper provided them with two rooms and shared how one was intended to be for the lone lady while the other would house the rest, though they found a pair of beds in each space. Will went into the first and Coura the second, as it seemed both were exhausted from the trek.

"I'll stay with Coura," Marcus offered. From the way he spoke, Byron could tell the young man grew concerned about her too, especially given how offended he seemed after the meal.

Clearshot snorted and put an arm around his fellow soldier's shoulders with a grin. "Oh, I see. An opportunity to be alone with a girl."

Obviously, Marcus had not thought about the implications since his cheeks flushed and he stammered, "N-no, that's not it!"

Clearshot continued to chide him until he gave up and stormed into the first room.

"I'll stay with Coura," Byron decided.

"And I'll keep an eye on the boys," his friend replied with a wink, leading Byron to roll his eyes.

It's always a game with him, isn't it?

Once inside the space, he noticed his student had curled up and fallen asleep, much to his disappointment. With his attempt to converse foiled, he relaxed on the second bed and soon lost himself to sleep.

***

On the seventh day of their travels, the group stopped in a town Coura had never heard of called Twindela. Instead of spending the night in the previous city and settling before sunset, Byron insisted they use the rest of the daylight.

"From Twindela, we can reach Dala within two days," he claimed.

Nobody protested his judgement, but she remained on constant alert because of Grace's news. She conferred with Soirée all the time when they weren't trying to sense the angels' presence. Her memories of the previous pair she fought and defeated provided motivation and support for her urgency. While she contemplated their origin as Yeluthians and what little she knew about their country, Soirée made nasty comments involving Grace.

{It would be easy for her to lie to you. Where else would there be angels hiding in the country?}

What about the letter from Yeluthia that never reached Hernan? I bet Grace is telling the truth.

{Did anyone see or hear of a letter beforehand? How can you be so sure the girl isn't just manipulating everyone? Besides, she hasn't contacted you for days.}

Coura tried her best to deny the accusations, yet some points were difficult to refute, and she hated herself for believing her friend could betray their relationship.

Beneath her own thoughts and Soirée's debating, a self-doubt started to suffocate her. She ignored the men and women who brought up the "demonic weapon in the palace" and her companions' concerned glances when they thought she wasn't paying attention. Although she and Soirée didn't care about the rumors, she still had to interact with the others. Worst of all, she knew Byron had been trying to get her alone to talk about it.

I can't keep behaving this way, or else I'll lose my mind, she realized as she stood between Marcus and Will just inside the tiny inn.

"We got three rooms available. I'm afraid we aren't large enough for a kitchen," she heard their older host mention.

Byron reassured him the rooms would be fine, and the five broke apart.

Coura's stomach growled, and she wished for a light meal before relaxing as the days of constantly moving on the road were taking their toll. *I don't know what's worse: the fact that I could fly to Dala within a day or two, the itching on my shoulder blades when I remember I can use magic, or the pounding in my head from too much thinking.*

Her mentor followed her into their shared space, just as he had over the past week, and promptly closed the door while she collapsed onto the closest mattress.

"Would you like to eat first?" he asked without hiding his amusement.

She groaned into her pillow, unable to decide whether she needed food or rest more, but nearly wept with gratitude when Byron ordered her to stay awake long enough for him to procure them a meal. Shortly after, he returned just as she struggled to force herself into a sitting position.

"That smells delicious," she commented.

He handed her a bag containing a portable meat pie. "It's all the tavern next door had to carry out."

After diving into his food, he relaxed on his bed and finished eating right away. While Coura nibbled on the remains of her meal, he made small talk until the room fell silent. She figured he meant for them to converse then since they had the time.

"What's been going on?" Byron began, confirming her suspicion.

"What do you mean?"

She took a bite following those words to hide her reluctance. Byron saw through her attempt to dismiss the conversation and gave her an unimpressed look.

"Fine, I'll say it," he continued without hiding his annoyance when she chewed the same mouthful for a full minute. "You've been secluding yourself ever since we left the capital. You hardly speak unless spoken to, and I know you're avoiding me. I understand you don't like King Hernan, but these are his orders."

"It's not that," she responded and abandoned her stubbornness. She hated to see her mentor upset with her, especially when she didn't do anything wrong on purpose.

"Then, what is it?"

Despite her concern, she decided to share what the Yeluthian told her while making sure to keep her voice soft in the quiet atmosphere of the inn. "I would imagine you heard about Grace's goddess gift," she ventured first.

He nodded as his eyes widened. "What did she tell you?"

Coura explained the message regarding the angels and the stranger who ordered them away as best as she could. Once she finished, Byron pondered the issue until she found herself nodding off.

"Get some rest," she heard him say before he went into the hallway.

*

In the morning, Coura found she was the only one up at sunrise. Byron snored softly underneath his blankets, and she noticed a piece of scrap paper on the floor by their door. The message appeared to be scribbled in his handwriting, so she skimmed the words.

> *We're going to set out at noon today. Please find us lunch beforehand since I'm guessing you'll be awake before anybody else.*

Given how roughly the note had been written, she figured he stayed up for a hours after she fell asleep. She seized the opportunity to properly wash her body in the bathhouse behind the inn and wander through town in search of a decent breakfast.

Soirée, are you awake? She couldn't remember sensing the additional presence the previous night when she told Byron about Grace and the angels.

A faint tickle in the back of her mind told Coura the demon decided to keep to herself but with no hostility.

I guess she isn't mad at me then.

Twindela was by far the smallest place she had ever been to. It took less than an hour for her to stroll through the entire area, including the backstreets made up of single-story homes. The surrounding land consisted of tilled farming soil with people already at work planting and watering their crops.

"I should return to the main square," she mumbled to herself, stretched her arms above her head, and spun around.

By that point in the morning, about a dozen men, women, and even a few children strolled on every road, going about their business or setting up shops. Along the street exiting toward Dala, the scent of a bakery hit Coura with enough force to cause her stomach to growl. She put a hand on it with a smile and moved in the direction of the brick building. Even as she did so, a strange sensation came over her.

Have I been here before?

A handful of people entered and left with their purchases and waved over their shoulders to those inside. She stopped for a moment just in front of the entrance yet away from the flow of customers, then she closed her eyes and inhaled a deep breath; the warm, doughy scent was somehow nostalgic.

I visited other bakeries in East Hoover and Verona before, but why is this one so different? A familiar ache in the back of her mind provided the answer. *Another memory?*

She opened her eyes and hurried through the doorway with a desire to learn about that special place. Nothing looked out of the ordinary about the lobby, though the front of the building seemed uncomfortably cramped. A lone counter littered with papers and bread rolls stood at the far end while desserts and breads were being pulled from shelves underneath by a woman spotted white with flour all over her clothing.

The worker shouted a greeting while she scanned the items. A pair of skinny, well-dressed ladies were ahead of her in line, but they left with their own purchases rather promptly. Then, the hefty woman behind the counter addressed Coura.

"Haven't noticed you around. My name's Maude, and this is my husband's bakery. Come up and take a gander!" Her arms extended in a gesture at the remaining products.

Coura tentatively stepped forward and glanced at every pastry while the worker watched with a gaze comparable to a hawk's. When she looked up, she noticed a bit of impatience in Maude's expression. "They look delicious."

"Well, what'd you be having?"

The entrance opened and closed to remind them there would be more customers coming inside, which pushed her to make a decision. Although it was still morning, she desired a taste of the powdered donuts on display.

"I'll take one of those," she concluded and pointed to one of the round, fried dough balls dusted with white sugar.

"Oh? A bit early for sweets, isn't it?"

Maude plucked up the pastry and handed it to her while she retrieved her money pouch and laid a silver coin on the counter. The woman winked in a motherly manner that made Coura smile and her head inexplicably begin throbbing.

"I don't think any time is too early," she replied while Maude opened a box to count her change.

That comment spurred a laugh from the worker. "I like it! I shouldn't be saying too much, especially with another customer waiting behind you, but you remind me of my sister. She owns her own bakery in Neston, and she's got such a sweet tooth!"

Coura froze as a sudden chill passed through her entire body. "Where did you say she's from?"

"Neston, just a few days east. There's no direct road from here, though, so I hardly..." Maude paused when she noticed Coura's perturbed expression. "Are you ill? You're as white as a sheet."

The worker reached a wary hand toward her as her eyes went to Maude's face. Reality blended with memories to show Coura another, similar version of the baker.

I've seen a woman like her before. Did I used to know her sister? Could I have lived in Neston?

In response, a pain worse than what she previously experienced knocked her in the back of the head, as if somebody had actually taken a club and done so. Coura doubled over in front of the counter with both hands gripping her head as she gasped from the invisible blow. Maude cried in alarm before addressing her with words she couldn't hear due to an intense ringing.

This time, she was unable to pull herself from the flood of scenes that came rushing into the forefront of her mind. In most of them, her younger self held a soft hand while her wide eyes scanned each item in a bakery; in the rest, voices chatted while she nibbled on pastries. Someone called to her and gently placed a hand on her head. She looked up into a face nearly identical to Maude's.

That must be...

{*Coura!*}

If Soirée didn't interrupt, she might have fallen even deeper into the visions, and brought on more pain in the process. *I...remember it...*

Her thoughts sounded weak, and prompting them stung. No matter how slowly she breathed, she couldn't steady her mind, leaving the stabbing memories to continue.

{*This place is triggering them. Get out now!*}

At that point, Coura realized what a scene she caused. A bald, burly man behind her wrapped an arm around her shoulders and spoke to Maude, who pulled herself over the counter in order to gaze at where Coura slid to the floor. She wanted to tell them she would be all right, but her thoughts and voice seemed disjointed, and nothing came out.

Soirée said...I need to go...for this...to stop.

With a jolt, she pushed herself to her feet and away from the man, bumping into Maude's outstretched arm in the process and knocking the handful of bronze coins onto the floor. Coura kept a hand on her head while forcing her legs to move toward the door where she braced herself on its frame. Although she tried to apologize, no sounds could form into words. One of the two people inside yelled at her, but she stood gaping at them a moment longer before fleeing the bakery.

The buildings blurred together as she sprinted along the main street. No more scenes from the past distracted her, but for some reason, the pounding in her head grew worse instead of better, causing her eyes to water.

What's happening? she frantically whimpered in her mind.

{*Just keep running.*}

Coura noted how Soirée sounded as though she were hurting too.

Between her unclear vision and bowed head, she didn't see where she went, which prevented her from catching any glimpses that might set the memories off again. Gasps and curses followed as she pushed past those on the road. Before she knew what was going on, she ran straight into somebody, causing them both to tumble to the ground. For a moment, her thoughts stopped. Then, she coughed and pushed herself onto her hands and knees.

"Coura?"

She blinked, rubbed her eyes, and realized she had collided with Marcus, who sat up from where he landed on his back to her right. Her mouth opened and closed, but the apology in her head didn't vocalize; however, the stabbing returned with a new memory. In it, she heard a woman's voice ordering her to be careful while her younger self giggled and wrestled another child in the dirt.

"What's wrong?" he asked when she dipped her chin against a wave of dizziness.

Before she could figure out how to react, he crawled closer, pulled her over against his chest, and wrapped his arms around her in a comforting embrace. He held her firmly after, even when she threatened to break away.

What is he doing?

"Just relax," her friend instructed at a hushed volume. "Try to calm down."

For what seemed like hours, Coura remained still. Her body stayed tense and breathing labored. Meanwhile, Soirée continued urging her to leave the town since the pain continued, but the flashes of memories faded. Soon, she was able to think easier and noticed other voices behind Marcus' soothing comments, reminding her of where they were. With as much control and dignity as she could muster, she ducked out of the assistant general's arms, though he didn't try to restrain her again, rose, and began walking away. Several strangers stared at her but said or did nothing.

She couldn't remember the direction she escaped from, but she eventually reached the outskirts of the town. Only when she was safely hidden within a bunch of trees past the farmland did she stop and seat herself against the trunk of a budding tree overlooking Twindela. Somehow, at some point during that morning, she drifted off and woke from the nap just before noon feeling surprisingly refreshed with a single thought on her mind.

"I know where I'm from," she muttered while gazing at the white puffs in the sky.

Soirée didn't seem to be in as lax a mood.

{*You need to avoid prompting such hostile memories. They should be useless to you now and serve only to distract us.*}

To the demon's annoyance, Coura didn't care about the headaches or embarrassment because she found a sense of accomplishment in keeping a portion of her past.

"Neston," she mused over and over again with a slight smile. The throbbing in her head returned, but it wasn't nearly as painful.

Once she had her fill of the experience, she decided to fulfill her mentor's request and hurried toward the street with the inn and its neighboring tavern. Thankfully, nobody seemed to recognize her or comment on the drama that took place mere hours earlier. She purchased eight pies and brought them to their rooms. Everyone else had gotten up and seemed ready to depart.

"You actually read my note," Byron commented while grabbing a meal.

She shrugged and shouldered her pack with more energy than she had the entire trip.

He raised an eyebrow but led the way outside where Clearshot, Marcus, and Will were waiting. Coura expected the assistant general to go to her side like the noble soldier he was, yet he merely looked her over without showing any sign of worry, nodded, and focused on the remainder of their journey.

The Southern Base

Byron had never been to Dala before, which seemed astonishing given the amount of traveling he'd done throughout his life. All he knew about the city was it had been loosely modeled after Verona, keeping the army's quarters separate from the rest of the businesses and homes. Even on the map, a giant, block-like structure stood alone, but there were no details to glean. When the group spotted the base during the afternoon of the ninth day, he found himself awestruck by the sight, along with his companions.

The structure housing the southern troops appeared to be twice as wide as the palace in Verona, though it only rose three stories tall and was circular in shape. The walls looked to be composed of dark bricks or stone with metal shielding reinforcing the first level, which had been designed with no windows. That was all he could describe about the base itself. An empty grassland stretched between it and the city, and a forest surrounded both sections.

He became interested in seeing more since Dala established itself as a well-known farming community despite its size and wealth.

"It's huge!" Clearshot exclaimed with wide eyes.

Byron shared his agreement before initiating their hike toward the entrance.

The road they used continued into the city while another split off to the base, so they switched directions at the fork. They remained alone until the sound of hoofbeats ahead made them halt. A figure on a white horse hailed the group, stopped nearby, and dismounted. He wore the silver armor of an Asteom soldier but didn't remove his helmet.

"I believe you are Master Byron from Verona," he said before bowing and greeting each of the others just as formally.

"Your supervising general must be expecting us," Byron replied before they walked with the man as he retraced his steps beside the mare.

The soldier gave a curt nod. "Aye. Word spread of mages traveling to Dala. We've been awaiting your arrival ever since."

Although he wondered why their people were so enthusiastic about mages, he would save his questions for the person in charge.

"If you're still fresh today, General Casner would like to meet you and give a tour of the base. I'll take you to your rooms right now, though."

"What may we call you if you are to be leading us around?" Clearshot threw in casually as he took in the scenery.

The soldier introduced himself as Orin and brought them to a bridge Byron hadn't noticed before. As they neared the structure, his breath caught. A wide moat surrounded the entire base, yet it stayed inconspicuous at a distance because of the terrain.

Orin noticed their expressions and laughed. "Most outsiders are surprised by the water. It's sort of like a secret defense. The land's flat, so it's too shrouded by the tall grass to see clearly unless you know it's there. This bridge is the only solid ground connecting the edges."

The soldier acted proud of his home when he spoke, which intrigued Byron.

Once inside, the building felt similar to the palace in Verona. Torches and lamps lined the walls to keep the temperature relatively warm against the cooler stone. In the palace, crimson and gold flags, paintings, and various, patriotic pictures had been displayed to add color and life. The base's walls remained unadorned, giving the building a sense of dreariness.

In contrast, the soldiers wandering the corridors behaved as energetically as Orin. Echoes of confident conversations rang throughout the space to provide a homey atmosphere.

As they walked, Byron noticed Orin leading them along the outer hallways. When he commented on it, the man grinned before revealing the reason to the newcomers.

"Our base is three floors tall and four layers wide. That is, four halls are next to each other, like rings, with two intersecting crossways on the east and west sides. The entrance we came through to the south only leads to the outer ring. Clever, isn't it?"

"Whoever designed this place must have planned for defense," Marcus added.

I wonder why? Dala has never been under pressure to go to war, as far as I know. Perhaps it's a precaution, but I would like to learn the history, especially if we'll be staying for a while.

On the eastern and western sides of the base were staircases leading to the top floors. As Byron guessed, they held the bedrooms. King Hernan ordered him to inspect the living quarters and prepare for mages to be stationed there, so he took his time analyzing the corridors and his own room, which was fairly simple. The private space consisted of a bed, a wooden desk and matching chair, and a dresser. Besides a worn carpet and a faded, woolen blanket, the room lacked any personality.

I assume each room is the same, though it doesn't matter; once somebody moves in, they can make it their own. Besides, I don't believe soldiers own too many belongings.

He rejoined the group in the hallway and glanced around for Orin.

"He went to see where we're supposed to go next," Clearshot answered Byron's unspoken question with his arms crossed.

"What do you think so far?" he asked to spark a casual conversation. Despite his intent, he frowned when Will produced a displeased groan.

The herbalist pushed up his glasses and leaned forward to whisper, as if he were afraid his complaints would hinder their luck. "This room will never do. How can anyone stand living with so little space? There's not even a bookshelf! Not to mention the desk, which probably won't be able to hold much. I would wager they don't care to house scholars or researchers."

"This place is rather plain," Marcus added when Will paused to breathe. "I didn't expect a lot, but I bet the southern troops don't spend time in their quarters except to sleep."

"That's what I was thinking," Byron replied before they heard a pair of footsteps.

"Hey!" Orin called from farther ahead and ushered them forward. "I've been told to show you the courtyard before you meet General Tio. He'll be joining us there."

When the man mentioned a courtyard, Byron suspected a location similar to the queen's garden in Verona, or an open area by the city used for comfortable gatherings. He grew confused when Orin led them down to the first floor and through one of the passages leading into the center of the building. Through an arch in the wall, they moved out into a wide space encompassed by the base, which appeared to be a lavish garden mixed with a training ground. His breath caught at the unexpected sight.

Orin ignored their awe and continued moving.

"This is incredible!" Will muttered from behind.

Adult trees were scattered around while vegetable and flower gardens hid beneath them, flourishing in the shade. Benches had also been placed in the shadows to protect people from the heat of the sun. They heard the sounds of various weapons whacking and clinking together or becoming embedded in practice targets, yet Byron didn't spot the soldiers until their group went past the vegetation. Like another ring within the base, the trees and plants cleared to reveal an area similar to Verona's training ground possessing three stables.

Some eyes caught the strangers, but no one paid them any attention.

"Wait here a moment," Orin ordered. He bowed and left them to jog over toward the opposite side of the clearing where a wooden shed stood alone. Presumably, it stored weapons or gardening tools.

"Well, it's working," Byron commented as he tried to hide the smile creeping up on him.

"What's working?" Coura asked from where she stood at his side.

He paused to assess the men and women. Most seemed skilled with their chosen weapon, and he figured they could stand against the combatants he'd worked alongside at the capital.

"Think about it," he continued at a lower volume. "Why bring us to a crowded area to meet with somebody famous in this base?"

"I don't know. They did want to show us around."

"Yes, but why else?" he glanced over to watch as her eyebrows scrunched a bit while she tried figuring out an answer.

"They could be hoping we note what a threat they are. With mages in the capital now, perhaps they're reminding us they've been fine without them."

Byron nodded to show his approval then returned his eyes to where Orin and two other men left the building and headed in the group's direction.

"I also get the impression they don't expect us to behave like outsiders," Coura surprised him by continuing.

"What makes you say that?"

"Yes, they're showing off, yet nobody's giving us attention or attitude. Maybe it's in my head, but that level of respect comes from one soldier to another instead of to strangers."

He didn't comment as the trio approached.

"Master Byron and company, I would like you to meet General Tio and Assistant General Calin," Orin announced and swept a hand to gesture at his superiors.

"Thank you, Orin. You're dismissed," said the burlier, bearded man identified as General Tio. He slapped his subordinate on the back and grinned at Byron and the others after. His voice sounded gruff, as though he'd spent most of his life yelling.

As Orin left them, the general turned around and strolled toward the wooden building without a word. His assistant waited for them to follow and held up the rear while they crossed the garden area at the other end. Then, they entered the base. Byron noted how everyone they wandered past saluted the general before returning to their business.

"You've been shown your quarters already," the stocky man began once they were within the walls. "It's time to get food in your bodies and chat over a couple, decent drinks. I hear they're pretty soft in the capital!"

The sudden offer shocked Byron, yet he didn't respond; the rest of his group did the same.

That must have been the reaction the general expected because he glanced behind with a wider grin. His scraggly, brown beard peppered with gray, bright, hazel eyes, and wrinkled uniform highlighted by his matter-of-fact attitude spurred a genuine smile from Byron.

"That's what I thought," General Tio muttered before chuckling and leading them through the southern gate.

***

Although some suspicion and nerves trailed Coura into the giant tavern at the center of Dala, she found herself liking the base, its soldiers, and the general more by the hour. Ever since his comment to Byron when they left the courtyard, Tio confirmed her thought about how his troops behave.

Several men inside The Stinger's Tavern and Inn greeted the general with a customary salute, then they offered their group seats at a table. It seemed strange for her, and probably the others, to observe how Tio interacted with his subordinates. Unlike the generals and assistant generals in Verona who kept to themselves and nearly commanded respect, Tio and Calin acted no differently than their soldiers in public. Both drank heavily, despite it being early afternoon, and joked or shoved each other and the dozens of people storming the bar after their arrival.

At first, Coura and her companions remained reserved, asking questions about the city and its base while complementing the delicious fish that continued to be served long after they felt stuffed. Byron and Clearshot loosened up after their first mugs of ale and joined in the fun. Marcus ate and drank, but his darting eyes revealed how alert he stayed. Will and Coura couldn't choke down much of the alcohol yet savored the lively atmosphere.

The shuttered windows prevented them from knowing how late it grew until no light was visible aside from the lamps and candles. By that point, the place had filled with laughter and music. Even the most stoic-looking soldiers found themselves giggling uncontrollably as the general stood with arms around his men, sang off-key, and spilled his mug's contents all over the table.

Although the noise remained consistent throughout the evening, Coura found herself yawning, and Clearshot was the first to take notice.

"We'd best be off," he practically slurred and pushed himself up from the table, interrupting the current song.

"Now?" Tio asked with disappointment written across his face. "The night's just begun."

Clearshot shook his head and pointed a thumb into his chest. "I'm a father, so I know when children get sleepy. Look at 'em! They're sort of like my own sons and daughter. Not Byron. He's too old."

Coura put a hand over her eyes in an attempt to hide her embarrassment while everyone around them laughed, including Byron, who found his friend's drunken behavior amusing.

The general lazily eyed Clearshot, then Marcus, Will, and Coura, as if he were actually searching for familial similarities. "Ah, forget it," he grumbled and drank from his mug.

Their group took their leave of the busy tavern amid the soldiers' waves and cheers. It took what felt like half the night for them to stumble back to their beds, especially since the corridors looked the same and Clearshot and Marcus argued about what floor their rooms were on.

*

Without a window in her room, Coura felt trapped by the stone walls and didn't know what time she woke until she left for the washroom. By then, the sun had risen high in the sky, and the other people on their floor steadily came to life. Men with groggy faces and pink eyes yawned as they passed her in the halls without a word.

Once she returned to her space, she waited for somebody to come get her before growing annoyed. "Leave it to the adults to sleep in."

{Why don't we go explore a little? I'm curious about the layout of this base, as well as its fighters. Did you notice them yesterday?}

Yes, Coura thought solemnly and rose to exit.

As she made her way to the training ground, she contemplated the adequate weaponry skills of the troops with Soirée. The soldiers looked as well-trained as Marcus with precise strikes, swift movements, and poise. Once in the garden area, she grabbed a seat under one of the trees, hugged herself from the unusually chilly air, and watched. Unlike her companions, the Dalans were up and ready for the day without any sign of hindrance. Coura and Soirée, to her surprise, both became impressed with the combatants, who showed the same amount of skill that morning as the previous afternoon.

{How interesting.}

What's that? She felt Soirée's attention drawn toward a bulky figure in full padding standing across from another, shorter individual wearing even more protection. The second fighter charged with his wooden practice blade raised to strike.

He'll be knocked off his balance with a swing to his side, Coura noted.

Just as she expected, the heftier fighter brought his own blade down in a slow and controlled motion to meet the other's side. In an instant, the swords met with a loud whack.

The weaker-looking soldier blocked it?

{Much faster than either of us anticipated.}

She heard amusement in Soirée's words, as though the unexpected continuation entertained her, and they became invested in the duo's spar. The shorter figure was quick to block every blow, yet his movements steadily grew less controlled and often resulted in weaker strikes. His opponent remained tough and sturdy, but for some reason, it seemed obvious to Coura they didn't really try to land hits. Nobody else in the area appeared as captivated by the heated swordplay.

After half an hour passed, the two broke off the spar. She sat a bit straighter when they removed their helmets, revealing the general and his assistant, Calin. The pair grinned at each other before shaking hands and wiping the sweat from their brows as they chatted. Again, she scanned the training ground and found their subordinates directing no attention toward the base's leaders.

Soirée followed her observation and commented on the obvious reason.

{A most formidable man who is well-known by his troops. You should look into that familiarity. A skilled fighter and instructor, in addition to a respected leader, is a frightening combination.}

While Coura grew intrigued by the base's troops and their general, deep down she felt an inexplicable wariness.

Before she could consider why, Calin glanced over his superior's shoulder to catch her gaze. The exhaustion left his face at once, and he said something less light-heartedly to Tio. The general didn't even try to hide his curiosity. He spun to mirror Calin's stare and saw Coura. She expected him to approach or ignore her, but he surprised her by shouting.

"Hey!" His gruff voice blended in with the outdoors, and he wound his arm around in a gesture for her to join them.

At first, she froze, unsure of what to think. She eventually stood and hurried over while shaking some feeling back into her hands in the process.

"Come, Coura Galdwin," Tio began. "Let us experience what a lady of our capital city is capable of."

"How generous," she mumbled half-heartedly as she accepted the practice sword he offered and weighed the wooden blade in one hand.

As if on cue, the general stepped away right after, allowing Calin to charge at her without warning. The movement took her off guard mentally; however, years of training developed the instinct she needed to block the gentle strike in response.

They're not out to hurt me. Perhaps they're gauging my skill.

It became apparent he favored offensive blows, at least in that moment. When he swung, Coura blocked or parried and was able to push him back again and again. During those instances, both Tio and Calin's expressions appeared to desire something more.

{Why not finish him off?}

Soirée's voice projected enough boredom to let her know it was time. As the assistant general charged once more while raising his sword above his head in a repeat of the first attack, she decided to lean forward and sidestep the strike instead. He didn't expect her to dodge, leading him to hesitate following through. She used that opportunity to hit him in the gut with the wooden hilt of her weapon. Even with padding, her physical blow proved well-timed enough to knock the breath out of her opponent, leaving him to fall backward. By the time he could sit up, the tip of Coura's blade rested at his throat.

"I yield," Calin admitted, coughed, then relaxed onto his back with a poorly concealed smile.

Behind her, Tio began clapping.

"I'd expect nothing less from a soldier of the capital city. I will admit, though, I had my doubts about a mage being skilled in sword work." The sly tone of voice hinted at an underlying tension.

"Apparently, you expected just as much," Coura replied after tossing him the weapon and rolling her shoulders without meeting his eyes.

"What do you mean?"

She faced the general while several sets of eyes glanced their way. "What kind of general would let a young woman like me fight without armor while he's covered in several layers of protection? Unless, of course, he knew I would be fine without it. After all, it's not difficult to avoid bruises when Calin went easy on me. Why don't you tell me what you intended this sparring session to accomplish."

To emphasize the demand for an explanation, she put her hands on her hips to showcase feigned impatience and waited for an answer. Tio remained silent for a minute and stared at her with a serious expression. When it became obvious how she saw through his test, the general burst into a hearty laugh that even she couldn't keep from chuckling at.

"I didn't believe the capital housed clever fighters anymore," he shared and wiped his eyes with one hand as the other rested on his stomach.

Coura noticed the others in the area beginning to circle around the trio with interest. Meanwhile, Calin pushed himself to his feet and brushed off.

"I'm not one for politics and masks," Tio began while approaching her in a friendlier manner. "That's why I'm here and not in Verona. All they seem to know is crafty behavior and manipulating men and women into serving the kingdom. At least, that's what it was like when I last visited a few years ago. Here in Dala, we only care about loyalty and strength. You held your own against Calin, and pretty effortlessly it seemed!"

From behind, several people shouted in agreement as the assistant general moved to his superior's side.

"You ordered me not to take this seriously," Calin protested.

"Me? I said no such thing!" Tio exclaimed with mock innocence.

Everybody who heard him, including Coura, laughed as the two bickered. Then, the general placed a hand on her shoulder. His demeanor remained relaxed, but his expression shifted into one reflecting a sense of earnestness.

"The real reason I set this up is because King Hernan's council told us you're supposed to be some sort of special, magical soldier training in Dala."

A familiar tightness grew in Coura's chest at the reminder. *I almost forgot I'm different...*

{*He sure is vocal about it.*}

Soirée spoke true, as Coura soon realized the lack of surprise from those surrounding them.

The general caught her wandering eyes. "I don't hide information from my troops, especially regarding additions to our allies. I must say, we're pretty curious to see your magic."

They stood in silence after, obviously waiting for an answer.

She glanced up at the clear, blue sky when she became unsure of what to do. In her mind, the warnings from Byron and the insults Hernan threw in her face replayed.

Against her better judgement, she decided to ask the demon. *What should I say?*

Soirée's bizarre response lifted a weight off her shoulders.

{*What do you want to do? Not the master mages or the king of this country, but you, Dear One.*}

Without the burden of the demon's wrath if she revealed her power, Coura chose to follow her instincts and ordered everybody to stand back.

Tio and Calin nearly jumped with anticipation and retreated a few steps while urging their subordinates to do the same. In response, the solders verbally acknowledged the request and shuffled farther away.

{*It's as if they've never seen a mage at work before.*}

We're hardly going to show them the abilities of an ordinary mage, Coura replied. *Perhaps I should let them know that as well.*

"I must warn you, my magic is not like any other kind in Asteom," she shouted loudly enough for the onlookers to hear. "It uses dark, demonic energy, and others may sense this."

Part of her worried they might change their minds and turn on her once they learned of the power's origin; however, the reveal seemed to make them more eager.

"Get on with it already!" someone barked from the crowd, prompting a flurry of excited comments.

The tightness in her chest was joined by anxiety at the realization she would be revealing her secret in such a public manner. *It's been months since I used magic outside my room in Verona.*

Soirée's own, hovering presence pressed on her as she focused inward on her center to pull the energy out and led it to an exit point. The familiar weight of the black wings fell on her shoulders a moment later, warming her back and banishing the ill feelings with their appearance. A chill flowed through her veins when the demonic power worked within her body and proved to be as intoxicating as her first experience.

Gasps sounded around Coura after the spell. She noticed Calin and many others' mouths hanging open and eyes widening. A few even placed their hands on the hilts of their sheathed weapons. The only person who didn't show a hint of fear was General Tio. He studied her with an almost greedy gaze before beaming and clapping his hands together in delight.

"I knew you had more to you than just a pretty face. Simply excellent!"

Despite their leader's enthusiasm, his troops remained wary. Some nodded hesitantly, but most mumbled to their comrades.

Coura didn't let her unimpressed stare waver. Tio evidently caught her message and approached again. Though his eyes stayed on the wings, he stood toe to toe with her.

"Don't believe word from Verona ever escapes my ears," he told her at a hushed volume, giving her the impression he spoke truthfully. "I've known about you for weeks, so I'm less shocked. King Hernan warned me to keep an eye on you, but frankly I believe I'll value you thrice as much as they do there. As far as I'm concerned, you're just another one of my soldiers now. If you uphold the rumors of your abilities, my troops will come to accept you too."

The man's easy-going nature left Coura speechless since she expected nothing of the sort from anybody once they learned of the demonic power.

He winked before stepping away and lifting the wooden sword she forgot he held to catch the onlookers' attention. "Let's see if this is all for show!"

With a warrior's cry, Tio swung his weapon downward. Unlike his previous spar with Calin, the strike looked genuine. She leapt backward, pushing her wings forward to go faster, and dodged the blade's tip by a finger's length. The resulting gust startled those around them enough to spur annoyed curses. Their superior ignored them and charged as though she were an actual enemy.

Coura dodged each wide, heavy slash too close for comfort until she grew used to her increased dexterity. Soon, she moved quickly enough to count a full three seconds between his attacks.

I should demonstrate what else I can do, she thought while feeling the exhilaration of a challenge.

The general raised his sword above his head and prepared to drop it down on her again. Before it fell past his chin, she manifested the demonic blade and cut upward through the wooden weapon. The top half of his weapon plopped into the grass at Tio's feet, and he stared at it with genuine surprise. She couldn't stop herself from giggling, both at her wit and the general's stupefied expression.

Despite his visible embarrassment, he chuckled too before retreating a few steps to distance himself from her. "Back up!" he called to the crowd after.

The soldiers looked at each other in disbelief, but Calin alone didn't hesitate to join Tio with an excited grin and another, "Aye!"

Together, the pair provided enough entertainment for Coura to stay focused. Instead of taking them down during open opportunities, which she knew she could do, she blocked their blows using the flat side of her blade while ducking and weaving around with the wings pressed tightly against her back.

In that moment, Tio's words from earlier returned. *"If you uphold the rumors of your strength, they'll come to accept you." This is a demonstration for his troops. Once they view me as a fighter, as one of them, I think he means my life here will be more normal.*

{*Well, that's no reason to show mercy!*}

Coura agreed with Soirée's ruthless comment. In another heartbeat, she tripped the general up so he fell onto his left side while Calin cradled his hand after she knocked his practice sword out of it. The only sound was of the wood hitting the ground; everybody who saw seemed to be holding their breath. Meanwhile, she grinned at her cleverness despite the lingering worry that if she fought too hard they would begin to see her as a monster, just like the mages in Verona and at the MAA.

When Tio pushed himself to his feet, she expected him to end the spar. Instead, he repeated his order.

"Back up!"

This time, his request was met with dozens of responses. A flood of both armored and unarmored individuals carrying either real or wooden swords, spears, and clubs charged to support their leaders.

Coura's smile vanished, and she felt uncertain of the outcome if she put in real effort. *How do I take them on without hurting anyone? He can't be serious about this!*

In the next instant, she found herself dodging and disarming not for fun, but for her own safety. At first, the soldiers attacked from the front two at a time. Then, they realized she could handle them easily that way and began surrounding her. Weapons struck from all sides to leave minor cuts and bruises, which healed within seconds.

Meanwhile, her mind continued racing as she wondered what the best approach would be. Each thought frightened her. *What if I accidentally kill somebody? How long can I keep this up? Should I give it my all or quit before something bad happens? What is the general hoping to accomplish?*

The rising panic ceased abruptly as Soirée's presence swallowed Coura's, like water upon a flame. Her breathing steadied from a newly found, internal control, heightening her senses in the process. Her keen sight picked up on the features of her opponents, even in the height of battle, and her hearing sharpened enough to discern their voices. Above all else, she took pleasure in the constant humming of magical energy flowing through her veins. Every distraction holding her back, including deciding when and where to strike, disappeared.

Perhaps the change altered her physical appearance as well because the troops nearest to her hesitated, which allowed her to either disarm them or knock them off their feet. The cycle continued since wherever one fell, another appeared to take their place.

Eventually, she remembered her wings and what they could do in such a situation. She shot them outward, shoving anyone in their way to the ground or startling the soldiers into backing away. When she created a decent amount of room, she fanned them, leapt upward, and pumped to climb higher into the air. It was then learned how untrained she was for flying when she bobbed around in an attempt to stabilize herself. Those below stared upward, oblivious to her lack of skill in the sky. Still, she contemplated her next attack, even going so far as to consider conjuring elemental magic in order to show them the extent of her abilities.

A few seconds later, her vision grew blurry. She blinked several times, yet her eyesight remained unclear, and her breathing grew heavy.

{*Descend, Coura. Your body's not used to this yet.*}

Soirée's disappointment reflected her own as she lowered herself to the ground. Even before reaching it, Tio's voice rang out.

"You've more than proven yourself against us. Let's end it here for today!"

Half the group showed their relief through sighs and chuckling while the others groaned or whined about pausing such an enthralling fight.

No one went to Coura after she landed, but most waved in her direction while they exited the area. Her legs refused to move, so she remained standing with an exhausted smile. The demonic energy retracted into her center, leaving behind a numbness against the physical weariness. At Soirée's reminder, she released the spell on her sword and wings, and the unbound energy faded, as it always had.

Once the space cleared, Calin and Tio came over. By that point, her legs gave in, and she dropped to her knees.

The assistant general hurried to kneel beside her. "What's wrong?"

Tio leaned forward to slap her on the back before she had a chance to answer. "She'll be fine! Just worn out, I bet."

He laughed when she agreed while wincing from the pain and embarrassment.

With their help, Coura was able to stand. When they were certain she wouldn't collapse again, they brought her to where a majority of the soldiers had gathered in the mess hall. If she thought she had been exhausted before, it became a true test of endurance being there with the general and his troops. While she ate, she had questions, compliments, other comments, and even pieces of food during their jesting thrown at her. Never had she dealt such a high level of attention, let alone *positive* attention, in her life. Despite her awkwardness stemming from that fact, she felt more welcome in that moment than any before.

The tables emptied over the course of the afternoon, and her popularity waned for the time being. She didn't feel her arms or legs throughout the meal; even with food in her body it seemed only sleep would cure her physical weariness. When she mustered the energy to rise, she hobbled out the door and managed to find her room without making a fool of herself. Her last concern as she fell into bed revolved around what Byron, Marcus, Will, and Clearshot were doing and what they would think once they found out about her actions in front of the Dalan troops.

Danger in Dala

Coura's pleasant dreams were interrupted by a pounding on her door. As expected, Byron, followed by Clearshot, Will and Marcus, stormed inside and demanded to hear about the scene in the training ground. Based on the older men's pink eyes and stuffy noses, she guessed they were still recovering from the night before, so she kept her story simple and pretended to mind their reproaches before offering to accompany them to the mess hall for dinner. The kitchen served a vegetable stew that she found delicious and exactly what she needed after the restful nap.

"I would like a word with General Tio when he arrives," Byron muttered to Clearshot as Coura cleaned her bowl and sighed in contentment.

"You haven't touched your food," she commented with as much of an innocent smile as she could manage, knowing his stomach and head were deterring him.

He frowned at her and continued stirring the contents of his bowl. "You really need a full-time babysitter. I can't believe we arrived yesterday and you managed to turn the base upside down."

Coura rolled her eyes but held her tongue. Even if she planned to argue, any words would have been cut off by the group of noisy soldiers, led by the general and his assistant, filing into the room.

"Well, it's about time we see some life from you today!" Tio roared at the sight of them.

He stole a spot next to Marcus while the others either pulled over chairs or stood around their table, and fresh bowls of stew were served. If the noise bothered Byron or Clearshot, the pair never showed it. Calin asked about their quarters, how they found the base, if they understood the layout, and other formalities until everyone finished eating.

"We should apologize for last night," he finished and rubbed the back of his neck in a bashful manner. "We don't celebrate often. Then again, we usually don't host guests from the capital."

That must have been the final comment he planned to mention, for the conversation turned elsewhere thanks to Tio. The general raised his fists into the air and let out his signature, heartfelt laugh.

"Speaking of celebrations, what a show we witnessed this morning!"

All around, the soldiers supported their leader's words with nods and a few cheers that made Coura blush. It deepened as he continued on at length about the extent of her performance.

When Tio seemed winded, Clearshot found an opportunity to sneak in a thought.

"I must say, few people in the palace are as comfortable with demonic energy as you and your troops. Even I found Coura's abilities suspicious at first."

The general tugged on his beard. "I can imagine how nervous that makes you folk, what with demonic creatures prowling about. To be honest, we haven't seen one of them around Dala in months. Every once in a while a beast pops up, but nothing we can't handle."

Clearshot raised his eyebrows in amazement when Calin nodded.

"It's true," the assistant general added after noticing their bewildered expressions. "That's why it doesn't bother us. Not to mention, she's on our side. As long as events play out in our favor…" He shrugged before tipping back his bowl.

***

Despite Coura earning a formidable reputation with the soldiers in the Dalan base, it took another week before Byron felt comfortable letting her practice dark magic. Even then, he remained cautious about when they worked and what spells they would cast. Many passing eyes lingered to study the new, strange power, and this made him nervous. In the end, it benefited Coura.

She always cared when there was an audience. Actually, she seems to thrive under that kind of pressure.

It took him another few days to get used to seeing her manifest the infamous, black wings and sword teeming with malice. Their presence grew less irritating than when he first encountered them while her magical energy stayed suppressed with an impressive level of control, which he didn't remember her having in the past.

The appearance seemed blasphemous in the general sense, yet it never troubled anybody in Dala, as far as he knew. Later, during a meal with several, aged soldiers, he learned no one in the area had ever seen a Yeluthian, and as General Tio mentioned, few ever dealt with demonic creatures. Even so, Byron forced himself to continue viewing Coura as his student first.

Fortunately, nothing about her behavior changed, and she acted as impatient as ever. He could train her in strengthening her dark magic and building endurance while the Dalan soldiers, Marcus, and even Clearshot kept her physical combat skills in check.

The only part they couldn't help her with were those wings. Like a bird confined to a cage, Coura wanted to jump into the sky at every opportunity and practice aerial motions and strikes. General Tio had been hesitant about this since the citizens in Dala weren't familiar with her like the soldiers in the base. After a month of explanations and negotiations, the general informed everyone in Dala that she wasn't a threat, so they didn't need to panic when they noticed a figure flying through the sky.

Life in the south became more relaxing for Byron than he realized as summer came and went. His student enjoyed herself and didn't seem afraid of her unique features. Although he felt initially hesitant to join the soldiers' business, Marcus warmed up to the other assistant general and peaked physically under his new direction. Even Will participated in exercises with them and the younger combatants. Clearshot remained observant and listened intently whenever General Tio held meetings or brought up news regarding the capital to catch what Byron missed. Nothing of concern reached them, which proved to be both a relief and worrisome.

As Byron watched Coura spar with Marcus and Calin, his mind wandered to the months prior when Grace contacted their group. *Still no word from the Yeluthian ambassador about the four angels moving south or the whereabouts of Prince Aaron. I wonder if sending us here had been King Hernan's way of keeping one issue away from another. All we can do is wait.*

"Again," he barked once his student stood panting alone after she managed to set her two opponents off balance.

Blood dripped from a slash across her left wing, but they became used to her healing ability by that point. With a grunt, the younger men rose and faced her to initiate another bout.

No matter what happens later, if an enemy does come here with ill wishes, I'm at least thankful we have the opportunity to prepare.

*

The first snowfall waited until they had been in the base for exactly eight months. Winter in Dala felt milder compared to Verona, which made sense considering how far south it was located.

Byron watched as fat, fluffy flakes descended from the gray sky in the training ground. That morning, he spent some time practicing his own magic with Coura before the soldiers took to their daily sessions. Though he joined for a while until he warmed up, he used a fair portion of his energy earlier and now sat under a leafless tree to catch his breath.

How calming these past weeks have been, he mused before a sharp wind cut through his cloak. Pulling it tighter prevented the chill from striking again moments later, yet he decided to pursue lunch since the weather didn't seem favorable for lounging about.

He rose and noticed Marcus and Coura tumbling around during their physical combat lesson until the former pinned his student to the ground. The sight of her exposed skin against the frozen ground caused him to involuntarily wince. Without proper clothing for her to be able to manifest the wings, she was forced to accept that the spell's energy burned two holes into the back of her shirts. Nearby, Will ran through offensive motions with a soldier to break down the movements of an attack. Byron found himself pleased with the inexperienced herbalist's progress and hurried inside after noting how well everyone's work appeared to be going.

A trio of soldiers in uniform saluted when they passed Byron. He did the same, as was customary in the base, though he didn't believe it necessary. *General Tio never ignores those minor gestures, and I think it means a lot to his troops.*

An alluring aroma wafted down the hallway to interrupt his concentration. He hurried his steps once his mouth began watering and nearly collided with another, cloaked man entering from the right.

"My apologies," he hurried to comment. "My stomach got the better of me."

"All is forgiven, Master Byron," answered the figure.

"Assistant general, is that you?"

Calin pulled back the hood of his cloak with a grin. "I thought you'd be out in the center area."

"You've been looking for me?"

The soldier nodded and started back the way he came, to Byron's dismay. His stomach growled in response, but Calin's next words took precedence.

"A messenger from Verona is here and requested you join General Tio and I."

"Is it urgent?" Byron pressed. He wasn't expecting anybody, and Grace's message had not been forgotten.

Luckily, Calin's lax manner and smile reassured him as much as a headshake. "Don't worry. He says it's just a visit to hear about everyone's progress and your observations of the base."

Byron expressed his relief, and they reached the double doors of the main office within minutes. General Tio had invited him inside three times to go over housing for the upcoming mages organized to be stationed there. Since then, they laid the topic to rest.

Perhaps that's all. Our last meeting was two weeks ago, so it makes sense for a messenger to confirm what we discussed.

Calin knocked before the two entered. A couple lamps it the room while General Tio stood across the circular table beside another, cloaked figure. Once they stepped in, the man waved him over.

"I'm glad we were able to find you."

"I didn't expect anybody from Verona," he admitted to both the general and the stranger.

"I would have been here sooner, but you know how unpredictable matters can become," replied the cloaked figure in a familiar voice as they reached up to pull the hood back.

The last person Byron expected to see was Prince Aaron, yet the young man stood in front of them with a smile and ran his fingers through his blond hair.

Has it only been a few months? He's gotten taller.

"Your Highness." Byron bowed before approaching to shake their guest's hand.

"Knowing what I do about you, I assume you imagined the worst," Aaron commented with a glance at Calin.

The assistant general shrugged without admitting how accurate the guess had been. Both he and his supervisor didn't appear uptight or nervous in the presence of royalty, something Byron steadily became accustomed to.

"I wouldn't expect your father to send you this far south," he said to continue the conversation. "At least, not without a letter first."

"Calin and I will grab us lunch," General Tio interrupted and stomped over to the door. "You two can catch up before we tend to business."

With that, the Dalans slipped out into the hallway.

"Now, why don't you tell me what you've been up to," Byron began and gestured at the table.

The prince understood the hint, so they took seats across from each other.

"There's not much to share," Aaron replied while looking around the room. "Father wanted me to travel to each of the main cities and survey the amount and level of guards posted."

"Don't they already keep track of that?"

"Yes, but many neglected towns have been begging for extra aid in recent years, especially with the increase in demonic creatures. My father and his advisors feel an imbalance between where the soldiers and mages are already stationed. The council hopes to completely restructure and reassign the positions before sending mages to this base."

"You've been meeting with the mayors around Asteom then to gauge their thoughts and recommendations," Byron concluded.

"Exactly. I left the day after your group and have been on and off the road ever since. Once I met with a city or town's leaders, we discussed their needs, then I stayed undercover until the additional support arrived. Dala is my last stop because I plan to spend a few days setting up the mages to be stationed here, rations, and whatever else is needed. After, I'll return to Verona and visit each town along the way."

"What about the far east and west?"

To the east, under where Yeluthia was said to float, the Ghurun Mountains stood tall and housed the Mintelian people. The land remained Asteom's territory, but those who chose to live around the mountains kept to themselves, unless the king requested their presence. To his knowledge, dozens of clustered villages were spread out in the area yet housed less than a hundred inhabitants each.

The expansive Western Woods hid the Sie-Kie people. Not much was known about them because of how uninhabitable the forest seemed to be. Like the Mintelians, their aid had never been required in recent years, so most of the kingdom left them alone.

Aaron shook his head. "For the time being, we assume they're fine without our guards. If they do need soldiers, we can work it out."

During the resulting pause, Byron considered the difficulties involved with reassigning and stationing the many mages filtering in and out of the palace and what his role would be since he had to stay in Dala for a while longer. *I can't imagine they would ignore the opportunity for my input, yet it would be easier if I returned to Verona.*

He decided to leave the problem for when the general returned and instead asked Aaron how he enjoyed traveling, knowing full well it would be the longest period of time the prince stayed away from home. Then, they laughed as Byron recounted his stories about Dala, and General Tio in particular.

"He's a valiant man with a kind heart under that rough exterior," Byron shared at a lower volume after realizing the man could waltz in at any moment.

Aaron grinned, as though he understood. "I'm glad you're making the most of life here. I couldn't imagine moving around as often as you seem to be doing."

"We've all been able to adjust."

Byron noticed the prince's expression soften and eyes light up a bit. "How has the rest of your group been? Are they getting along fine?"

While he informed Aaron of their statuses, he found himself reflecting fondly on the heir's character. *I've had the opportunity to visit the palace many times, and on each occasion, he's steadily grown into his own person. He may look like his father and possess his mother's charm, but I also believe he represents King Hernan's finest qualities. I wonder if that will change when he begins such a demanding position.*

He pushed his concern aside for the moment and offered a brief summary of their experiences. "The only person I don't get the chance to speak with often is Will. Then again, with this location's new information, I doubt he wants to spend a second away from his work."

"I'm just relieved to hear nobody changed much." Aaron leaned back in his chair and crossed his arms in a content manner.

Byron tilted his head at the prince. "Why don't we request a private meal together with them? I'm sure you would love to catch up."

A slight sadness crept across the young man's face. "I'd like to, but I'm supposed to remain as unnoticed and cautious as possible. If word reaches the wrong ears that the heir is outside the capital, I can imagine the unfavorable outcomes."

"Even so, these are your friends. I doubt they would speak of your arrival to anyone." Byron raised an eyebrow and sensed another reason behind the prince's shyness.

He never heard Aaron's reply, for a knock at the door signaled the return of General Tio and Calin.

*

By the time they cleaned the trays laden with food, the four discussed the proper living arrangements, training schedules, and other factors for the fifty mages scheduled to be sent to the base in late spring. The general had little to say about Aaron's journey and refused additional mages or soldiers for Dala or the surrounding towns.

"If circumstances worsen, we'll just get stronger," he said matter-of-factly, and that was that.

"In that case, I believe everything is in order," the prince concluded as he pushed himself up and extended a hand to the general, who stood and stretched. "I expected to stay for a few days, but you are an easy person to deal with, General Tio."

The burly soldier grasped Aaron's hand firmly and slapped the prince on the arm hard enough to make the young man jump. "You're the spitting image of King Hernan, you know that? Ah, excuse me...*Prince* Aaron. I've never been one for manners, you know."

After they shared a laugh, the four prepared to exit until a hurried knock at the door made them hesitate.

407

An armored soldier burst in without waiting for approval, panting as he saluted them. "General Tio! My apologies for interrupting-"

"Out with it!" the general roared, startling everyone except the newcomer.

"A soldier from the underground passageway returned from his post and claims there's an army of monsters in The Valley Beyond. He's hysteric!"

"The Valley Beyond," the general muttered with his brows knit in concentration. After a moment, he marched forward to push past the man in the doorway while shouting, "Take me to him!"

Although Byron wasn't familiar with the layout of the land, he certainly he knew what the so-called monsters likely were and hurried behind General Tio, the messenger, and Calin with Aaron on his heels.

***

Coura caught her breath from where she sat on the ice-cold ground while those outside waited for the general to make an appearance. Marcus joined her shortly after. Both were heavy with sweat from a regular afternoon of training.

"You suppose he's talking about demonic creatures?" the assistant general leaned closer to whisper.

She nodded. "I can't think of anything else that fits the description better."

Not even five minutes ago, the soldier, an awkward-looking, middle-aged man with shaggy, blond hair, burst into the middle of the training ground, grabbed somebody's arm, and begged them to bring him to Tio. He would only say an army of monsters appeared where he had been posted. After, he stood twitching or paced in circles while ignoring everyone's questions.

I'm lucky I wasn't using my magic or else he'd fall over on the spot, she realized with a yawn. A gust of wind blew against the holes in the back of her shirt to send shivers throughout her body.

"Want my coat?" Marcus offered. Without waiting for an answer, he slipped off the crimson jacket and handed it to her.

She thanked him and wrapped the covering around her shoulders.

"What's this about monsters in the Valley Beyond?"

At the sound of the general's booming voice, those who were seated jumped to their feet, and those already standing rushed over. They expected a confrontation, especially since he didn't sound pleased.

The frantic soldier briefly saluted Tio before going off without taking a breath. He repeated many phrases, including "their frightening, purple eyes," but Coura got the impression a horde of demonic creatures were preparing to attack Dala through an underground tunnel system.

The base's leader must have reached the same conclusion since he interrupted the soldier and ordered another to take the man to the infirmary.

"That's enough thumb-twiddling for you lot!" he shouted to the entire field in an authoritative voice she hadn't heard him use before. "Outer squad, prepare yourselves to depart. Defensive squad, head to the city before I blink twice. Base squad, secure the area while I'm gone. Everyone else, find a ranked soldier and ask what you can help with. What are you waiting for? Get moving!"

Coura's mind went blank upon hearing such commands. While the soldiers rushed out of the training ground, she remained unsure of what to do until Marcus grabbed her arm and pulled her along toward the general.

"I see Byron," he explained. "Let's hear our assignment."

That's right, he's used to this life. I guess we've been spoiled by a lack of action for so long I'd forgotten.

As they pushed their way past a growing crowd surrounding Tio, Coura tugged her arm free and removed Marcus' coat to return it before they were issued orders. She spotted Byron and Will waiting behind the general and a cloaked figure lingering farther back. Marcus called to the master mage as they approached.

"For now, be patient," her mentor answered their unspoken question.

{Why don't we scout ahead?}

Coura opened her mouth to ask then abruptly closed it. *I'll see if I can sense the creatures instead.*

Soirée expressed her disappointment yet let Coura scan the surrounding area. *I don't sense demonic energy.*

{*You searched in all directions?*}

She tried again while they continued to stand around, but still no power revealed itself as far as she could look. *Perhaps the valley is farther away.*

As Soirée shared her doubtful thoughts, Coura caught Byron's eye. He seemed to understand the dilemma yet didn't comment on the lack of hostile energy. Before she could speak, Tio turned to the four of them with an unreadable expression.

"What are you wasting time for? I said, prepare to head out!" He flashed them a grin and faced Calin, who hovered near his side the whole time, before shouting more orders.

Byron tried to hide a smile but nodded and addressed their group. "Meet here once you're all set. If any of you see Clearshot, tell him the same."

They agreed and hurried inside with the master mage following close behind.

"I'm going too," another voice declared.

"Absolutely not," Byron responded in a firm tone.

"You could use the help."

Coura glanced over her shoulder and caught a glimpse of the cloaked figure keeping pace with them. When she faced forward again, she practically ran into Marcus when he stopped in the middle of the hallway to stare at the stranger.

"What are you doing?" she snapped at him after stumbling to a halt.

"I'd recognize that whining anywhere," the assistant general replied with widening eyes.

Will, Byron, and the cloaked figure slowed too. The master mage pressed a finger to his lips as a signal for them to be quiet and continued down the corridor. Meanwhile, the figure put an arm on Marcus' shoulder and lifted his hood just enough for them to make out his face.

"Aaron?" Marcus whispered. "What are you doing here?"

Will and Coura glanced at one another with a mixture of surprise and alarm, and the prince responded by offering a relieved smile.

"I'll catch up with you later," he promised, replaced the hood, and followed in Byron's footsteps. That seemed to satisfy Marcus, so the three moved on and parted for their own quarters.

Once inside her room, Coura dug out her uniform and eagerly donned the clothing while remembering the comfortable feel. She held the unworn, crimson coat in her hands for a moment before donning it. The golden buttons still shined as though they had just been polished, and she wished for a mirror since she instantly became self-conscious.

What am I doing? I don't have time for this!

She remembered the situation's urgency and tied her hair into a slim ponytail before departing. As she jogged down the hallway, she heard Will's voice calling her from behind and slowed to meet his pace. His clothing had been given to him for the combat exercises, but he also threw on a cloak and carried a satchel underneath.

"You're staying at the base, right?" she asked despite already sensing his response.

"It's like Aaron said: You're going to need all the help you can get."

While he continued ahead, Coura paused in the corridor and shook her head. "I'm not letting you go."

Will challenged her words with a determined look. "I know I can't do much, but I've been working on my combat skills. I want to record what happens and explore the valley."

"This isn't a vacation. We're dealing with demonic creatures. People will probably get hurt or die. Remember how I looked at Clearshot's home after saving Mace and Lexie? Remember how they described the creatures? *That's* what we're facing."

Her friend paled but refused to back down. When he started walking again, Coura shouted for him to stop twice, swore to herself when he didn't, then jogged to his side.

"Say what you want. I'm making this choice," he argued when she reached him.

"Will…"

"I haven't been useful, but I hope to be now. Besides, you once said you would protect me." He met her eyes with a smile, despite the obvious nerves. "I trust you with my life."

Coura stared at him for a moment before dropping her head into her hands. "That doesn't mean you should throw yourself into danger," she muttered yet gave up on trying to convince him.

*

Byron spoke to Clearshot and Marcus with Aaron in the courtyard when Coura and Will arrived. The area was otherwise empty, giving it a haunted presence. The morning snowfall let up, so a thin layer crunched under their feet as the pair approached the others.

Upon spotting them, Clearshot let out a long whistle. "The uniform suits you, Coura!"

She looked down at herself and felt her cheeks growing warm. "You've got the same outfit on," she pointed out. Both Clearshot and Marcus wore uniforms identical to hers while Byron dusted off his royal blue cloak and Aaron one in a gray color.

"Let's join the troops," her mentor instructed and pulled his hood down against the wind. Although the others eyed Will, no one commented on his appearance within their group.

They found Tio and what he referred to as the outer squad, which consisted of fifty soldiers armed with swords and shields, at the southern exit. Each wore a suit of silver-colored, metal armor with protective padding underneath and a helmet. All eyes fell on the six since they were the last to arrive.

"About time you showed up," Tio yelled from the front. Coura noticed his eyes dart to Aaron, but he didn't comment on the addition.

412

"All right," Calin began. "As you know, the underground tunnel system is east of Dala. Once we reach it, we'll set up camp inside and head to the Valley Beyond at dawn. According to the scout posted there, the creatures seem to be waiting for something, perhaps a command or nightfall. Either way, we'll be between them and the city."

"I expect nothing less from the southern troops," Tio belted after.

With those final words, he lifted his sword and produced a mighty cry echoed by his soldiers. Together, they marched across the bridge above the moat, through the forest lining the grassland, and into the open fields beyond.

Friends or Foes

As dusk approached at their backs, Coura wondered if the squad would ever reach the aforementioned tunnel entrance. Outside Dala were fields with farmers and their families waving the troops off, and flat land stretched past those. The only notable objects in sight afterward became two trees next to each other and a hill away in the distance.

"I wonder how much longer it is until we get there," she grumbled to no one in particular.

"Just be patient," Byron reassured her and pointed ahead. "See those trees? I'm guessing they're a sign we're close."

"Why?"

Both her mentor and Soirée spoke at the same time and with an equal amount of impatience.

"Use your head, Coura."

{*Idiot, use your head.*}

"Fine," she replied and rolled her eyes at their comments. For a brief moment, she pondered the hill and its trees until an idea sprouted. "I get it. There aren't trees around here, so it's odd that not just one but two are able to grow. It's a method for people to find the system at a distance."

"Exactly."

"There's more to it," Will jumped in with an envious amount of energy.

Byron raised an eyebrow at him. "Oh?"

"I've been reading about the surrounding areas. The people who founded Dala became so used to flat land that when they came upon the forests just outside the southern border, it proved difficult to transport their crops to various cities, including Clearwater. I always knew that much, so I decided I could learn more from the people while we're here."

"So, they built tunnels to transfer produce and products? It makes sense to me," Coura summarized.

"That's half of it," Will continued while beaming with pride. "Part of the tunnel branches off to the south while one opens to the north, to what they call The Valley Beyond."

"I've heard of that place," Aaron added from where he listened behind Coura.

Byron nodded in agreement. "I'm not surprised. Most people in the north have, including myself."

"I haven't," she said pointedly.

As Tio approached the pair of trees, he was the first to climb over the hill and disappear. His troops followed, including their group. On the other side of the natural landmark, a hole opened into a tunnel wide enough for four people to walk through at once and twice Coura's height. She marveled at the smooth, clean walls carved into the dirt and instantly became chilled once they moved below the surface. Torches had been placed at equal distances along the walls and were lit by those at the front as the squad progressed.

Despite wearing a coat, her body began to shiver. Coura asked Will to go on about the valley in order to distract from the temperature.

"The Valley Beyond, let's see. It was used as a trading route to Fester in the northeastern part of Asteom, but one part of the tunnel collapsed a decade or so ago. Nobody knows why or how, but the accident killed a group of traders. I guess Dala, Fester, and some of the other towns it passed through argued about who was to blame. Because they couldn't reach a clear answer, no city offered to pay to fix it, even if it meant cutting off a portion of their trading business."

"That explains why Dala remains separated from the north," Aaron muttered.

"I agree," Will continued with a brief nod. "Now, there's no use for this tunnel system, except to go to Clearwater. The Valley Beyond is where the tunnel's second route comes out to. I think travelers used it as a camping ground before they entered the next section of the tunnel, which is what collapsed."

After a pause, Byron spoke at a lower volume, seemingly more to himself than the others. "Dala must have claim over the land, which explains why someone is posted to survey the valley. The stories I heard were about spirits wandering aimlessly through the tunnels or lost souls waiting to go beyond our world."

Their group fell silent and actively listened for unusual noises within the echoes of shuffling feet and mumbled conversations. A while later, Tio halted the squad for the night. Some soldiers propped themselves against the walls while others carrying sleeping rolls or blankets sprawled onto the floor. Although her body felt exhausted, Coura's mind wandered aimlessly with thoughts of transparent faces watching her from the shadows. It wasn't until her eyes began to burn that she allowed herself to nod off into an uneasy sleep.

*

It seemed as if Coura slept for a few minutes before she woke with a start. Her skin had goosebumps and tingled, like a prickly branch glided gently across her body; it irritated her how familiar the sensation felt.

Outside Fester, when the angels stalked us, I picked up on their presence. Only this is twice as powerful…

She glanced around and caught Byron sitting up.

"You can sense it too," he said without looking at her.

She hugged herself and took deep breaths in order to calm down as a grip of panic loomed over her. "It's worse than before."

His head turned in her direction, and his eyes widened in alarm. She didn't understand what startled him, but he hurried to the front of the group where Tio's gruff snores echoed above the others.

The sound stopped, followed by grumbling, and people began rising and lighting the torches with the master mage's assistance.

"Get up," Tio ordered and lightly kicked those closest to him.

Within minutes, snores shifted into groans and yawns. The soldiers packed their items and prepared to set out as Clearshot roused Marcus, Aaron, and Will. It didn't take much for the squad to be ready to move on.

Meanwhile, Coura remained farther away at the light's edge, stretching and flexing her arms. Similar to the first time they encountered the angelic presence, it bothered her center of power and made it seem as though a pair of eyes watched her from every direction. Unlike before, though, Soirée's predatory behavior overwhelmed Coura and threatened to sweep her away. The demon's killing instinct seemed even more active due to the dark, damp tunnel. Coura had to keep a grip on the energy as a suffocating rage grew in her chest; fighting this caused her whole body to grow tense and quiver.

In the other half of her mind, she became petrified at the reminder of the angels outside Fester who were responsible for attacking Will and Marcus. *Last time, I fought two angels separately. Grace claims she saw four. If these are as powerful as the last ones…*

"I sure didn't assign you to this squad for your speed, you sad excuses for soldiers. Let's be on our way!" Tio's voice rang twice as loud in the tunnel and faded once his troops started marching.

At the rear of the squad, Marcus, Will, and Aaron talked in hushed voices. Word spread about the unseen, possibly hostile angels, but Coura didn't bother listening. It took all her self-control just to keep herself sane. Soirée hissed and growled for vengeance, cursing the unseen beings while her demonic energy sparked within Coura's body. Once, Byron asked her how she was doing and received a curt nod in response. No one else bothered her after.

*

It proved impossible to distinguish the time underground, but Coura figured it had to be nearly sunrise when the squad reached a fork in the path. Without hesitation, the general turned left, leading them north.

At that moment, the unseen presence vanished, as if cut it off. A great amount of stress lifted from her body, though not immediately, and she slowed to a stop.

"Byron…"

"I know," he replied and appeared just as baffled. Neither of them spoke, and those around the two took notice.

Clearshot rubbed the bridge of his nose before releasing a sigh. "It's times like this you make me wish I had magical powers."

"The energy we sensed just disappeared," the master mage explained.

"What does that mean?"

"It means the enemy has the ability to suppress their power. Coura and I picked up on it because they let us, and I'm sure they wouldn't make the mistake of revealing their presence without precise control. I can't tell where it came from since we're underground, but now I wonder what we'll find in The Valley Beyond."

"Perhaps they knew the demonic creatures were waiting and came to help," Clearshot offered in his regular, optimistic tone.

"I doubt it," Coura heard Byron mutter.

Before long, they heard Tio shouting from the front.

"I see the end. Ardel here led us back to his post, and now he'll lead us into battle against these scum. Prepare yourselves!"

The soldiers' enthusiasm doubled after their general's motivational update. Coura saw the aforementioned scout named Ardel huddled uncomfortably at the front with Tio's hand on his shoulder. The pair spun around and strode toward a growing light.

Swords were drawn with slick hisses, and shields had been raised. Clearshot slipped his bow off his back and knocked an arrow, shifting his attitude into a deadly calm she had not experienced before. Marcus held his sword in a similar, still manner, like an animal ready to pounce, and Aaron did the same, though it became obvious by his lesser poise and balance he lacked the extra training both soldiers experienced. Will had procured a sword from the shed in the base before their group left and held it at the ready. Although his hands visibly shook, his face remained set with the determination he showed the previous afternoon.

Coura kept behind Byron, who wore an expressionless mask while keeping a hand on the hilt of his sheathed sword, and contemplated manifesting her own weapon. Soirée urged her to do so, yet she couldn't convince herself.

{*Get ready.*}

Not yet. Something doesn't seem right about this.

She constantly blinked to adjust her eyes to the growing brightness while searching for any unnatural shadows as the squad reached the end of their protective walls. Will's explanation of the tunnel's collapse years ago stayed fresh in her mind to add additional anxiety. Everyone else appeared tense as they all passed into the open area.

*

The Valley Beyond rested in a bowl surrounded by structures too short to be considered mountains but standing higher than any hill Coura had ever seen. Its vibrant, green grass tickled her ankles once the troops tentatively stepped out. Amid the threats, she wondered how this place managed to escape the gray of winter. No wind passed either, and dozens of stars still twinkled in the approaching light of dawn.

She soon forgot the rumors Byron mentioned about spirits in favor of savoring its tranquility. *This place is beautiful. I can't imagine inhuman beings haunting such a serene stretch of land.*

The silence lingered as their squad halted far from the mouth of the tunnel. Several boulders ranging in height were scattered across the field to hide much of the space, yet the other end of the valley remained visible, albeit vaguely. She longed to comment on its extensive width, but everyone seemed determined not to make a sound.

It stayed quiet long enough that Soirée's voice startled her.

{*I sense no demonic or light-blooded energy. This valley is in waiting.*}

Coura prepared to ask what she meant when a distressed cry broke out from the front of the squad. The soldiers expected some sort of attack, yet it was Ardel who moved.

"What are you doing?" she heard Tio demand without hiding his wrath.

The soldier shrieked before sprinting toward the opposite end of the valley while gasping and panting, as though he were already exhausted.

"Hold your positions!" the general ordered and held up a fist.

Ardel didn't run fast. He stumbled blindly through the grass and let out several sobs each time he pushed himself to his feet. It became downright pathetic to watch, but he stopped beside one of the closest boulders and fell to his knees.

"I brought them here," he whined loudly enough for the troops to hear. "Just as you requested!"

The resulting pause filled with the man's heavy breathing and sniveling before he repeated himself while expressing more emotion. "I did what you asked!" he cried then buried his face in his hands.

A clear, tenor voice came from near the boulder, projecting to the entire area. "I suppose you did, human, though I wish you would have had enough patience to do *specifically* what I requested."

As the words ended, a slim figure revealed himself from behind the rock to place a hand on Ardel's head. The lingering darkness hid his features, yet Coura knew by his condescending tone and the way he called Ardel a human that he had to be a Yeluthian. A bead of sweat dropped down her temple to slide along her neck in response. To her amazement, Tio and his men appeared unaffected by the newcomer.

"Are you in allegiance with the demonic creatures plaguing this valley?" the general yelled without a trace of fear.

The stranger ignored the question. Instead, he bent forward to say something to Ardel, which sent the man into another fit of weeping. The soldier picked himself up after and stumbled away from the troops a minute later. For a moment, everybody stared across the valley until Tio repeated his question more forcefully.

"What a noisy human," the tenor voice rang. He approached the squad and stopped a safe distance from the general. His clothing consisted of ordinary, dull colors on a material helping him to appear less conspicuous; however, he had a thin blade strapped around his waist.

Tio said nothing but raised his sword higher, as if to show he wasn't intimidated.

This amused the stranger, who laughed and crossed his arms. "I despise demons as much as you, if not more, General Tio."

If he expected Tio to be surprised by the direct address, the general didn't show it.

"What are you doing here then, and what did you ask my soldier to do?" His voice remained set with a firm authority, though it probably sounded neutral to the stranger.

"I guess you could say we bargained for his help to draw you and your outer squad here."

The word "we" stood out from the rest of his answer. Before Tio could question it, the stranger's smile stretched wider, and he whistled over his right shoulder. Three more figures emerged from other boulders, each wearing the same type of outfit and challenging grins.

As they lined up with their companion, Byron sidestepped to slip himself in front of Coura, blocking her view.

"Hey!" she whispered in protest.

Her mentor turned his face slightly to the side so she could hear his mumble. "Don't act yet. I'm sure they know you're with us in Dala, especially since they came from the palace, but they might not think you're here now."

Although she disliked the idea of staying hidden, she pressed her lips together and said no more. The soldiers murmured to one another in the meantime, and General Tio dropped his patient façade.

"You used Ardel to lure us here with a fake story about demon creatures." His tone shifted into casual annoyance. "Are you ready to tell me what this is about and who you are?"

Coura peeked around Byron's arm to catch the irritated frowns of the Yeluthians. Apparently, they intended to stretch the suspense out for as long as possible, which she assumed would have been for their entertainment, just as the two she faced before had done.

"If you must know, we were sent to eliminate you and your base. Of course, it would be too messy for the other humans in town to witness, so the best idea was to lure you here where another tunnel accident wouldn't raise questions."

They intend to kill us.

The stranger's eyes shifted to gaze behind Tio and at the faces of his troops. The men and women fidgeted in response while the general didn't comment on the angels' plan.

"Our second mission is to capture the prince hiding among your soldiers."

A stab of alarm pierced Coura's heart at his mention of Aaron. She glanced over at him, but his face stayed hidden by the hood of his cloak. His stance gave nothing away either.

While they conversed, the sun rose to brighten the sky in a vibrant collection of purples, reds, and oranges. It rested behind the rock walls to the east yet provided enough light by that point so she could make out the strangers' faces. Each looked like the other two angels she encountered, flaunting flowing, blond hair of differing lengths, blue eyes visible even at a distance, and lean builds. One was female and reminded Coura of Grace; her gut twisted at the idea of fighting someone who looked familiar.

"Who are you?" Tio demanded.

"I am Drake." The leader bowed in a dramatic fashion before gesturing to his companions. Next to him, the female he called Thelma scanned the squad with visible curiosity. A shorter male named Hector stood on his other side. Lastly, he introduced the tallest of the four as Urvin. Unlike the other males, this one's unbound hair trailed down his back.

"That doesn't answer my question," Tio growled and took a fighting stance.

Drake's expression twisted into a devious smile, then he manifested a pair of pure white wings. The other three did the same a second later.

"I believe the time for idle conversing is over."

They suppressed their energy, just as Byron predicted, which actually benefited Coura because it didn't distract her again. Still, none of the soldiers, including the general, expected to be engaging in combat with the angels. While some froze or gazed in awe, others were visibly startled and began backing up.

As the four stepped forward and drew their swords, Tio released a battle cry and charged. Coura almost called for him to wait and not go alone; however, his troops snapped out of the trance upon hearing the sound to follow with their own shouts.

Once the sound of clashing metal began, Byron spun around to face her. "Take Will to the tunnel!"

Before she could protest, or even consider what to do next, he sprinted ahead and drew his sword. Clearshot, who already let several arrows fly, appeared at his side after.

She hesitated to join before muttering a curse, knowing her unique abilities and inexperience could prove detrimental to the squad if she rushed in. Will appeared to be struggling to decide as well, so she hurried over to grab his arm. To her relief, he understood her intentions without an explanation and allowed her to pull him toward the tunnel as the battle continued at their backs. Soon, pain-filled shrieks and shouting merged into the original noise.

Once inside, the pair pressed against the wall, attempted to catch their breath, then glanced out of the opening. The female angel, Thelma, hovered in the sky to launch fire and lightning at the soldiers, who dodged within what appeared to be a hair's length. The impact of her magic sent some flying and rumbled the ground, yet Tio's subordinates proved well-prepared for action. None went down, as far as she could tell, making her appreciate the time they had to train with her up until that point.

*

The fighting stretched without positive change. Each moment ticked by sluggishly, and every second wore at Coura's hope and patience.

They can't keep this up.

The thought repeated in her mind as her eyes lingered on one of the soldiers. He screamed after being stabbed in the leg, and the jarring sound brought her back to her senses.

"We need to do something," she said aloud, both to herself and Will. When she looked at him, she found he was staring outside with wide, horrified eyes.

"What can we do?" he muttered. "They're going to kill us."

"I don't know," she admitted and faced the combat again.

Every person seemed covered with blood and opened their mouths to breathe heavily beneath their helmets. The four angels became visible now that the silver suits of armor were continually being knocked down, which made her heart sink as she understood how weary they grew.

{*The enemy might not know you're here, so let's surprise them.*}

Because of her apprehension, Coura tuned out Soirée's wrath against the angelic race. Now that she noticed it, the rage welled again and gave her an idea.

You're right. We can distract them until everyone retreats into the tunnel!

{*We'll kill them before that!*}

The demonic energy pounded from the rising bloodlust spurred by the thought of fighting. It devoured Coura's fear and indecisiveness, allowing her to focus for the first time that day.

"I'm going to help," she announced and stripped off her crimson coat.

Will's eyes darted to her. "What? You can't go!"

I need him for this to work.

She put her hands on his shoulders to shake him a bit until he seemed more alert. "They can't survive out there. I'm going to distract the angels until everybody is in the tunnel. You have to let them know to retreat."

Will started trembling worse than before and looked from Coura to the valley and back again. "I can't," he whimpered after.

She ground her teeth as precious seconds passed and contemplated what she could say to convince him. Once she recalled what motivated him to accompany the troops in the first place, Coura latched on to the words she spoke before they left the base.

"Remember what I told you?" she asked and met his eyes. "I said I would protect you. I want to help you and the troops, but I can't do that while they're out there. More people are going to get hurt unless we bring them into the tunnel. Please, we need you!"

Will swallowed and stared at the ground. Coura's heart beat louder in her ears as she forced herself to wait for his answer. At last, she heard his timid response.

"What should I do?"

She released a brief sigh of relief before pointing outside. "I'm going to distract the angels for as long as I can. I need you to tell every soldier to move back into this tunnel. If they argue, just tell them General Tio said so. Help carry those who are hurt, but don't get caught in the combat, understand?"

He nodded. That was all the confirmation she could wait for, yet she trusted he would fulfill her request. Before her doubt could catch up, she moved outside.

*

If she didn't feel Soirée's enthusiasm when it came to violence, Coura would have become immobile as soon as she moved into the open. Of the fifty soldiers, at least half knelt or lied on the ground and showcased fresh blood. Byron began using dark magic and kept the female in the sky preoccupied by matching her spell for spell. She caught Clearshot tending to the injured since he emptied the quiver along his back, and everyone else stood with Tio against the three grounded opponents.

Meanwhile, the angels obviously toyed with their human prey. When a soldier swung their sword, the trio would slip aside at the last second to dodge the attack before striking with the flat sides of their blades, causing a sickening ringing noise against the metal armor.

I have to hurry, Coura told herself and glanced around.

Far to her right, she spotted a lone boulder, which she decided would provide the best cover, and sprinted in that direction. As soon as she reached it, she heard a stream of agony-filled curses from Tio; the sound prompted wild and uncertain thoughts about her next course of action.

{Calm down. I will take control of this.}

She felt a flow of demonic energy spread from her center to each part of her body, like an icy river. With it, the fear holding her captive washed away until she was filled with the eagerness accompanying the indulgence of her power and a lust for combat. Underneath the sensation rested Soirée's unending bloodthirst noticeable in the demon's next thought.

{Now we can have some fun!}

Deadly Ambitions

Even after Coura left the safety of the tunnel, Will stared outside, praying for the courage to act. Then, General Tio's voice snapped him into his right mind.

What now? I must go, and quickly!

He became so used to analyzing every situation that the idea of charging into a fast-paced, unforgiving battle left him unable to move, no matter how many times he internally screamed at his body. Somehow, he managed to peek out of the opening once more, though he regretted this when he saw the crimson-stained bodies and the sight of General Tio. The man held up his right arm with the other so everybody could see how it had been cleanly sliced at the wrist. Blood squirted and dripped from where his hand had been moments ago, and the general's face looked pale.

Will turned away and squeezed his eyes closed.

What should I do? The question repeated in his mind until he heard Coura's voice and remembered her shaking his shoulders.

"Please, we need you!"

The words helped him feel more grounded, and he opened his eyes with a slightly stronger resolve. One leg followed the other through the opening until the dirt walls no longer protected him.

"We need you!"

He spotted the closest soldier lying in the grass and hurried over while remaining careful not to draw attention to himself. The man's helmet had been dented in two places, making it impossible for Will to pull it off.

"What do I do now?" he asked himself absentmindedly.

"Who's…there…"

Will started at the rasping voice. "Are you all right?"

"Head…hurts…but I'm fine."

After searching for any other injuries, he struggled to think of a way to carry the soldier. In that moment, a shadow moved into his line of sight. An angelic silhouette paused against the clear sky above before diving into the valley. He noted its black color, and a sense of relief washed through him once he realized Coura was following through on her promise.

The Dalan soldiers must have recognized her as well, for they let her land in front of them and fan a gust of air at their opponents. In response, the trio of male combatants leapt away to put distance between themselves and the newcomer. After, she walked forward to meet them. Although he couldn't see her face, Will imagined the sadistic expression she wore the night outside Fester; the memory made his heart beat faster despite his attempt to reassure himself of their friendship.

"It's…about time," came a grumble.

The man on the ground coughed and tried sitting up, so Will put the metal-clad arm around his neck to assist. Then, the soldier groaned and relaxed against Will, who didn't expect to be helping with such a simple movement. Together, they continued to watch the scene unfold.

The angel's leader named Drake released a sniveling laugh before his companions joined in. "I was wondering when you would show up, imposter," he teased Coura once she stopped.

Even though he addressed her, she didn't respond.

"You really do have a knack for being where you are not wanted. I suppose this does provide us with an opportunity to avenge our fallen companions, though. Do you remember Elsa and Devon?"

Again, silence from Coura.

One of the other angels scoffed before Drake continued.

"If you plan on ignoring us, we can go ahead and kill you."

"I'm sorry. I was waiting for you to say something worthwhile," she replied at last in an unusually carefree tone. "If you're done rambling, I would like to know why the Yeluthians are plotting to attack Dala's base and kidnap the prince?"

Drake raised his chin to visibly ponder whether or not he should reveal any information. He shrugged after and caved in. "I am sure you figured out we are not from Asteom. Still, our leader is pretty fond of keeping the peace in this kingdom. I suggest you leave, demon-blooded. We have no use for you right now."

"You want me to squander the opportunity to slaughter four of you? That is, if none of you flee from here."

While the angels chuckled at her boldness, a black blade appeared out of nowhere in her hand as the dark wings extended to display what Will assumed to be anticipation. The already humid air grew heavier, and he held his breath. Nobody moved a muscle as the magical beings stood their ground.

Coura decided to attack first. She launched herself at Drake and brought up her sword to the angel's throat. He raised his in time to stop her slice, then they remained in that position, pressing against the other's blade until she dropped her left arm. Her palm opened to reveal a bright light. When Drake glanced down, a bolt of lightning burst forth to strike him in the hip, sending his body flying backward. He landed on one side with a thud and didn't rise.

Will wanted to cheer and felt his voice in the back of his throat, yet no one made a sound except for the female angel named Thelma, who stayed in the sky above Byron. She shouted her fallen companion's name and glared at his body before extending both hands toward Coura. This time, Will began to shout a warning, but his friend was already on the move.

Before the angel could summon her magic, Coura jumped into the air. She flew above and over her opponent, dodging the resulting fireballs with a satisfying grace. Witnessing such inhuman agility captivated Will until the soldier against him groaned, pulling his attention away from the fight.

We're supposed to be evacuating, he remembered with a surge of guilt while he helped the man to his feet.

"Come on. I'll get you to safety."

He managed to make it a few steps with the extra weight before walking became difficult. As he wondered how he would be able to do more for the rest of the troops given his lack of strength, Will felt part of the man's weight slide to the other side. At first, he thought the soldier was falling over, but a glance to his right showed a cloaked figure supporting the opposite side.

"Let's hurry."

Will recalled seeing Aaron in a hallway at the base before the squad's departure and took comfort in being around someone familiar. Working together to accomplish the same goal also motivated him as they continued toward the tunnel. All the while, he prayed none of the angels would notice the fleeing troops.

The trio made it inside and went far enough from the opening until they felt safe. Once there, Will and Aaron set the injured man down.

"Thank you, Your Highness," Will managed to say. A hand flew up to cover his mouth after he remembered the prince's need to stay inconspicuous, as well as Aaron's hatred of formal titles.

He sensed his friend's annoyance; however, they mutually understood it wasn't time for a reunion. Plenty of other soldiers limped behind to enter the tunnel and collapse against its walls.

"We need to get everybody in here, especially the injured," Aaron announced for those inside to hear before issuing orders to either return to the valley or tend to those they would bring back.

Will hurried to the opening, suddenly empowered by the support. Whatever happened with Coura and the angels went on in the background once he focused on his mission. He did notice Byron using spells to shield those nearby or attack, and the troops still able to fight began condensing into a fortified cluster. The general remained in that mix as well.

Aaron caught up when he knelt beside and inspected a pair of soldiers lying on the ground. "Their wounds aren't life-threatening," he explained.

"Good, then let's move," his friend urged in the same, commanding manner.

Neither of the men questioned him, but they both needed assistance. Will looked around and found Clearshot approaching.

"I told those around me to head for the tunnel. The angels haven't tried to finish off the wounded, but Byron's protecting them," he shared with the most serious expression Will had seen from the archer.

The prince nodded. "Without a healer, our best option is to retreat, especially if they intend to attack the base. Help us with these men."

Clearshot managed with a single, stumbling soldier while Will and Aaron repeated their previous process with the one in a worse condition. In his head, Will counted all the people still scattered around the valley who weren't already being brought inside the safety of the tunnel by others.

Ten are around General Tio, and seven bodies aren't moving on the ground. We need to keep going. That is, until the Yeluthians decide to intervene.

While Clearshot dropped off his burden and turned to exit, Aaron and Will set down the soldier hanging over their shoulders. The former rushed out again, but Will took a moment to catch his breath and look at himself. After seeing the spots of fresh blood staining his clothes, he had to shut his eyes and turn inward in order to find his courage once more.

A blast against the outside of the miniature mountain caused the tunnel to shudder, and Will forgot about his emotions as he jogged toward the opening. Coin-sized pieces of dirt fell from the ceiling around him after, raising a new fear.

What if they cause this entrance to collapse?

He didn't know which side of the tunnel he would rather be on if that happened, leading him to contemplate staying until he heard somebody call his name. Without thinking, he exited and met Aaron. The prince, though covered with sweat and blood, didn't seem fazed. Will grew embarrassed by his earlier disgust and constant panting.

"We need to hurry," his friend reminded him.

They glanced at the damaged rock above the tunnel's opening then at the clearing just in time to catch one of the angels land a slice along Coura's right wing. A stream of dark liquid poured from the wound, but she didn't seem to notice and retaliated with a slash of her own against her opponent's chest. Will heard the male's startled cry, but before he could respond, she raised a leg to kick him in the stomach. The unexpected blow had him stumbling in the opposite direction.

Even though Will liked to see another threat fall, Coura's unbothered expression distracted him, and he wondered if she ever tired.

Nearby, Byron and Thelma continued hurling bolts of lightning and ice shards at one another. The master mage's strength had weakened, so he could barely bring up a shield to block her attacks or dodge them. The ground around him was scorched and torn from the spells, but he had the foresight to stay away from everyone else.

Aaron began moving, prompting Will to follow. The two approached the final grouping of soldiers where Clearshot and another man carried a limp body with hardened faces that made him shiver. They passed without a word.

"You go there and wait for me," Aaron instructed once they were close. He pointed to a trio of soldiers at their right before hurrying in another direction.

Although he wondered why the prince would leave him alone, Will mustered his energy before reaching the bodies. He checked their breathing first and felt a weight drop from his shoulders when he discovered they were all still alive. Even so, he couldn't move them on his own. He perked up as Aaron jogged to meet him with General Tio. The image of the man's hand being cut off remained fresh enough in Will's mind to make him queasy.

The prince opened his mouth to speak, but an explosion from above caught their attention. Thelma and the angel with the longer hair named Urvin engaged in combat with Coura, and Will grew dizzy trying to watch their swords. When one attacked, the other prepared to strike, preventing her from pausing the bout. Her speed amazed him when he noted it, for every blow was met with the black blade, though she couldn't seem to get a hit in retaliation.

She's only supposed to keep them occupied, he reminded himself.

"We need to get back to the tunnel," he said without taking his eyes off the fighting.

Aaron and General Tio ignored the message and gazed upward with a mixture of concern and awe.

Coura still blocked the continuous blows until, in the blink of an eye, she leaned into one of the angel's swords. Will heard himself gasp when the blade sunk deep into her left shoulder. Although she winced, she turned her body sideways, pulling the injured shoulder away in a sharp motion. Then, Will understood what she planned to do.

The weapon had been embedded deep enough into her flesh that when she turned, she yanked the hilt out of the angel's hands. The unanticipated jerk and the loss of his weapon startled him enough to forget about dodging her sword, which stabbed through his torso a second later. His partner shrieked as she removed her blade, leaving her victim to fall to the ground with his wings covering him like a sheet.

During that time, Thelma didn't react fast enough either. While she watched her companion, Coura grabbed the second angel's arm, threw her in the direction of the tunnel, and launched a series of fireballs, which exploded on impact. Each blast pushed the female backward until she slammed into the miniature mountain and dropped to the ground, sending more rubble tumbling down.

An eerie silence fell over the area after. Suddenly, General Tio let out a whoop followed by a hearty cheer that scared Will. He chuckled once it dawned on him the enemy had been defeated. Even Aaron breathed easier as he continued watching their friend.

"What a show!" came an exasperated voice from behind. Clearshot stood with a hand above his eyes to shade them from the newly risen sun and grinned like his normal self.

"I'll say," the general added and raised his right arm instinctively before growling in pain and clutching it to his chest. More crimson blood oozed from the open wound.

The sight concerned Will. "We need to get you treated!"

The man shoved his comment aside. For the moment, he chose to celebrate the battle's end and break down the fight, both what he participated in and witnessed. Those nearby listened before searching for their comrades.

Then, their eyes fell on Byron, who stood alone staring toward the opposite end of the valley. Even from a distance, Will could tell the master mage remained alert. He then looked up at Coura and saw the same behavior. Without flinching, she removed the sword buried in her shoulder and held it in her left hand. Its silver blade became the light to match her dark, demonic weapon. Her wings cupped to allow her to descend to the ground farther away from them.

"What's going on?" somebody asked, but no one answered the question.

Upon hearing crunching footsteps, they turned when Byron approached from where the grass had burned away. Before Will, Clearshot, General Tio, or another onlooker could speak, the master mage fixed them with a stern expression, held up a hand, then put a finger to his lips as a signal for them to be quiet.

"There's another one," he explained, and his tone reflected his apprehension.

In the resulting lull, Will wondered why this additional angel made both Byron and Coura nervous.

***

Despite the dreamlike state she was in, Coura found herself growing uneasy while she faced the empty end of the valley and waited for the final figure to emerge. Soirée's energy gave her body a surreal feeling, as though she could feel no pain. Each wound delivered by the previous foes healed almost immediately and used little of her reserves. At the moment, her worst injury, the shoulder wound, had almost closed.

As each enemy fell, a presence similar to theirs imposed itself on the valley until both Coura and Soirée were certain it wouldn't go away. She decided to stay in the hope of buying as much time as possible before fleeing and gripped each sword tighter. It took all her patience to keep from shouting into the morning air while the unknown source of energy irritated her.

A few minutes passed before the angel stepped out from behind a nearby bolder. He appeared to be younger than the previous four and bore similar features, except his hair had been braided and he wore a white robe instead. His voluntary reveal surprised her, especially when he came closer, though he kept his hands together at the waist under the draping sleeves.

"Although I wish no ill will on my companions, I am glad I could witness such abilities from you," he began with a slight smile.

"Who are you?" Coura demanded. Even beyond Soirée's hatred, she sensed a wrongness coming from him and prayed the retreating troops were already moving toward Dala.

"I am called Jaspire."

When he said no more, she narrowed her eyes. "Why are you here?"

This time, she didn't receive an answer, so she raised the swords in her hands as a threat.

At the sight, Jaspire's smile faded. "Believe me, I do not wish to fight you."

"Then tell me what you're doing here," she growled in response.

"It is as they told you. We were ordered to dispose of the base in Dala and capture Prince Aaron. Although eliminating you was not our top priority yet, I think we might need to bend our orders a bit."

He smirked, spun around, and retraced his steps to hide in the mix of boulders. Before Coura could move to attack, she caught him glance over his shoulder at something behind her. She heard a flap of wings and a warning cry from someone after.

{*Look out!*}

She twisted around, caught a glimmer of metal, and raised both swords in a crossed motion just in time to stop a blade from slicing open her skull. Their leader, Drake, grinned down at her with wings outstretched and dried blood covering his face and arms.

He's still alive? Coura thought before leaping backward.

It became too late to pursue Jaspire by that point. Drake dashed to strike but not before she spotted another set of white wings behind his. She manifested her own pair then ducked under his blade, sliced at his thigh, and leapt into the air. His mad laugh echoed after her.

Their newcomer was buying time too? Soirée, what's going on?

Coura felt the panic and doubt doubling, but the demon snuffed them out with her own frustration and loathing.

{*I don't know, but if they wish to die again, we'll oblige them!*}

That newfound determination halted her flight, and she turned to see the shortest of the angels named Hector meet her in the sky. Like earlier, she blocked and dodged his blows until he made a wrong move she could take advantage of. Her sword rose to pierce his throat during that opening, then she left him to tumble to the ground.

As soon as she rid herself of the previous opponent, Drake caught up and lunged at her. He struck with all his weight in a physical attack to collide with her in the air instead of using a weapon. Together, they spun and fell uncontrollably. Coura wasn't able to steady her wings or her limbs because Drake grabbed hold of her wrists and tried wrapping his legs around hers. With no other options and the ground growing closer, she let go of her swords and drove a knee into his stomach. Although he didn't release her arms, that distracted him enough for her to push her fist and punch him square in the nose. *That* caused him to yell and loosen his grip.

They already dropped too far down for either to land without injury. She snapped her wings open and gasped as several of the fragile bones broke from the sheer force of her fall. The support did slow her body down so she landed hard on her feet, and the black wings sagged at her sides before the demonic energy stretched to heal what bones and muscles had been damaged. Across from her, Drake crashed into the ground where he remained unmoving. Coura continued watching him despite that.

My reserves are starting to wear out; I can feel it. These injuries are taking longer to heal.

Soirée growled with displeasure, but her silence meant she agreed.

"Over here," a female voice chimed from above.

She glanced upward to where Thelma stretch a hand toward her, and Urvin hovered behind, wielding a different sword than the one he lost.

With a curse, Coura forced her right wing above her head to act as cover when the female released a barrage of fireballs. Before the spell reached her, she cast a thin shield, which proved to be all she could manage at the moment. Upon making contact with her barrier, the energy cracked the protective wall, and the flames singed some of her feathers. She ignored the resulting stings to push her wing away only for Urvin to swoop for her with his new weapon poised to strike.

Instinctively, she manifested her demonic blade. Just as she had done with Hector, Coura dodged and blocked as many blows as she could, though far too many landed to make her feel comfortable. Unlike the smaller opponent, Urvin's attacks showcased his precision, limiting the amount of opportunities for her to deal a lethal strike.

She blocked his next swing with the flat side of her blade, then she used as much strength as possible to hold his sword against hers for a moment. While he grinned into her face, she ground her teeth in frustration. Each combatant struggled to overpower the other, but soon her weapon moved his. With a final grunt, she put her weight behind a shove also helped by a sweep of her nearly healed wings. It provided enough force to knock Urvin off his feet. The angel rolled over before catching himself on one knee.

At first, she wondered what to do next. Her back faced the tunnel, so she knew her allies remained protected from the enemy for the time being; however, her heart sank as she watched Drake and Hector stand from behind Urvin while wearing their confident smiles. Thelma descended to fall in line with her companions after.

Coura's eyes darted to the bloody spots on Drake's stomach and Hector's throat, as well as the dark blotches on their clothing. *How are they still alive? Not all of them possess a healing ability, do they?*

A surge of the unsettling energy nearby provided an answer.

{The other one. He's been healing them from a distance, which is why we felt his presence growing around us.}

Soirée's confirmation only elevated Coura's present fear. *What do we do now? There's no way we can find and defeat Jaspire before getting rid of these four.*

Another surge of the sickly, demonic energy began flowing from her center.

{I will die from exhaustion before I let a light-blooded kill me!}

The wrath in Soirée's voice drowned out Coura's resulting thought.

It's not just you who will die.

The Golden Dagger

oura expected the four to attack at once, but for some reason, they paused, as if waiting. During the break, she mentally traced the tendrils of demonic energy to make sure each minor wound healed, then she fanned her wings to release some of their built up tension. Still, the angels didn't move. They grinned while staring at her, and she caught their lips moving while they spoke to one another.

They're plotting a trap. I just know it... She mentally summarized the situation, remembered the tunnel, and considered her escape plan.

{*I didn't give you this power to flee, you pathetic coward!*}

Despite Soirée's anger, she contemplated flying away from the valley until deciding the best course of action would be to do so after incapacitating her opponents. She would regroup with the Dalan soldiers later before pursuing their attackers once everyone recovered.

I'm not the only person involved in this, Soirée. Besides, I'm certain we'll meet them again.

Coura opened her wings and leapt backward, launching herself in the opposite direction with the help of her extra limbs' momentum. She didn't intend to leave outright but instead lead her opponents far from the tunnel, which was why she chose to keep her front side to them and move without hurrying. Although she half-expected them to pursue her, they remained in place and continued mumbling. Twice more she repeated this backtracking until she sensed the mouth of the tunnel nearby. It bothered her that the Yeluthians hadn't followed, and she hesitated to go farther.

What are they waiting for? she wondered anxiously.

Her first explanation went to the possibility of a trap they laid on that side of the valley. When she reached out and sensed no stray energy, she decided to chance glancing around for a physical attack. Nothing appeared to her right except more boulders in the distance, and a group of people stood to the left.

What?

Coura did a double take to make sure she hadn't lost her mind. Her face fell at the sight of those lingering in the valley to watch the fight, oblivious to her weakening power. When she noticed several bodies lying on the ground, her mind and frustration caught up to replace her initial shock.

Will was supposed to tell them to retreat into the tunnel. Can't they see how much danger they're in? Her head snapped forward toward the angels as the sound of their snickering reached across the space between them. All her emotions, concern, irritation, and fear, rose at once.

"What are you still doing here?" she shouted at her comrades. Her voice strained and threatened to break on the last word.

Based on how their captive gazes dropped into dumbfounded stares, she figured they had not realized the angels would overtake her soon. Their opponents' chirping laughter grew louder, and they finally began stalking in her direction.

They were waiting for that moment to attack the stragglers. If we stay...

No one besides the four moved.

Coura ground her fingernails into the palms of her hands and cursed in her mind.

{*Strike while we have the chance!*}

Soirée's desire to confront them tugged at Coura's heart, but she knew matters would remain complicated if the soldiers remained.

No. We need to protect the troops until they're in the tunnel, or everything we've done will be for nothing.

{Fool, we will kill the light-blooded first!}

She shoved Soirée's words and the bloodlust behind them down and instead raised a hand in front of herself. With the rising energy the demon provided, she cast a shield that stretched to cover her and those nearby in a half dome. The angels were not expecting this, and their amused noises ceased.

Although she longed to pour more energy into the barrier, she turned away, pressed her wings against her body, and sprinted over to the soldiers. As she did so, she yelled for them to leave; this time, she saw Byron grab Tio's arm and pull the general toward the tunnel.

"I'll not flee," the man started, but she noticed him wince, as well as the bloody stump where his right hand was missing. He followed her mentor after the outburst.

Meanwhile, the rest began to put the bodies around their shoulders or carry them off. Clearshot was one of the last to go and gave her a curt nod before he hauled another body away.

A second later, a tremor shook the ground. At the same time, she felt her shield weaken. Thelma had leapt into the sky to launch magical projectiles while the males struck the glimmering wall with their swords. The energy cracked under their strength, wearing down her spell until it shattered and faded into the sunlight. Coura gripped her weapon, mustered her courage and Soirée's desire to kill, then threw herself at the three on the ground.

***

What an idiot! How could I just stand there like that?

Will gasped for breath after he and Aaron returned to the valley for one of two remaining soldiers. No one said a word as they hurried back and forth to retrieve bodies either squirming in pain or regaining consciousness.

In his mind, he berated himself for acting carelessly and leaving Coura to fight for them. *I should have kept going. I should have argued when no one would listen.*

Aaron and Will kept an eye on the angels while they moved. At the moment, three of them fought their friend on the ground at once. She proved fast enough to avoid their fatal blows, but a lump grew in his throat with each scrape and slice that found its mark. In a matter of seconds, a flurry of white feathers blocked his view of the figure underneath.

"Let's hurry," the prince urged from ahead with a worried expression, doubling Will's fear.

They reached the soldiers and repeated the process of throwing one of their arms over a shoulder and hauling them to their feet. Will almost slipped as his legs began to give out under the added weight, but he managed to keep up with Aaron's lead. Clearshot and another soldier passed them along the way to retrieve the last person.

Steadily, the mouth of the tunnel crept closer. He kept his eyes on it to avoid losing focus and noticed somebody standing against the wall just inside. He squinted and recognized the crimson color was Marcus' coat, not the blood he became used to seeing. The assistant general held his side with one hand and ushered them toward him with the other in a somewhat hopeful gesture.

I didn't even notice where Marcus had gone.

All at once, his friend's head swung to the side, and the waving stopped. He shouted a warning, and Will looked up just before one of the angels fell to the ground directly in his path. The body rolled away with their wings beneath them. Right after, another plummeted near the same spot as the first, but this male had Coura wrapped in his arms. Her wings appeared to slow their descent before they hit the ground and tumbled together.

Will froze and hoped to remain unnoticed, like a startled hare.

The angel with the unbound hair pinned her to the ground after a rough tackle and punched her across the face. He raised his fist to deliver another blow, but in the next instant, the black blade protruded from his back, passing right through the center of his chest. His entire body went stiff, then collapsed onto Coura.

Both Aaron and Will shifted to go in her direction until Marcus' voice rose above the noise. He shouted for them to keep going and again gestured with more urgency.

"Move!"

The voice from behind had Will glancing around to where Clearshot and his partner dragged the final soldier on their shoulders.

"She'll be fine," he reassured them while passing by.

Still, Aaron hesitated with him until Coura pushed the limp angel off herself with some effort. She sat up and paused to catch her breath for a moment and wipe away the blood on her face.

The Dalan troops were well aware of her healing ability, so Will put his faith in that in order to stay calm. He took the lead toward the tunnel when Aaron didn't, and the pair soon reached their destination. Out of the corner of his eye, Will caught their friend rise and jump into the sky again just as they entered the shelter of the dirt walls.

With how hopeless the situation seemed at first, the progress inside amazed him, and they were soon relieved of their burden by others in the squad. A survey of the torch-lit space showed most of the troops on their feet wrapped in bandages or helping to patch up their comrades. Calin had taken to issuing orders while the general sat along the wall groaning as his arm was being tended to.

Next to Will, Aaron seemed to approve of the situation, then the prince turned away to walk back the way they came.

"Where are you going?" Will asked apprehensively as he thought of what took place beyond the opening.

"To get Coura."

Byron and Clearshot were near enough to overhear and stepped in to stop him.

"Absolutely not," the master mage said first. "Did you forget they're after you?"

Aaron frowned. "So you'll let them kill her?"

Clearshot moved forward before Byron could answer. "I'll go."

"Me too." Marcus hurried over, along with three other soldiers.

Will wanted to help as well but remembered Coura's purpose for staying behind. "Wait, that's not what she planned," he began to protest, but his reasoning became drowned out by the others, who raised theirs.

"You're injured enough as is. Clearshot and I can handle it."

"Byron, you're exhausted! I've worked with you enough to know."

"You can't go alone, so I'm coming too."

"Prince Aaron, please…"

As their arguing filled the passage, it caught Calin and General Tio's attention. The former dismissed them to continue his supervising duties while the latter pushed away his helpers and rose to approach them.

"What's all the fuss about?" he demanded in a raspy voice.

"Nothing," Marcus and Clearshot said together.

Evidently, the general understood what they were plotting and pushed to march toward the opening.

"No, please wait!" Will begged again despite it being too late.

The people around him crept closer to the light of the valley until they could see Coura beyond. She stood facing south between two opponents whose clothes were caked with dried blood, making him wonder how they were still alive. When she noticed them, he could sense her disappointment because they were pursuing the enemy and disrupting her original idea.

Those who lingered inside bickered about what to do and drew their weapons, which distracted the angels from their current target. Will's heartbeat picked up when it seemed like a fight for survival was imminent.

We can't beat them if they haven't been killed after everything so far. Does Coura believe that too? What happens if they get inside the tunnel with the injured?

As he began to give up hope for a successful retreat, Will sent his friend an apologetic look but noticed her analyzing them with an oddly thoughtful expression. She mouthed an inaudible message in their direction, then raised a hand toward the rocky hill.

"What is she-"

"Move farther inside!" Byron shouted and stepped back.

The others stared at him then out into the valley before registering the warning.

"Retreat!" the general cried after.

Will caught a bright light and spun around to scramble away. A crack of thunder chased them and echoed throughout the underground system, followed by tremors causing so many fragments to fall that they needed to stop and cover their heads in order to avoid serious injuries. The air became a cloud of dust that had everybody coughing in an attempt to inhale cleaner air. Behind, the sound of a resulting rockslide grew deafening.

Out of both caution and fear, Will dropped to huddle against the wall until only a haunting silence filled the tunnel. He trembled when he stood and began brushing himself off in a mindful manner, as if a false movement would cause the whole passageway to collapse. Then, he decided to search for the others who were at the entrance.

Voices from the rest of the squad picked up, but no one sounded anything worse than stunned. On the opposite end, Byron, Clearshot, General Tio, Marcus, and Aaron stood in front of a wall of fallen rocks that closed the opening.

"Hey!" someone called to draw their eyes away. Calin jogged over to meet them, shaking out the bits of dirt resting on his head. "What happened?"

The master mage answered with a sadness hanging over him like a rain cloud. "Coura sealed us in."

"They won't be able to follow," Clearshot added to project a bit of hopefulness.

"We also can't help her now," Marcus protested and extended a hand to touch the massive boulders blocking their path.

With what confidence he could muster, Will recalled his promise to Coura and used the opportunity to inform them of her intentions. "Clearshot's right. *This* was her plan all along."

Every face turned to him with questionable expressions.

"It's true," he went on and shared her idea to distract the angels then flee after every soldier went inside the tunnel. "That's probably what she's doing right now."

General Tio seemed to be the only person able to understand and move forward. He cleared his throat before crossing his arms. "My troops need medical attention, and there's just one way to go at the moment. Let's regroup and head back to Dala."

With that, he gestured for Calin to lead the way, and the pair returned to the awaiting soldiers where the general barked orders like his usual self. After a moment, Will was the first to join them with Clearshot immediately behind. The archer placed a hand on his shoulder and leaned closer to speak at a lower volume.

"If there's anything I learned about Coura in the short time I've known her, it's that she's determined to win and survive. You've known her for a while too, so you should feel more reassured than I am, right?"

Although Will agreed out loud, his thoughts continued to wander elsewhere.

***

The air in the valley chilled as Coura stood with her hand outstretched toward the rubble-sealed tunnel entrance. Her breathing grew heavy and painful while her vision blurred. Despite reaching her limit, her lips stretched into a weak smile as she surveyed the damage.

There, now everybody is safe.

{*Wonderful. How do you suppose we deal with the light-blooded being?*}

Soirée's bitterness at the angelic race wore down as their energy faded and peaked again and again. Each time Coura thought they had nothing left, another surge of power would rise to revitalize her, yet it put additional stress on her body. This time, the demon's energy had been thrown into the lightning spell used to prevent the angels from going after the Dalan troops. Of course, Soirée criticized her decision the entire time.

I knew as soon as I saw people returning they would be preparing to help, she reflected. One look at Will's face confirmed her suspicion that they disregarded her attempt to let them escape, and she whispered an apology to him before releasing the spell.

What made the whole situation worthwhile, aside from the squad and her friends being protected, was seeing the dumbfounded expressions of the four surrounding her. None spoke when the rockslide fell over the mouth of the tunnel; even moments later, they continued to assess the result. The lone sound in the valley became Coura's labored panting against a breeze. Blood caked her face and limbs, and her healing ability slowed to a crawl.

{*I hate the idea of fleeing, but...*}

The fifth angel, Jaspire, interrupted Soiree's grumbling from where he crept behind Coura.

"Why did you go and do that? I told you before, we had no business with you yet." His voice reflected the irritation displayed on his face.

She tried to stand taller and faced him.

The angel sighed, shook his head, and shot each of his companions a knowing look.

I'll have to make a run for it, she thought and prepared to leap into the sky again.

At Jaspire's nod, the four others charged. They were completely healed from their earlier injuries, making their movements as fast and precise as when they first started fighting. Coura jumped and tried pumping her wings to climb higher, but someone grabbed her ankle and tugged her down. Without the full strength behind her wings, she couldn't break free and landed on a knee.

Once on the ground, Drake, Hector, and Urvin swarmed her while Jaspire and Thelma observed. The three males preferred physical blows instead of using their swords, a change she wasn't prepared to defend against. Each punch and kick hit hard enough to create bruises, drawing her mind away until she couldn't think clearly against the pain. It took all her remaining concentration to stay steady on her feet.

The assault stopped at once, and the three stepped aside when Jaspire approached with a golden dagger in his hands, which glittered in the sunlight.

Soirée instantly reacted negatively to the weapon.

{*It's not right, whatever it is.*}

Coura grew too tired and hurt to comprehend what the demon said anymore. Her eyes drooped before closing. Then, she relaxed, preparing for it to end.

{*Has it come to this already? Well, I suppose this time you weren't stabbed through the chest and left to die against a rotting tree.*}

Coura's eyes shot open, but not by her choice.

Jaspire had moved to stand over her with the shining, gold dagger raised to strike. Her hand balled into a fist and snapped at him, connecting with his elbow and sending the weapon flying. The angel stumbled backward while cradling his arm and directed several curses at her; however, Coura wasn't the one in control. Just like during the horrific evening outside Fester when she believed her life had ended, Soirée came to her rescue.

In response to the blow, the other males pounced. Her body sprang with newfound life, dodging their physical blows until they finally drew their swords. Then, she became an observer in her own body. Her consciousness watched helplessly as Soirée manifested the demonic blade and danced as only a demon could with the angels.

Still, it remained Coura's body. She felt every muscle protest the movements, every wound sting and burn, yet she could do nothing except endure the pain and weariness without a choice.

In a short amount of time, Soirée cut down two of the three, leaving the fourth combatant to draw her sword and join. The demon giggled with a wild, crazed glee as her energy rose so their shared body resumed its healing process. It seemed as if they stood a chance.

For a heartbeat, Coura thought they would live.

Out of the corner of her eye, they caught a hint of gold before Drake plunged the dagger into Coura's left side. They expected to stagger, prepared for the blood loss, and predicted how soon it would take to recover.

The demon had been right though; something *was* wrong with the weapon.

Time seemed to stop once the point broke skin. The world slowed as Coura stared at the short blade while it sank deeper into her body until only the hilt stuck out.

Soirée, what's happening?

She called to the demon but only heard her voice in her mind. Any trace of Soirée or the demonic energy vanished, and a numbness took over.

Without the second presence, she regained control of her body yet couldn't move. Not even her mouth would open to speak while Drake grinned and yanked the blade out. Then, Coura felt herself break. All the energy flowing throughout her body and center poured forth from the wound until nothing was left, leaving her a hollow figure.

Shadows danced in her sight while the angels began shouting; to her or one another, she didn't know, though the sound became muffled. Every part of her began to shut down. Her breathing came in shallow wheezes, and her eyes fluttered as her consciousness faded into the barrenness beyond.

*

In the empty space, something flickered from Coura's center.

She barely felt the spark, even dismissed it, yet the wisps of energy lingered. Soirée's demonic power always remained stable but gave her a confident, merciless mentality. This became warm and filled with a different sort of strength.

What do you want? it seemed to ask.

She desired safety and rest, which shaped into a memory of the underground tunnel's torchlight where she remembered heading north toward The Valley Beyond. The energy responded to her vision before she could imagine more and went forth from that space. As Coura lost consciousness again, it manifested into some sort of spell, then she experienced the sensation of falling.

***

General Tio stopped the squad in the tunnel at the fork to debate where they should go next before ultimately continuing west toward Dala. A strange homesickness swept over Will that interrupted his worries as they turned.

I wonder how everyone is doing in Clearwater. Mother, Father, are you still healthy and happy? I remember when we would play by the sea together.

He closed his eyes to picture the foamy waves against a cloudless sky and the sounds of seagulls. His feet dragged as he trudged on until a foot caught on a piece of fallen rubble, causing him to stumble a bit.

"Are you all right?" Aaron asked from behind when Will halted.

"I just got distracted," he admitted sheepishly.

The prince and assistant general held up the rear of the squad with Marcus leaning on Aaron for support. Will learned afterward how one of the angels cut his friend's side before knocking him in the head with the bottom of their sword. Although the wound didn't prove serious, he lost a lot of blood while unconscious and blamed himself for being careless.

Everybody else seemed to feel the same.

The three adjusted into a line after switching directions. Their slower pace left them farther away from the others, but no one voiced their concern. For the most part, they were all exhausted and defeated with the knowledge that their home remained under the threat of being attacked.

"How much longer do you think we have left?" Marcus asked into the silence broken only by the squad's low mumbles.

"I don't know," Will answered and sighed. "It's difficult to tell when we stopped last night."

I can't believe it's only been a few hours...

He wanted to keep talking in order to keep their minds off Coura and the hostile Yeluthians, but his throat felt raw. In his mind, he told himself he was lucky to escape without injury and everything would be fine once they reached the base. The wounded would be treated, their friend would rejoin them, and he could recover under the protection of an entire army.

There's no reason for me to complain. After all, it's not like I'm a fighter. At the reminder, a wave of self-pity came over Will, threatening to bring him to tears. *I'm weak. If I could do more, perhaps the mission wouldn't have ended this way.*

The other half of his mind ordered him to be quiet and focus on the task at hand. He obeyed that part easily and stared ahead at the approaching light of one of the torches. It seemed to flicker and fill the tunnel for a second before returning to its normal brightness. He blinked and rubbed his eyes before questioning his sanity.

"Did you see a flash?" Aaron asked to confirm the odd phenomenon.

Still, Will remained in denial. "What flash?"

"I noticed it too," Marcus added, showing more enthusiasm than the other two. "A bright light appeared back the way we came."

Before Will could caution them, the two began retracing their steps. The assistant general pushed off Aaron so the prince could draw his sword and limped close behind despite his obvious pain.

Will glanced between the two and the rest of the squad, who moved on without noticing the missing members. He swallowed his worries and hurried to catch up with his friends. It took a few minutes to reach the fork in the tunnel system, which became as far as he prepared to go.

"What is it?" he asked while moving to stand beside Aaron and Marcus when they halted and peered ahead. He did the same and noticed a shape on the ground at the split in the path, but it remained too far away to identify.

"I think it's a body," the assistant general said without hiding his surprise.

Aaron sheathed his sword and strolled forward. This time, Marcus told him to wait before following behind with Will.

"It *is* a person," the prince called from ahead.

As he stepped closer, Will froze at the sight of a female figure possessing dark hair. Her body faced away from the trio, but he spotted a pair of holes in the back of her shirt.

Could it be ...

About the Author

Courtney Lillard was born and raised in Appleton, Wisconsin as the middle of five children. Growing up, she loved music and theater, and participating in both allowed her to develop a deeper interest in the arts. She graduated from Quincy University in 2015 with a B.A. degree in Broadcasting and Public Relations Communications and from Western Illinois University in 2018 with a M.A. degree in Communication Studies.

Aside from writing, Lillard is a fan of reading fantasy stories and the classics. Her other hobbies include cooking, playing video games, and doing puzzles, at least until her cats knock the pieces off the table.